THE
SELECT

ALSO BY F. PAUL WILSON

Healer (1976)*
Wheels Within Wheels (1978)*
An Enemy of the State (1980)*
Black Wind (1988)
Soft & Others (1989)
Dydeetown World (1989)
The Tery (1990)
Sibs (1991)

The *Adversary* Cycle (six volumes):
The Keep (1981)
The Tomb (1984)
The Touch (1986)
Reborn (1990)
Reprisal (1991)
Nightworld (1992)

Freak Show (editor)

*combined in *The LaNague Chronicles* (1992)

the SELECT

F. Paul Wilson

WILLIAM MORROW AND COMPANY, INC.
NEW YORK

ISBN 0-688-04618-5

Printed in the United States of America

To Mary,

who makes it all possible

ACKNOWLEDGMENTS

The author wishes to thank Albert Zuckerman, agent, editor, and friend, for his encouragement and guidance from the first outline to the last revision.

Thanks also to Daphne Stamos for checking out the medical student's perspective and Steven Spruill for the usual.

CHRISTMAS BREAK

THE INGRAHAM COLLEGE OF MEDICINE
Laurel Hills, MD

Known as the "24-karat medical school," the Ingraham (pronounced "ING-gram") College of Medicine has become one of the most respected and prestigious institutes in the nation. Nestled in the wooded hills of Frederick County, Maryland, less than an hour's drive from both Baltimore and Washington, D.C., it has built its teaching staff by culling the great names from all the medical specialties. The Ingraham faculty is considered without peer.

The same can be said of its student body. Every December, the nation's highest scorers on the MCAT are invited to The Ingraham (as it is known) to take a special entrance exam. It is a highly coveted invitation: The Ingraham is entirely subsidized by the Kleederman Foundation—its students pay no tuition, no book or lab fees, and receive free room and board. (A strict condition of acceptance is that you must live on the Ingraham campus the entire four years.) But academic excellence is only part of The Ingraham's requirements. The Admissions Office stresses that it is looking for "well-rounded individuals with something extra, who will be

committed to the *practice* of medicine in a primary care setting, especially in areas where it is needed most." Academic
brilliance is, of course, an important requirement, but they
state The Ingraham is not looking to turn out academic physicians who will spend their careers hunched over microscopes and test tubes. The ideal candidates are pre-med
students who were not only top in their class academically,
but who were also class officers or active in campus affairs.

The Ingraham alumni are considered the cream of the
crop. Without exception, its fifty annual graduates are offered
the medical world's most highly regarded residencies. Yet an
extraordinary number of alumni eschew the high-paying sub-
specialties for primary care and can be found practicing in
the nation's poorer areas, especially the inner cities. They
have earned The Ingraham an unequaled reputation for academic excellence and social commitment.

from *American Medical Schools in Perspective*
by Emmett Fenton (Bobbs-Merrill, 1993,
reprinted by permission)

CHAPTER · 1

"Quinn! Quinn, come on!"

Quinn Cleary heard the voice but continued to stare out over the cluster of buildings below her and at the surrounding fall-dappled hills beyond. From here on the hilltop, the high point on campus, she'd been told she could see three states: Maryland, of course; West Virginia to her right, and Virginia due south, straight ahead.

And down the gentle slope beneath her feet, perhaps a dozen yards below, sat the circle of beige brick-and-stone buildings—the classrooms, the dorm, the administration and faculty offices, all clustered around the central pond—that made up The Ingraham.

A touch on her arm. She turned. Matt Crawford stood there, dark curly hair, deeply tanned skin, dark eyes looking at her curiously.

"Are you in a trance or something?"

"No. But isn't it beautiful?" She looked again at the manicured sloping lawns, sculpted out of the surrounding wooded acres. "Isn't it almost too good to be true?"

"Yeah, it's great." He gripped her elbow gently. "Come on. We don't want to get too far behind."

Reluctantly, Quinn let herself be turned away from the grand view. Her long legs easily matched Matt's strides as they hurried to catch up with the other hopefuls following Mr. Verran on the campus tour. She was tall and slender—too slender, she thought whenever she'd catch a look at herself in a full-length mirror. Almost boyish-looking with her short red-blond hair and her mostly straight-up-and-down body. She'd look at herself morosely and think that the only rounded things on her body were all above the shoulders: a round Irish face with clear pale skin and high-colored cheeks, a round, full-lipped mouth, and big round blue eyes. She'd

never liked her face. A dopey Campbell-Soup-Kid face. She'd especially disliked her lips, had always thought they were too fat.
She'd looked at her face as a teenager, and all she'd seen were
those lips. But now her lips were the in thing. Full lips were all
the rage. Movie stars were getting their lips injected with silicone
to get them to look like the lips Quinn had been born with and
had always hated.

Who could figure out fashion? Which was why Quinn was
rarely in fashion, and when so, purely by accident. She favored
loose and comfortable in her slacks, blouses, and sweaters. No tight
jeans or stretch pants, and good God, no Lycra bicycle pants. She'd
look like a spray-painted Olive Oyl. She glanced down at her
slacks and her sweater. A little behind the times, perhaps, a bit
generous in the cut, but good quality, bought on sale.

Most people wear baggy clothing to hide bulges, she thought.
I'm hiding the lack of them.

But Quinn knew neither looks, body type, nor fashion sense
would make a difference when she and the others sat for the entrance exam tomorrow morning. What would count then was what
was between the ears. And she was pretty sure she had good stuff
between her ears.

But was it the right stuff? Was it the stuff the Ingraham College
of Medicine wanted from its students?

They've got to take me, Quinn thought. They've just *got* to.

The Ingraham was like a dream waiting to come true.

Medicine was Quinn's dream—had been since she'd been old
enough to dream—and The Ingraham was the only place that
could make that dream come true, the only medical school she
could afford.

Suddenly she heard running footsteps behind her.

"Hey, Matt! Wait up."

She turned and saw a vaguely familiar-looking guy trotting up
the walk from the main campus.

"Timmy!" Matt said, grinning as he held out his hand. "I
thought you weren't going to make it."

"Almost didn't," he said. "Got a late start from A.C."

"Atlantic City?" Matt said. "What were you . . . ? Oh, no. You
didn't."

Now the newcomer was grinning. "Pass up some easy cash?
How could I?"

Matt shook his head in wonder. "You're nuts, Timmy. Completely nuts." He turned to Quinn. "You remember my roomie, Tim Brown, don't you, Quinn?"

Where Matt was average height, dark, and broad-shouldered, Tim was a fair, lanky six-footer with sandy-brown hair and impenetrable, wire-rimmed, aviator-style dark glasses.

Quinn remembered meeting Tim along with some of Matt's other friends at Dartmouth last year.

"I think so. Green Key Weekend, right?"

Tim lifted his shades and looked at her. His blue eyes were bloodshot.

"If you guys say so. I don't remember much from that weekend." He extended his hand. "Nice to meet you again, Quinn. Is that your first name or your last?"

His hand was cool and dry as Quinn briefly clasped it.

"My last name's Cleary."

"Quinn Cleary." Tim dropped the shades back over his eyes. "That has a nice sound to it."

Quinn felt the sudden warmth in her cheeks and knew their already high color was climbing higher.

"My folks thought so."

She cursed again her tendency to blush at the drop of a hat, even at a throwaway compliment like Tim's. She didn't want him to get the idea that she was attracted to him or anything like that. She might be unattached, but no way was she attracted to Tim Brown. She didn't know him personally, but what she'd heard from Matt during the years those two had roomed together at Dartmouth was more than enough.

Timmy Brown: wild man.

From all accounts he probably had a gambling problem on top of a drinking problem.

But what was he doing here at The Ingraham? He couldn't have been invited to sit for the entrance exam. They only took the MCAT's top scorers. Hadn't Matt told her Tim was a business or economics major? How . . . ?

She'd worry about that later. No, she wouldn't. She wouldn't worry about it at all. It was none of her business. Her business now was the tour. They were finishing up at the science center. So far the tour had been a fantasy. The dorm rooms were like luxury hotel suites; the labs were state of the art; the lecture halls were equipped with the very latest in A-V technology. And now they were about to tour the major medical-research facility right on campus. This was a medical Disney World.

But Matt and Tim were hanging back, talking and laughing at some story Tim was telling about the casino he'd been thrown out of last night. They'd last seen each other only days ago, yet they were acting like two old war buddies who'd been reunited after years of separation.

Quinn felt a twinge of jealousy. Matt was *her* friend, had been forever. Their mothers had gone to high school together. She and Matt had fumbled through an attempt at something more than friendship when they were both sixteen, but once they put that behind them, they'd continued on like brother and sister. Or better yet, because there was no hint of sibling rivalry, like close cousins, with Matt coming from the rich wing of the family tree, and Quinn from the poor.

She sighed and told herself to get real. Why was she suddenly feeling possessive about Matt? There had to be things—lots of things—that he shared with Tim that he couldn't share with her.

"Listen," she told them. "I want to catch this end of the tour. I'll meet you later."

She caught up with the rest of the hopefuls. There were about fifty in the group—another fifty had taken the tour this morning—all of them going for their interviews this afternoon and sitting for the test tomorrow. And this was only one of a number of groups taking the test this week. An awful lot of applicants. Quinn had known there would be fierce competition for each seat in next year's class, but this was a bit daunting. The Ingraham took only fifty a year.

I'll make it, she told herself. I have to.

She joined the lead section, all following close behind The Ingraham's chief of security, Louis Verran.

Mr. Verran was a short, dark, balding, stubby man with what looked to be five o'clock shadow even though it was only early afternoon. He could have been some sort of middle manager at a bindery or the like. Smoking was not allowed anywhere on the Ingraham campus, he'd told them at the outset, and one of the duties of his office was the strict enforcement of that rule, yet that didn't stop him from carrying an unlit cigar everywhere. He chewed on it once in a while but generally used it as a pointer.

Quinn could not see a cigar without thinking of home—or rather home as it used to be. Her family's Connecticut farm had once grown the tobacco that wrapped cigars like Mr. Verran's, but not anymore.

She returned her attention to Mr. Verran, whose body apparently ran on a different thermostat from everybody else's. Despite the chill December wind, he was dressed in a short-sleeved white shirt, no jacket, and seemed perfectly comfortable. Maybe the extra pounds kept him insulated. He was overweight, but brawny rather than blubbery—except for his face and neck. Rolls of fat rode his open collar, pushing up on his jowls and cheeks. He reminded Quinn of a Shar Pei.

"The Campus Security Office is also located in the science center," Mr. Verran said as they passed the five-story building on their way to the hospital. He had a whiny voice for such a burly-looking man. "On the second floor."

Quinn had noticed security cameras mounted on the walls of all the campus buildings; the science center was no exception. Apparently, she wasn't the only one who'd noticed.

"Is security a problem here?" someone asked. "Has there been trouble?"

"No, and there never will be. Not with me in charge," he said, flashing a lopsided grin. "It's my job to make sure that anybody who's on this campus belongs here, and to keep out anyone who doesn't. We never lock the labs, libraries, or study halls. They're available to students around the clock. It's my guarantee that as a student here you'll be able to walk anywhere on this campus at any hour of the day or night and not give a second thought to your personal safety. You'll have other things to worry about." Another grin here. "Like your grades."

Nervous laugher from the Ingraham hopefuls.

Quinn had noticed that the group was pretty ethnically balanced. There'd never been many blacks in the rural area where she'd grown up, but she'd become accustomed to black faces everywhere at UConn. There were plenty here, along with some Hispanics and Orientals. The Ingraham seemed color-blind but not sex-blind: There were very few women in the group.

Mr. Verran led them past a guardhouse that watched over a gate in the ten-foot-high fence that ran around the campus.

"It's all public access beyond this point," he said, gesturing to the looming eight-story medical center and its multilevel parking lots, all gleaming white in contrast to the masses of beige brick behind them, "but not the campus. You need special ID to get on campus."

He led them on a quick tour of the first floor of the medical center, reeling off facts about the place as they trooped down the wide center corridor: 520 beds, 210 physicians on staff representing every specialty and subspecialty, drawing patients from Washington, D.C., Virginia, West Virginia, Pennsylvania, and, of course, Maryland. He whisked them past the labs—hematology, special chemistry, virology, parasitology, toxicology, cytology, and on and on—and past the radiology department with its array of every imaging device known to man, and skirted the bustling emergency room.

Quinn didn't understand much of what she was shown—she knew it would take years of medical school before she would *begin* to understand—but she'd learned enough from her pre-med courses and her outside reading to know that she had entered a tertiary medical center working on the cutting edge of medical technology.

As they were leaving the center, Quinn heard the sound of an approaching aircraft. She turned with the rest to see a medevac helicopter settling on the helipad. She watched breathlessly as a group in whites ran from the hospital and removed a patient on a stretcher.

"How great is this!" someone murmured behind her. Quinn could only nod agreement.

They've got to take me, she thought. I've *got* to go here.

Mr. Verran dragged them away from the medical complex and back through the gate to the campus. At the entrance to the science center, a motion detector opened the double sliding-glass doors for the group.

"All right," he said once they were clustered in the lobby. "Everybody wait here while I make sure they're ready for us upstairs."

Quinn watched him walk to the security desk, centered in the lobby like an island in a stream, and speak to the two blue-uniformed security guards stationed there. It occurred to her that they looked fairly young and fit, not like the dumpy ex-cops who passed as a security force at the UConn campus where she'd spent the past three and a half years.

She wondered why they needed this sort of security—the ten-foot-high cyclone perimeter fence, the guard posts at all the gates. She could see it in an inner city—downtown Baltimore or D.C., maybe—but out here in the woods?

Her musings were interrupted by Mr. Verran's return.

"Okay," he said, clapping his hands and rubbing them together. "They're ready for us. Take the elevators and we'll reassemble on the third floor."

Quinn followed the rest of the tour in a state of rapture. The Ingraham's five-story hilltop complex was a temple to the art and science of medical research. The third floor was actually a miniature pharmaceutical plant, producing experimental compounds for trials in the treatment of lupus and cancer and AIDS.

They've got to take me, she thought again. I've *got* to go here.

The fourth floor was a vivarium housing the center's experimental animals. The pungent odor of its inhabitants filled the air. The stacked cages full of doomed rats and mice didn't bother her. As a farm girl she'd learned early on not to get attached to the livestock. But the array of whining dogs, meowing cats, and wide-eyed monkeys made her acutely uncomfortable. She was glad to move up to the top floor.

"This is Dr. Alston," Mr. Verran said when they reached the fifth floor. He presented a tall, sallow, gaunt, balding, fiftyish man in a lab coat. He had watery hazel eyes, slightly yellowed teeth, and a string tie. "He's not only director of medical education at The Ingraham, but one of the country's foremost dermatological pathologists." He glanced at Dr. Alston. "Did I say that right?"

Dr. Alston smiled and nodded tolerantly.

"Looks like Uncle Creepy," a voice whispered near her ear.

Quinn glanced around and saw Tim Brown standing close behind her. He was still wearing his dark aviator glasses. Indoors. Maybe he wanted to hide his bloodshot eyes.

"I'm going to place you in his hands for the final leg of the tour," Mr. Verran was saying. "The research they're doing up here is so secret even I don't know what's going on."

Dr. Alston stepped forward. His smile toward the security chief was condescending.

"Mr. Verran has a tendency to exaggerate. However, we do try to keep a lid on the data from the fifth floor. Our projects here have commercial applications, and we wish to protect the patents. Any profits from those applications will, of course, be plowed back into more research and to maintain funding of the school and the medical center. Follow me, please."

As they trooped after him down the wide hallway, he continued speaking over his shoulder. "I can't show you much, I'm afraid. My own project is in the human-trials stage, and we must respect the subjects' privacy. But I can tell you that I'm working with a semisynthetic, rejection-proof skin graft which I hope, once perfected, will completely change the lives of burn victims all over the world. But perhaps . . . there he is now."

Down the hall ahead of them, someone in a lab coat stepped into the hallway.

"Oh, Walter. Just a moment, please."

The other man turned. He was older, shorter, and plumper than Dr. Alston. He sported an unruly mane of white hair and bright blue eyes.

"Oh, great," Tim whispered again. "Here's Cousin Eerie."

Quinn turned and gave him a hard look that told him to knock it off.

The man called Walter looked up at Dr. Alston over the tops of his reading glasses, then at the crowd of applicants. He smiled absently.

"Oh, my. Another tour."

"Yes, Walter. Walk us through your section, won't you?"

The shorter man shrugged. "Very well, Arthur. As long as you do the talking."

"This is Dr. Walter Emerson," Dr. Alston announced. "Very possibly the world's top expert in neuropharmacology."

"Really, Arthur—"

Dr. Alston half turned and began moving his shorter, heavier companion down the hall. The group followed, Quinn on the left end of the leading phalanx.

"Dr. Emerson is too modest to tell you so himself, but the work he is doing with a new anesthetic compound is absolutely astounding. He hasn't named it yet, but it does have a code number: 9574. If our animal studies translate to the human nervous system, 9574 will offer total body anesthesia and selective skeletal-muscle paralysis. I can't say more than that, but if we're successful, 9574 will revolutionize operative anesthesia."

The tile wall to Quinn's left became plate glass and she stopped, staring.

A room beyond the glass, a ward, filled with hospital beds. And in those beds, pure white bodies. Quinn blinked. No, that wasn't pale skin, it was gauze. The bodies were gauze-wrapped from head to toe. Blue, green, red, and yellow patches on the gauze. They didn't move. Seven beds, seven bodies, and not a sign of life. They looked dead.

But they had to be alive. Nurses—gloved, gowned, masked—glided among them like wraiths. There were IVs and feeding tubes running into the bodies, and catheters trailing out from under the sheets down to transparent bedside collection bags filled with clear golden fluid.

She felt someone bump against her back and knew it was Tim. "Jesus," he said. His voice was hoarse.

What? No crack about mummies? She glanced at his face, saw his awed expression, watched his Adam's apple bob as he swallowed. He seemed genuinely moved.

Quinn stared again into the ward and was startled to see a bed directly before her on the other side of the window. The body . . . patient . . . person in the bed was wrapped head to toe in thick white gauze. Only the bridge of the nose and a pair of dull, rheumy blue eyes remained uncovered. Those eyes were staring up at Quinn. They searched her face as if seeking something there. The patient looked vaguely male . . . the shoulders were broad, the chest flat.

"What . . . who . . . ?" Quinn said.

The entire tour had stopped and gravitated toward the window, crowding behind Quinn.

"Oh, dear. Oh, my." It was Dr. Emerson, squeezing toward the front. He looked flustered. "This is Ward C. Dr. Alston's ward. The curtain should have been drawn on this window. Not that there's anything confidential going on, but for the sake of these patients."

"Wh-what happened to them?" Quinn said.

"Burns," Dr. Emerson replied, his voice soft as he stared through the window at Quinn's side. "Third-degree burns over eighty or ninety percent of their bodies. Not fresh burns. They'd be in hyperbaric chambers at our burn center in the hospital if they were. No, these are burn-center survivors. They're alive, but so covered with stiff, thick scar tissue that they can barely move. Some of them are brain-damaged; all of them are in constant misery." He sighed. "Arthur is their last hope."

Quinn could not take her eyes off the patient before her. Her gaze seemed to be locked into his. His eyes seemed to be trying to tell her something.

"Their beds are rotated by the outer windows and by this hall-way window," Dr. Emerson was saying. "They can't move. Very few of them can even speak. It has to be boring beyond belief to spend all day staring at the ceiling. So they're moved around, to let them see the outdoors, let them watch the hustle and bustle of the hallway here. It stimulates them. The nurses have been trained to speak to them constantly. Even if they're not sure their words are being heard or understood, they're communicating continually with these patients."

Communicating . . . that was what the blue eyes of the patient before Quinn seemed to be trying to do. They were reaching out to her. They narrowed with the effort. Quinn sensed a silent desperation there.

The patient began to move. Just a little. Twisting, writhing, ever so slightly.

"Dr. Emerson," Quinn said, pointing through the window. "Is something wrong?"

Dr. Emerson had turned away. He looked through the glass again.

"Oh, dear. He seems to be in pain."

He moved away and spoke through the door to a nurse in the ward. Then he returned to Quinn's side.

"He'll get some relief now."

Quinn saw a nurse approach the bed with a syringe. She poked the end of the needle into the injection port on the Y-adapter in the IV line and depressed the plunger.

"Will he be all right?"

"As right as anyone can be with that amount of skin damage," Dr. Emerson said. Gently he took her arm. "Come, my dear. These patients and their pain are not on display. Don't rob them of what little dignity and privacy they have left."

As Quinn allowed herself to be drawn away, she glanced back and thought she saw tears in the patient's eyes, and could have sworn she saw his chest heave with a single sob before the inner curtain was drawn across the window.

The remainder of the tour was a blur. All she saw were those eyes, those pain-racked, plaintive blue eyes staring at her, calling to her from within their gauze cocoon.

She knew she had to get back to that patient. Someday, some way, she would. Easing pain, healing the unhealable. That was what it was all about. That was what The Ingraham was all about.

They've got to take me, Quinn thought for the hundredth time today. They've just *got* to.

Matt stared at the board on the wall of the cafeteria.

WHERE ARE THEY NOW?

"Jesus," Tim said over his shoulder. "This place cranks out its share of dedicated docs, doesn't it?"

Matt read down the list. In any urban area of any size across the country, Ingraham graduates manned inner-city clinics. And never too far away was a Kleederman-owned medical center or nursing home.

"That it does," Matt said, then lowered his voice to a Ted Baxterish baritone. "Wherever the health of America is in need, the Ingraham graduate is ready to serve."

"So where are the real medical students?" Tim said as they turned and joined Quinn at a small table in a corner of the cafeteria.

Cafeteria? Matt thought. To call this a cafeteria was like calling the "21" Club an Automat.

Matt looked around at the white tables of varying shapes and sizes, scattershot occupied by hopefuls, but no medical students. The Ingraham's cafeteria was a large, open, two-story affair. You could enter from the attached classroom building, in which case you had to walk down a long, curved stairway, or you could enter directly onto the floor from the grounds outside. The three outer walls were all glass—twenty-foot-high panes flanked with white curtains, offering a panoramic view of the sky and the wooded hills rolling away to the north. No expense had been spared in outfitting The Ingraham's facilities, even the cafeteria. And the food . . .

They sipped diet Pepsi or Mountain Dew as they picked from

a communal plate of french fries in the center of the table. Not
ordinary french fries. These were curlicue fries, perfectly crisp outside, soft and hot inside, salted with some sort of crimson season-
ing, tangy and peppery. A wedge of Camembert had been placed
on the side. Matt had always figured caf food was caf food everywhere. Not so at The Ingraham.

"They're home for Christmas break," Matt said. "Like we
should be."

"Right," Tim said, his eyes unreadable behind his shades. "But
we want to go to The Ingraham so bad we give up part of our
vacation to come here and take their test. Are we all that desperate?"

Matt glanced at Quinn and could almost read her mind. The
Ingraham was her only chance. His family could send him to any
med school that accepted him. His father could probably take it
out of petty cash. Tim's family could help him out with the tuition,
and he'd get the rest. Tim was resourceful that way. But Quinn's
family, they were just getting by.

"I heard there was a group like this on Monday and another
coming in Friday," Matt said. "That's a lot of applicants for fifty
places."

Matt saw Quinn flinch and wanted to kick himself. He wished he
knew some back-door way to get her in, but people said The Ingraham was influence-proof. Only the best and the brightest. Well,
Quinn certainly qualified there. He'd never known anyone who deserved more to be a doctor, who was more *right* for medicine. She
was born for it. But she looked so scared. He could all but see the anticipation of rejection in her eyes. He wanted to tell her it would be
okay, it would all work out. But he didn't know that.

Tim drained his Pepsi and looked around.

"They ought to serve draft beer here. Might liven up the place."

Uh-oh, Matt thought. Tim's getting bored.

And when he got bored he got strange. He saw Quinn staring
at Tim, probably wondering if he was for real. The answer was
yes—and no. Matt tried to change the subject.

"How'd you do in A.C. last night?"

"About a thousand."

"Blackjack?"

"That's my game."

Quinn's eyes were wide. "A thousand *dollars*? In one night?
Just like that?"

Matt wondered how many weeks she'd slaved at her two wait-ressing jobs during the summer to earn a thousand.

"Yeah," Tim said, "but I can't do that too often, or else my name'll get around and they'll ban me." He looked around again. "There's got to be some beer here."

"It's a medical-school cafeteria," Quinn told him. Matt detected a hint of annoyance creeping into her voice. "There's no beer here."

Tim smiled. "Wanna bet?"

"Are you serious?"

"Of course I'm serious. Ten bucks says I can get us some beer."

"Real beer—not root beer?"

"Real beer. And I'll have it before the interviews start."

"Okay," she said finally. "Ten—"

Matt knew it was time to step in. He couldn't let her throw away ten bucks. He laid a hand on her arm.

"Uh-uh, Quinn."

"What? Why not?"

"Never bet against Tim."

"But—"

"Never." He patted her arm. "Trust me on this one. I spent years learning that lesson—the hard way."

Quinn sat back and crossed her arms across her chest. Matt knew what she was thinking: She didn't have ten bucks to throw away but this seemed like such a sure thing. And besides, she wanted to take the wind out of Mr. Cocksure Timothy Brown's sails.

"Oh, well," Tim said, rising. "Looks like I'll have to get it any-way. It would appear my integrity is at stake." He looked at Quinn. "I suppose you want a light of some kind?"

"I don't want any kind," she said. "I've got my interview in twenty minutes."

He grinned. "I'd better get you a couple. You're awfully up-tight. You'll do better if you're relaxed."

As Tim wandered away toward the kitchen, Quinn turned to him, eyes blazing.

"Do you actually live with him?"

Matt tried but couldn't hide his laughter.

"What's so funny?"

"You!" Matt said, gasping. "You should have seen your face when he said you were uptight."

"I *am* uptight, Matt. This means the world to me. You know that."

Matt sobered immediately. He reached over and put a hand over hers, then gave it a squeeze. He loved the feel of her skin. There were times—and this was one of them—when he wished they were more than just friends.

"Yeah, I do know. And I'm pulling for you. If this place is half as discerning as it's supposed to be, you're in, no sweat."

She seemed to take heart from that. Good. He wanted her to believe that this time something would go her way.

"Thanks," she said. "But what about Tim? I thought you told me your roomie was a business major or something. I can't believe he wants to be a doctor."

"I don't know if he really does. He's an economics major, but he squeezed in the required science courses for med school last year to give him the option in case he wanted it. I guess he decided he wanted it."

"Great!" she said, leaning back. "I spend three and a half years breaking my back as a pre-med bio major so I can nail the MCATs; he 'squeezes in' a few science courses and gets invited to sit for The Ingraham's exam. How does that happen?"

Matt grinned. This was familiar territory for him.

"Tim's not like the rest of us mortals. He has an eidetic memory. Never forgets a thing. That's how he wins at blackjack—remembers every card that's been played."

"All fine and good, but that's not enough to—"

"*Plus* he has a keen analytical mind. You remember calculus—all the binary equations you had to memorize? Tim never bothered. He'd go into the test and *figure them out*."

Quinn glanced toward the kitchen door where Tim was in deep conversation with a heavyset black man in a white apron, then turned back to Matt.

"You could hate a guy like that."

Matt sighed. "Sometimes I do. Not easy to be friends with a guy who can ace every test without breaking a sweat."

"You're no slouch in the grade-point department yourself."

"I've done all right." Matt had calculated that by this semester's end his overall GPA at Dartmouth would be 3.75. "But I've had to crunch for those grades. Yet here's Tim, who spends his time gambling, drinking, and polishing his car, whose idea of studying is pulling one all-nighter before an exam, and he's going to graduate Phi Beta Kappa. If he weren't such a nice guy—"

"Nice guy?" Quinn said, her voice rising half an octave. "Matt, he's got to be one of the most irresponsible, self-centered, inconsiderate, egotistical—"

"He's just testing you," Matt said. "It's a game he plays, but only with people he likes. Likes to see how far he can push them, how much they can take. Once he finds out, he backs off. He's pushing you, Quinn—gently. He must like you."

He saw her cheeks begin to redden and hid a smile. She blushed so easily.

"That kind of like I can do without."

"Go with it. Once you get to know him he's a lot of fun. And believe me, he—" Matt glanced up. "Speak of the devil, here he comes now."

Tim glided up and set three sixteen-ounce paper cups on the table.

"Rolling Rock for the men, and"—he pushed one of the cups toward Quinn—"a Coors Light for the pretty lady."

Quinn glanced down at the white foam riding an inch below the rim, sniffed—

"How on earth . . . ?"

"Nothing to it, my dear. I used to work in a kitchen. The help always have a corner of one of the coolers reserved for their own private stock, three cans of which these folks were more than happy to part with for a mere ten dollars." He lifted his cup. "Cheers."

"No, thanks," Quinn said. She pushed hers across toward Tim. "But please don't let this go to waste. As Matt said, there's a lot of people vying for The Ingraham's fifty places. I need all the edge I can get. Do drink up." Quinn rose from her seat. "Excuse me. I've got my interview."

Matt was startled—this wasn't the Quinn he knew—but as she turned to leave, she winked and gave him a little smile. Matt relaxed. So that was it. Tim had started pushing Quinn, so Quinn was pushing right back.

Good for her.

Matt glanced at Tim and saw that he was staring after Quinn. He turned to Matt and grinned.

"I *like* her. Where'd you find her and are there any more like her where she came from?"

"Known her since we were toddlers, and she's one of a kind. But not *your* kind."

Tim's eyebrows rose above the frame of his aviator shades. "Oh, really? You staking out that territory for yourself? Because if you are, just say the word and I'll—"

"Nah," Matt said. "We've known each other too long and too well to be anything more than good friends." *At least that's the way Quinn sees it,* he thought.

"Good," Tim said, watching her retreating figure. "Because I think I like being around her."

Matt wasn't sure how he felt about that, but Quinn was quite capable of taking care of herself. She had her sights set and wouldn't let Tim Brown or him or anyone distract her from becoming a doctor.

He watched the door close behind her and silently wished her well on her interview. She'd need all the help she could get. The Ingraham was known—and widely criticized—for peopling its student body with mostly males. He hoped she got somebody with enough perception to recognize what a prize The Ingraham would have in Quinn Cleary.

Dr. Walter Emerson rubbed his eyes and waited for the next applicant to arrive. These interviews were tiring but a necessary evil. Current wisdom ran that you could tell only so much from test scores and application data. You had to meet these people face-to-face, see how they presented themselves, and look them in the eye to decide whether they would make the kind of doctor worthy of the enormous amount of time and treasure invested in each one of them, who'd go out into the world and practice frontline medicine.

But it pained him to know that so few of the hopeful, eager faces he'd seen this week were going to be asked to return to The Ingraham in September.

He yawned. He always got sleepy this time of the afternoon. He hoped he didn't doze off during the next interview.

A soft knock.

"Come in."

He immediately recognized the slim strawberry blonde who entered as the girl he'd seen on Fifth Science this afternoon. He remembered her staring at Ward C through the window, the high color in her cheeks, the wide blue eyes so filled with wonder and empathy. He glanced down at her file: Quinn Cleary, twenty-one, Connecticut, full academic scholarship to the University of Connecticut, pre-med biology major; president of the Biology Club, stringer for the school paper; excellent GPA, high MCATs. A fine catch for any medical school. Too bad she was lacking a critical factor: a Y chromosome.

Walter had gone around and around with the board for years on this thing its members had for males. Sure, twenty years ago when The Ingraham first opened its doors, males ran American medicine. But things were changing. Hell, things had *already* changed. Women were gaining now, and their influence would continue to grow. If The Ingraham was to maintain its status as a premier training center, the foundation's board would have to alter its antiquated sex preference.

So far the board had paid him a little lip service, but no new admissions directives had been issued.

Well, he'd see what he could do for this young thing. For some reason he could not quite fathom, Walter felt attached to her. Maybe he'd seen something of his old self in this youngster as she'd looked at those patients, something in her eyes, the desire to do something for them, the *need* to act.

And then an epiphany: his daughter. This girl reminded him of Clarice. Clarice was twenty-five in Walter's mind. Would always be twenty-five. That was when a drunk had run a Stop sign and brought her life and her mother's to a fiery end. A void had opened in him then. He still carried it with him every minute.

"So, Miss Quinn Cleary," he said after she'd seated herself across from him. He smiled to allay the tension he sensed in her. "Let me ask you the question I must ask, the question you know you're going to be asked, and get that one out of the way: Why do you wish to become a doctor?"

"Because I . . ."

Her voice trailed off. She sat there with a tortured expression, twisting her hands together.

"Is something wrong?" he said.

"I . . . I had a whole speech prepared, and now I can't remember a word of it."

"Good. I've been listening to speeches all afternoon. Let's deviate from the prepared text, as the politicians say, and get down to the real you. Why a doctor?"

"Because I can't remember ever wanting to be anything else."

"That doesn't answer the question."

"Well . . . because I know I can do it and do it well. I can be the best damn doctor you've ever seen."

Walter couldn't help but believe her.

"Now we're getting somewhere. Because you can do it and do it well . . . I haven't heard that one in a long time. I hear a lot of altruistic jimmer-jammer but competence *is* the bottom line, isn't it. A doctor who can't get the job done is no doctor at all. But what about helping people, bettering the lot of your fellow man?"

Walter had heard that *ad nauseam* this week . . . and last year . . . and the year before. . . .

Quinn Cleary shrugged. She seemed to be relaxing.

"That's important, I guess."

"You guess?"

"Well, benefiting mankind is great, but that's not what's driving me. I mean, you don't spend four years in pre-med, four years in medical school, then two, three, maybe five more years in a residency just to 'help' people. Plenty of people need help right now, today, this minute. If helping people is all you care about, why put it off for ten years? Join the Peace Corps or go work in a mission feeding the homeless."

How refreshing she was. Walter felt his afternoon lethargy slipping away.

"You're not an altruist, then, I take it?"

"I care a lot about people—sometimes too much, I think—but there's got to be more to becoming a doctor than that."

"Oh, yes," Walter said, allowing a smile. "How could we forget? There's the status, the respect, and maybe most important, the money."

The girl returned his smile. "Money . . . that would be a new experience. But at the risk of sounding holier-than-thou, when I visualize myself as a doctor, it's not driving a Mercedes, it's in a hospital or an examining room. *Doing* it—doing the job, and doing it *right*. That's what matters."

Again Walter found himself believing her. But he made himself sound dubious. "Does it really now?"

"Yes," she said, her cheeks coloring. "And if that sounds corny or phony, I'm sorry, but that's the way I feel."

Spunky too. Walter decided he was going to do his damnedest to get this young lady into The Ingraham.

But he could do only so much. A lot—everything, one might say—depended on the test tomorrow. She'd have to correctly answer those special questions. He couldn't help her with those. Nobody could.

MONITORING

Louis Verran sat at the main console in the monitoring room in the basement of the science center and struck a match. Elliot and Kurt weren't due in for another thirty minutes, so he had the place to himself. He held the flame to the tip of his panatela and puffed. This was his domain, the only place on the whole goddamn campus where he made the rules, and he did not have one against smoking here. Never would. He savored the coolness of the early puffs, even inhaled a little.

Nothing in the world like an after-dinner cigar. All he needed was a snifter of VSOP to feel 100 percent mellow. But that would have to wait. No booze while he was on the job. *His* rule.

He scanned the readouts, checking to make sure the pickups were tracking their target data.

The dorm was hopping. The hopefuls had all been fed—nicely stuffed on chicken française and all the trimmings—and escorted to their rooms. Now time for them to settle in, settle down, and go beddie-bye by lights out at 11:00 P.M.

Everything was operative. One hundred and four sets of readouts, one for every room in the V-shaped dorm's two wings. Half of them were occupied by hopefuls tonight. A pair in each of those rooms. One hundred nervous, twitchy bodies in all.

He decided to run some random checks. He activated the audio in 241. A couple of girls in that one . . .

". . . think this could be some sort of test too?"

It was the third time Trish had asked that since dinner—which Quinn was still marveling at. She glanced over at where her roommate for the night sat with an MCAT review-course manual open on her lap. Trish was pudgy, with long frizzy hair and mild acne. The seams of her jeans, made for someone two sizes smaller, were stretched almost to the breaking point over her thighs.

"I don't know what you mean."

Trish rolled her eyes and sighed as if it were all so obvious.

"This." She gestured around her. "This room. Spending the night in the med students' rooms. They could be testing us to see how well we respect their rules. What do you think?"

A handsome room—a two-room suite, actually. Cedar-paneled walls, a thick rug on the floor, and their own cheerfully tiled bathroom. The outer room had the beds and a view of the woods; the elaborate headboards looked like mahogany and were built into the walls, with drawers and bookshelves and compartments of various sizes; two huge closets also built in. The inner half was a sitting room with two built-in desks that also seemed like mahogany, plus a neatly upholstered, Laura Ashley–looking couch, a round table, and two comfy chairs. A far cry from the cinder-block box she called home at UConn.

"Isn't this the most incredible dorm room you've ever seen?" Quinn said.

"Got to be. Do you think it's true about the daily maid service?"

"That's what I've heard."

"But do you think they're testing us by putting us in here?"

"Could be. They certainly have enough rules around here."

The Ingraham, she'd heard, had a reputation of exerting an

unusual amount of control over its students, and that seemed to stretch to its applicants as well. All applicants—and they reminded you endlessly that you'd been *invited* to be an applicant—had to attend the full orientation and spend the night prior to the test in The Ingraham's dorm.

As soon as she'd arrived, Quinn had been handed an orientation booklet that had laid down the rules in no uncertain terms. And in bold type had been the requirement of spending the night here. As if to say: If you don't stay the night, don't bother showing up for the test. Why, Quinn wondered, were they so adamant about that?

And these dorm rooms, all that stuff about not opening any drawers or closets, respecting the residents' belongings and privacy—as if she had any intention of prying into people's drawers.

Quinn was grateful for the free room and board. But why were they so strident?

"Well, the whole thing beats me," Trish said, "but I'm going to keep my hands off everything in here. Not even going to use the desk lamp."

"Maybe we shouldn't even get *in* the beds," Quinn teased in a near whisper. "Maybe we should just leave the spreads pulled up and sleep on top."

"You really think so?"

"Or maybe we should sleep on the floor," Quinn continued, wondering when Trish would catch on. "That way we won't wrinkle the spreads."

"Oh, I don't . . ." Finally she caught it. She smiled. "You're putting me on, aren't you! I must sound a little nuts, huh?"

"No. Just nervous. Like me."

"You too? You don't show it."

Next to Trish, anyone would look calm, but Quinn saw no need to point that out.

"I guess I have a different way of showing it."

"So, aren't you going to study?"

"I don't think this is the kind of test you can study for. But you go ahead. I think I'll take a little walk."

She strolled out into the hall and headed for Matt's down on the first floor. The hall was almost like an expensive hotel corridor, well lit, carpeted, and clean—no graffiti, no cigarette burns, no litter. She wondered at the size of the maintenance crew it took to keep things in this shape.

Tim and Matt had somehow finagled a room together. Quinn begrudgingly admitted to herself that she had warmed to Tim over dinner. She'd actually had fun laughing at his unsuccessful attempts to conjure up some white wine to go with the chicken française. She found him stretched out on the couch, reading a *Cerebus* comic—and still wearing his shades. Matt sat with his feet up on the table, listening to his Walkman. He looked up and waved.

Tim said, "The Mighty Quinn. Welcome!" He plucked up a fold of a new sweatshirt he was wearing emblazoned with THE INGRAHAM. "How do I look?"

" 'Like a patient etherized upon a table.' "

"Ah! A T. S. Eliot fan."

"But what poem?"

" 'The Love Song of J. Alfred Prufrock '—first stanza." He lifted his sunglasses and looked at her cross-eyed. "You saw the comic book and thought you'd slip one by me, huh?"

"Not if it's a *Cerebus*, but isn't it hard to read with those things?"

"Very. Especially at night."

"Then why wear them?"

Matt lowered the headphones to the back of his neck and answered for his roommate. "Because as Andre Agassi says, 'Image . . . is everything.' "

Quinn had her own idea about that: Image had nothing to do with it; Tim Brown was hiding behind those lenses.

"How'd you two manage to get assigned to the same room?" she asked, dropping into a chair.

Tim said, "I traded with the guy who was originally here."

"You sure there isn't a rule against that?" Quinn said.

"I didn't see one," Matt said, "but I'll bet there's one somewhere."

Tim put down his *Cerebus* and sat up. "Hell of a lot of rules, don't you think?"

"Their ball, their gloves, and their playing field," Matt said. "So they call the shots."

"Yeah," Tim said, "but what's this deal with you've *got* to sleep over in the dorm the night before the test? Where's that come from? If you don't like institutional food, or you'd rather stay at that Quality Inn down the road, why should they care?"

Quinn had been thinking about that. "Maybe they want us all to start off tomorrow morning on equal footing. You know, same dinner, same amount of sleep on the same kind of mattress, same breakfast, that sort of thing. Another level of standardization for the test.''

Matt nodded. ''Maybe. Their booklet does say they've learned over the years that they get the best results from their applicants under these conditions.''

''Well, I don't know about you guys,'' Tim said, ''but this kind of thing makes me feel like some sort of a lab rat.''

''Maybe the whole point,'' Quinn said, ''is seeing if you're willing to do things their way.''

''Obviously this place isn't for the wild and free spirits of the world,'' Matt said.

''But the price is right,'' Quinn said. *The price is* very *right.*

Tim shrugged. ''No arguing that.''

''What's not to like?'' Quinn said. ''The place is like a resort. The dorm is like a Hyatt, the caf is like a fine restaurant, you've got a physical-fitness center with a lap pool, a great game room, and a top-notch faculty—''

''Even a pub,'' Tim said.

''Makes you wonder, though, doesn't it?'' Matt said. ''I mean, what are *they* getting out of it?''

''Simple,'' Quinn said. ''The cream of the crop.''

''Yeah . . . maybe.''

''TANSTAAFL,'' Tim said, and pointed to Quinn with raised eyebrows.

She guessed it was her turn to identify a reference.

''Easy,'' she said. ''It means There Ain't No Such Thing As A Free Lunch. From *The Moon Is a Harsh Mistress* by Robert A. Heinlein.''

''Hey, very good,'' Tim said, nodding and mock-applauding. ''The lady knows SF too.''

Quinn was surprised to find herself enjoying his approval. She shook it off and said, ''Who *wouldn't* want to go to medical school here?''

''Nobody,'' Matt said, ''until you realize that you *must* spend all four years right within these walls.''

Quinn felt a flash of resentment. Easy to say when money was no object. But she knew Matt didn't deserve that. He was a sweet guy despite the silver spoon he'd teethed on.

''My point exactly,'' Tim was saying. ''What's the big deal? Why *must* you spend all four years in their dorm?''

Quinn shrugged. "I don't know. But they're *very* serious about it. I understand they make you sign a contract to live on campus all four years. You don't sign it, you don't register."

"And if you quit, you pay," Tim said.

Quinn was startled. She hadn't heard about that. "Pay? Pay what?"

"All your back tuition, room, board, book and lab fees."

"But that could be—"

"*Lots*," Tim said. "Upward of thirty thou a year."

"But if you get sick or hurt—"

"No. Only if you transfer to another medical school. If you get sick or hurt or change careers, it's good-bye and good luck. But if you want to graduate from another med school, watch out."

Quinn figured Tim must have read every line of fine print in the booklet.

"What if you want to get married?"

"You wait," Tim said.

"Or you marry a fellow Ingrahamite." Matt laughed. "But seriously, speaking as the son of a high-priced lawyer, let me assure you: Contracts can be broken."

"Not this one," Tim said. "Not yet, anyway. Some parents took The Ingraham to court a few years ago. Their kid wanted to transfer to Cornell after two years here. They spent years battling it and lost. They had to pay."

"Well, they won't have to worry about me," Quinn said. "If I get in, I'm staying." And she meant it with all her heart.

But Tim's remark about no free lunch nagged at her.

Matt was staring at Tim. "Where'd you learn so much about the Ingraham contract?"

"*Time* had an article on it a while back." Tim lifted his sunglasses and rubbed his right eye with his index finger. "Let's see . . . it was the October fifteenth issue, page twelve, lower right-hand corner."

Quinn stared in amazement, then glanced at Matt for his reaction. He was grinning at her.

"He's kidding, isn't he?" she said to Matt.

"Didn't I tell you?"

Tim sat up. "Tell her? Tell her what?"

"About your weird memory."

Tim placed a hand over his heart and let out an exaggerated sigh. "You had me worried there. For one very bad moment I thought you'd told her about my . . . *other* weirdness.''

"Never!" Matt said.

Quinn knew when she was being put on. She stared at Matt with feigned shock.

"Sure you did. You said he's got a shoe fetish, and his philosophy of life is somewhere to the left of 'Whoopee!' "

Matt laughed, but Tim was on his feet, wagging his index finger at her.

"I know that line! I know it! It's from . . . *A Thousand Clowns*. Murray Burns discussing his sister. Right?"

"Incredible," Quinn said. Matt hadn't exaggerated. Tim Brown's memory was phenomenal.

"But how do *you* know that line?" Tim said.

"For a long time it was my favorite movie."

"Yeah, well, Jason Robards was great, but—"

"It just was."

Quinn didn't want to get into how as a teenager she'd fantasized about taking the place of Murray Burns's nephew—she'd have been Murray's niece—and being raised by such a lovable nonconformist. Her parents were such staid, stick-in-the-mud, *normal* people. For years she'd longed for a little kookiness in her home.

She glanced at her watch. It was 10:50. "I'd better be getting back."

"Right," Tim said. "I've heard you turn into a pumpkin if you're late."

"Really? Was that in the *Time* article too?"

"A curfew!" Matt said, sitting up on his bed. "Can you believe it? I haven't been here a full day yet, and already this place is getting on my nerves. And have you seen all the security cameras around the campus?"

Tim pressed a finger to his lips. "Careful, my friend. The walls may have ears."

MONITORING

"You bet they have ears, wise ass," Louis Verran muttered as he switched to another set of pickups.

"Mattress sensors positive all over the place, boss," Kurt said from his console.

"All right," Verran said. "It's almost eleven. Nighty-night time. Let's get some slow waves going."

He flipped the power switch and gave the rheostat a clockwise turn on the slow-wave inducer. Getting them to sleep before midnight was always the trickiest part of entrance-exam week. Most of these kids were uptight about the test tomorrow and wired on their own adrenaline. That was why all the coffee in the caf had been decaf—even the pots marked Regular. Without a little help, too many would spend the night chewing their fingernails and tossing and turning on the unfamiliar mattresses. Big no-no. They had to sleep. All of them. For at least five full hours.

So each suite was hard-wired with—among other things— slow-wave/spindle inducers. A huge expense, considering that they were used only one week out of fifty-two. The inducer created an electromagnetic field in the rooms that connected with human brain waves, inducing sleep spindles on the EEG, and making the pattern most comfortable in the slow-wave form—the sleep pattern. Worked great on the kids if they were lying in bed: thirty to sixty seconds and they were in dreamland. Took a little longer if they were sitting up, but eventually they'd give in to a sudden, overwhelming urge to lie down . . . just for a few minutes . . . just to rest their eyes.

"Good evening, gentlemen," said a voice behind Verran. "It's lights-out time for the students, I believe."

Verran suppressed a growl of annoyance as he turned to face
Dr. Alston. The ghoul was always meddling. Seemed to think being director gave him the right to stick his nose into everyone's
business. Didn't know the first thing about running security, but
he always had two cents' worth of nothing to contribute.

"Dr. Alston," Verran said, forcing a smile. "Back again for another evening of fun and games, I see."

"Hardly, Louis," Alston said grimly as he sniffed the air. His
gaze came to rest on Verran's smoldering cigar. "Louis . . . is that
another cigar?"

Louis held it up before him, appearing to scrutinize it. "Good
Lord, Doc, I believe you're right!"

Elliot leaned on his console and coughed to hide a laugh.

"Really, Louis, how many times must I remind you of the rules
against smoking on this campus?"

"And how many times must I remind *you*, Doc, that this is the
one place on campus where that rule doesn't apply?"

And how many times, you tightass, are we going to butt heads
on this? Verran thought.

"We'll settle this some other time," Dr. Alston said. "Right
now, how are we doing?"

Verran clamped the cigar between his teeth and leaned left so
he could see Kurt behind Alston.

"What's the status on the Z Patrol?"

"Getting there," Kurt said. "Twenty percent down already."

Verran glanced at the timer. The slow-wave inducers had been
running just shy of fifteen minutes.

"Right on schedule."

Dr. Alston pulled up a chair and sat down on the far side of
the control room, fanning the air with a manila folder every time
some of Verran's cigar smoke drifted his way.

Half an hour later Kurt slapped his palm on the top of his
console.

"There goes the last of them. They're all down."

Verran nodded his approval. Amazing how well those inducers
worked. No one could hold out against them for long—unless they
were on anticonvulsant medication. And The Ingraham's pre-
invitation screening process culled out any such kids long before
the first invitation was sent.

"Excellent!" Dr. Alston said, rising and moving to the center of the control room. "Let the music begin!"

"Gimme a break," Verran muttered as he nodded to Elliot.

Elliot began to work the switches on his own console, and soon "the music," as Dr. Alston called it, began to filter through the occupied dorm rooms.

"How can you guys eat?" Quinn said.

Tim looked up from his blueberry pancakes. They were, quite literally, melting in his mouth.

"Are you kidding? These things are fabulous. I'm going back for seconds."

Matt was already back on line, rejoining the bustle around the buffet area. The morning sun shone brightly through the tall windows, but Tim's shades filtered the glare. All around them the Ingraham hopefuls clustered at scattered tables, creating pockets of nervous chatter or pools of silence. Tim watched Quinn grimace as she picked at her shredded wheat.

He said, "Why don't you try something a little more substantial? The scrambled eggs look good."

She pressed a hand over her stomach. "Please. They're not even real eggs."

"Sure they are. They're egg whites—real eggs with the yolks removed. Looks like anybody who goes here will be on low cholesterol, like it or not."

"I'm all for that," Quinn said.

Tim swallowed another bite. "No smoking, low-cholesterol food . . . looks like they want us to live forever."

"Makes sense, doesn't it? They're investing a lot in their students."

Tim studied Quinn out of the corner of his eye. She looked good this morning, dressed in a navy-blue sweater that deepened the tint of her eyes, and white slacks that hugged the curves of her buttocks. Tim decided he liked those buttocks. Her short strawberry-blond hair looked just right; she wore a hint of eye makeup, just enough to draw attention to her eyes. She looked well-put-together, but then, watching her fidgety hands, he could see the stress she was putting on herself. This test was too important to her. Tim had an urge to put his arm around her shoulder, hug her close, and tell her not to worry. But he didn't know her well enough for that. Yet.

"Didn't you sleep well?" he said.

"Like the dead. Which is weird, because I'm usually up and down all night before a big test. But last night I hit the pillow and that was it till morning. Maybe they put something in the food."

"Maybe," Tim said. He'd slept like the proverbial log himself, but he'd expected to. He'd had next to no sleep the night before.

"So we're all well-rested," he said. "And if you're well-fed you'll do better on the test."

She shook her head. "My stomach's in a square knot. I—" She broke off and stared toward the far end of the caf. "Say . . . isn't he somebody?"

"Most people are," Tim said, looking around for whom she meant.

"No, I mean somebody famous."

He spotted him. Tall, lean, striding toward the curved stairway with Dr. Alston. Tim lifted his dark glasses for a better look. Strong features, dark hair graying at the temples, distinguished-looking in a tailored gray suit.

Matt returned then, carrying a plate heaped with scrambled eggs and hash browns. He cocked his head toward the newcomer. "Isn't he . . . ?"

At that instant the name clicked. "Senator Jefferson Stephen Whitney," Tim said. "Or I guess I should say, *former* U.S. senator Whitney."

"And I'll bet he was in that private helicopter that just landed," Quinn said.

Tim nodded. They'd all stood at the windows watching it whir down at the heliport behind the medical center.

The image of an article from *The Wall Street Journal* flashed before Tim's eyes with a photo. He'd come across it while researching an economics paper on the inflationary recession of the 1970s. He saw the header now:

SEN. WHITNEY CANCELS CAMPAIGN
ACCEPTS NEW FOUNDATION POST

"He was a hotshot, Young Turk senator in the seventies," Tim said. "Made lots of waves in trying to revamp the FDA. Wasn't

popular nationally but people in Wisconsin loved him. Looked like
he was going to be right up there for a long time, but when it came
time for reelection, he opted out and took a position with the
Kleederman Foundation. He's been on its board ever since."

"That explains why he's here," Quinn said.

"Right. The Kleederman Foundation is paying for this breakfast
we're eating—"

"That *two* of us are eating," Matt said pointedly as he eyed
Quinn's barely touched shredded wheat.

"—and all the rest of The Ingraham's bills."

Dr. Alston and the former senator had mounted the stairway
to the landing at the halfway mark and stopped to face the cafeteria. Tim noticed that a microphone and stand had been rigged
on the landing.

"Good morning, everyone," Dr. Alston said. "I trust you all
slept well and are enjoying the breakfast that The Ingraham's staff
has prepared for you."

Polite scattered applause.

"We are privileged this morning to have a surprise visit from
former United States senator Jefferson Whitney, a director of the
Kleederman Foundation, the magnanimous organization responsible for the founding and funding of the Ingraham College of
Medicine. Senator?"

Tim noted that this round of applause was less scattered and
more vigorous. Even he joined in. After all, this guy represented
the deep pockets that supported this place.

"Good morning," Whitney said, flashing an easygoing smile
that gleamed even through Tim's shades. "I know you're all on
tenterhooks and anxious to get to the test, and I know I won't have
your rapt and undivided attention, so I'll be brief." Whitney
paused, then: "You see today as an all-important day for your
future."

Tim glanced at Quinn and saw her blond head nod once, almost imperceptibly.

"But you should not lose sight of the fact that this is an important day for The Ingraham as well. You are the cream of the
crop. Your college careers are testimonies to your desire to strive
for and your ability to achieve excellence. You are the people we
want as Ingraham students, as Ingraham graduates. This is not a
situation of you, the individual, against us, the institution. We're
not trying to keep any of you out. We *want* you here. We'd love

to take you all. We wish we could *afford* to take you all. Unfortunately, the Kleederman Foundation's funds are finite.

"But for those of you who are accepted, what a world will be opened to you! Not only will you receive the gift of the finest medical education in the world, but you will have a chance to go out and shape the future of American medicine, to make it the model and envy of every country on Earth.

"So I wish you all well in today's examination. And please remember that no matter what happens in the coming months, each and every one of you is already a winner. I know I speak for the Ingraham College of Medicine and the Kleederman Foundation when I say that we are proud of all of you."

More applause. Tim clapped mechanically.

"Amazing," he said. "Platitudes trip off his tongue as if they'd sprung into his mind *de novo*."

Quinn looked at him sharply. "I think it was very nice of him to take the time and come speak to us. I mean, we're just applicants. None of us has even been accepted yet. Give him a break, will you?"

Tim winced. He was *not* scoring points with Quinn.

Why was he attracted to this twitchy type-A ingenue anyway? She was sweet-looking, bright, and she had a nice butt. So what? The same could be said of plenty of other girls he knew. Obviously she disapproved of him and his style. So what else was new? Plenty of people disapproved of him. He liked it when uptight people disapproved of him. He *reveled* in it. So why did her little put-down bother him?

And why the hell was he racking his brain now for a way to mollify her?

Matt, ever the peacemaker, said, "Tim doesn't trust politicians."

"Senator Whitney isn't a politician. He heads a foundation."

"The fact that everybody still calls him Senator Whitney says something," Tim said. "I hear he spends most of his time lobbying his old cronies at the Senate. Once a politician, always a politician." Tim raised his orange-juice glass in Whitney's direction. "But if he's going to foot the bill for med school for me, he's a prince."

Another cool look from Quinn. This was going nowhere. He took his empty plate and stood up.

"Seconds anyone?"

* * *

Tim chewed the eraser on the back end of his number two pencil as he considered question 200.

The test was a bitch.

A lot like the MCAT, only worse. The biology questions were off the wall. The chemistry questions were even tougher. This baby was out to separate the men from the boys, not to mention the women from the girls.

Tim glanced around. About twenty-five of the hopefuls had been seated in this classroom; the rest were scattered through the class building. Nothing special here. Green chalkboard across the front of the room, gray tile floor, overhead fluorescents, a pair of TV monitors suspended from the ceiling, and one-piece desks. Only the life-size skeleton hanging in the rear corner offered any clue that the room was on a medical-school campus. In the seat to his left Quinn's brow was furrowed in concentration as her foot beat a soft, nervous tattoo on the floor. To his right Matt was hunched over his exam booklet, scribbling figures on his scratch sheets. All around Tim, nervous people trying to score for their future.

He could almost hear them sweat.

Not that Tim was taking this lightly himself. His folks could manage to send him to med school, but it wouldn't be pocket change like for Matt's family—not even close. They'd have to make some sacrifices, maybe get a home-equity loan, but they'd find a way to come up with it. And gladly. Still, it would make things a hell of a lot easier for them if Tim got accepted here.

But taking pressure off his family was only part of why he was sweating this exam. A small part. The big part was being free. Making it into The Ingraham would be a sort of declaration of independence. No more checks for Dad to write for tuition, room, and board. For the first time Tim would be 100 percent self-sufficient. He'd feel like a man. That would be great.

But question 200 was strange.

It asked for the first corollary of the Kleederman Equation. No problem there. Tim knew the answer. Trouble was, he couldn't figure out *how* he knew it.

Usually he could simply picture the book, page, and paragraph where he'd read about any given subject. It just came to him, as naturally and easily as breathing. He remembered how as a kid he used to wow the grown-ups at family gatherings. Someone would hand him a driver's license, he'd glance at it, hand it back, then reel off every letter and number on it. Next he'd do a page from a magazine, and then go to his grand finale: a page from the phone book. They thought he was a genius, but Tim came to understand that his ability had nothing to do with intelligence—it was simply the way his brain worked.

But what about now? Johann Kleederman—Tim could see before him a page from *U.S. News & World Report*, an article on Kleederman and his foundation. Born in Switzerland in 1935, where he and his wealthy parents weathered World War II. Johann took over the reins of the family pharmaceutical company after his father's death in 1960 and immediately began a rapid extension into the U.S. market. He set up his foundation in 1968 and became a pioneer of managed health care during the seventies. He'd spent the latter half of the eighties and early nineties buying up nursing homes and turning financially troubled hospitals into medical centers, a move considered by many to be eccentric and financially risky. Still, the medical centers and nursing homes controlled by Kleederman Medical Industries, a multinational conglomerate that included the innovative and extraordinarily profitable Kleederman Pharmaceuticals, were considered the best managed, most cost-effective health-care facilities in the world. Tim even could see an old photo of the reclusive, balding, mutton-chop-sideburned Kleederman in the upper-left corner of the page.

But the Kleederman Equation? Nothing in the article about that. No picture came. Just the answer.

Tim gave a mental shrug and blackened the *B* box next to 200 on his answer sheet. Who cared? When the sheet went through the grading computer, the machine wasn't going to ask how anyone got the answer. It was only going to note if the response was correct or incorrect.

And correct was definitely better.

The next two questions also referred to the Kleederman Equation. These answers too popped unbidden into his mind. So be it. He marked them down and went on.

The questions changed after that. Science segued into general knowledge. Tim had seen some of this on the MCAT, but there was much more of it here—from who won last year's World Series to the name of the Impressionist who painted *Starry Night* to the first name of the eighteenth-century British cabinetmaker for whom the Chippendale style was named.

Tim smiled to himself. He knew what The Ingraham was up to: trying to weed out the science nerds, the oddballs who spent their entire lives hunching over microscopes or squinting at computer monitors without ever looking out the window to see what was going on in the world. They might be brilliant, they might be able to breeze through the toughest p-chem questions, but they fit the definition of culturally deprived. They'd make great researchers, but a medical degree would be wasted on them. They could be *doctors* but never *physicians*. And The Ingraham wanted to graduate *physicians*.

After the general-knowledge section the questions got weird.

They baffled Tim. Strange questions involving values and decision making: about being a general in a battle and deciding who was expendable, about being a surgeon in a M.A.S.H. unit surrounded by wounded soldiers—instead of goofy jokers like the TV show—and having to decide who would be treated now and who would have to wait until later.

Triage.

There didn't seem to be any one correct answer to these.

Tim felt paralyzed. He'd spent years matching the right answer to the right question. But now there was no right answer.

Maybe that was the point. Maybe The Ingraham wasn't looking so much for answers to the questions as it was looking for answers about the person taking the test.

The realization galvanized Tim. This was great. All he had to do was dive into these and cut loose. But not too loose. He had to consider the kind of answer these folks were looking for.

Finished.

Tim glanced at his watch. Ten minutes to spare. Everything done. All his four hundred multiple choices had an *A, B, C, D,* or *E* box blackened to the right of it. No sense in going back and rechecking. Too many. And besides, he was drained. He couldn't bear to read and answer one more goddamn question about anything.

He glanced over at Quinn. She was still working down at the bottom of the last row. She'd finish in time. He was turning away to check on Matt when he noticed two unanswered questions at the top of one of her columns. He checked his exam booklet. Those were two of the Kleederman questions.

It hit him that maybe Quinn wasn't familiar with the equation. Maybe she'd drawn a blank on Johann Kleederman. Why else would she leave them unanswered?

And Christ, the Kleederman Foundation was the pocketbook for The Ingraham. They might dump on anyone missing those.

Tim looked around for the proctor. She was standing by her desk now, arranging her papers, preparing to collect the test pamphlets. Tim slipped his answer sheet inside his exam book, replaced his shades over his eyes, and waited. When her back was turned, he rose and, in one continuous movement, leaned over Quinn's shoulder, blackened the *B* and *C* boxes next to questions 201 and 202, then straightened, and strode down the aisle. Over and done with before anyone saw him.

My good deed for the day.

Quinn stared down at the two marks Tim had made on her answer sheet. He'd blackened in choices on two of the three questions that had completely stymied her. What on God's earth was the Kleederman Equation? She'd never heard of it.

Obviously Tim had. Probably could tell her the page and paragraph where he'd read about it. God, she wished she had a memory like that. Wouldn't that be great? Like having an optical CD-ROM reader in your head.

She stared at those little blackened boxes. They weren't her answers. She felt queasy about handing them in.

Instinctively, Quinn reversed her pencil and moved to erase them. She had always done her own work, always stood on her own two feet. She wasn't going to change that now.

Almost of its own accord, her pencil froze, the eraser poised half an inch above the paper.

Her whole future was at stake here. This was real life. The nitty-gritty. Doing "good enough" wouldn't cut it; there were just so many places in the next class. Fifty, to be exact. She had to score in the top fifty.

The Kleederman questions could mean the difference between acceptance and rejection.

And she didn't have a clue as to how to answer them.

But still . . . they weren't her answers.

As she lowered the eraser to the paper, the proctor's voice cut through the silence.

"Time's up. Pencils down. Any more marks and your test will be disqualified."

* * *

Tim stood with Matt around the central pond and waited for Quinn to come out of the class building. A chill wind had come up, scraping dead leaves along the concrete walks. He pulled his jacket closer around him. Winter was knocking.

Finally she showed up, walking slow. He wondered at her grim expression.

"How'd you do?" Matt asked.

Quinn shrugged. "You ever hear of the Kleederman Equation?"

"Sure," Tim said. "It's—"

"I know *you* did." The look she tossed him was anything but friendly. "I want to know about Matt."

That look unsettled Tim. He'd thought he'd be her knight in shining armor. What was eating her?

Matt scratched his head. "It has to do with distribution of medical services among an expanding population."

"You've heard of it too? You've both heard of it?" She shook her head in dismay. "Why haven't I? Three questions, and I couldn't even guess at an answer."

"Cheer up," Tim said. "You got two of them right, anyway. At least I hope they were right."

Her head snapped up. Her expression was fierce. Her eyes flashed as she looked into his.

"No. *You* got two of them right. Not me. I didn't have a clue. I don't hand in other people's work, Tim."

He groaned. "Oh, no. You didn't erase them, did you?"

There was pain in her eyes now. "No. I didn't. And I'm not too proud of myself for that."

She turned and walked off toward the dorm. Tim started after her but stopped after two steps. He wanted to be with her, but what was the use? She'd put up a wall.

"You marked a couple of answers on her sheet?" Matt said.

"Yeah. They were blank. Thought I was doing her a favor." He didn't want to show it—didn't even want to admit it—but he was *hurt*, dammit. "Boy, I just can't win with her."

"With nine hundred ninety-nine other people you'd be a hero. But Quinn's got her own set of rules. You tested her on her own standards, and she feels she failed."

Tim was jolted. "Jesus . . ."

"Didn't I tell you she's one of a kind?"

"You got that right. Kind of old-fashioned though, don't you think?"

"Yeah," Matt said softly. "She's an old-fashioned girl."

"I didn't think there were any of those left."

To his dismay Tim realized he was becoming enthralled with Quinn Cleary.

SPRING
BREAK

Adrix (adriazepam), the new non-habituating benzodiazepine with strong anti-depressant properties from Kleederman Pharmaceuticals, has quickly become the second most widely prescribed tranquilizer in the world.

Medical World News

In what had become a daily ritual, Quinn sat on her window seat in her cozy little bedroom, raised the binoculars, and aimed them across the front yard toward the end of the driveway. And with each new day the suspense grew. It had swollen to a Hitchcockian level now.

The front yard wasn't much—a hundred feet deep, rimmed with oaks and elms, filled with laurel and natural brush and a patch of winter-brown grass. Pretty drab and lifeless now, but soon spring would bring the forsythia into buttery bloom, and then there'd be lots of color. The house was old, the foundation even older—the first stones had been placed a century and a half ago. The superstructure had been built and rebuilt a number of times since then. The current structure had been completed sometime in the Roaring Twenties. Over the years Quinn had lined her little bedroom nest with photos, pennants, posters, honor certificates, medals, and trophies from her seasons as a high school track star. And many a night she had spent fantasizing about the children who had occupied the room before her—where they were now, what they had done with their lives.

They hadn't all stayed farmers, she was sure of that.

The farm. The acres stretched out behind the house. Lots of land. If this kind of acreage were situated near the coast, or better yet, along the inner reaches of Long Island Sound, they'd be rich. Millionaires. Developers would be banging on their door wanting to buy it for subdivision. But not here in the hinterlands of Northeast Connecticut.

The farm had changed crops since Quinn was a child, and that had changed the look of the place. Dad grew hay, potatoes, and corn now, but back in the seventies the Cleary place had been a tobacco farm—shade-grown tobacco, for cigar wrappers. Quinn had helped work the farm then, feeding the chickens, milking the cows, sweeping out the barns. All of that had stopped when she went off to college. She no longer thought of herself as a farm girl, but she could still remember summer days looking out the door at acres of pale muslin undulating in the afternoon breeze as they shielded the tender leaves of the tobacco plants from the direct rays of the sun.

Thinking of those fields of white triggered the memory of another color. Red . . . blood red.

It had been in the spring. Quinn had just turned seven and she was out in the fields watching the hands work. A couple of the men were stretching the wire from post to post while the others followed, draping the muslin between the wires. Suddenly one of the men—Jerry, they called him—shouted in pain and fell to the ground, clutching at his upper leg. He'd pulled the wire too tight and it had snapped back, gashing his thigh. He lay in the dirt, white-faced as he stared at the blood leaking out from under his fingers. Then he fainted. And with the relaxation of the pressure from his hands, a stream of bright red sprayed into the air, glinting in the sun with each pulsating arc. One of the men had already run for help, but the other three simply stood around their fallen fellow in shock, silent, staring.

Quinn too stared, but only for a heartbeat or two. She knew Jerry would be dead in no time if someone didn't stop his bleeding—you couldn't grow up on a farm without knowing that. As she watched the spurting blood, the story of the little Dutch boy flashed through her mind. She leaped forward and did the equivalent of putting her finger in the dike.

The blood had been hot and slippery. The feel of the torn flesh made her woozy at first, but she knelt there and kept her finger in the dike until Dad had come with a first-aid kit and a tourniquet.

For a while people referred to her as the gutsy little girl who'd saved Jerry's life. The accolades faded, but the incident had a lingering effect. It had swung open a door and allowed Quinn to peer through and view a part of herself. She had *done* something. Because of her, life would go on with Jerry around; if she had done nothing, he would have died. Up to that time she'd had a vague image of her future self as a veterinarian, caring for the livestock on the family farm and all over Windham County. From then on there was never a question in Quinn's mind that one day she would be a doctor.

Quinn shook off the memories and focused the binocs on the mailbox where it sat on its post in the afternoon sun. The red flag was still up. She lowered the glasses and tapped an impatient foot.

Where is he?

"Is there no mail yet?"

Quinn turned at the sound of her mother's voice, still touched with the lilt of her native Ireland. She was standing in the doorway, a pile of folded towels balanced in her arms. Quinn had inherited Dad's lean, straight-up-and-down body type and Mom's fair skin and high coloring. How many times had she wished things were reversed? Her mother was fair-haired too, but with a womanly shape, a good bust and feminine hips—she was only in her mid-forties and she still turned heads when she was out shopping. Dad was built like a bean pole, but his skin type never blushed.

It seemed to Quinn that she had wound up with the leftovers of her gene pool.

"Henry's late today."

"He'll get here," Mom said. "A watched pot never boils."

Yes, it does, Quinn wanted to say. And an unwatched pot boils over. Instead she nodded and said, "I know."

No sense arguing with Mom's Old Sayings.

"I'm very proud of you," her mother said. "Who'd have ever dreamed when you were born that my little baby girl would be in demand by the finest medical schools in the world?"

Sure. Great. She'd heard from Harvard, Yale, and Georgetown. All acceptances. All wanted her. Which was fine for her ego but didn't get her any closer to being a doctor. Each called for $20,000–$25,000 a year. She couldn't come up with even half of that.

Quinn said nothing. What could she say? Her father broke his back every day working this farm, and what did it get him? He met expenses. Food, clothes, seeing to the cars, repairing the machinery, insurance, mortgage payments, pretty much took it all. If she hadn't won a full ride at UConn, she'd never even have come this far.

Dad's ego had taken a real beating during the past dozen or so years, so she couldn't even hint at how she'd die inside if she couldn't go to med school. It would crush him.

But Mom knew. And although her mother never said it, Quinn suspected she was secretly glad they couldn't afford it. But not through any malice. She'd probably hurt for Quinn as much as

Quinn would hurt for herself. But Mom had her own agenda, her own reasons for wanting Quinn home. And none of it made any sense to Quinn.

"It's got to come today," she said, raising the glasses again. She wished there weren't so many trees out by the road so she could spot the white mail Jeep as it rounded the curve half a mile down. The way things were, she had to wait until he was within a dozen feet of the box before she saw him.

"Don't be forgetting the old saying," her mother said. "Be careful what you wish for—you may just get it."

Quinn kept her face toward the window so her mother wouldn't see her rolling her eyes. That was Mom's *favorite* Old Saying.

"If I get what I'm wishing for, I'll be really, really careful," Quinn said. "I promise."

The phone rang.

"I'll get it," Quinn said.

She dashed down to the kitchen and grabbed the receiver off the wall. It was Matt.

"Quinn! Did you hear yet?"

"No, Matt. No mail yet today."

He'd called every day this week, ever since he'd received his acceptance to The Ingraham. She wished she could tell him to sit back and wait until she called him, but he was pulling for her, almost as anxious as she.

"Damn. You said it's usually here by this time."

"I probably won't hear today either."

"Maybe. But when it comes, it'll be a yes. Has to be. How could The Ingraham turn you down when Harvard and all those others want you? You're in, Quinn. No sweat. So don't worry. It can't go any other way."

Then why are you calling every day? she wanted to say.

"If you say so."

She wished she could share Matt's optimism. Maybe then she wouldn't feel like an overwound spring. And every day her insides seemed to wind tighter.

Matt had heard last Saturday. Here it was Friday, and she still hadn't. Every passing day had to decrease her chances.

"I don't . . ." The words caught in her throat but she managed to force them out. " . . . think I made it."

"No way, Quinn. That's—"

"Look, Matt. You've got to figure all the acceptances went out in one wave. It's not like they were mailing two thousand of them. There's only fifty spots. And it's not like I live in California. I mean, you're in New Haven and I'm in the boonies, but we're both in Connecticut. So let's face it, Matt. The acceptances all went out and I wasn't in there."

"I don't believe that, Quinn. And neither does Tim."

"Tim?"

"Yeah. He's staying over for some golf and a sortie to the reservation casino."

The memory of the exam last December, the answers Tim had marked on her sheet, and how she'd passed them in still rankled. She'd resented him—and her own weakness—for a long time. Now it didn't seem to matter.

Unless they'd been wrong answers.

"Matt . . . did Tim . . . make it?"

She was almost afraid to hear his reply.

"Yeah, Quinn. Tim made it too. That's why you've got to make it."

Quinn slumped into one of the ladder-back chairs at the rugged, porcelain-topped kitchen table. Her gaze wandered, unseeing, from the worn linoleum floor to the stark white cabinets that had been painted and repainted so many times the edges of the panels were rounded and the type of wood beneath had long since been forgotten.

Tim had made it. That meant the two answers he'd given her probably had been correct.

Then why haven't *I* made it? she thought.

"Listen," Matt said. "Tim wants to talk to you. He—"

"Can't talk now," she blurted. "I think I hear the mail truck."

Not really true, but she didn't want to talk to Tim. Was it because she felt embarrassed?

"Great. Call me right back if you hear anything."

"Okay. Sure."

Quinn hung up and sat there drumming her fingers on the tabletop. This waiting was driving her nuts.

And then a faint squeak filtered in from the front of the house. She knew that sound. The mail truck's brakes. She ran to the front door.

There it was, the white Jeep pausing at the end of the driveway. She waited until it had rolled on—no sense in appearing *too* anxious—then she stepped out into the bright afternoon sunshine and, as casually as she could manage, strolled the one hundred feet to the road.

She flipped down the mailbox door and withdrew the slim stack of letters and catalogs from the galvanized gullet. Electric bill . . . phone bill . . . bank statement . . . the Ingraham College of Medicine . . .

Quinn's heart stumbled over a beat. She shoved the rest of the stack back into the box and stared at the envelope. It was light, no more than a single sheet of paper folded in there. She wished she'd asked Matt some details about his acceptance notice. Had it come in a bigger envelope with instructions on the how, where, and when of registration?

It's got to be a rejection, she told herself. It only takes one page to tell you to go pound salt.

Her mouth was dry and her fingers trembled as she tore open the envelope.

Dear Ms. Cleary:
Every year, the Ingraham College of Medicine reviews hundreds of applications and entrance exam scores. It is a most difficult task to select the fifty applicants who will attend The Ingraham. The Admissions Office regrets to inform you that, although you are most highly qualified and will certainly be a credit to any institution of medical learning, after careful consideration, your name was not among those selected for acceptance to next year's class. However, since your scores were ranked within the top one hundred, your name has been placed on the waiting list. This office will inform you immediately of any change in your status as it occurs. If you do not wish your name placed on the wait list, please inform the Admissions Office immediately.

There was another paragraph but Quinn couldn't bring herself to read it. Maybe later. Not now. Her vision blurred. She blinked to clear it. She fought the urge to ball up the letter and envelope and shove them back into the mailbox, or better yet, hurl them into the road. But that wouldn't do. She'd turned twenty-two last month. She was supposed to be an adult.

Biting back the sob that swelled in her chest, Quinn retrieved the rest of the mail from the box and forced her wobbly legs to walk her back toward the house.

What am I going to do?

She felt dizzy, half-panicked as her rubbery knees threatened to collapse with each step. All those bleary nights of cramming, the cups of bitter black coffee at 4:00 A.M., the endless sessions in the poisonous air of the chemistry labs . . . hours, days, her whole *life* had been about becoming a doctor. And suddenly it was all gone . . . in a few seconds—the time it took to tear open an envelope . . . gone.

She stumbled but kept her balance, kept walking. She clenched her teeth.

Get a grip, Cleary.

She slowed her breathing, cleared her head, brushed aside the panic.

Okay, she told herself. Bad news. The worst. An awful setback. But there were other ways. Loans, and maybe work-study programs. Maybe even the military—sell a piece of her life to the army or navy for medical-school tuition. She was not going to give up. There had to be a way, and dammit, she'd find it.

And besides, The Ingraham hadn't slammed the door on her. She was on the waiting list. There was still a chance. She'd call the Admissions Office and find out how many were ahead of her. She'd call them every month—no, every *week*. By September, when registration day rolled around, everyone in that Admissions Office would know the name Quinn Cleary. And if any name was going to be moved off the waiting list into acceptance, it was going to be hers.

She quickened her stride. That was it. She would not let this get her down. She wasn't beaten yet. One way or another she was going to medical school.

As she stepped onto the front porch she glanced up and saw her mother standing there, waiting for her. Her mother's eyes were moist; her lips were trembling.

"Oh, Quinn."

She knows, Quinn thought. Does it show that much?

Then her mother held out her arms to her.

Quinn held back for an instant. She was an adult, a woman now; she could handle this on her own. She didn't need her mother cooing over her like a kid with a scraped knee.

But somewhere inside she wanted a hug, *needed* one. And the understanding, the shared pain, the sympathy she saw in her mother's eyes tore something loose in Quinn. Inner walls cracked and crumbled. Everything she had dammed up, the agony of the months of waiting, the hurt, the crushing disappointment, the fear and uncertainty about what was to come, all broke free. She clung to her mother like a drowning child to a rock in the sea and began to sob.

"Oh, Mom . . . what am I going to do?"

She felt her mother's arms envelop her and hold her tight, and she cried harder, cried as she hadn't since her dog Sneakers had died when she was ten years old.

"You're secretly glad I was turned down, aren't you?"

Quinn said it without rancor. She'd pulled herself together, and now she was sitting at the battered kitchen table while Mom brewed them some tea.

Mom looked at her for a few seconds, then turned back to the whistling kettle.

"Now why would you be saying such a thing, Quinn, dear? Glad means I take some pleasure in your hurt. I don't. Nothing could be farther from the truth. I feel your hurt like my own. I want to go down to that Ingraham place and wring somebody's neck. But, well, yes, deep down inside some part of me is . . . relieved."

Over the past couple of years Quinn had sensed in her mother an unspoken resistance to her dream of becoming a doctor. Now she felt oddly relieved that it was out in the open.

"Why . . . why don't you want me to be a doctor?"

Mom brought the teapot to the table and set it on a crocheted pot holder between them.

"It's not that I don't want you to be a doctor—I'd love to see you as a doctor. It's just that I . . . " She paused, at a loss for words. "Oh, Quinn, I know you're going to be thinking this sounds crazy, but I'm worried about your going to medical school."

Quinn was baffled. "Mom, I've been away at UConn for the past four years and—"

"Oh, it's not the going away that bothers me. It's just this . . . *feeling* I have."

Uh-oh. One of Mom's *feelings.*

"Sure and I know what you're going to say, how it makes no sense to let this kind of feeling affect your life, but I can't help it,

Quinn. Especially when the feeling is this strong."

Quinn shook her head. No use in arguing. Mom sometimes thought she had premonitions. She called it "the Sheedy thing." Some turned out true, but plenty of others didn't. She tended to forget all the ones that didn't and cling to the ones that had panned out. Mostly they were just apprehensions, fears of what might go wrong. She almost never had premonitions of anything good.

Mom seemed to think this sort of sixth sense ran in the family. If it did, it clearly was one more useful gene Quinn had missed out on. She wished she could have seen that letter coming. She would have prepared herself better.

Watching Mom pour the tea, she decided to play along, just this once.

"What's it like, this bad feeling about med school?"

"Nothing specific." Her eyes lost their focus for a moment. "Just a feeling that you'll never come back."

Is that it? Quinn thought. She's afraid of losing me forever to some faraway medical center?

"Mom, if you think I'll ever forget you and Dad or turn my back—"

"No, dear. It's not that sort of thing. I have this feeling you'll be in danger there."

"But what danger could I possibly be in?"

"I don't know. But you remember what happened with your aunt Sandra, don't you?"

Oh boy. Aunt Sandra. Mom's older sister. The two of them had been teenagers when the Sheedy family came over from Ireland. Aunt Sandra was always having run-ins with "the Sheedy thing."

"Of course." Quinn had heard this story a thousand times. "But—"

"She awoke one night and saw this light in the hall outside her bedroom. . . . "

Mom wasn't going to be stopped, so Quinn leaned back and let her go.

"The glow got brighter and brighter, and then she saw it: a glowing hand, and clutched in that hand was a glowing knife. It glided past her bedroom door and disappeared down the hall. Three nights in a row she saw it. The third night she tried to wake your uncle Evan but he was sound asleep, so she got up alone and followed the glowing arm with the knife down the hall. It glided past your cousin Kathy's room and went straight to your cousin Bob's, passed right through the oak door. She rushed inside and saw it poised over Bob's bed. And as she watched, it plunged the knife blade into Bob's stomach. She screamed and that woke everybody up. But the hand was gone as if it had never been. Your uncle Evan thought she was going crazy, and even Bob and Kathy were getting worried about her." As she always did, Mom paused here for effect. "But the next day, your cousin Bob was rushed to the hospital and taken to surgery where he had to go *under the surgeon's knife for a ruptured appendix*." Another pause, this time accompanied by a meaningful stare. "Thank the Lord everything turned out okay, but after that no one ever doubted your aunt Sandra when she had one of her premonitions."

Silly, but the story yet again gave Quinn a chill. The thought of being the only one awake, sitting in the dark and seeing a glowing, knife-wielding hand float past your bedroom door . . .

She threw off the frisson.

"Mom, you haven't had any, uh, visions about me, have you?"

Mom stirred honey into her tea. "No. Nothing like that. Just a . . . feeling. Especially that Ingraham place. Giving you everything free. That seems . . . unnatural."

She was sounding a bit like Matt.

"Well," Quinn said, "I don't think you have to worry now. Nothing bad is going to happen to me at med school."

Saying those words, "med school," triggered a pain in her chest. Crying it out, talking it out, having a cup of tea with her mother had helped her put aside the crushing loss. But only for a moment.

"I've got to call Matt," Quinn said around the newly formed lump in her throat. Which was the last thing she wanted to do. She hadn't made it, and he had. So had Tim. She felt humiliated, ashamed. But might as well grit her teeth and get it over with. "He's waiting to hear from me."

Tim sat in Matt's bedroom and watched his friend hang up the phone. He stared at it accusingly, as if it had lied to him. After a moment he turned and faced Tim.

"They turned her down," he said, his voice hushed. "The Ingraham fucking College of fucking Medicine turned down Quinn Cleary. I don't believe it."

Tim already had gathered that from what he'd just overheard.

He felt a pang, almost like a soldier who'd just lost a comrade. His hurt, he realized, was a little selfish: He'd been looking forward to spending some time with Quinn.

"Doesn't seem right," Tim said. "I mean, I don't know her as well as you, but she strikes me as someone who was born to be a doctor."

"Damn right," Matt said, his lips thinning as he spoke—Tim could tell he was getting angry now. "What the hell's wrong with them, anyway? Turning down Quinn—what kind of bullshit is that? Where are their heads? What are they *thinking* about? Do they have any idea what they've just done to her life?"

"Probably not," Tim said. "They—"

Matt stood up and kicked his wicker wastebasket against the far wall, then began to stalk the room. No mean distance, that. Matt's bedroom was the size of the living room in Tim's home, which wasn't exactly a shack.

"Damn, this pisses me off! I've had reservations about that place from the start, all their prissy rules and regulations, but this ices the cake! If they don't want Quinn Cleary, I've got to ask myself if The Ingraham even knows what the hell it's doing."

"And what's worse," Tim said, silently tipping his hat to Groucho Marx as he tried to lighten things up a bit, "they accepted me. I'm not even sure *I* want to go to a medical school that'll take me as a student."

Matt didn't smile. "I'm not kidding, Tim. I'd like to turn those bastards down, just for spite."

Tim saw that he was serious, and the seed of a scheme began to germinate in his mind.

"Hold that thought," he told Matt.

SUMMER

Fenostatin (Hypolip—Kleederman Pharm.) has surpassed lovastatin as the number-one selling lipid-lowering agent. In long-term clinical studies it has consistently lowered LDL by 50% and triglycerides by 40% while raising HDL by as much as 60% with a daily 10 mg dose, without the risk of rhabdomyolysis or alterations in liver function studies seen with other HMG-CoA reductase inhibitors.

Medical Tribune

C H A P T E R · 6

"I ngraham Admissions, Marge speaking. How may I help you?"

"Hi, Marge. It's Quinn Cleary."

"Quinn! How are you, dear?"

"Still hanging in there. Any word?"

"No, honey. I'm sorry. Nobody's called. As I told you, it's very rare that someone turns down an acceptance here. I've been here ten years now and I can only remember two. And one of those had a serious neck injury that was going to lay him up for a year."

"I know. But I can still hope, can't I?"

"And we're hoping right along with you, sweetheart. Listen, you know if it was up to us, we'd have you in here in a jiffy."

"That's nice, Marge. Thanks."

"It's the truth. Look. You keep calling, you hear? I can't call you— I have to account for my outgoing long distances, and they'd kick my butt out of here for something like that—hell, they might even do that yet if they find out I told you your spot on the wait list."

Quinn had been crushed to hear she was eleventh on the list. Even if she were first or second, her chances of getting in were slim to none. But *eleventh . . .*

"They won't hear it from me, Marge."

"I know that, dear. But there's no law says you can't call again. So don't you hesitate a minute."

"Thanks, Marge. I appreciate that. Talk to you soon."

"Any time, Quinn, honey. Any time."

Quinn shook her head as she hung up. Couldn't be too many applicants who got to know the Admissions Office staff on a first-name basis. She'd called so many times since spring break she actually felt close to those secretaries. Couldn't hurt. Just too bad they didn't decide who got in.

August was boiling the potato fields outside and baking her here in the kitchen. She yawned and rubbed her burning eyes. She was beat—mental fatigue more than anything else. She was working her usual two waitress jobs plus hustling after student loans from anyone who had money to lend. She'd even tracked down a Connecticut Masonic Lodge with a student-loan program. She spent her free hours filling out applications and financial statements until she was bleary-eyed.

Money was tight. The bankers she spoke to said student loans had been easier years ago, but with the economy the way it was and the ongoing trouble some of the government programs were having with deadbeats, a lot of the funds had dried up. And they all told her the same thing: All the purse strings would loosen considerably once she reached her third year in med school; she'd have passed through the flames of the first two years when the shakeout occurred, when those who couldn't cut it were culled out, and would then be considered an excellent financial risk. But that didn't do much for her now.

There was still the Navy. It was beginning to look as if they were going to approve her for their program. If so, they'd pay her way through med school, but in return they'd want her to take a Navy residency in the specialty she chose plus a year-for-year payback— one year of service for every year of medical education they funded.

So that was Quinn's situation on this steamy summer morning. If she was approved for the Navy plan, she'd get her degree in exchange for six to eight years of her life. A stiff price, but at least it was a sure thing.

The other course was riskier: Gamble that she could scrape together the tuition for the UConn school on a year-by-year basis through work, loans, and anything else she could think of, and come out of medical school $75,000 or $80,000 dollars in debt.

The panic and heartbreak of March were gone. She'd got her act together and devised a plan. Her dream had not been snatched from her as she'd thought on that awful day, merely pulled further away. She'd get there; she simply was going to have to work a lot harder to reach it.

But getting into The Ingraham would be so much better. She'd be able to devote all her efforts to the massive amount of learning that had to be done and not worry about chasing after tuition dollars. Or she wouldn't be stuck in a Navy uniform, doing whatever they told her to do, going wherever they sent her.

She sighed. The Ingraham . . . she still got low when she thought about what she'd be missing. Here it was the middle of August and no one who'd been accepted was going elsewhere.

Better get used to it, she told herself.

"I'm not going to The Ingraham," Matt said.

Tim sat up and stared at him.

"Bullshit."

They were stretched out on white and canary-yellow PVC loungers beside the Olympic-sized pool in Matt's back lawn. Each had a tall gin and Bitter Lemon on the ground beside his chair, a pile of fresh-baked nachos cooled on the Lucite table between them. Tim had been drifting slowly away on a soft golden mellow wave.

"No, I mean it," Matt said, keeping his eyes closed against the glare of the sun. "I told you there were all those things I didn't like about the place. But I sloughed them off. I mean, The Ingraham is such an ego trip. Then the other night my father sits me down and says he and Mom really wish I'd consider going to Yale."

"Yeah, but Yale isn't offering you any incentives."

"They don't care. My father went to Yale and Yale Law, my grandfather too, and I hadn't realized how much the place means to him. And my mom . . . I think she just wants me closer than Maryland."

Tim felt bad. Hot. Suddenly the sun was getting to him. Hell, he was so comfortable with Matt, and now the guy was dumping him, which he knew was not really the case.

Tim tried to imagine his folks telling him to kiss off over a hundred thousand bucks' worth of tuition, room, and board just to attend NYU, where his father had gone to night school. Fat chance.

"What did the Ingraham folks say when you told them?"

"Haven't yet," Matt said. "I've been trying to figure a way to slip Quinn into my spot. Think I could demand that they substitute Quinn for me?"

"Yeah, right," Tim said. "That'll work. They'll jump her over ten names on your say-so."

"You got a better idea?"

"I might." A half-formed scenario had been lurking in the back of his mind since the spring.

"Well, let's have it. I need the input of that devious mind."

"Give me a minute."

Tim lay back and closed his eyes.

The Ingraham ... he'd really been looking forward to having Matt around, even finagling him as a cadaver partner. All down the tubes now. But that did leave ...

Quinn.

He'd spoken to her twice this summer. She'd seemed a little friendlier each time, but still reserved. Perhaps on guard said it better. He'd tried to wrangle a date but she'd always been too busy with her jobs or her tuition hunting. If he could come up with a way to get her into The Ingraham ...

What had she said during that last call? Something about how she'd become best friends with the Admissions Office staff, how they were all pulling for her.

He bolted upright on the lounge.

"I've got it!"

Matt opened his eyes, squinting up at him.

"Yeah? What do we do? What do I tell The Ingraham?"

"The first thing is, you tell The Ingraham nothing. The second is hand me that phone. I have to call Ms. Quinn Cleary."

Quinn felt awkward, uncomfortable, scared too about this off-the-wall scheme, yet she felt she had no choice but to accept Tim's offer to drive her down to Maryland. He raced along 95 in a gray 1985 Olds Cierra that he seemed to love. He even had a name for it.

"Griffin?" she said when he told her the name. "Why a griffin?"

"Not *a* griffin. Just 'Griffin.' The gray 1985 Olds Cierra is the invisible car. GM sold a zillion of them, or Buicks and Pontis that look just like it. I've parked this car in some terrible neighborhoods and it's never been touched. Nobody wants to steal it or bother it—nobody even *sees* it. So I named it Griffin, which, if you know your H. G. Wells, is the—"

"Name of the Invisible Man." She smiled. Griffin—the Invisible Car. She liked that.

After checking Tim's name on a list, the guard in the gatehouse raised the gate and admitted him to The Ingraham's student lot. Stiff and achy as she was after almost six hours of confined sitting, Quinn didn't move from her seat when they pulled into a parking slot. She stared ahead at the tight cluster of beige brick-and-stone buildings that made up The Ingraham. She hardly recognized the place. The trees had shed most of their leaves the last time; now the oaks and maples were lush and green. She watched a couple of new students hurry up the slope to register.

They've got to take me, she thought. They've just *got* to.

"Here we are," Tim said, glancing at his watch. "Right on schedule."

"Do you think this has even a slight chance to work?"

"Of course. The plan was designed by the Master Plotter. It cannot fail."

"If you say so."

Quinn didn't want to hope, couldn't *allow* herself to hope.

Matt had said Tim had cooked up this whole scheme. Why? What was his angle? She'd actually cried when Matt told her how he was trying to help her get his spot at The Ingraham, but she hadn't been all that surprised. This was the sort of thing Matt would do.

But Tim . . . What was Tim Brown getting out of this?

"All right," Tim said, gathering up his papers. "Registration's in the class building. That's where I'll be. You head for the Admissions Office and do your thing. I'll catch up with you there."

Quinn still couldn't move. Now she was terrified.

"What if this doesn't work?"

"It will. Ten to one it will. But even if not, what have you lost? By tonight you'll either be registered here or right back where you were two weeks ago when we cooked this thing up. And you haven't risked a thing."

"But I'll *feel* awful." And I'll have to hustle back to Connecticut and sign my life away to the Navy.

"Yeah, but you'd feel worse if you never gave it a shot."

Quinn nodded. He was right. Pass this up and she risked being plagued the rest of her life wondering if it would have worked.

As she made herself step out of the car, Tim said, "Good luck, Quinn."

"Thanks. I'll need it."

She walked up the slope to the administration building and followed the little black-and-white arrows planted in the grass to the Admissions Office. She paused in the empty silent hallway outside the oak door. Her heart began to pound; her palms were suddenly slick with sweat. Intrigue was not her thing. How on earth was she ever going to pull this off?

Quinn shook herself. How? Because she couldn't afford *not* to pull it off. She stepped inside.

The Admissions Office turned out to be a small room, fluorescent lighted, with a dropped ceiling. A long marble counter ran the width of the room, separating the staff from the public. A woman sat at a cluttered desk just past the counter. She appeared to be in her fifties with a lined face, a prominent overbite, and graying hair that might have been red once. A plastic nameplate on her desk read MARJORY LAKE.

"Are—" The word came out a croak. Quinn cleared her throat. "Are you Marge?"

The woman looked up, fixed her with bright blue eyes, wary, not welcoming. "Some people call me that. If you're looking for Registration, it's—"

"I'm Quinn Cleary," she said, reaching her hand over the counter. "It's nice to talk to you face-to-face for a change."

Marge bolted out of her seat. "Quinn? Is that you, sweetheart? Oh, you look just like I imagined you! Claire! Evelyn! Look who's here! It's Quinn!"

Two other women, both short, plump brunettes, left their desks and crowded forward, shaking her hand, welcoming her like a relative. Quinn was sure if the counter hadn't been there they'd have been hugging her.

When all the greetings and first-meeting pleasantries had been exchanged, Marge looked at her with a puzzled expression.

"But what are you doing here? We didn't . . . I mean . . . no one's . . . "

"I know," Quinn said. "I just decided I wanted to be here in case someone doesn't show up."

Claire and Evelyn went "Aaawww," and glanced at each other. Marge gripped her hand.

"I don't know how to say this, Quinn, honey," Marge said, "but that sort of thing just doesn't happen around here."

"I know," Quinn said. "But I haven't anyplace else to go at the moment so I thought I'd give it a shot."

More quick that-poor-kid glances were exchanged, then Marge said, "Well, might as well make the best of it. Have a seat. Make yourself comfortable. You're welcome to wait as long as you like. Want some coffee?"

Quinn would have preferred a Pepsi but didn't want to turn down their kind offer.

"Sure. Coffee would be great."

Tim showed up an hour later. Quinn introduced him to "the girls," as they called themselves. They knew his name—after all, they had processed his acceptance. She told them she was going out to stretch her legs but would be back in a while to see if there was any news.

"How's it going in there?" Tim asked when they were outside.

"They're sweet. I feel like a rat deceiving them like this."

"Who's deceiving anyone? You're hanging around to try and take the spot of anyone who doesn't show up. That's an absolutely true statement."

"But—"

"But nothing. It's true. The fact that we know something they don't is irrelevant."

They found a shady spot under an oak by the central pond and sat on a wooden bench. The sun was in and out of drifting clouds; the air was heavy with moisture. A bathing sparrow fluttered its wings at the edge of the pond, disturbing the still surface of the water with tiny ripples and splashes. Off to her left Quinn saw a parade of sweaty new arrivals lugging suitcases, boxes, and stereos into the dorm. She looked around and was struck by how *planned* The Ingraham looked. The dorm, the caf, the administration, class, and faculty buildings were all two stories, all of similar design and color. And off to her right, up the slope, rose the science building; and rising beyond that, the medical center. Each set higher than the one before it, like steps to knowledge and experience.

"Where do you fit into this, Tim?"

He swiveled on the bench and faced her. She wished he'd take off those damn sunglasses. She wanted to see his eyes.

"What do you mean?"

"I mean, what's in it for you? You don't know me. Sure, we've met a couple of times, but we're not what you'd call close by any stretch. Why should you care if I get into The Ingraham?"

He smiled. "I'm the compleat altruist. My *raison d'être* is to help others. That's why I want to become a doctor."

"Not."

"You doubt my devotion to the human species? Okay, try this: I'm hoping that my getting *you* into The Ingraham will help *me* add you to my near-endless list of beautiful female conquests."

"Very funny."

"Hey, don't sell yourself short. I think you're a knockout. And you've got a very nice butt."

"And you need glasses," Quinn said. She was annoyed now. "I ask you a simple question . . ."

She pushed herself off the bench to head back to the Admissions Office. This was dumb. Tim's hand on her arm stopped her.

"Okay, okay," he said. "Forget everything I just said—except the part about your having a nice butt—"

"Tim . . ."

"Well, I meant that. But as for the rest of it . . . " He paused, as if searching for the right words. "Look. Places like The Ingraham, they're systems. A bunch of nerdy little dorks get together and figure out a way to set someplace up so they can push all the buttons, pull all the levers, call all the shots—run the show. They've got the bucks, that gives them power, and they think they can make everybody jump through their hoops. But they couldn't make Matt jump. With his family's kind of clout, he can tell *them* to go jump. People like you and me, though, Quinn . . . if we want to get into their system, when they say, 'Jump,' we've got to ask, 'How high?' "

"That's the way the world works, Tim. You can't change that."

"I'm not saying I can. But I make it a point to screw them up every chance I get."

"Oh," Quinn said slowly, wondering if she should feel insulted. "And I suppose helping me get into The Ingraham is screwing them up."

Tim slumped forward and rested his forehead on his forearms. He spoke to the grass. "This conversation is heading for the tubes. Maybe we should just go back to saying that I thought it was a shortcut to adding another notch in my, um, belt and leave it at that."

"No," Quinn said softly. "You're going out of your way to do me a favor. We've only met three times, talked on the phone a few more. Can you blame me for being curious as to why? TAN-STAAFL, remember?"

Tim lifted his head. The blank sunglasses stared at her again.

"Fair enough. Okay. I like you. I like you a lot."

Quinn felt herself flushing. Now she *really* wished she could see his eyes.

"And I don't know of anyone," he continued, "who wants to be a doctor more than you. I mean, it shines from you. And with your MCAT scores and GPA, I can't think of anyone—with the possible exception of myself—who *deserves* to be a doctor more."

"Really, Tim—"

"No, I mean it. And I was pissed, really pissed, when I heard that these jokers had turned you down. Not as pissed as Matt, of course. I mean, he wanted to nuke the place. Neither of us could figure it out. Every other med school you applied to took you, but not The Ingraham. Why? What is it about you that doesn't fit into their system? Was it because you're female? Do they have something against nice butts?"

"*Please* stop talking about my butt!" She did *not* have a nice butt or a nice anything. "Can't you be serious for two consecutive minutes?"

"I'll try, but . . . I don't know, Quinn . . . show me an anal-retentive system like this one that's screwing somebody I know, and it's like waving a red flag in front of a bull. I want to beat that system."

"So, if you're Don Quixote, who am I? Sancho Panza?"

"Hardly. Take the casinos as a for instance. They're a system. They set up the rules so that the percentages are always with them. Somebody wins big once in a while, but that's the exception. They publicize those exceptions to bring in more losers. But systems aren't set up for wild cards. I'm a wild card. Their blackjack system has no contingencies for someone with an eidetic memory. Fortunately for them, we're rare birds. But with my memory, I can screw up their system and *win* most of the time instead of *lose*."

"But The Ingraham is not a casino."

"Right. But it's a system. And Matt is the wild card here. His family's got—pardon the phrase—fuck-you money. He qualified, they accepted him, but they can't buy him. They can buy you and me, Quinn. We'll gladly put up with their bullshit rules for a free medical education. Hell, we'll fight for it. We need them. But Matt doesn't. He's the chink in their armor. How many people did you say have turned them down?"

"Two in the last ten years."

"Right. But they're well prepared for that contingency anyway: They've set up a highly qualified waiting list. But I'll bet they've got no contingency plan for what Matt's going to do." His expression was gleeful as he pounded his knees. "And that's when we stick it to them."

"Tim Brown . . . radical."

"Not a bit," he said, raising his hands, palms out. "I'm not out to destroy anything, or throw a monkey wrench into anybody's works. The whole idea is to stick it to them without them even knowing they've been stuck. If you cause noticeable damage, or you make a big deal about it and strut yourself around bragging how clever you are, you queer it for the next wild card. Because they'll fix that weak spot in their system. But if everybody keeps their mouths shut, someone may get a chance to stick it to them again."

"Is sticking it to them so important?"

"How important is it to you right now?"

"Touché."

"All right. Then let's do it." He checked his watch. "Registration's pretty well closed. Any minute they ought to be realizing they're shy one body."

She headed back to the Admissions Office feeling anxious, scared, thinking about Tim and how he was turning out to be a lot deeper than she'd originally thought, and wondering if he really thought she had a nice butt. She knew she didn't, but there was no accounting for taste.

"Don't you have to unload?" she said as Tim ambled by her side.

"We'll unload together. This plan is my baby. I want to be present in the delivery room."

Quinn sensed the change in the Admissions Office as soon as she walked through the door. The air was charged. Claire and Evelyn were trundling about between their desks and the file cabinets. Marge look frazzled. Her eyes went wide when she saw her.

"Quinn! We've just heard from Registration. They're getting ready to close and somebody hasn't shown up. I can't believe it. I've been here ten years and nothing like this has ever happened."

She felt Tim's elbow bump her ribs.

"Wink, nudge, poke," he whispered.

Quinn ignored him. "Maybe that's my chance," she said to Marge. "What's his name?"

"Crawford. Matthew Crawford."

"Are you going to be calling him? Maybe he's just had car trouble or something."

"Well, then," Marge sniffed as she picked up her phone, "*he* should have called *us*. Whatever the cause, I'll have to check with Dr. Alston first. Then we'll call." She smiled at Quinn. "This could be your lucky day, hon."

Quinn stepped back so as not to appear to be listening. She dragged Tim with her to the row of chairs by the door, then sat there straining to hear. Marge's end of the conversation was garbled, but she heard her hang up and dial another number. Matt's?

If so, Mrs. Crawford, Quinn's mother's old high school friend, would tell Marge the truth—as she knew it.

Quinn crossed her fingers and waited.

She heard Marge slam her receiver into its cradle.

"Matthew Crawford's not coming!"

Quinn heard cheers from Claire and Evelyn. She grabbed Tim's hand and squeezed, then realized what she was doing and let go.

"It's okay," Tim said. "I wash them regularly. Twice a week sometimes."

Marge was up at the counter, motioning Quinn closer. Her face was flushed.

"He's not coming!" she said as Quinn approached. "He decided to go to Yale Med instead!"

"And he didn't let you know?" Tim said, leaning against the counter beside her. "What a cad!"

"He wasn't there—off to Yale already—but I spoke to his mother and she said as far as she knows he sent us a letter last month. She couldn't imagine why we never received it."

"Probably never sent it," Tim muttered with convincing disgust. "You know how these rich kids are—"

Quinn kicked his ankle. He was getting carried away.

"Can I take his spot?" Quinn said.

"If it was up to me, honey, you'd be on your way to the registrar. But it's up to Dr. Alston and the admissions committee. I'll do my damnedest for you, though."

As she returned to her desk and tapped a number into her phone, Tim leaned closer.

"Why'd you kick me?"

"You're overdoing it."

"You mean Robert De Niro doesn't have to worry about me?"

"It might be better if you hung back a little . . . like in one of the chairs."

Tim shrugged. "Okay. But you're having all the fun."

Some fun. This was murder. Quinn turned and clung to the counter, hanging on Marge's every word.

"Dr. Alston? It's Marge, down at the office. . . . Yes, we called him. . . . No, apparently he's decided to go to Yale instead. . . . That's right, sir. . . . No, I don't know why. . . . Yes, sir, I certainly can do that, but I think you should know, one of the wait-list students is right here. . . . Dr. Alston? Are you there? . . . Yes, sir, she's been hanging around all day in the hope that something like this would happen. . . . I know, sir. Not in my memory either. Her name's . . . let me see . . . " Marge smiled and winked at Quinn as she made a noisy show of shuffling through the papers on her desk. "Here it is: Cleary . . . Quinn Cleary. Yes, sir. I'll do that, sir. Do you want me to start making those calls now? . . . Okay. I'll wait. . . . Right, sir."

She hung up and approached Quinn. Her air was conspiratorial.

"Well, Quinn, honey, you've sure thrown Dr. Alston a curve. He wanted me to start calling the waiting list immediately, starting with number one and working my way down. When I told him you were here, he was actually speechless. And if you knew Dr. Alston, you'd know that he's *never* speechless. He's never heard of a wait-list student hanging around on registration day. He's going to check your application and talk to the committee."

Quinn felt light-headed. Her knees wobbled. She struggled for a breath to speak.

"Then I have a chance?"

"You sure do. Better than you think. Because just between you and me, if I get the word to start calling the waiting list, there's a *very* good chance that most of them will already be committed to other schools, and those that aren't, well"—her voice sank to a whisper—"they may not be home, if you know what I mean."

"I wouldn't want you doing anything like that for me," Quinn said. "You might be risking your job."

Marge patted her hand. "You let me worry about that. Meanwhile, take a seat by your friend over there and we'll see what happens."

"I smell a rat."

Dr. Walter Emerson was startled by Arthur's vehemence. He'd known Arthur Alston for years and had always thought of him as a phlegmatic sort.

"Do you, Arthur? I'm the one who does most of the rat studies here, so if anyone should recognize that smell, it's me. And I don't."

"Really, Walter," Alston sniffed. "This is serious business. I don't think any of us should take it lightly."

Walter glanced around the conference room at the "us" to whom Arthur was referring. The Ingraham's admissions committee—or at least most of it—all top specialists in their fields, sat around the polished table in the oak-paneled conference room: Arthur Alston, Phyllis Miles, Harold Cohen, Steven Mercer, Michael Cofone, and Walter himself. Although Arthur was the director, Senator Whitney was the powerhouse; he represented the Kleederman Foundation and had veto power. He would be flying in later for his annual welcoming address to the first-year students.

"I'm not taking it lightly, Arthur," Walter said. "But I see no point in viewing this as some sort of conspiracy."

"You've got to admit it looks suspicious," Arthur said, tapping the tabletop with the eraser end of a pencil. "The applicant who turned us down and the wait-listed one in question are both from Connecticut. I don't know about you, but I find it a little hard to swallow that as mere coincidence."

So did Walter, but he wasn't going to admit it. Not just yet. He'd been oddly thrilled when he'd learned that the unorthodox student sitting on their doorstep was Quinn Cleary, that bright young woman with whom he'd been so taken when he'd interviewed her. He'd recommended her highly and had been disappointed when she'd been wait-listed.

"Granted, they're both from Connecticut, but they live nowhere near each other. They went to different high schools in different counties, went to different colleges. There may be a connection, but it's certainly not obvious."

"Exactly. That's why I said I *smell* a rat. I haven't found one yet." He looked around the table. "Does anyone else have anything to add?"

Cohen and Mercer said no; Cofone and Miles shook their heads. They seemed largely indifferent. And why not? None of them had ever met Quinn Cleary. But Walter had. If only there was some way he could convey his enthusiasm for her.

"All right, then," Arthur said. "We'll follow the usual procedure and start calling the wait-listed applicants in order. And if by some stretch of the imagination we have no takers by the time we reach Miss Cleary—"

"Can I say one more thing, Arthur?"

"Walter, we haven't got all day."

"Just hear me out," Walter said, rising and walking slowly around the table. "Last winter we made out a list that we put on hold for possible admission to The Ingraham. All but one took that lying down. Miss Cleary did not. She took the initiative of coming down here on registration day in the hope of being admitted. Her chances were slim to none, but she did it anyway. That takes determination; that takes *desire*.''

"Or insider knowledge," Arthur said. "She might very well have known that this Crawford was not going to show up. The two of them might have cooked up this entire scenario together."

"Then I say, '*Bravo!*' More power to her. If your suspicions are true, then all the more reason to accept her. We're always saying we want students with something extra, something that's not reflected in the grade-point average, aren't we? Well, here it is. In spades. This young woman is utterly determined to come here. She will not take no for an answer. Isn't this the caliber of student we're looking for? With the training and direction The Ingraham can give her, won't she be one *hell* of a force in the outside world? Nothing is going to stand in this woman's way. Isn't this what The Ingraham is all about?"

"But—" Arthur began.

"Plus she's female," Walter said, pressing on. He had the other committee members' attention, could see the growing interest in their eyes. He was not going to let Arthur break his stride now. "The Ingraham is constantly criticized for not taking enough women. Here's a chance to accept a woman who has the potential of doing more than any ten other students on that wait list combined. I say to hell with the rest of the wait list. We accept Quinn Cleary now."

"But the Kleederman Equation questions," Arthur said. "She missed one."

"Negative thinking, Arthur," Walter said, wagging his finger. "She may have answered only two of the three, but she got them both right. And if she'd got all three, she would have been one of our first choices for acceptance, am I correct?"

"Yes." His tone was reluctant. "But—"

"But nothing. She got two right. That's enough. She didn't get the third wrong, she simply didn't do it. Maybe she missed it. Maybe she wasn't sure and she was going to come back to it but ran out of time. It doesn't matter. She got two *right*. She qualifies, Arthur. And she'll be a credit to The Ingraham."

"I don't know, Walter. . . . "

It was Arthur's first show of uncertainty. Walter leapt to the advantage. He faced the other four.

"What do you say?" He met the stares of Cohen, Mercer, Cofone, and Miles one by one. "Do we take her in, or do we tell her that initiative, tenacity, and determination have no place at The Ingraham and send her packing? Which will it be?"

"Accepting a woman in place of a male will cause rooming problems, but that's why we have extra rooms," Mercer said. "I'm for taking her."

Cofone nodded. "Sure. Why not?"

"After all, she's already here," Cohen said.

Phyllis Miles frowned. "I'm not saying this because I'm the only woman here, but The Ingraham could use another female in the incoming class. It's terribly unbalanced."

"Then it's done!" Walter said.

Arthur cleared his throat. "Not quite. I'll have to run this by the senator. He should be arriving within the hour. I'll show him Cleary's record and convey to him the sentiments of the committee."

"And what are your sentiments, Arthur? Are you actively opposed?"

"I don't like prospective students to try and pull a fast one, but since I have no hard proof, I shall not contend against her. If she meets with the approval of you five and with the senator, then I shall go along."

Good, Walter thought. Only one more hurdle, and that might be a tough one. It was difficult sometimes to predict how the senator and the Kleederman Foundation would react.

The wait didn't just *seem* endless—it *was* endless.

Hours on those hard, narrow chairs in the Admissions Office. Quitting time had come and gone for Marge and Claire and Evelyn, but all three had stayed on, encouraging her, warning her not to give up hope.

"Dr. Alston didn't tell me to start polling the waiting list," Marge kept saying. "That's got to mean something—something good."

Tim was optimistic too: "As long as they haven't sent you packing, you're still in the game."

And then someone was walking down the Administration Building's deserted main corridor, coming their way. The five of them huddled on their seats, waiting. Quinn could barely breathe. A graying head with thick white eyebrows poked through the doorway.

"Miss Cleary?"

"Yes?" Quinn said, rising, trembling.

"There you are." He smiled. "Do you remember me?"

"Of course. You're Dr. Emerson. You interviewed me last winter."

"Right. And recommended you very highly."

"Thank you."

"Well, it didn't do you much good on the first round, I'm sad to say. But that's all water under the bridge now. The committee has voted to let you take the place of the no-show." He thrust out a gnarled hand. "Welcome to The Ingraham, Miss Cleary."

Marge cried, "Yes!" and Evelyn cheered and Claire said, "Praise the Lord!" over and over as Quinn stepped forward on wobbly knees to shake Dr. Emerson's hand.

His grip was firm and his eyes twinkled.

"Looks like you've gathered quite a cheering section here," he said.

"It's been a long afternoon and we've all become well acquainted."

"People seem to warm to you very quickly. That's a valuable asset for a doctor. Don't lose it." He gave her hand one final squeeze. "You can register officially here in this office tomorrow. Welcome aboard."

Then he was gone, walking back down the hall. And suddenly Marge and Claire and Evelyn were all over her, hugging her, patting her on the back. Quinn stood in a daze, barely aware of them. The full import of what she'd just been told was seeping slowly through to her, like water soaking into a sponge. She'd made it.

I'm in! I'm going to be a doctor!

Christmas, New Year's Eve, her sixteenth birthday, all at once. She felt tears spring into her eyes as she glanced at Tim. He was still in his chair, legs crossed, arms folded across his chest. Everything she'd read about body language told her he was blocking something out—or locking something in. But then he smiled and gave her a thumbs-up.

Quinn began to cry. Matt and Tim—such good friends. They'd saved her life—or the closest thing to it. How could she ever repay them?

She couldn't. Ever. But the least she could do was call Matt and let him know the plan had worked.

She broke away from the Admissions Office ladies, thanked

them with all her heart for their support, then leaned over and kissed Tim on the forehead.

"Thank you," she whispered.

He seemed embarrassed. "Nothing to it."

She turned back to the ladies and waved. "I've got to call home and tell everybody the news. I'll see you all tomorrow."

She ran for the phone booth in the hall and dialed home.

MONITORING

Louis Verran sat amid his blinking indicator lights, twitching meters, tangled wires, and flashing readouts, dreaming of France. He'd spent July in Nice, with side trips to the Camargue and Bourgogne. He'd gone alone, stayed alone—except for those nights when he found a companion—and returned alone. Four weeks had been plenty. As much as he loved Nice and its people, he loved this room even more. All his toys were here, and he missed them when he was away. He'd spent most of August tuning up the electronics. Everything was working perfectly now, everything set for another year. This was the way it was supposed to be: everything under control, and all the controls at his fingertips.

Get a life! That was what his ex-wife had told him the last time she'd walked out. Yeah, well, someday he would. When he re-. tired, it would be to France. He spoke French like a native, loved their wine, their cheese, their gustatorial abandon. They knew how to *live*. But until then, Monitoring was where he felt truly alive. *This* was his life.

He was reaching for a fresh cigar when Alston walked in with Senator Whitney. He shoved the cylinder out of sight.

"There's been a change in the roster," Alston said. "Room two-five-two in the dorm won't be empty as originally planned. We're sticking a female in there. Her name is Cleary, Quinn."

Verran nodded. "No problem. It's all tuned up and ready to go, just like the rest of the dorm."

"Good," the senator said. He smoothed the streaks of gray at his temples. "I want you to keep a close eye on that girl for the first few months."

"Looking for anything in particular?" Verran said, hoping for a clue.

"Anything out of the ordinary," Senator Whitney said. "Her advent is a bit unusual, so we just want her under scrutiny for a while."

"You got it."

Anything out of the ordinary. Big help. But when the senator said, Keep an extra close watch, he didn't have to say why. The senator represented the folks who wrote Verran's biweekly check, so Louis would get it done. Pronto.

Verran tracked her down to one of the pay phones in the Administration Building. He had remote taps on every phone in the Ingraham complex. Once he isolated the tap, he adjusted his headphones and listened in.

The first Quinn Cleary call was nothing special. Five-point-six minutes to her mother, burbling and sobbing over how happy she was about getting in at last. The Irish-sounding mother wasn't exactly overjoyed. Didn't sound happy at all, as a matter of fact. Strange. You'd think a mother would be jumping for joy that her kid had just got herself a full ride to the best medical school in the country—in the freaking *world*.

Well, you couldn't choose your parents. Couldn't choose the name they gave you either. What the hell kind of first name was Quinn, anyway? It made Verran think of *Zorba the Greek*. Some parents were weird. Louis's mother, for instance. He shook his head sadly at the thought of her tight-lipped mouth and wide, wild eyes. There was one lady who'd been a few trestles shy of a full-length bridge.

The second call was more interesting. To a guy named Matt Crawford. The name sounded familiar, and Louis had to smile when he checked it against the name of the kid who hadn't showed today. Wouldn't tightass Alston like to know about this. The little bitch had pulled a fast one on him.

Hadn't really broken any rules—bent a couple into pretzels, maybe, but no harm done. And even if she had trampled a few of Alston's rules, it made no never mind to Verran. In fact, he kind of admired her ingenuity. She had what his father used to call pluck. Verran wasn't sure exactly what pluck was, but he was pretty sure this girl had it.

All the more reason to keep an eye on her. Not just because the senator had said so, but because kids with pluck were unpredictable. Louis Verran didn't like unpredictability, and he loathed surprises.

She finished her call to Crawford and left the hall phone. Verran cut the feed from the tap.

Yes, Miss Quinn Cleary could bend, break, even mutilate all the Dr. Alston rules she wished, just so long as she didn't mess with any of the Louis Verran rules. Those were the ones that kept The Ingraham operating smoothly and efficiently and, most crucially, quietly.

You've had your fun, Quinn Cleary, he thought as he removed his headphones. Now be a good little med student and keep your nose clean for the next four years, and we'll all love you. But if you don't, I'll know. And I'll land on you like a ton of bricks.

FIRST
SEMESTER

Second-quarter sales reports place Kleederman Pharmaceuticals firmly in the top spot as the highest-grossing and most profitable pharmaceutical company in the world.

The New York Times

"I don't think I can go in there."

Quinn couldn't believe she was reacting like this. She stood with her knees locked and her back pressed against the tiled wall of the hallway. She was afraid she'd tip over and fall if she moved away from the wall. The tuna-fish sandwich she'd had for lunch seemed to be sitting in the back of her throat; it wanted out. She hoped her panic wasn't evident to the other first-year students passing by in their fresh gray lab coats.

"Sure you can," Tim said. "There's nothing to it. You just put one foot in front of the other and—"

"There are dead bodies in there," she said through her tightly clenched teeth. "Twenty-five of them."

"Right. That's why they call it the Anatomy Lab."

Quinn's euphoria at becoming a member of The Ingraham's student body had been short-lived. It had floated her along through the first night. All sixteen women enrolled in The Ingraham—seventeen now, with Quinn—were housed in what they called Women's Country, a cluster of rooms at the end of the south wing's second floor. The four women The Ingraham originally had accepted into the new class already had been paired off together. Since she couldn't very well move into the room that had been allocated to Matt—despite the protestations of the guy set to be Matt's roommate that he had absolutely *no* objections to bunking with her—Quinn wound up with a room all to herself, which she did not mind. In fact she liked the idea of having her own private suite. But the daily maid service . . . she wondered if she'd ever get used to that.

Her high lasted through most of the following day's orientation lectures, but it began to thin when she checked in at the student bookstore and received her microscope, her dissection kit, and a three-foot stack of textbooks and laboratory workbooks.

The last wisps were shredded by her first anatomy lecture. The professors at The Ingraham weren't holding back, weren't about to coddle anyone who might be a little slow in adjusting. Their attitude was clear: They were addressing the best of the best, the cream of the intellectual crop, and they saw no reason why they shouldn't plunge into their subjects and proceed at full speed. They covered enormous amounts of material in an hour's time.

Quinn's concentration was taxed to the limit that first morning. At UConn she'd had to put in her share of crunch hours to get her grades, but all along she'd known she was somewhere near the high end of the learning curve in her class. The courses had been pitched to the center of that curve. She'd sailed through them.

Perhaps the courses here too were being pitched toward the center of a curve, but Quinn was quite sure she was not at the upper end of this curve. She hoped she was at least near the middle. She would not be sailing through these courses. She'd be rowing. Rowing like crazy.

You're playing with the big boys now, she told herself.

But she'd handle it. She'd take anything they threw at her and somehow find a way to toss it right back at them.

Except perhaps a dead human being.

She'd never really thought about the fact that a good part of her first year would be spent dissecting a human cadaver. Human Anatomy Lab had been an abstraction. She'd grown up on a farm, for God's sake. She'd delivered calves on her own and helped slaughter chickens, turkeys, and pigs for the table. And in college she'd dissected her share of worms and frogs and fish and fetal pigs and even a cat during comparative anatomy as an undergrad. No problem. Well, the cat had posed a bit of a problem—she'd known it had been a stray, but she couldn't help wondering if it had ever belonged to someone, if somewhere a child was still waiting for her kitty to come home. But she'd got past that.

This was different. Starting today she'd be dissecting a human being—slicing into, peeling back, cutting away the tissues of something that once had been *somebody*. Intellectually, she'd been able to handle that, at least until she'd approached the entrance to the Anatomy Lab, felt the sting of the cool, dank, formaldehyde-laden air in her nostrils as the double doors had swung open and closed, and caught a fleeting glimpse of those rows of large, plastic-sheet-covered forms lumped upon their tables under the bright banks of fluorescents.

Suddenly the prospect was no longer abstract. There were corpses under those sheets, and she was going to have to touch one. Put a knife right into it.

She didn't know if she could. And that angered her. Why was she being so squeamish?

"Come on, Quinn," Tim said, taking her elbow. "I'll be right beside you."

"I'll be okay," she said, shaking him off and straightening herself away from the wall. She was not going to be led into the lab like some sort of invalid. "I'm fine. It's just . . . the smell got to me for a moment."

"Yeah. I know what you mean." Tim grimaced. "It's pretty bad. But we'd better get used to it. We've got three afternoons a week in there for the next two semesters."

"Great." Quinn took a deep breath. "Okay. Lead on, MacDuff."

"Easy: Shakespeare—*Macbeth*—the eponymous character."

"If you say so."

As they pushed through the swinging doors, the formaldehyde hit her like a punch in the nose. Her eyes watered; her nose began to run. She glanced at Tim. He was blinking behind his shades and sniffing too.

He smiled at her, a bit weakly, she thought. "How you doing, Quinn?"

Quinn coughed. She swore she could taste the formaldehyde. "They say we'll adjust. I'd like to believe that."

Tim nodded. "Just be glad the air conditioning's working. It's ninety-five outside. Can you imagine what this place would be like if we had an extended power failure?"

Quinn couldn't—didn't even want to try.

She said, "Let's check the list and see where we're—"

"I already did. Our table's over here."

"*Our* table?"

"Number four."

"How'd we happen to get together?" she said. "Did you pull something . . . ?"

"Not my doing, I swear. Check the list yourself. Brown is the last of the *B*'s. There's only two *C*'s, and Cleary comes before Coye. They put us together."

Quinn stepped over to the bulletin board. Sure enough: Brown, T. and Cleary, Q. were assigned to table four.

"Come on," Tim said. "Stop dragging this out. Let's go meet Mr. Cadaver."

Table four was in the far left corner. As they made their way toward it, Quinn took in her surroundings. The Anatomy Lab was a long, high-ceilinged room, brightly lighted by banks of fluorescents. Twenty-five tables were strung out in two rows of ten and one row of five; a lecture/demonstration area took up the free corner.

She and Tim were among the last to arrive, but no one was looking at them. They all were standing at their assigned metal tables, one on each side, flanking their cadavers—inert mounds beneath light green plastic sheets. Quinn studied the faces of her fellow students as she passed. Some grim, some green, some as gray as their lab coats, some avid and animated, all a bit anxious.

Quinn took heart. Maybe she wasn't such a wimp. She felt a sampling of each of those same emotions swirling within her: As much as she loathed the idea of cutting up a human body, she yearned for what she would be learning. And as eager as she was to get started, she dreaded her first look at that dead face.

"Here we are," Tim said. "Table four." He moved around to the far side of the green-sheeted form. "And here's Mr. Cadaver." He lifted the edge of the sheet and peeked beneath. "Oops. Sorry. *Mrs.* Cadaver."

"Tim," she whispered. "Knock it off. Aren't you . . . the least bit . . . ?" Words failed her.

Tim lowered his dark glasses and looked over the rims with his blue eyes.

"Want to know the truth?" he said softly. "I'm terrified. And I'm completely grossed out." Then he snapped the glasses back up over his eyes and gave her a steely smile. "But don't tell anyone."

Well, we've all got our own ways of dealing with things, I guess, Quinn told herself. This must be his.

Better than throwing up, which was what she felt like doing.

She jumped as the overhead speakers came to life.

"All right, gentlemen and ladies. We're about to start the first dissection. But before we begin, I want each of you to listen very carefully to me."

Quinn looked around and saw their anatomy professor, Dr. Titus Kogan, short, balding, puffy, looking as if he'd spent some time in the formaldehyde baths himself. He stood in the lecture/ demonstration area, holding a microphone.

"For the next nine months you will be dissecting the cadavers at your assigned tables. They are no doubt intimidating now, but you will soon enough become familiar with them. Do not become *too* familiar with them. I will repeat that for anyone who might have missed it: Do not become too familiar with your cadaver.

"Never forget that you are dismantling the body of a fellow human being. This is a rare and precious privilege. Many of these people donated their bodies for this purpose. Others belonged to the least of our species—the homeless, the unidentified, the un-claimed. All of them are anonymous, but that doesn't mean they didn't have names, didn't have friends and family. Remember that as you carve them up. No matter what their past histories, no matter what their socioeconomic status when they were alive, or what route they took to get here, they all deserve our respect. And I shall demand that you accord them that respect.

"I should inform you that this lab will be open at all times. One good thing about an enclosed campus with its own security force is that it allows students access to the labs whenever they need them. Do not hesitate to take advantage of that.

"Now. Roll your cover sheets down to the foot of the table. It is time to begin."

Quinn looked at Tim across the table. He raised his eyebrows. "Ready, partner?"

"Sure," she said, steeling herself. "Now or never. Let's get to it."

They each grabbed a corner of the green plastic sheet and drew it swiftly toward the end of the table.

Gray hair . . . sallow, wrinkled, sagging, turgorless skin . . . flabby buttocks . . . skinny legs—the images, strobed close-ups, bits and pieces, catapulted into her brain. She blinked, got the whole picture. Female. A thin old woman. No jolting surprises in the appearance of their cadaver except that it was lying facedown on the table.

Quinn glanced around at the other tables. All the cadavers were facedown.

She turned back to her table. Whoever the woman was—or had been—Quinn felt embarrassed for her, laid bare like this under these pitiless lights. She wanted to edge the sheet up, at least to cover her buttocks, but she left it where it was. As she tucked the plastic sheet under the cadaver's feet, she noticed a tag tied to her left great toe. She turned it over and read the print:

FREDERICKSON FUNERAL HOME
TOWSON, MD

A name had been block-printed in blue ink below the heading:

DOROTHY HAVERS

Dorothy Havers . . . that couldn't be anything but the woman's name. They weren't supposed to know their cadaver's name. Nobody was.

Quinn pulled her dissection kit from her lab-coat pocket, removed the scissors, and snipped the string. The back of her hand brushed the cold, stiff flesh. She shuddered.

"What are you doing?" Tim asked, leaning over from his side.

"Nothing." She stuffed the tag into her pocket. "Just checking out my kit."

"Good afternoon, Miss Cleary."

Quinn turned and recognized the white-haired figure standing by the head of their table. He wore a stained, wrinkled lab coat and had a battered hardcover copy of *Gray's Anatomy* clamped under his left arm.

"You lucked out," he said, looking over the cadaver. "You got yourself a thin one."

"Dr. Emerson. I didn't expect to see you here."

"Oh, you'll see a lot of me around here," he said, smiling. "Neuropharmacology is my field and my love, but you can spend only so many hours a day calculating minuscule changes in the reuptake rates of sundry neurotransmitters without going batty. A few afternoons a week it does me good to get back to the basics of gross anatomy."

Quinn was glad he was here. She liked Dr. Emerson. She had a feeling he'd played an important part in her acceptance, but she would have liked him anyway. He radiated a certain warmth that invited trust. And it was certainly good to know that she had someone willing to go to bat for her at The Ingraham.

She introduced him to Tim.

"Do you have a photophobic condition, Mr. Brown?" he said, eyeing Tim's shades.

"Yes," Tim said slowly. "In a way."

Quinn then asked the question that had been plaguing her since they'd removed the plastic sheet.

"Why is she facedown?"

"Because the first dissection you'll be doing is the nuchal region, the back of the neck. You'll be looking to isolate the greater occipital nerve. Dr. Kogan will be starting you off momentarily, but if you want to get a jump, take a look at Section One in your lab workbook."

"Okay," Quinn said. "But first . . . "

She freed the end of the plastic sheet from under Dorothy's feet and drew it up to the middle of her back.

Dr. Emerson was looking at her curiously. A faint smile played about his lips. "Are you afraid your cadaver's going to catch a chill?"

She's not just a cadaver, Quinn thought. She's Dorothy.

She shrugged. "We'll only be working on the neck, so I just thought . . . " She ran out of words.

Apparently she didn't need any more. Dr. Emerson was nodding slowly, his eyes bright.

"I understand, Miss Cleary. I understand perfectly."

Quinn made the first cut.

With Dr. Kogan instructing over the loudspeaker and Dr. Emerson watching, Quinn gloved up, fixed a blade to her scalpel handle, and poised the point over the white-haired scalp. The diagram showed a central incision running from the back of the head down to the base of the neck.

She hesitated.

"Want me to do it?" Tim said.

She shook her head. She was going to have to get used to this, and the quickest way to acclimate to the water was to jump in.

"Press hard," Dr. Emerson told her. "Human skin is tough. And human skin that's been in a formaldehyde bath can be almost like shoe leather."

Quinn gritted her teeth and pushed the point through the skin. Dr. Emerson hadn't been exaggerating. Even with a brand-new scalpel blade it was tough going. The honed edge rasped and gritted as she dragged the blade downward to the base of the skull and along the midline groove above the vertebrae of the neck.

"Very good," Dr. Emerson said. "Now you've started. From

here on you're each on your own, each responsible for the dissection of your own side. Later, of course, when we get to them, you'll have to share the unpaired internal organs." He patted Quinn on the shoulder. "I'll be back later to see how you're doing."

"Wow," Tim said to the air when Dr. Emerson had moved on to another table. "Only just got here and already she's teacher's pet."

She flashed him a grin. "Some of us have engaging personalities, some of us don't."

"Is that so?" Tim raised his scalpel in challenge. "Race you to the greater occipital nerve?"

"You're on."

Quinn won.

In fact, she had to stop her own dissection a couple of times to help Tim with his.

Finally she told him, "I would venture to say that your manual dexterity is inversely proportional to the accuracy of your memory."

"Am I to take it then that you don't think neurosurgery is the field for me?"

"Only if you keep the world's finest malpractice defense attorney on permanent retainer."

"Who knows? I may decide to *be* the world's finest defense attorney."

"You have to go to law school for that. This is a med school, in case you forgot."

"Didn't I tell you? I'm going to law school as soon as I graduate from The Ingraham."

Quinn was about to ask Tim if he was joking when one of the second-year student teaching assistants strolled up to the table. The name tag on his lab coat read HARRISON. He was thin, with longish blond hair and pale, pockmarked skin that glistened under the fluorescents. His attitude was condescending, bordering on imperious. Quinn disliked him almost immediately.

"Not bad," he said as he inspected their dissection.

He smiled as he pulled a penlike instrument from the breast pocket of his lab coat, telescoped it into a pointer, and began quizzing Quinn on the local anatomy. She did all right on the tissues they'd already covered in class, but then he began to move into unknown territory.

"We haven't got there yet," Tim said, coming to her aid.

"Oh, really?" Harrison said, his gaze flicking back and forth between the two of them. "Well, maybe you ought to consider showing some initiative. One way to get ahead at The Ingraham is to work ahead."

"Thank you for that advice," Tim said softly. "Now, if you don't mind, what was the origin and insertion of that last muscle you pointed to?"

Harrison smirked. "Look it up," he said, then turned and almost walked into the man standing directly behind him.

"Oh," Harrison said. "Excuse me, Dr. Emerson."

Dr. Emerson's expression was not pleased.

Quinn wondered how long he'd been standing there. Long enough to hear Harrison's last remark, apparently. Quinn hadn't noticed him come up. But Tim obviously had. His lopsided smile told her he'd bushwhacked the second-year student. He cocked his head toward Harrison as he mouthed the words *Dumb ass.*

"I'd like to speak to you a moment, Mr. Harrison," Dr. Emerson said.

He took the younger man aside and did most of the talking. Quinn couldn't hear much of what was being said but caught brief snatches, such as, "—if you wish to keep your stipend—" and "—no place for one-upmanship—"

Finally Harrison nodded and turned away, moving toward the far side of the lab. Dr. Emerson too moved on, not bothering to stop at their table.

"You set that up, didn't you," Quinn said.

" 'Hoist with his own petard.' "

"Easy," Quinn said. "*Hamlet.* But does this mean I have two guardian angels here?"

Tim smiled. "Could be."

"I don't know if I can handle this."

Judy Trachtenberg was speaking, holding a forkful of prime rib over her plate and staring at it. Her dark hair was pulled back into a ponytail; she wore no makeup and looked very pale. She and her roomie, Karen Evers, occupied the room next to Quinn's. She'd hooked up with them on the way to the caf. Tim and his roommate, Kevin Sanders, a big black guy, a quiet type who didn't say much, had joined their table.

"If it's too rare for you," Tim said, "I'll take it."

Judy rolled her eyes and returned the fork to her plate.

"I'm not talking about the *food*. I'm talking about this . . . this whole medical-school thing."

"This is only the first day," Quinn said. "It'll get better. It has to."

She said it to encourage herself as much as Judy. She knew exactly how she was feeling. Like Judy, she'd found today almost overwhelming.

"I can handle the courses easily enough," Judy said. "I mean, give me a textbook, put me in a class, and I can *learn* anything. But these *labs*. Have you *seen* the lab schedule? Every afternoon! And anatomy lab has got to be the *worst*! Am I right?"

A chorus of agreement from the table.

She went on. "I mean, I've washed my hands half a dozen times since we got out of lab and they *still* smell like formaldehyde—and I was wearing *gloves*! My God, I *still* smell it. It must have gotten into my *nose*. I mean, even the *food* tastes like formaldehyde. I don't know if I can handle a whole year of this."

Quinn sniffed her own fingers. Yes, there was a hint of formaldehyde there. She'd thought she'd tasted it for a while, but that was gone now. Maybe Judy was more sensitive to it—or more dramatic. Either way, she was not a happy camper.

"Does that mean you're not going to eat your meat?" Tim said, eyeing Judy's plate.

Judy shoved it toward him. "Here. Be my guest. Eat till you burst. Doesn't any of this bother you?"

Tim speared the prime rib from Judy's plate and placed it on his own.

"Sure," he said. "It's sickening. But I don't dwell on it. It's something you've got to get through. And if you can't handle it, maybe you shouldn't be a doctor."

Judy reddened. "I don't intend to practice on preserved corpses. I plan to have *living* patients."

"Right. But you've got to have a certain amount of intestinal fortitude, got to walk through some fires along the way to get to those living patients. If you can't handle this, how are you going to handle spurting blood and spilling guts when people are calling you Doctor and looking to you for an answer?"

Quinn watched fascinated as Tim somehow managed to cut his meat, poke it into his mouth, chew a couple of times, and swallow, without breaking the rhythm of his speech. His expression was intent—on his food—but his words struck a resonant chord within Quinn: *You do what you have to do.*

Maybe she and Tim weren't so different after all.

"Looking at the way you eat that red meat," Judy said, "I can see you've got no fear of blood and guts."

Amid the laughter, Tim grinned and held up his knife.

"Okay. How about this? We've all met the estimable Mr. Harrison, haven't we?"

Nods and groans all about the table.

"A dork of the first water," Judy said.

"Indisputably. But consider the fact that he's a second-year student. That means he took whatever The Ingraham threw at him in his first year and came through. In your moments of self-doubt, gird yourself with this little thought: I will not be less than Harrison."

Judy stared into Tim's sunglasses for a few seconds, nodding slowly; then she reached across the table and retrieved the remainder of her prime rib.

"I will *not* be less than Harrison," she said.

Amid the applause Quinn looked at Tim and made a startling discovery.

I like you, Tim Brown. I like you a lot.

But she'd never tell him that.

T im's head was killing him as he pulled into The Ingraham's student parking lot. He leaned forward and gently rested his forehead on the steering wheel.

Jack Daniel's . . . too much Jack Daniel's. It happened every time someone talked him into trying some sour mash.

He shook himself and straightened. He'd made it from Baltimore in forty minutes—record time—but he hadn't raced all that distance just to take a nap in the parking lot. He glanced at his watch. Two minutes to get to Alston's lecture. He jumped out of the car and hurried toward the class complex. He eyed the security cameras high on the corners of the buildings, wondering if they were eyeing him.

As the days had stretched into weeks, Tim had found himself falling into the rhythm of The Ingraham's class and lab schedule. The basic first-year courses were mostly rote. Anatomy, pathology, and histology were purely memory. Biochemistry and physiology were more analytical but still mostly regurgitated facts. And regurgitating facts was Tim's specialty. Poor Quinn needed hours of crunch study to master what he could absorb in minutes.

So he'd found himself getting bored. Sure there was the roving bull session in the dorm, but he could take only so much of speculating and arguing about the future of medicine. Novels and his tape collection could hold his interest only so long. With everybody's head but his own buried in a book most of the time, he'd begun to feel like the only seeing, speaking person in a land populated by the deaf and blind.

The only answer was to get off campus. The nearby county seat of Frederick was little better than staying on campus. He needed a city. Baltimore and Washington were the two obvious choices.

He was passing the pond when he heard a familiar voice.

"Where have you been?"

He turned and saw Quinn hurrying up the walk behind him. He stopped to wait for her, nodding to others he knew as they swirled past him. She looked great, but he didn't want her to get too close. He figured he had a terminal case of morning mouth.

"Miss me?" he said.

"I was looking for you last night. Kevin told me you took off after dinner. God, you look awful. Where on earth have you been?"

"Baltimore."

He knew a little about the city. Some guys he'd hung with in high school had gone to Loyola, and he'd made a few trips down there during his four years at Dartmouth. But last night he'd headed for downtown, far from Loyola's suburban neighborhood. He'd hit Baltimore Street: the Block. Baltimore's downsized equivalent of New York's West Forty-second Street or Boston's Combat Zone.

He hadn't gone there for the porn shops, the peep shows, the strippers, or the whores. He'd gone for the games. He'd learned on his past visits that there were a couple or three backroom card games in progress on any given night, games with stakes high enough to make things interesting.

Trouble was, they hardly ever played blackjack. Poker, poker, poker, was all these guys cared about. Tim knew he was a decent poker player, but nothing close to what he was in blackjack. Still, he was desperate for some action, and Atlantic City was too far.

"Did you get mugged or something?" Quinn said, looking him up and down.

He smiled and thought, In a way, yes.

He'd stayed up all night playing five-card stud. The other players had been standoffish at first—because of his youth, Tim assumed—but after they'd seen he could play, they'd warmed to him. Even started buying him drinks after a while. Jack Daniel's. Many Jack Daniel's.

Good ol' Tim. C'mon back anytime.

They loved him. Why not? He'd dropped a couple of hundred. Poker. Not his game.

"No. Just not enough sleep."

"Well, come on. You're late, and Dr. Alston will cut you up into little pieces."

"You go on ahead. I'm going to sit in the back. *Way* in the back."

He watched her cute butt hurry off and followed at a slower pace.

Dr. Alston's medical ethics: the semester's only nonregurgitant course. It was scheduled for only one hour a week, but that hour fell at 7:00 A.M. on Wednesday mornings. Some days it was hell getting there, and today was pure murder, but Tim had never missed it; not simply because attendance was required and strictly monitored, but because the class actually was stimulating.

I could use some stimulating now, he thought, as he slipped into the last row and took a seat in a shadowed corner.

Dr. Alston seemed to take delight in being provocative and controversial. His manner was brusque, witty, acerbic, and coolly intellectual, as if he were contending for the title of the William F. Buckley, Jr., of the medical world.

Tim vividly remembered the first lecture a couple of weeks ago. . . .

"Most medical schools don't offer this course," Dr. Alston had said on that first morning. He'd looked wolfishly lean in his dark business suit and one of his trademark string ties. The overhead lights gleamed off his pale scalp. His movements were quick, sharp, as if his morning coffee had been too strong. "I guess they expect you to become ethical physicians by osmosis—or pinocytosis, perhaps. And a few schools may offer something *called* medical ethics, but I assure you it's nothing like my course. *Their* courses are dull."

Amid polite laughter he'd stepped off the dais and pointed at one of the students.

"Mr. Kahl. Consider, if you will: You have a donor kidney and three potential recipients with perfect matches. Who gets the kidney?"

Kahl swallowed hard. "I . . . I don't have enough information to say."

"Correct. So let's say we've got a nine-year-old girl, a thirty-five-year-old ironworker with a family, a forty-seven-year-old homeless woman, and a sixty-two-year-old CEO of a large corporation—who, by the way, is willing to pay six figures for the transplant." He pointed toward the rear of the room. "Who would you give the kidney to, Mr. Coye?"

"The little girl."

"She has no money, you know."

"Money shouldn't matter. I wouldn't care if the CEO was willing to pay *seven* figures for the kidney."

"We wouldn't be indulging in a bit of reverse discrimination against a rich, older man over an indigent child, would we, Mr. Coye?" He turned to another student. "How about you, Mr. Greely? Think carefully and unemotionally before you answer."

Tim was impressed. This was Dr. Alston's first lecture to the class and already he seemed to know every student by name.

"I believe I'd also give it to the little girl," Greely said.

"Really? Why?"

"Because she's got the most years ahead of her."

"Years to do what? You don't know what she'll do with her life. Maybe she'll perfect cold fusion, maybe she'll die at eighteen with a needle in her arm. Meanwhile you tell the homeless woman, the ironworker, and the CEO to go scratch?"

He turned toward the second row. "Who would you choose, Miss Cleary?"

Tim leaned forward when he realized Quinn was on the spot. He saw her cheeks begin to redden. She wasn't ready for this. No one was.

"The ironworker," she said in that clear voice of hers.

"And why is that?"

"Because he's got a family to support. Other people are depending on him. And he's got a lot of productive years ahead of him."

"What about the CEO? He's very productive."

She paused, then: "Yes, but maybe he'll get twenty years out of the kidney. The ironworker might get twice that."

"Perhaps, perhaps not. But the CEO's present position places him in charge of the livelihoods of thousands of workers. Without his management expertise his corporation could go under."

Quinn obviously hadn't thought of that, but she didn't seem ready to back down. Tim decided to buy her some time.

"Are doctors supposed to be playing God like this?" he called out.

Dr. Alston looked up and pointed at him. He didn't seem annoyed that Tim had spoken without being recognized.

"An excellent question, Mr. Brown. But 'playing God' is a loaded phrase, don't you think? It implies an endless bounty being doled out to some and withheld from others. That is not the case here. We are dealing with meager resources. There are barely enough donor organs available at any one time to fulfill the needs of one *tenth* of the registered recipients. No, Mr. Brown, we are hardly playing God. It rather seems more like we are sweeping up after Him."

He returned to the dais and surveyed the class for a moment before speaking again. Tim found Dr. Alston a bit too pompous, but the subject was fascinating.

"In an ideal world," Dr. Alston said, "there would be a donated organ waiting for every person who needed one, there would be a dialysis machine for every chronic renal-failure patient who was a difficult match, bypass surgery for every clogged coronary artery, endarterectomy for every stenotic carotid, total replacement surgery for every severely arthritic hip and knee . . . I could go on all morning. The sad, grim truth is that there isn't. And there never will be. And what is even grimmer is the increasing gap between the demand for these high-tech, high-ticket, state-of-the-art procedures and society's ability to supply them.

"Consider: There are now around thirty million people over age sixty-five on Medicare. In the year 2011, when you are in the prime of your practice years, the first baby boomers will hit Medicare age. By the year 2030 they will swell the Medicare ranks to sixty-five million. That is nothing compared to what will be going on outside our borders where the world population will have reached ten *billion* people."

Dr. Alston paused to let his words sink in, and Tim struggled to comprehend that figure. Ten billion people—almost twice the planet's present population. Who the hell was going to care for all of them?

As if reading his mind, Dr. Alston continued.

"Don't bother cudgeling your brains to figure out how to care for the world's population when you'll be hard-pressed enough satisfying the demands of the geriatric baby boomers. And believe me, those demands will be considerable. They will have spent their lives receiving the best medical care in the world, and they will expect to go on receiving it."

"*Is* it the best?" a voice challenged from the rear.

"Yes, Mr. Finlay. It is the best. You can quibble about delivery, but when those who can afford to go anywhere in the world need state-of-the-art treatment, where do they come? They come to

America. When foreign medical graduates want the top residencies and postgraduate training, where do they apply? To their own countries' medical centers? No. They apply here. The U.S. can't handle more than a fraction of the foreign doctors who want to take residencies here. Conversely, how many U.S. medical-school graduates do you hear of matriculating to Bombay, or Kiev, or even Brussels, Stockholm, Paris, or London? Have you heard of *one*? At the risk of sounding chauvinistic, this is where the cutting edge of medicine gets honed."

Tim felt a guilty surge of pride. If the United States had the best, then certainly he was enrolled in the best of the best. He made a little promise to himself to put what he learned at The Ingraham to good use.

"But back to our elderly baby boomers: Who is going to supply their enormous demand for medical care? That demand will eat up a proportionally enormous portion of the GNP. The national debt was one trillion in 1980. It is now approaching five trillion. Who can guess what it will be by the time the twenty-first century rolls in? Who is going to pay for all that medical care? In an ideal world it would be no problem. But in this world, the real world, choices will have to be made. In the real world there are winners and losers. Some will get their transplant, their endarterectomy, their chance to resume a normal life; others will not. Who will decide? Who'll be making the list and checking it twice, deciding which ones receive a share of the finite medical resources available, and which ones do not?

"Is that playing God? Perhaps. But someone must make the decisions. Ultimately the guidelines will be drawn up by politicians and administered by their bureaucrats."

Tim lent his groan to the others arising from all sides of the lecture hall. Dr. Alston raised his arms to quiet them.

"But you *can* have a say. Ultimately you *will* have a say. Often the final say. Look at the tacit decision you all made this morning. How many of you considered the homeless woman for the transplant?"

Tim scanned the hall from his rear seat. Not a hand went up.

Dr. Alston nodded slowly. "Why not, Mr. Jessup?"

Jessup started in his seat as if he'd been shocked. "Uh ... I ... because it seemed the other candidates could put the transplant to better use."

"Exactly! Societal worth is a factor here. There are individuals who give much more to the human community than they receive, and there are those who put in as much as they take out. And then there are those who contribute absolutely nothing but spend their entire existence taking and taking. In the rationing of medical resources, what tier should they occupy? Should they be classed with the hardworking majority where they can siphon off valuable health-care resources in order to continue their useless lives at the expense of the productive members of society?"

"No one's completely useless," said a female voice. Tim recognized it as Quinn's.

Good for you, babe.

Dr. Alston's eyes gleamed. "How right you are, Miss Cleary. And someday it might fall to you to help these people become useful, to guide them toward making a contribution to the society they've sponged off for most of their lives. But more on that another time. The purpose of this course is to give you the tools, the perspectives to make the monumental moral and ethical choices which will become an everyday part of medical practice in the future."

So saying, Dr. Alston had ended his introductory class in medical ethics. Tim had felt intellectually alive for the first time since classes had begun. He'd vowed then never to miss one of these classes.

He was remaining true to that vow this morning, hangover and all.

WHERE ARE THEY NOW?

Quinn and Tim had stopped before the huge pin board in the main hall of the administration building, the companion to the one in the caf. She'd glanced at the display in passing on a daily basis, but this was the first time in a while she'd stopped to look at the list of graduates of which The Ingraham seemed the proudest. Tim stopped beside her.

As she read through the names and their locations all across the country, she was impressed at how far and wide The Ingraham's graduates had spread from this little corner of Maryland. They ran inner-city clinics or nursing homes from Los Angeles to Lower Manhattan to Miami, Chicago, Houston, Detroit, and all points between. And all were active staff members of a KMI medical center that was never far away.

A thought struck her.

"Doesn't anybody come out of The Ingraham and practice medicine in the suburbs?"

"Maybe," Tim said. "But I don't think they're listed here."

"Weird, isn't it," she said as they walked on. "Dr. Alston's always talking about ranking patients according to societal value, and the way he talks, you'd figure he'd place inner-city folks at the bottom of the list. But here you've got all these Ingraham graduates spending their professional lives in inner-city clinics."

She couldn't say exactly why, but somehow the "Where Are They Now?" board gave her a vaguely uneasy feeling.

The World's Longest Continuous Floating
Medical Bull Session

(I)

"Not tonight," Quinn told Tim as he tried to get her to sit in on the bull session when it moved into his room. "I've got to crunch path."

"Lighten up or you'll wind up like Metzger," said a second-year student she didn't know.

"Who's Metzger?" Quinn said.

"Someone from our year. He studied so hard he began hearing voices in his head. Went completely batty."

"Or how about that guy in the year before us?" said another second-year. "The guy who went over the wall. What was his name?"

"Prosser," said the first. "Yeah. Work too hard and you might pull a Prosser."

"What does that mean?" Quinn said.

"One night he upped and left. Vanished without a trace. No one's heard from him since."

"Okay," Quinn said. "I'll stay. But not too long."

"All right!" Tim said, making room for her beside him. "Where were we?"

It was some sort of tradition. No one knew how it got started, but it had been going as long as anyone could remember. The floating bull session, wandering from room to room, from floor to floor, changing personnel from night to night, hibernating during class hours and sleep time, but reawakening every night after dinner to pick up where it had left off.

Quinn rarely got involved in the sessions; she had too much work to do, always seemed just on the verge of—but never quite— catching up. But when she did sit in, the topic almost always gravitated toward Dr. Alston's lectures. Like tonight.

"I was up," Judy Trachtenberg said. "I was just saying that if rationing of medical services is inevitable, maybe the elderly should be put at the ends of the waiting lists."

"Sure," Tim said. "I can just see you telling your grandmother she can't have that hip operation because she's over seventy-five."

"So, I'd find a way to squeeze her in," Judy said with an expressive shrug.

Her casual attitude offended Quinn. As much as she wanted to avoid getting mired in one of these endless conversations, she had to speak.

"Either you believe in what you're proposing or you don't," she said. "You can't say this is how we're going to do it, these are the rules, and they apply to everyone equally—except my friends and family."

Judy laughed. "Quinn, where have you been for the past thousand years? This is the way the world works. *What* you know is nowhere near as important as *who* you know."

Quinn felt herself reddening but pressed on.

"But then you run into the corruption of the magnitude of old USSR-style Communism, where the size of your apartment and the amount of meat on your plate depended on how buddy-buddy you were with the local commissar. I don't think that kind of system is the answer."

"Well, we need *some* kind of system," Judy said. "Like a national health-insurance program that will keep costs down so we can distribute the services as broadly as possible."

"And end up like the Brits?" Tim said. "No, thanks. Their system is broke and they're already rationing care to the elderly. A million people on waiting lists. Nobody over fifty-five gets dialysis. Chemotherapy and coronary bypasses are strictly rationed too. That's pretty cold. That kind of system seems to ensure that everyone gets *some* health care, but no one gets *great* health care. And I'm one hundred percent against rationing."

"So am I," Judy said. "But since I don't plan to practice in

Shangri-La, what do we do when we can't treat everybody on demand?"

"Do it on a need basis," Tim said. "The guy whose heart has the worst coronary arteries and is just about to quit gets first spot on the list, and the next worst gets second, and so on."

Quinn said, "But what about the guy who's far down the list with only one bad coronary artery, but his angina's bad enough to keep him from running his forklift? Does he have to wait till he's in cardiogenic shock before he gets some help?"

"If he gets worse, we move him up the list."

"In other words, under your system people will have to get sicker before they can get well?"

Tim scratched his head, his expression troubled. "You know, I never looked at it like that."

"Okay, Quinn," Judy said. "Now that you've shot everything down, what's your solution to the mess?"

"The *coming* mess," Quinn said. "Dr. Alston talks like it's already here, but it's not. And with the way medical knowledge and technology are advancing, the entire practice of medicine could be revolutionized by 2011. It might be nothing like what we see today. We'll have new resources, new methods of delivery, we might be able to handle—"

"You can't count on that," Judy said.

"Technological growth is exponential," Quinn said. "As the base broadens—"

"You still can't count on it."

Quinn sighed. Judy was right. No matter what happened, the Medicare population was going to double in the next thirty to forty years, but medical resources weren't going to double with them.

She had a sudden vision of the future. She found herself in the worn-down and rusted-out body of an elderly woman, seventy-six years old, with a failing heart, gallstones, and arthritis, trudging from specialist to specialist, clinic to clinic, hospital to hospital, trying to find relief, and being told repeatedly that none of her conditions met the established criteria that would allow immediate medical intervention, so she'd have to wait her turn.

True enough, perhaps, on paper. True enough according to the numbers the medical facilities had used to encode her diagnoses for the government computers.

True enough: Her heart failure had been gauged as Grade II, which meant the old pump was failing, its reserve low enough to make a breathless chore of walking a single block, but still pumping well enough to keep her from being completely incapacitated; Grade II heart failure warranted only a limited workup and certainly not aggressive therapy.

True enough: Her Grade II gallbladder disease did not trigger attacks of sufficient severity to yellow her skin or generate enough unremitting pain to warrant emergency surgery, but her rattling gallstones did cause her daily abdominal distress and incessant belching, and she lived in constant fear of another attack, so much so that each meal had become a form of gastric Russian roulette.

True enough: The Grade III arthritis in her hip elicited a bolt of pain whenever she went up or down a stair, and her spine was arthritic enough to cause it to stiffen like a rusty gate whenever she sat or reclined for more than fifteen minutes, which made rising from a chair or getting out of bed each morning an excruciating ordeal; but her symptoms—when adjusted for age—did not code severe enough (you needed Grade V) under the federal guidelines to warrant hip surgery or even one of the newer, more potent anti-inflammatory medications that were in such short supply; she'd have to make do with the older, more tried-and-true (and lower-priced) generics.

All true enough—when each condition was considered one at a time. If she had been afflicted with just the arthritis, or merely the gallstones, or simply the heart failure, she could have handled it. And she even might have coped fairly well with a combination of any two of them.

But all three?

The triple whammy was slowly doing her in, melting her days into exhausted blurs, nibbling away at her quality of life to the point where she'd begun to wonder whether life was worth living any longer.

Why wasn't there a code for the quality of life? Why couldn't the computers add up a person's Grade IIs and Grade IIIs and send up a red flag that said *Help* when they reached a certain critical number—regardless of age?

Was that what it was going to be like? Number-coded doctors treating the number-coded diseases afflicting number-coded patients? There had to be another way.

But what?

"Quinn?" It was Tim's voice. "Yo, Quinn. Where are you? Come back to us."

Quinn shook herself. "I'm, uh, thinking," she said.

"Good," Tim said. "I thought you were in a trance. Come up with anything?"

"No," she said. "No solution. Sooner or later the politicians and bureaucrats are going to take over completely. They can control the funds and the distribution of their so-called resources—and they'll consider us 'resources' too—but they can't control the delivery of compassion, can they?"

Judy groaned, but Tim cut her off with a karate-chop wave of his hand.

Tim nodded. "You said it. The empty suits will try to get into the hospital charts, into the operating rooms, into the office records, even into the examining rooms." He tapped his chest. "They'll even try to get in here, and believe me, plenty of times they'll succeed, but they can't get a piece of that special chemistry that happens between a doctor and a patient unless we let them. And part of that chemistry is compassion. Empathy."

"The floor's getting gooey with idealism," Judy said. "How about a little realism here?"

"We're still students," Tim said. "We're not supposed to be realists. That comes later. For the moment let's believe in the healing power of compassion."

Quinn saw the fire in his eyes, the ferocity in his tight smile, and knew she'd found a kindred spirit. She raised a fist to chin level and responded with a smile of her own.

"Compassion," she said. "Let 'em find a procedure code for *that*."

MONITORING

"I believe it's time to start the night music," Alston said. "What do you think?"

Louis Verran concealed his annoyance as Alston stood with his hands behind his back and leaned forward over his shoulder, studying the main console.

Right, Verran thought. Like he almost knows what he's looking at.

"You're the boss," he said, not meaning a word of it. In this room Louis Verran was the boss.

Alston pointed to one of the readouts. "My goodness, what's going on in room one-oh-seven?"

Verran glanced up. The mattress-weight sensor for bed B had risen into the red.

"Looks like some extra bodies on the bed. I'd guesstimate about four."

Alston's eyes widened. "Really? What on earth could they be doing?"

"Probably an orgy," Verran said, keeping his face deadpan. "Don't you wish we had video?"

"Certainly not. Turn up the audio and let's hear what's going on."

Verran activated the audio. All of the rooms had been wired with tiny electret microphones. The sound of male voices quizzing each other on hepatic histology swelled through the speakers.

"Orgy indeed!" Alston said. He pointed to another readout panel. "Look at room two-twenty-four. What's—"

Verran took a deep puff on his cigar and floated a trio of blue-white smoke rings. He watched with concealed amusement as Alston backed away, waving his hand through the air.

"Must you, Louis?"

"If you can't stand the smoke," Verran muttered, "stay away from the console."

He glanced at Alston and was startled by the fury that flashed across his features. It showed only for an instant, then was gone as if it had never been, and the prissy, supercilious expression was back in control. But Verran realized his remark had caused the mask to slip and allowed a darker side of Dr. Arthur Alston to peek through.

Verran glanced at Kurt and Elliot. Both of his assistants were busy at their own consoles, checking the mattress sensors to see who was in bed and who wasn't. They gave no indication that they had heard or seen anything. Good. They'd learned quickly to act oblivious to the squabbles between their boss and Dr. Alston. Verran had known them both when he'd been with the CIA. He'd hired them away from the Company when he'd landed this job.

Elliot and Kurt—the tortoise and the hare.

Elliot was careful, meticulous, one of the best electronic-surveillance jockeys in the business. He could bug a room six ways from Sunday with no one the wiser. But he'd been stopped on the street in Costa Rica one night and couldn't explain all the electronic junk in his trunk. Spent one very rough week in an Alajuela jail before the Company could extricate him. Elliot never spoke of that week, but even now he got quiet and twitchy whenever anyone mentioned jail. After the Costa Rica incident, he refused any and all foreign assignments. Which meant his career was dead in the water.

Kurt was fast on his feet but a little flaky. He had gained a reputation around the Company as something of a loose cannon and had been passed over a number of times when promotions came around. It was obvious he wasn't going to move any further up the ladder.

Neither had hesitated when Verran offered them jobs at The Ingraham. He'd never regretted it, and neither had they.

But he did regret having to deal with Alston. Even so, Verran wouldn't have made that kind of crack if Alston were his direct superior. But after seeing Alston's ferocious reaction, Verran was suddenly very glad that he didn't have to answer to the man. He had a feeling life could be pretty shitty for an underling who got on the good doctor's bad side. Fortunately, security had its own responsibilities, separate from Alston's education bailiwick. They both answered to the foundation, however. And the foundation, of course, answered to Mr. Kleederman.

Verran had never met Mr. Kleederman and had not the slightest desire to do so.

"I assure you, Louis," Alston said levelly, "I wouldn't be here if I didn't have to be. I don't enjoy your smoky presence any more than you enjoy mine."

Verran put his cigar in the ashtray—he would let it sit there and go out as a peace-making gesture. Besides, he needed peace to function in this job.

Maybe he'd been letting Alston get too far under his skin. The creep was a long-term irritation, like his ulcer, and he'd have to learn to live with him, just as he'd learned to live with the gnawing, hungerlike pain in his gut. But if the undercurrent of hostility between them broke out into the open, it could impinge on Verran's concentration. And he couldn't allow that. Security at The Ingraham was a seven-days-a-week, around-the-clock process that ruled his life ten months a year. And he was good at his job. Damn good. There'd been a few glitches over the years, and a couple of close calls, but he and Alston had been able to keep them nice and quiet, with no one—except the foundation—the wiser.

So, like it or not, he and Alston had to work together, or their heads could wind up on the chopping block.

"I've got nothing against you, Doc. It's just that we're dealing with delicate equipment here. State-of-the-art sensors and pickups. Very temperamental. I get nervous when anybody but me or Kurt or Elliot gets near it. This stuff is my baby and I'm a protective daddy. So don't take it personal."

Alston accepted the truce with a slight nod of his head. "I understand. No offense taken. It's forgotten."

Right, Verran thought. Tightasses never forget.

"So," Alston said, clearing his throat with a sound like a record needle skipping to another track, "it seems to me that we've given them enough time to acclimate to their new surroundings. A few weeks should suffice for anyone. All the equipment is in a state of readiness, I assume?"

"The SLI units are ready and waiting. Every room in the dorm is on-line and working like a dream."

"Excellent. And our new charges, are they all behaving themselves? No bad apples in the bunch?"

"All but one: the Brown kid."

"Timothy Brown? The high-IQ boy from New Hampshire? What's he been up to?"

Alston's ability to recognize each student's face and reel off his vital statistics never failed to amaze Verran. It was the one thing about Alston he envied.

"All-nighters," Verran said.

"We certainly don't discourage studying, Louis."

"No. I mean *out* all night. Off campus."

"Really?" Alston frowned with concern. "That's not good. Where?"

"Baltimore, I think."

"How often?"

"Twice, so far."

"Weekday nights?"

"Let me check." Verran swiveled to his computer keyboard and punched in Brown's room number. His data file scrolled down the screen. "One Tuesday into Wednesday, and one Saturday into Sunday."

"Hmmm. I don't like that midweek absence. Let's hope he doesn't make a habit of it. We'll have to come down on him if he does, but we'll let it go for now. I don't particularly care about the weekends. Any night music they hear on weekends is a lagniappe anyway. But do keep a close watch on young Mr. Brown. I do *not* want another fiasco like two years ago."

Verran's stomach burned at the memory. Neither did he. One of those was enough for a lifetime.

"Will do," he said. "You're the boss."

Alston smiled and it looked almost genuine. "You sound so convincing when you say that, Louis."

"Well, you *are* the DME, after all."

"Yes. The maestro, as it were. Very well, strike up the band and let The Ingraham's nocturnal concert series begin."

He turned and headed for the door, humming a tune Verran recognized from *The Phantom of the Opera* . . . "The Music of the Night."

OCTOBER

Carbenamycin (Carbocin—Kleederman Pharm.), the new macrolide released just two years ago, has become the most prescribed antibiotic in the United States.

P.M.A. News

A warm day for October, with a high, bright sun cooking the asphalt of the parking lot like summer. Good driving weather.

"Are you *sure* you don't want some company?" Tim said, leaning against the driver's door of his car and speaking through the open window. "I'll even do the driving."

"Any other time and I'd say yes," Quinn said as she adjusted the seat belt. "But this is personal."

He reached through the window and gripped her shoulder. His voice rose in a panicky quaver.

"Oh, no, Quinn! Not another abortion. This makes three this year! I *told* you I'd stand by you!"

A fellow student who had a seat near hers in histology lab was passing nearby. His head whipped in their direction and almost tripped on the curb, but he recovered and hurried past.

Quinn fixed her eyes straight ahead as she felt her cheeks go crimson. She tried to keep her voice level.

"I hate you, Timothy Brown. It's as simple as that. Even if you lend me this car every day for the next four years, I will still hate you forever."

He flashed his boyish smile and slapped the roof.

"Take good care of Griffin for me, drive carefully, and wear shorts more often—you've got dynamite legs."

Her cheeks didn't cool until she reached the highway, then she smiled and shook her head. *My third abortion?* How did he come up with things like that?

She checked the gas gauge and saw that it read full. He was a clown, but a considerate clown.

She found Route 70 and followed it east. Company would have

been nice, but how could she explain to Tim this need to learn about their cadaver?

She took the inner loop on 695 to York Road in Towson and followed that south. She almost cruised past the Towson Library without seeing it. Not because it was small. It was huge, but it looked as if the town had used the same architect as the Berlin Wall. With all that bare, exposed concrete it looked about as warm and inviting as a bomb shelter.

Inside wasn't much better, but the friendliness of the librarians went a long way toward countering the bunker decor. They gave her a stack of back issues of the Towson *Times*, the local weekly, and she began to search through the obits. There weren't many. Quinn was beginning to worry that the *Times* might print only select obituaries when she spotted the heading:

DOROTHY HAVERS, LONGTIME
TOWSON RESIDENT, AGE 82

Dorothy O'Boyle Havers, the only daughter of Francis and Catherine O'Boyle, both Irish immigrants, died on July 12 of natural causes at the Laurel Hills Medical Center. Prior to that she had been a resident of the Towson Nursing Center for seven years. Mrs. Havers was predeceased by her husband, Earl, and by her two daughters, Catherine and Francine. No plans for viewing or burial were announced.

Ireland . . . Dorothy came over from Ireland . . . just like her mother. And she'd died right next door to The Ingraham.

Quinn reread the obit and was swept by a wave of sadness. Of course no plans for viewing or burial were announced. There was nobody to view her remains, nobody left to mourn at her grave side. Husband dead, children dead, seven years in a nursing home, probably without a single visitor, completely forgotten, no one caring if she lived or died. So she'd willed her body to The Ingraham.

Poor woman.

But what had she died of? That might be interesting to know during the dissection. She wondered if they'd know at the Towson Nursing Center. How far could it be?

Quinn photocopied the obituary, then went looking for a phone.

*   *   *

"Dorothy Havers?" said Virginia Bennett, RN, head nurse at the Towson Nursing Center. "I remember that name. You say you're related to her?"

"Her great-niece," Quinn said.

She'd discovered the Towson Nursing Center was a couple of miles from the library, so she'd stopped in to learn what she could. The one-story dark brick building seemed about as pleasant as something called a nursing home could be. Elderly men and women sat in wheelchairs around the foyer while others inched by with the aid of four-footed canes. A vague odor of urine suffused the air, like olfactory Muzak.

"Well, I'll be." Nurse Bennett scratched the side of her neck with short scarlet fingernails. She had ebony skin, gray hair, and a bulldog face, but seemed pleasant enough. "We searched high and low for a next of kin last year when we were getting ready to transfer her to the medical center. Couldn't find anybody. Figured she was alone in the world."

"We have a common relative in Ireland," Quinn said, amazed at how easily the lies tripped off her tongue. She'd figured no one would tell her a thing about Dorothy unless they thought she was related. "I just happened to come across her name while I was researching the family's medical history. Was she very sick?"

"Just a little heart failure, if I remember. But Dr. Clifton—he's one of our doctors—is very conservative. He refers patients to the medical center at the first sign of trouble. But he's top-notch. A graduate of The Ingraham, you know."

"Really? That's good to know."

"But what sort of family history were you looking for?"

"There's ovarian cancer in one of my aunts, and I was wondering . . . "

"Very important," Nurse Bennett said, jabbing a finger at Quinn. "But I don't know a thing about Mrs. Havers, so I can't—" She glanced past Quinn. "Wait. There's Dr. Clifton now. Maybe he can help you. Dr. Clifton? Could we see you a minute?"

Quinn turned and saw a young, dark-haired doctor, surely not much older than thirty, entering through a rear door, dressed in a sport coat and carrying a black bag.

"Dr. Clifton," Nurse Bennett said as he approached the desk. "You remember Dorothy Havers, don't you? This is her great-niece."

It almost looked to Quinn as if Dr. Clifton stumbled a step. He blinked twice, then smiled.

"I didn't know Dotty had a great-niece, or any kind of relative at all."

Quinn repeated her story about the Ireland link, and about researching the family medical history. The lies came easier the second time around.

"No," Dr. Clifton said. "Dotty had no history of cancer of any sort. Her main problem was arteriosclerosis—coronary and cerebral. We were sorry to lose her this summer. She was a nice lady."

"I wish I'd known her," Quinn said, and that wasn't a lie. "Was she in bad heart failure when you transferred her to the medical center?"

"Bad enough in my clinical opinion to need more intense care than a nursing home could provide," he said stiffly. "Is there a point to these questions, Miss . . . ?"

"Sheedy," Quinn said, barely missing a beat. "No. Just curious."

"Well, then, as much as I'd like to satisfy your curiosity, Miss Sheedy, I have rounds to make. Excuse me."

"Not much of a bedside manner," Quinn said after he'd hurried off.

"Must have had a bad day," Nurse Bennett said. "Usually he's very easygoing."

Not today, Quinn thought. Today he's downright defensive.

As she left the Towson Nursing Center, she noticed the small print on the entry plaque: OWNED AND OPERATED BY KLEEDERMAN MEDICAL INDUSTRIES.

KMI is everywhere, she thought. I guess I'll be pretty well connected after I graduate.

She wondered why she took no comfort in that.

She pulled the folded copy of Dorothy Havers's obituary from her pocket and reread it.

"There's no one left to remember you, is there, Dorothy Havers," she said softly. "Tell you what. I'll remember you, with gratitude, for the rest of my life. And maybe I can get someone else to remember you too."

"Well, now. Look at you."

Quinn glanced up from her dissection of the accessory nerve

to see Tim peering at her from the other side of their cadaver. He'd just arrived, late as usual.

"What's the matter with me?" she said.

"Here she is, the gal who was turning three shades of green out in the hall before her first an lab last month, and look at her now: having lunch with her cadaver."

Quinn paused. Tim was right. She hadn't given it any thought, but she had come a long way since that first day when she'd feared she was going to toss her cookies as soon as she stepped into this room. She hardly noticed the smell anymore, and here she was, barely a month later, sitting with her nose in her dissection of the rhomboid muscles, a Pepsi to her left by the cadaver's shoulder, and a half-eaten Twinkie to her right by the hip.

"A testament to the human organism's adaptability, I suppose," she said.

"And how."

Quinn watched him open his kit, pull the damp cloth off his dissection, and sit down. Only his head was visible on the far side as he got to work. She'd been debating how to broach a certain subject with him and figured now was as good a time as any.

"I've been thinking," Quinn said.

"Careful. That can be dangerous. Habit-forming, even."

"Seriously. I want to name our cadaver."

Tim glanced up at her. "Yeah? Well, why not? Kevin and Jerry named theirs Auntie Griselda. We can name ours Skinny Minnie."

"No. I mean give it a real name. A person's name."

He went back to his rhomboids. "Any particular name in mind?"

"Dorothy."

"Dorothy . . . like Dorothy of the Oz variety?"

"Exactly."

"Should we scare up a little dead dog and name it Toto?"

God, he could be annoying at times. "I don't know why I even bothered."

Tim must have tuned in to her tone. He glanced up again. "Okay. Dorothy it is. We can call her Dot."

"No," Quinn said firmly. "Not Dot. Dorothy."

"Why is this suddenly so important?"

Quinn had hoped he wouldn't ask that. She couldn't tell him, That's her name, and she wasn't sure how to answer otherwise without sounding like some sort of wimp.

"I've got my reasons," she said. "But you're going to think they're corny and sappy."

Tim set down his instruments and leaned forward. "Try me."

"All right." She took a deep breath and rattled off her rationale: "I want to call her a real name because she was a real person when she was alive, and I think it's only fair that we think of her as a 'she' or a 'her' instead of an 'it.' And as we whittle her away and she stops looking like something even remotely human, maybe we can still think of her as a person if she's got a person's name. Dot isn't very human. It's like a punctuation mark. But Dorothy sounds pretty neighborly and very human—even without a dog."

Tim's lips were struggling against a smile as he stared at her. Finally it broke through.

"You're right," he said. "Those are *very* corny and sappy reasons. But if it's important to you, then it's a done deal. From now on, our friend on the table is Dorothy. Do we want to give her a last name?"

"No." God, no. The first name was already too close to reality. "Just Dorothy should do fine."

She'll like that. I hope.

Tim was still staring at her.

"What?" she said.

"Dorothy's her real name, isn't it. How did you find out?"

She was stunned. How did he know? "Tim, you're nuts. I—"

"Truth, Quinn: How'd you find out?"

She hesitated, then decided he should know. After all, he was dissecting her too.

She told him everything, from finding the toe tag to Dr. Clifton's cool response to her questions.

Tim grinned. "Probably afraid you were some money-hungry relative fishing for a hint of malpractice. I hear it's a jungle out there."

Harrison walked up then, his teaching-assistant smirk firmly in place.

"Late again, Brown?"

"Was I?" Tim said. "I didn't check the clock when I came in."

"I did. And you were late—the third time this week. You're batting a thousand, Brown." He pointed to Tim's dissection. "Let's see what you've learned here. The accessory is which cranial nerve?"

"The twelfth," Tim said.

"Name the other eleven."

Tim rattled them off.

"Okay," Harrison said. He withdrew a pointer from his pocket and poked at Tim's dissection. "Identify these tissues here."

Tim scorched through them without a miss. Quinn knew he was comparing his dissection to his mental photographs from the pages of *Gray's*.

"Well, apparently you've learned something from this, although I don't see how. Looks like you've been working with a chain saw instead of a scalpel. Where is your technique, Brown?"

"I think I left it with your tact," Tim said with his little-boy smile.

Harrison stood statue-still for an instant, as if not quite sure that he had heard correctly and listening carefully in case it might be repeated. Then his smirk curved into a reluctant but genuine smile.

"One for you, Brown." He turned to Quinn. "By the way, Cleary. Dr. Emerson asked me to tell you to stop by his office in the faculty building after lab."

The words startled Quinn. "Me? Did he say why?"

"Something about a job."

Harrison strolled away toward another table.

"There he goes," Tim said in a low voice, "leaving a trail of slime as he—"

"He almost seemed human there for a moment," Quinn said.

"Almost. What do you think Emerson wants with you?"

"I haven't the faintest."

"Got to watch out for these old guys."

"What do you mean?"

Tim winked. "Wear an extra pair of panty hose."

Quinn almost threw her scalpel at him.

Walter Emerson sat in his oak-paneled faculty building office, poring over the latest printouts on 9574. The new data were good, better than he'd hoped for. This compound was going to revolutionize—

"You wanted to see me, Dr. Emerson?"

He glanced up and saw the slim young strawberry blonde standing in his doorway, exactly as she had last December when she'd arrived for her interview. And looking no less apprehensive now, as well might any first-year student who'd been summoned to the office of one of the professors.

A sight for sore eyes, he thought. That is, if you don't mind clichés and have a weakness for slim young strawberry blondes.

"Miss Cleary. Yes. Yes, I did. Come in. Have a seat. Do you want some coffee?"

She shook her head as she seated herself in the leather chair opposite his desk. "No, thanks."

"Just as well," he said. "By this time of day the coffee's not fit for human consumption. Even the lab rats won't touch it."

She was gracious enough to smile politely at his weak attempt at humor.

"Harrison mentioned something about a job," she said.

"Yes. I need a research assistant. The pay is modest, to say the least, but it's respectable."

"Really?" she said, her already large blue eyes widening further. "You want me?"

"That is, after all, why I asked you to come here."

"But what about my studies?"

"It's a part-time job and the work is easy. Actually, you'll soon find out that 'research assistant' is a euphemism for dishwasher and all-purpose gofer. But you'll be working on the sacrosanct fifth floor of the science center, and between bouts of scut work you'll get a firsthand look at neuropharmacological research that I promise will prove useful later on in your schooling here. And we can arrange your hours around your class and lab schedule."

Walter watched her chew her lower lip, weighing the pros and cons. The student who had been his assistant last year had moved on to his clinical duties and was now spending his afternoons learning from the patients in the medical center. Walter needed an extra hand around here and he knew she needed the money.

"How much . . . ?"

"Ten dollars an hour."

"Can I give it a trial run?" she said after another, briefer pause. "I'd really like to do it, but I don't want to commit to the job and then find out it's eating into my study time too much."

"That would be fine," Walter said. "We'll give you three or four weeks—till the first of November, say. At that point you can either sign on for the year or send me looking for someone else."

She smiled. The room brightened. "Okay. Great."

"Wonderful. Tomorrow's your early afternoon. Come up to Fifth Science and I'll show you around. You can officially start then."

"I'll be there," she said, rising. She turned at the door, her expression troubled, hesitant. "But . . . why me?"

"Pardon?" He wasn't prepared for that question.

"There are forty-nine other students in the class. Why'd you ask me?"

"Because . . . "

How could he put this? He didn't want her to think he looked on her as a charity case. Of course he'd checked out her parents' financial statement, and it was obvious she could use the income. But that wasn't the prime criterion. Walter had watched her in the an lab, spoken to her, eavesdropped on her interaction with her fellow students, and he'd come to realize that his first impression had been correct: Quinn Cleary was one of the good ones, one of the rare birds that came along only once in a great while. She was going places. And once she got out of here and into the real world, she was going to buff the shine on The Ingraham's already bright name. Walter didn't want anything—especially the shortage of a few dollars—to get between Quinn Cleary and her medical degree.

And of course it didn't hurt that she reminded him so much of Clarice.

"Because I think that not only can you do the job, but perhaps you can make a contribution as well."

That smile again. "Okay. I'll sure try."

And then she was gone, and Walter Emerson's office descended into relative gloom.

"So it's legit?" Tim said. "He's not just some dirty old man?"

He had stopped by Quinn's room to see what Dr. Emerson had wanted and was stretched out on the extra bed, hands behind his head.

"Actually, he's a rather clean old man," Quinn said. She swiveled quickly in her desk chair and pointed to him. "Source?"

"Easy: *A Hard Day's Night.* I think McCartney said it first, but each of them used the line eventually."

Quinn shrugged resignedly. She should have known. If Tim could spot a line from *A Thousand Clowns,* a Beatles movie would be easy pickings.

Tim sat up on the edge of the bed. He worked a folded envelope out of the back pocket of his jeans and held it up.

"And now *my* news. My folks sent down a bunch of my mail from home, and guess what? The Taj comped me a room."

"What language are you speaking?"

He smiled. "English. The Taj Mahal—that's Trump's big casino in A.C.—has offered me a free room any night I want between November first and February twenty-eighth."

"Why would they want to do that?"

"I used to be a regular winner there last winter and spring, right after I turned twenty-one. But I haven't been back for some time. They probably think I'm gambling at that new place the Indians opened in Connecticut and they want me back."

"Why would they want you back if you won money from them? I'd think they'd be glad you went somewhere else."

"Because the odds are in their favor. They don't care if I've won in the past. All they want is my action."

"Action?"

"Yeah. My play. They figure if I play there long enough, they'll get their money back. What they don't like is my taking the money I won from them and losing it at a competitor's tables. They want me to lose it at *their* tables."

"Are you going?"

"Of course. And you're invited."

Quinn laughed. "To spend the night with you in an Atlantic City hotel room? *Now* who's the dirty old man?"

"I'm not old. And besides, the room'll have two double beds. You could have your own."

"That's good of you."

"Of course, if you got lonely during the night and wanted me to—"

"Dream on, Brown."

"Okay, but seriously, I'd like to show you how I work these places. It'll be fun."

"And what'll I be? Your good-luck charm?"

"Quinn, babes, if I had to depend on luck I wouldn't get within ten miles of a casino. Luck is a sucker bet. What do you say?"

She looked at his eager face and wondered. She'd turn down a similar proposition from anyone else she'd known for so brief a time. Turn it down flat. But Tim . . . somehow she trusted Tim.

"I'll give you a definite maybe. Let's think about it."

"Great. I was looking at the second weekend in November,

right after the big anatomy midterm. We'll need a break then. How's that sound?"

"We'll see."

He waved and headed for the door. "Okay. It's a deal. Second weekend in November. Don't forget."

"Tim—"

But he was already out in the hall.

Quinn couldn't help smiling as she swiveled back and forth in her desk chair. A weekend in Atlantic City with Tim. That could be fun. She'd never been to a casino in her life.

But sharing a room . . .

What am I afraid of? Tim?

No. That wasn't it. She liked Tim—found herself liking him more each passing day. Liked him too much, maybe. Sometimes, when he was sitting near her, she had this urge to reach over and stroke his cheek, or the nape of his neck.

Maybe she was afraid of getting carried away. Maybe it went further than that. Maybe it was involvement she was afraid of. Hadn't George Washington told the country to avoid foreign entanglements? That was what she'd managed to do through her four years at UConn. She'd dated plenty—sweet guys, determined gropers, and the whole spectrum between—but through it all she'd kept her emotional distance. No foreign entanglements.

And frankly, no one had really moved her.

The last time she had been involved—really *involved*—had been in high school, and that had been a disaster. Maybe that was the problem. Maybe it all went back to Bobby Roca.

She turned back to her desk and cleared thoughts of men and hotel rooms and November from her head and concentrated on her pathology notes. *Tomorrow* was the immediate concern. She had to do some extra booking tonight to make up for the loss of study time tomorrow afternoon when she'd be starting in Dr. Emerson's lab.

MONITORING

Louis Verran cursed around his cigar as he adjusted the volume from room 252. It didn't help, just made the static louder. He'd heard Atlantic City mentioned and that was about it.

Alston wanted a close watch on those two first-year kids, Brown and Cleary. They were being nice and cooperative about it by spending lots of time together in either Cleary's room or Brown's. Verran appreciated the two-fer. Too bad they weren't boffing each other. That would have made the surveillance a little more interesting.

And now the pickup in 252 was so full of static, he probably couldn't even tell if they were screwing. Electret mikes were just about the hardiest on the market. Weren't supposed to go bad early in the first semester.

Damn. He resisted the impulse to bang on the control panel—the problem wasn't here, it was in the dorm—and turned to Kurt.

"The audio from two-fifty-two is for shit. When was the last time it was replaced?"

"I'll check." He tapped his keyboard a few times, then looked up at Verran. "Two years come December. What's up? It checked out fine during the summer."

"It's dying."

"I'll put it down for replacement over Thanksgiving break."

"Can't wait till then," Verran said. "I'll do it myself tomorrow."

"Elliot can stay late and—"

"I'll handle it."

Kurt and Elliot were capable, but Verran believed in keeping their exposure to the student body at a minimum. Especially Kurt. He was good-looking and all the more memorable for his shaggy blond hair. Someone would remember him wandering through the dorms. And if challenged, Kurt could be trouble. He had a mean streak.

But as chief of security, Verran had the entire campus as his stomping grounds. And sometime tomorrow morning he'd be stomping through Ms. Cleary's room while she was out.

The beige brick front of the science center loomed over Quinn as she hurried up the slope. The double-wide glass doors slid open at her approach. She hurried through the high-ceilinged, marble-floored lobby and headed directly for the elevators. Usually her energy was scraping bottom by this time in the afternoon, but today she was up and excited. Today she started her new job.

"Excuse me," said a woman's voice to her right.

Quinn turned and saw a heavyset black woman looking at her from behind the circular counter of the security desk.

"Me?"

"Can I help you, miss?"

Quinn stepped closer. The woman's badge read CHARLENE TURNER. She wore a smile but her eyes and manner were all business.

"I'm supposed to meet Dr. Emerson upstairs this afternoon," Quinn told her.

"Fifth floor?" she said, her expression dubious. "He's going to meet you on Fifth? What's your name?"

"Cleary."

The woman tapped something into her keyboard and checked her screen.

"You're not down for an appointment. What time he tell you?"

"No time. He just said to come by after class this afternoon. I'm going to be working for him."

"Ah. Why didn't you say so?" More tapping on her keyboard. "Now I got you. Cleary, Quinn—student assistant to Dr. Emerson."

"Right," Quinn said. "I can go upstairs now?"

"Not so fast. You're not official yet." Charlene Turner flipped through a file drawer and withdrew a manila envelope. From it she produced an ID badge and something that looked like a credit card. She compared the photo on the badge to Quinn.

"Yeah, that's you all right." She handed both across the counter. "The badge goes on your coat or blouse or some other visible place as soon as you enter this building, and it stays there as long as you're in here. The other goes in your wallet. Don't lose it. Big trouble if you do."

The ID badge listed her name and Department of Neuropharmacology assignment next to a photo that looked like a copy of the one she'd submitted with her application. Quinn immediately clipped it to the belt on her slacks. But the card . . .

"What is this?"

"Your security key," Charlene Turner said. "You can't get to the fifth floor without it."

"Key?"

The card said SCIENCE CENTER on the dark blue side, with an arrow pointing away from the *S*; the other side was white with a brown strip running across on the flip side of the arrow.

"Yeah. It's got a magnetic code in that little strip at the end. That's the business end. Just stick it faceup into the slot in the elevator and you'll be on your way."

"Okay. Thanks."

They do go a little overboard on their security here, Quinn thought as she headed for the elevators.

One of the pair was standing open when she got there. The car was deep—deep enough for a hospital bed. Inside on the control panel were six buttons for floors 1 through 5 plus the basement. Next to the 5 and the *B* were pairs of little indicator lights. The red one was glowing next to each. On a hunch Quinn inserted her card—her *key*—into the slot above the row of buttons and pressed 5. To the accompaniment of a soft click, the red light next to 5 went off, and its companion lit up green. The elevator doors closed and the car started up.

"All right," Quinn said, smiling as she removed the key and slipped it into her pocket. She had a key that let her go where only a select few were allowed. It was exciting. She felt as if she'd arrived, as if she belonged.

Stepping out on the fifth floor, she was lost for a moment. No one was in the hall, and she didn't know where to turn. She tried to remember the layout from the tour last Christmas and got the feeling she should head to her right.

And then she saw the glass plate in the wall—the window onto the place called Ward C.

She stopped in the center of the hall. She'd forgotten completely about Ward C. Now it was all back, especially the eyes. She remembered peering through that window and meeting that pair of dull blue eyes staring up at her from within their gauze frame, remembered the questing look in them, remembered the tears as she'd moved away.

How had she forgotten? *Why* had she forgotten? Too painful a memory? Too disturbing?

As if in the grip of some invisible hand that had reached through the glass from the burn ward and taken hold of her, Quinn gravitated to the window. She couldn't resist. She stopped before it and gazed within.

It was the same . . . the gauze-swathed bodies on their air mattresses, still white shapes under their sheets, the IVs, the feeding tubes, the catheters, the blue, green, red, yellow, patches on their limbs and trunks, the nurses gliding among them like benevolent phantoms, turning them, examining them, ministering to their unspoken needs. Not a whisper of sound penetrated the glass . . . like watching a silent movie.

Quinn hesitated, then forced herself to look down at the bed directly before the window, fearing yet yearning for the sight of that same pair of blue eyes, wondering if that person was still here, still in pain, still alive.

The form on the bed by the window was sleeping. Yet even though the eyes were closed, Quinn knew it wasn't the same patient. This one seemed female. Smaller, narrower in the shoulders, a hint of breasts mounded under the gauze—

"Miss Cleary?"

Quinn spun, jolted by the voice. Dr. Emerson was standing behind her.

"I didn't mean to startle you, but they called from downstairs to let me know you were on your way up. When you didn't show . . ."

"I wasn't sure where to go."

He smiled. "My fault. I should have realized that and had someone watching for you." He glanced at the burn-ward window.

"This is where we first crossed paths, I believe."

Quinn remembered . . . the blue-eyed patient, his obvious pain, Dr. Emerson directing the nurse to medicate him.

"Yes. The orientation tour."

"And now you're back in the same spot."

"It's these patients. They're . . . "

Quinn didn't know how to express her feelings without sounding theatrical, but something about these unknown, faceless, helpless people was drawing her to them. She sensed a need in that ward, and an urge within herself to fulfill it.

"The other patients in the medical center next door come and go," Dr. Emerson said. "But these are our orphans, the homeless, the ones nobody wants. They need more care than a nursing home can provide, yet no hospital can afford to keep them. So they wind up here, at the science center, where they allow us to try experimental cures for their damaged skin."

Quinn swallowed. "Experimental?"

He laughed. "You say that as if we're mad scientists, Miss Cleary. All the patients here on Fifth are experimental subjects. They or their families have applied to come here. There's even a waiting list."

"For experimental treatment?"

"Every new drug and every therapeutic advance such as Dr. Alston's semisynthetic skin grafts goes through exhaustive testing on mice and dogs and monkeys before it's even considered for use in a human being. And once all that testing has been reviewed by the FDA and found suitably safe, *then* it's tested in human volunteers. Very carefully tested."

Quinn glanced through the window. "But these—"

"Are all volunteers. Or have been given over to our care by their families. You hear about new AIDS drugs being tested. Who do you think they're tested on? AIDS victims. And cholesterol-lowering agents. Who are they tested on? People with high cholesterol. And on whom else can you test new skin grafts but burn victims? Here Dr. Alston and his staff have taken on the toughest burn cases, the ones who've been failed by conventional therapy." He moved up to the window and stared into the ward. His voice softened. "And for the residents of Ward C, The Ingraham is their last, best hope."

"Why the colored patches?" Quinn asked.

"Color coding for different strains of Dr. Alston's grafts. You see, he takes samples of a patient's healthy skin—and on some of these poor devils that's not easy to find—and grows sheets of new cells in cultures. Then he coats the micromesh he's synthesized with the patient's own DNA. The body's immune system does not react against its own DNA; therefore there's no rejection of the mesh. The skin cells in the mesh begin to multiply, and soon you've got a patch of healthy skin. It's worked wonders in the animal studies. He's maybe two years away from approval by the FDA."

Quinn almost wished she were working for Dr. Alston. Dr. Emerson seemed to be reading her mind.

"I never told you, but your duties in my department will have an impact on the burn patients."

Quinn pointed through the window. "You mean . . . ?"

He gestured down the hall. "Let me show you my lab and things will be clearer."

The prospect of dealing with real live patients pumped up Quinn's already soaring excitement as she accompanied Dr. Emerson down the hall. She followed him past the nurses' station and through a narrow doorway.

"Not very glamorous, I'm afraid," he said. "But here's the front section of my little domain."

A small room, its walls lined with desks and computer terminals. A middle-aged woman was hunched over a keyboard, typing madly.

"Alice," Dr. Emerson said, touching her on the shoulder. "This is Quinn Cleary, the student assistant I told you about."

Alice turned and extended her hand to Quinn. She looked about fifty; she wore no makeup, had gray-streaked hair and unusually dry skin. But her smile was warm and welcoming.

"Am I glad to see *you*! Are you starting today?"

Quinn glanced at Dr. Emerson. "I'm not sure."

"You're on the payroll as of today," he said, "so you might as well."

"Great!" Alice said. "We're so backed up on data entry, you wouldn't believe! Take a seat and I'll—"

"I think I'll give her the tour first, Alice," Dr. Emerson said with a tolerant smile.

"Oh, right. Sure. Of course. Go ahead. I'll be here when you're through."

Dr. Emerson then led Quinn through a door at the rear of the office. Immediately she noticed a pungent odor. She sniffed.

"Still noticeable?" Dr. Emerson said.

"Something is."

"This used to be the vivarium. Lined with rat cages. But we moved the little fellows back down to the fourth floor. Not many left. We're long since past that stage." He gestured to the work-stations where two technicians were measuring minute amounts of amber fluid into pipettes and inserting them into a wide as-sortment of autoanalytical machines. "This is where we used to sacrifice them. Now we've converted this area to analysis of the sera we draw from the patients."

"The Ward C patients?"

"Yes."

Quinn's face must have reflected her confusion because Dr. Em-erson nodded and motioned her back the way they had come.

"Follow me."

They again passed Alice, who turned and looked up at them expectantly.

"Not quite yet, Alice."

Quinn followed him out into the hall to the nurses' station.

"Marguerite," he said to the slim, middle-aged, mocha-skinned nurse at the counter. Her black hair was pulled back into a tight bun; her light eye shadow emphasized her dark, penetrating eyes. "One of the 9574 vials, please."

The nurse reached behind her and plucked a two-ounce bottle from a pocket in the top of the medication cart. She handed it to Dr. Emerson, who in turn handed it to Quinn.

"This," he said, "is the reason Dr. Alston and I have our labs on the same floor. It's the new anesthetic I'm developing. We have no name for it yet, so we refer to it by its entry number in the log when we isolated it. This is the nine thousand five hundred and seventy-fourth compound we've registered at The Ingraham."

Quinn stared at the bottle of clear fluid in her hand. It looked like water.

"So many."

"We've synthesized *tens* of thousands, but we only register the ones we feel might have human therapeutic potential."

"It's good?"

"Good?" His entire forehead lifted with his eyebrows. "It's *wonderful*. Works like a charm. And you know the best part?"

Quinn placed the bottle on the counter. "What?"

"It's nontoxic. That's because it's not a foreign chemical compound but a naturally occurring neuroamine, secreted in minute amounts in the brain stem during REM sleep."

Quinn couldn't help but smile at him. His enthusiasm was catching. He was like a little boy talking about a rocket voyage to Mars. She didn't want to slow him down, so she prodded him on.

"Really?"

"Yes. You're paralyzed during dream sleep, you know. Oh, yes. Almost completely paralyzed. Otherwise you'd be talking, laughing, and generally thrashing all about in your dreams. Yet your eyes move. You've heard of rapid eye movements—REM sleep— of course. And your chest wall moves, allowing your lungs to breathe. So what you've got is a selective paralysis, affecting all the skeletal muscles except the eyes, the intercostals, and the diaphragm. And of course, you're unconscious."

"It paralyzes," Quinn said. "I thought you said it was an anesthetic."

"It is. At higher doses it produces total anesthesia. I'm working on the mechanism for that now, but I do know it's active in the higher centers as well as the brain stem." The years seemed to drop away from him as his enthusiasm grew. "But do you understand what we've got here, Miss Cleary? A potent general anesthetic that causes complete paralysis but allows the patient to continue breathing on his own. The anesthesiologist won't have to intubate and ventilate the patient. It can be used in every kind of surgery except chest procedures; there's zero chance of allergic reaction because 9574 is a human neurohormone—everybody's got their own. And perhaps best of all, there's no postanesthesia side effects. You come to in the recovery room like someone awakening from a nap." He put his hands on his hips and stared at the bottle like a proud parent. "So. Those are the properties of the neurohormone you'll be working with here. What do you think?"

"It sounds almost too good to be true."

"It does, doesn't it." He began gesturing excitedly with his hands. "But that's not the whole of it. It would be almost perfect with just those features, but it's also completely nontoxic. Its LD_{50}—"

"Elldee . . . ?"

"LD_{50}," Dr. Emerson said. "You'll learn all about that as we go. Stands for the lethal dose of a given compound for fifty percent of the experimental animals. Every drug meant for human use

must register one. For instance, I take the Kleederman Pharmaceuticals product fenostatin for my cholesterol, a dose of twenty *milli-*
grams per day—total. I happen to know that the LD_{50} of fenostatin
is twenty *grams* per kilogram. In other words, if I gave a hundred
lab mice a dose of twenty grams of fenostatin per kilogram of their
body weight, fifty of them would die. That's a good LD_{50}. It means
that if I became suicidal and stuffed seventy thousand twenty-
milligram fenostatin tablets down my throat, I'd still have only a
fifty percent chance of dying from fenostatin toxicity. Probably
rupture my intestines first. But the wonderful thing about 9574 is
that it's even less toxic. We haven't *found* a lethal dose yet."

Triumphant, he threw out his arms and struck the bottle of
9574, sending it skittering toward the end of the counter. Marguerite the nurse leapt out of her seat, knocking it over as she lunged
for the bottle. She caught it just as it went off the end and dropped
toward the floor. Then she slumped there, shaking her head, panting as if she had run a race.

"Thank God you caught that, Marguerite," Dr. Emerson said.
He seemed quite upset.

Marguerite straightened and carefully replaced the vial in its
slot on the meds cart.

"Dr. Emerson," she said as she righted her chair. "That was
too close."

"Amen," he said, then turned to Quinn. "We have precious
little of 9574 available. Synthesizing it in quantities would be a
simple matter for a commercial lab, but our tiny operation down
on the third floor is taxed to its limits to produce what we need
here for research purposes. Consequently, we treat it like gold."

"But who are you using it on?"

"Why, the Ward C patients, of course. It's perfect for them."

Quinn was confused. "But why would you want to paralyze
them?"

"It's not so much the paralysis we want for them," he said.
"It's the anesthesia. Most of the Ward C patients have horrific scarring, thick wads of stiff tissue that resists movement because it's
got minimal elasticity. We use 9574 on them during their physical-
therapy sessions. It allows the therapists to stretch their limbs and
exercise their joints to prevent flexion contractures. If left alone,
most of them would end up curled into the fetal position. Without
9574 the pain of physical therapy would be unendurable."

"But didn't you say the lower dose paralyzes, and the higher

dose anesthetizes? Wouldn't that mean they're completely paralyzed during therapy?" Quinn was starting to feel uncomfortable.

Dr. Emerson turned and looked at her closely. A wry smile
worked across his lips.

"You're a quick study, aren't you."

Quinn was suddenly flustered. Had she angered him?

"Well, I don't know . . . I just—"

"I like that. I like that a lot. Shows you've been listening. But
as it works out, the paralysis with 9574 is a harmless side effect
for some of the Ward C patients and an absolute necessity for
others." He gestured down the hall. "Let me show you."

They moved the dozen feet or so to the window and stood
looking into Ward C. Quinn counted the gauze-wrapped shapes.
Seven. All lying still and silent, looking . . .

"Are they paralyzed now?"

"No," Dr. Emerson said. "Just resting. They sleep a lot. There's
not much else they can do. Their scarring is so extensive that they
can't move on their own. But for four of them the therapists need
the skeletal-muscle paralysis that 9574 offers. Those four are brain-
damaged from their burns."

Quinn tore her eyes away from the ward and looked at him.

"How . . . ?"

"Anoxia. Either the smoke and heat of the fire itself stole their
air, or the shock that goes along with such extensive third-degree
burns robbed their brains of sufficient blood flow for too long—
either way, lack of oxygen damaged their brains, permanently. All
four are disoriented and confused; two are frankly psychotic. The
physical therapists would have to fight them all the way without
9574. But with 9574 they can work those limbs and keep the muscles from complete atrophy."

Quinn stared back into the ward and her heart went out to
them. "Those poor, poor people." And then a thought struck her.
"But even if Dr. Alston's grafts repair their skin, they'll never get
any benefit from it."

"True. Their bodies may improve but not their brains. However, their lives will not be wasted. Other burn patients will reap
the benefits of what we learn from these poor devils' tragedies."
He put a hand gently on her elbow. "But enough philosophizing.
It's time to drag you down and introduce you to the more mundane aspects of the daily grind that is medical research. The nitty-
gritty of gathering raw data, sorting and analyzing it, and

organizing it seven hundred different ways in order to satisfy the bureaucrats at the FDA.''

That's the trouble with Women's Country, Louis Verran thought as he waited outside the dorm and watched the windows of the south wing's second floor. Too much of a class mix.

Women's Country. Sounded so uppity. The kind of name his ex-wife would have been into after her conversion. Elizabeth, the born-again feminist. She took to the women's movement like a convert to a new religion. Took him to the cleaners, then took off. Good riddance.

Women's Country? Broads' Country was more like it.

It had been Alston's bright idea—not a bad one, really—to room each class as a unit, generally one class per floor per wing, allowing them to work out study groups, make friends, and generally build a sense of camaraderie. The third- and fourth-year students were out more than they were in due to their clinical-training schedules at the medical center, but first- and second-year wing floors went to class together, attended labs together, and ate together. One quick look at the class schedule told you when a certain wing would be deserted.

But Women's Country was different. The broads had formed an enclave of first-, second-, third-, and fourth-year students there, which made it almost impossible to find a time when everybody was out.

Except dinnertime. Hardly anybody on campus missed dinner.

This was Verran's third trip over here today. On both his previous ones he'd found girls wandering about. This time the place would be empty. Had to be. He did not want to come back again.

He had his walkie-talkie on his hip and Kurt watching the elevators over at Science, ready to let him know as soon as the Cleary girl left the building. She'd probably go straight to the caf, but Verran was not taking any chances. As soon as he got word that she was leaving Science, he'd be outta here.

Watching the dorm door, he saw a couple more of the broads leave and decided to make his move.

The hallway in Broads' Country looked deserted. He checked the walkie-talkie to make sure it was on. No word from Kurt, so that meant the Cleary girl was still up on Fifth. He checked up and down the hall to make sure no one could see him, then used the master key to let himself into 252.

He was glad he didn't have to turn on the lights. You never knew who might notice. He had his flashlight and the sunset was glowing through the window of the bedroom, where the problem mike was located. Plenty of light.

Quinn looked up from the computer screen at her new workstation and glanced at the clock. Dinnertime already. Time to hang it up.

She rubbed her eyes. Dr. Emerson hadn't exaggerated about how mundane the nitty-gritty would be. Alice had set her in front of a computer, showed her how the data-entry end of the program worked, then given her a ream of readings from the analytical lab next door and set her to work.

Not the least bit exciting, and hardly medical or even scientific. Nothing more than keyboard pounding. She'd been discouraged at first, but Dr. Emerson had forewarned her that this sort of scut work would be part of her duties and that this was a good way to get herself familiarized with the doings in his little department. Once the data entry was caught up, he would involve her in the analysis of that data, and if all went well, she might even earn herself a credit on one or two of the scientific articles these mountains of numbers were going to generate.

Dr. Emerson had left the department a little while ago and Alice now was on her way out. She showed Quinn how to do a final Save on her work and sign off her console. She left while Quinn straightened up her work area. When she had everything looking reasonably neat, she headed for the elevator.

On her way down the hall she noticed that the curtains were drawn across the Ward C window. She was almost glad she didn't have to see those poor souls again.

When she got to the elevators she saw that the floor indicator showed both cars on the lobby level. There was a slot next to the call button. She slipped her card in and pressed the button a couple of times, but neither light moved off its L. She noticed the Exit sign over the stairway door a short way down the hall.

Why not? She'd spent most of the day sitting in lecture halls, perched over her microscope, or in front of that computer. Her legs could use a good stretch.

At the door she found a little red light and a card slot in the lock assembly. She plugged in the card, the light turned green, and the door opened. She noticed a similar assembly on the other side. Seemed you couldn't get on or off the fifth floor unless you had a card. Seemed a little excessive. God, what if there was a fire?

A few minutes of bounding down the flights, and she reached the first floor. The stair door opened into a hall around a corner from the lobby. She started to round that corner when she noticed the red steel door of a side exit. Going out this end, she realized, would save her a lot of steps. But as she approached it she saw the standard warnings:

THIS IS NOT AN EXIT
ALARM WILL SOUND IF OPENED

But she also noticed a familiar slot in the door's lock assembly, identical to the one on the fifth-floor door. The little light was red. Quinn wondered . . .

She stepped up and slipped her security card into the slot. The lock clicked and the light turned green.

She grinned. "Yes!"

She let herself out and saw another slot and indicator lamp on the outside. She could enter here as well as exit. All right. Her little key card was going to come in very handy, especially in bad weather.

She turned and paused for a moment in the mild October air to take in the orange glow of the sunset. Beautiful. She was hungry but she felt grubby. She decided to make a quick trip back to the room to freshen up before dinner.

It would take only a couple of minutes.

Verran palmed the defective electret mike and withdrew its replacement from his coat pocket; he stuck the new one's pin into the same hole in the insulation of the wire just occupied by its predecessor.

"Piece of cake," he said softly.

He was checking the bedroom to make sure it looked untouched when he heard a rustle in the hall on the far side of the door. He froze. Who the hell . . . ?

And then he heard the key slipping into the lock. He dived for the floor on the far side of the bed near the window and lay there, holding his breath, sweating. The door opened and the light came on in the front room. Then the overhead in the bedroom. Its glare hit him like a kick in the head. He winced.

Shit! Why hadn't Kurt called? That son of a bitch! Probably admiring his reflection in the glass door when he should have been watching the elevator. Verran vowed to kick his preening butt when he got back.

But what about now? He was going to get caught for sure. He resigned himself to that. But what the hell was he going to say?

The bed moved as something bounced on it. Not heavy enough for a person. Books? Christ, this was it. He could feel it coming. He was going to look like an ass. He tried thinking of some sort of explanation. He had a flashlight—he could say he was looking for something. But even if he came up with a remotely plausible story, it still would be all over campus before morning: Chief Verran found huddling on the floor of a female student's room. Tight-ass Alston would have a field day. He'd never live it down.

Fucking Kurt ought to be fired for this. Except he knew too much. Well, he'd see to it that Kurt *never* screwed up again.

But now . . . now he clenched his teeth and waited for the scream that would—

A door closed. Water started running in the bathroom.

Hope burst in Verran's chest like a flare.

He risked popping his head up and checking the room. Empty. She was in the john. He didn't hesitate. He jumped up and hurried toward the front room, gliding his feet. He made it to the door, grabbed the handle, gave it a slow, careful twist, then slipped through and into the hall. He closed it very slowly, very carefully, behind him, letting the latch catch with a barely audible click.

Panting, sweating, his heart pounding at two hundred miles an hour, Verran checked out the hall. Empty. He hurried toward the exit, his sweaty palms enclosed in fists.

Goddamn fucking Kurt.

MONITORING

"She didn't come by me, Lou. I was watching the whole time and I *swear* she never stepped out of those elevators."

Verran stared at Kurt. They were facing off in the center of the control room. Elliot was at his console, munching a sandwich, trying to make like a chameleon and blend in with the background. Kurt was awful convincing with his hurt eyes and whiny voice. If Verran himself hadn't been in room 252 a few moments ago, he'd be ready to believe him. A first-class performance.

"Then who was it who came into Cleary's room, dropped their books on the bed, and went into the bathroom? Little Red Riding Hood? The Tooth Fairy?"

"Maybe. But it wasn't the Cleary broad, I'll tell you that. I never left the security station for a fucking minute. Not even to take a leak."

"Oh, I believe you were there, all right. But you were too busy admiring yourself in some piece of glass to notice her when she passed by."

"Not fair, Lou."

"Admit it, Kurt. You fucked up. And I'm warning you now, one more screwup and you're out on your ass."

"Bullshit. I'm not taking the rap for something I didn't do. Especially since you never forget, Lou."

That last part was true, at least. He did have a tendency to carry a grudge. And why not? Guy screws up and damn near makes him look like an ass and he should just say, What the hell, shit happens? No way. He wanted to grab a handful of Kurt's perfect blond hair, rip it out, and feed it to him.

"Then how did she get past you, Kurt? Fly out a fifth-floor window? Answer me that or—"

"Wait a sec," Kurt said. "I'll prove it to you." He fairly leapt to his console and began typing furiously.

"What now?"

"The locks. We issued her a key, right? Let's see where she used it."

Verran stood over Kurt's shoulder and peered at his screen. The electronic locks in Science weren't just for show. They were linked to this control room, not merely for security, but for monitoring as well. The system kept an ongoing record of each time one of the locks was opened, not only of the time and location, but whose key was used.

He watched as Kurt called up a list of current key holders, highlighted Cleary's number, then plugged it into an activity search with today's date.

The console beeped, and when the results popped up on the screen, Kurt slammed his palm on the counter.

"There! What'd I tell you?" He sprang from his chair and pointed. "What'd I fucking tell you?"

Verran stared at the screen. It listed three locations where Cleary had used her key today. The first was the fifth-floor access slot in the elevator at 3:12 P.M.; the second the fifth-floor west stairwell door; the third the fire door on Science's west flank at 5:16.

Shit. It hadn't been Kurt at all. The bitch had gone out the fire door.

So now what? Verran felt like a jerk.

Only one thing to do: Pull a Swann.

Good old Ed Swann had been Verran's direct superior at the Company. Back in the Iran hostage days, he'd chewed Verran up and down for following the wrong Syrian embassy car around D.C. all day. But when it was discovered that he'd given Verran the wrong license-plate number, what did Swann do?

He turned to Verran and offered his hand.

Which is just what Verran did now.

"My apologies, Kurt," he said, keeping any hint of sheepishness from his tone. "She fooled us both. I shouldn't have jumped on you like that. I'm sorry."

Kurt stared at him in shock for a few seconds, then shook his hand.

"Yeah . . . okay, Lou," he said, completely disarmed. "I guess if places were reversed I probably would have thought you'd screwed up too."

Verran smiled—inwardly as well as outwardly. Kurt had been poised to jump all over him, but Verran had rocked him back on his heels with a matter-of-fact apology. The tactic had worked for Swann, and it still worked like a charm. Kurt had gained the high ground, but the apology made Verran look like the bigger man—*and* defused a tense situation that might have affected the usually relaxed working atmosphere of the monitoring room.

He didn't want *anything* to interfere with his operation.

He gestured to the screen. "She's a tricky one. Almost caught me with my hand in the cookie jar. Better not take anything for granted with that one."

Elliot finally must have thought it was safe to open his yap. "You able to get the bug, chief?"

"Of course." He reached into his coat pocket. "It's right . . . "

The pocket was empty. He tried the other side. Empty too. He patted his pants pockets, pulled them inside out.

"What the hell?"

"What's the matter, Lou?" Kurt said.

"The bad bug. I know I had it."

"You lose it?" Elliot said. "Shit!"

Shit is right, Verran thought as he pawed through his pockets again. He prayed he hadn't lost it; there'd be hell to pay if the wrong person found it.

Kurt rummaged in the cabinet under his console. At first Verran thought he might be looking for the electronic sweeper, which would do no good since electret mikes were nonradiating. Instead, he came up with a metal detector. He turned it on, adjusted the controls, and approached Verran.

"Here. Empty your pockets and I'll give you the once-over. If it's on you, we'll find it."

After Verran had dumped all his change on the counter, Kurt began waving the business end of the detector over his clothing. As the wand worked its way around his body, Verran watched the indicator needle in the handle. It would start to move when it crossed something metal. It lay dormant.

"It's not on you, Lou," Kurt said. "You must have dropped it somewhere."

"How could I drop it?" Verran snapped. "I distinctly remember putting it in my pocket."

"Well, it ain't in your pocket now."

Elliot chimed in: "Which means it's gotta be somewhere between here and the room."

"All right, all right." Verran was pissed, and there was no one to get pissed at but himself. "Let me think."

Kurt and Elliot stayed mum while Verran retraced all his moves since switching the bugs. He was sure he'd put it in his pocket, just before he'd put the chair back . . . which was just before he'd heard the key slipping into the door lock . . . .

Acid surged around Verran's ulcer.

"Christ," he said. "It must have come out of my pocket when I hit the floor."

Kurt held up the metal detector. "Want me to go back to the room and see if I can find it?"

"No," Verran said, glancing at the clock. "They'll all be wandering back from dinner now. No way you can get in and out without being seen."

"You can't just leave it there."

No, they couldn't just leave it there. The discovery of an electret mike in a dorm room might tip the first domino. The whole scenario played out in his head: questions asked, jokes made, talk about the place being bugged, people starting to search their rooms . . .

That one little mike could bring down the whole operation.

"It's small. If it's in the room, it's on the far side of the bed by the window. Nobody's going to see it there. We're okay. We'll pick it up tomorrow. No sweat."

No sweat? he thought. Then why am I shaking like a little old lady inside?

CHAPTER 12

Quinn pinned her ID badge onto her new lab coat—her *white* lab coat—and turned to Tim.

"How do I look?"

Tim glanced up from the spare bed in her room, where he was stretched out on the spread reading this morning's *Baltimore Sun*. He had his shoes off and looked perfectly at home.

"Very scientificky. But I still say you'd score more points in your running shorts."

"Fine," she said quickly. She didn't want him starting in on her legs again. "Be like that. While I'm out toiling to push back the frontiers of medical science, what'll you be doing?"

"Reading the funnies."

"You going to stay here?"

"Yeah, just for a little while, if you don't mind. Kevin's sacked out—he was up late studying last night—and I figured I'd let him sleep."

Quinn shook her head. She didn't mind at all. In fact, she wished he'd stay until she got back. Not just because she liked having him around; it had been kind of creepy coming back to the room during the dinner hour yesterday. The floor had been deserted, yet she'd had the weirdest feeling that someone was lurking about.

"Stay as long as you want. Why not hang out till I get back and I'll buy you dinner."

"Deal," Tim said, and stuck his head back into the newspaper.

Matt Crawford let himself into his New Haven condo and tossed his notebooks onto the couch. He dropped into the recliner, turned on the TV with the remote, flipped through the thirty-four channels in as many seconds, then turned it off. He sat there and stared at the blank screen.

He was feeling low and not sure why. A brand-new high-rise apartment with a panoramic view of the harbor and the Sound beyond, luxury furnishings selected and arranged by the decorator his mother had hired, a fully stocked fridge, all to himself.

Maybe that was the problem. Too much to himself these days. Never anyone around—at least not anyone he had anything in common with. Unlike The Ingraham, Yale and most other medical schools had no dorm. Students lived wherever they could find a place they could afford. Matt's dad had jumped on this condo not only as a great place for Matt to live, but as a great investment as well.

He was half-right.

At times like this, Matt almost wished he were at The Ingraham. But then if he were, Quinn would be somewhere else, sweating her tuition payments as well as sweating her courses.

He felt his mouth twist into a crooked smile. "'Tis a far, far better thing I do than I have ever done.'"

Quinn's strawberry-blond head with its wide blue eyes and red cheeks appeared in his mind, and suddenly he had to talk to her. He pulled out his address book and punched in her number.

A groggy male voice answered on the third ring.

"'Lo?'"

Matt wasn't sure what to say. "Is, uh, Quinn there?"

"Matt?"

Now he recognized the voice. "Tim? What are you doing there?"

"Didn't Quinn tell you? We moved in together. In fact, she's right beside me here in bed."

Matt was struck dumb.

Quinn and Tim . . . was it possible? He'd seen them both back in August before they'd left. Tim was being Tim and Quinn seemed to be barely tolerating him. Ms. No-nonsense and the goofmeister. A lot could happen in a couple of months, but this was too much. *Definitely* too much.

"Not."

Tim's laugh rattled over the line. "Had you going there for a second, didn't I."

"Not for a nanosecond."

Matt was surprised at his sudden surge of relief and asked himself, How come?

Tim went on, telling him that Quinn had just left, so they talked—compared courses, teachers, test difficulty, reminisced about the Good Old Days at Dartmouth—and as they spoke, an aching void expanded slowly in Matt's chest.

When he finally hung up, after asking that Quinn give him a call when she had a moment, Matt felt more alone than ever.

He felt as if he were being left out of something. Something good.

Quinn hurried over to Science. She was tempted to use the side door but decided to save that for when she was running late.

Charlene was at the security desk again. Quinn flashed her badge as she approached and Charlene waved her by.

Up on Fifth, Quinn tried not to look into Ward C as she passed the window but couldn't resist a glance.

The curtain was drawn shut.

Quinn intended to keep moving, but the sight of that blank beige surface brought her to an abrupt halt before the glass. She stepped closer and tried to peek around the curtain's edges but found no openings.

Frustrated, she proceeded around the corner to the nurses' station. Maybe Marguerite would be there. All Quinn wanted was for someone to tell her everything was all right in Ward C. Not that she could do anything if it wasn't, but she felt linked to those seven helpless patients, in some odd way partially responsible for them.

The nurses' station was deserted. Where was everybody? Wasn't anyone watching Ward C?

Behind the counter and to the left Quinn spotted a glass-windowed door. It had to open into Ward C. Why else the red-and-white warning sign under the glass?

AUTHORIZED STAFF ONLY

She glanced up and down the hall. Still no one in sight to ask. Shrugging, she stepped behind the nurses' station to take a peek through the glass.

What could it hurt?

Yes, it was Ward C, but it looked different this time. Brighter. Instead of backlit by daylight from the windows, the room was bathed in the fluorescent glow of the ceiling lights. Everything seemed to have a sharper edge. Otherwise, nothing had changed. The patients still numbered seven—at least no one had died—they still lay on their beds, immobile mounds of white with—

No. Not all were immobile. One patient lying on his side on a bed in the central area was moving slightly, twisting, shifting his weight, sliding his red-bandaged leg toward the edge of the bed. The red bandage on the thigh gripped Quinn's attention. Something about the way it glistened . . .

She gasped and pressed her face hard against the glass. That wasn't a bandage. That was blood. A patch of raw flesh, oozing red.

And then Quinn noticed that the safety rail was down on the side where the leg was moving toward the edge. The patient was trying to get out of bed. If nobody stopped him, he was going to land in a heap on the floor.

Quinn stepped back for another look up and down the hall. Still empty. She called Marguerite's name twice but no one answered. She thought of running down the hall for Dr. Emerson, but that would take too long. And what could he do then that she couldn't do now?

She returned to the door. The patient's bloody leg had moved farther along—the knee was jutting over the edge of the mattress. Another thirty seconds and he'd start sliding toward the floor.

Quinn realized she couldn't wait. Setting her jaw, she pushed through the door and hurried to the bed. She caught the lower leg by the calf just as the foot fell off the edge.

"Whoops!" she said softly, smiling and putting all the reassurance she had into her expression. "You're going to fall if you're not careful."

Gently she guided the leg back onto the mattress. She averted her eyes from the bloody patch of flesh and looked into the eyes. They were blue, yes, the same eyes she had seen here over Christmas.

Quinn jumped as a loud, angry voice rang out behind her.

"What the hell do you think you're DOING?"

She whirled and found Marguerite standing not two feet away, her dark eyes wide and angry above her surgical mask.

"He—he was falling," Quinn said.

"You're not allowed in here!" the nurse cried, her shout muffled by the mask. "Can't you *read*?"

"Just get her out of here, Marguerite," said a sharp voice from the far side of the room behind Marguerite. "Before she does any more damage."

Quinn knew that voice: Dr. Alston's. She looked past Marguerite's shoulder and saw him standing—masked, capped, gowned, gloved—in an alcove to the left of the door Quinn had entered. He was holding something over a tray, something that looked like a pink wet paper towel.

Quinn felt as if she'd been slapped in the face. "But I—"

"Get her *out!*" Dr. Alston shouted. "We'll deal with her later!"

"You heard him," Marguerite said. "Out."

Unable to speak, her cheeks afire, Quinn brushed past her and hurried for the door. What did she do that was so terrible? She'd only been trying to help.

Arthur Alston's face was livid as he pointed a shaking finger at Quinn Cleary.

"It will be days before we know the fallout from your irresponsible misadventure, young lady."

Walter Emerson watched Quinn closely, curious as to how she was going to respond. She had come to him with her story nearly an hour ago, visibly upset. He had listened, calmed her down, but had given no opinion, saying only that he would be with her when she faced Arthur.

That time came soon enough. Arthur stormed into Walter's lab with that insufferable attitude of his, demanding that "the ignoramus who invaded Ward C" be brought before him. Walter had sent Alice on an early coffee break and summoned Quinn. Now he was settled back in his chair, waiting to see how she handled herself. If she had half the gumption he thought she had, she'd stand her ground.

"I'm sorry, Dr. Alston," she said. "I know I entered a restricted area, but I saw no other choice at the time."

"The sign says 'Authorized Staff Only,' " Arthur said. "Can it be stated any more clearly than that?"

"No, but—"

"There are no 'buts' here, Miss Cleary. If you are to remain a lab assistant here—in fact, if you are to remain a *student* at this institution—you will follow the rules, or you will be out of here faster than you can blink your baby-blue eyes."

Walter watched Quinn's cheeks redden. He was tempted to

step in here before Arthur got out of hand, but no. He wanted to hear Quinn's response.

"I saw one of your patients in danger, Dr. Alston," she said through tight lips. "I saw his bed's safety rail down and saw him slipping over the edge of the mattress. What was I supposed to do?"

"You shouldn't have been at the door in the first place!"

"What was I supposed to do, sir?"

Very good, Walter thought. Stay polite, respectful, but keep the ball in his court.

"You should have called for a nurse," Arthur said.

"I did, sir. More than once. No one answered. What was I to do then, sir? Stand there and watch your patient hit the floor?"

"You should not have ignored the sign on the door, Miss Cleary. The health of those patients is extremely fragile. Their graft sites are highly prone to infection. We allow no one to enter Ward C unless they are wearing a surgical cap, a surgical mask, and sterile gloves. You were wearing none of those. God knows what you brought with you into that room."

"Correct me if I'm wrong, sir, but wouldn't he be worse off contamination-wise if he'd fallen on the floor?"

"That would not have happened, Miss Cleary. Marguerite was keeping an eye on him all the time."

"If you say so, sir. But I could not know that at the time. I acted as I thought best. I'm sorry it upset you or risked any harm to your patient. But may I ask you, sir: If I'd stood there and watched your patient bounce off the floor, would you now be here congratulating me for *not* acting?"

Arthur opened his mouth, then closed it, then opened it again.

"Do not enter Ward C again, Miss Cleary. Under *any* circumstances. Is that clear?"

"Very clear, sir." She turned to Walter. "I'm going to call it a day, if that's all right with you, Dr. Emerson."

Walter could see she was fighting back tears. He wanted to shake her hand and congratulate her on the way she'd handled herself, but he couldn't do that in front of Arthur.

"Fine, Quinn," he said. "Get some dinner and relax. It's Friday night. Have some fun somewhere."

She gave him a forced smile that said she was not in a fun mood, then she started for the door.

"Good night, Dr. Alston," she said as she passed him.

Arthur said nothing. When she was gone, he turned to Walter, but Walter spoke first.

"A little hard on her, weren't you, Arthur?" he said.

"Not hard enough, I fear," Arthur replied. "That girl is trouble, Walter, sticking her nose where it does not belong."

"She saw someone in trouble, she rushed in to help. A humanitarian gesture. Why do you berate a future doctor for a humanitarian gesture?"

"She could have contaminated the graft. She shouldn't have been in there, pure and simple."

Walter fixed Arthur with a stare. "And the safety rail shouldn't have been left down," he said pointedly. "Pure and simple."

Arthur returned the stare for a few heartbeats, then turned away.

"This is getting nowhere. But it does point up one problem: 9574 needs a longer half-life. The subjects seem to be developing a tolerance to it. The longer they're on it, the less efficacious it appears to be."

"I'm working on it," Walter said. "And with Miss Cleary as an assistant, I may be able to solve that problem for you."

Arthur looked at him and shook his head. "You do love to rub salt in a wound, don't you."

"Only your wounds, Arthur. Only yours."

They shared a laugh.

Tim had been dozing on Quinn's extra bed. The sound of the key in the lock roused him. He leapt up and tiptoed quickly to the door, where he flattened himself against the wall next to the hinges and waited. As the door began to swing inward, he grabbed the knob and yanked it the rest of the way.

"Booga-booga!"

Only it wasn't Quinn staring at him with an openmouthed, shocked expression. It was some fat, fiftyish guy instead. Tim yelped in surprise and took a step back.

"Who the hell are you?" Tim said.

"That's my question, buddy," the guy said in a whiny voice. "Who the hell are *you*, and what the hell are you doing in one of the female rooms?"

He looked rattled. He had a hangdog face and a bulging neck. He carried a flashlight in one hand and some sort of electronic baton in the other. Tim gave him a closer look and recognized him.

"You're Mr. Verran, the security guy."

"Chief of security. And you still haven't answered the questions."

"Oh. Yeah. I'm Tim Brown. First-year student here. I'm waiting for Quinn Cleary—this is her room—"

"I know that. Let's see some ID."

Tim fished his photo ID card out of his wallet and handed it to Verran. He noticed a tremor in the older man's hand as he examined it.

"Tell me something, Mr. Verran. What's the idea of sneaking in here?"

"I'm not sneaking in anywhere," he said sharply. He seemed to have regained his composure as he handed back Tim's card. "There's . . . there was a report of some guy hiding out in one of the girls' rooms. I came by to check up on it. Where's the assigned occupant?"

"She's over in Science, working for Dr. Emerson."

"She know you're here?"

"Of course. We're going to dinner together when she gets back. But tell me something: Who reported—"

"A concerned fellow student. But how do I know the assigned occupant knows you're here?"

"You don't. But we can wait for Miss Assigned Occupant, and she can tell you herself."

"Maybe I—" The walkie-talkie on Verran's hip squawked. He unclipped it from his belt and turned his back to Tim. "Yeah?"

"*She's on her way, Lou,*" said a tinny voice.

"Right." Verran turned back to Tim. "I've got to go. But I'll check up on you, buddy. If your story checks out, okay. If not, you're in big trouble."

Tim watched him hurry down the hall, then looked around. Women's Country was empty. Who would have called Security about a guy in Quinn's room? And how could anyone possibly have known he was here?

Tim closed the door and wandered back toward the spare bed.

Come to think of it, this Verran guy had looked pretty damn surprised, as shocked to see Tim as Tim had been to see him. Maybe more so. And why a flashlight and that other weird-looking gadget? Not exactly equipment for confronting a prowler.

What was he going to do with a flashlight in Quinn's room?

Tim stepped over to the window.

Something strange there. Some—

"Damn!"

Sudden pain in the sole of his right foot. Something had jabbed into it. Something sharp.

He dropped back onto the bed and pulled his foot up where he could see it. Some sort of pin had pierced his sock and was stuck in his sole. He pulled it out and held it up to the light.

A little black thing, a flat, circular hockey-pucklike knob, maybe a quarter inch across, stuck on a straight pin. What was it? A tie tack? One of those old-fashioned stickpins? He wondered if it was Quinn's. He doubted it. She wore about as much jewelry as she did makeup. And this thing didn't look very feminine anyway.

Then he heard the key in the door again. He hoped this time it was Quinn, not just because he didn't want to deal with Louis Verran's homely puss again, not just because his stomach was rumbling, but because he was hungry for the sight of her. Images of her face—talking, eating, bending over her books, concentrating as she wielded her scalpel—had been popping into his head at all hours.

As she stepped into the room, the sight of her sent a smile to his face and a wave of warmth through him.

What have you done to me, Quinn Cleary? he thought.

He said, "How were things at the office today, dear?"

She smiled, but it was a halfhearted smile, as if it were an effort. That wasn't like her.

"Something wrong?"

"Oh, nothing really," she said as she slipped out of her lab coat. "I just had a bad run-in with Alston over at Science a little while ago."

She told him about Ward C and the patient almost slipping off the bed, and about the dressing-down she'd received.

"The ungrateful bastard," Tim said when she'd finished. "That wasn't a fair or even a sane reaction."

"Tell me about it. But you know, I got the strangest feeling that he was almost as afraid as he was angry."

Tim was angry too. And the heat of his anger surprised him. He had an urge to find Alston and grab him by his dinky string tie and teach him a thing or two about the proper response to a young woman who tries to help a patient in trouble.

Was he so angry because that young woman was Quinn?

More evidence of how far she'd gotten under his skin.

But he bottled the anger. Confronting Alston was little more than an idle fantasy anyway.

"Forget about the creep," he told her. "Let's go eat."

"I've lost my appetite," she said, "but I'll keep you company."

Tim remembered the weird black stickpin he'd found and held it out to her.

"By the way, is this yours?"

She gave it barely a glance. "Nope. Never seen it before. What is it?"

"Beats me. I found it on your floor, over there by the window. Stuck me in the foot."

She looked at it again, more closely this time, but no sign of recognition lit in her eyes. She shrugged.

"Maybe one of the maids dropped it."

Tim shrugged into his sport coat and stuck the pin into the lapel, then he struck a pose.

"May I present the very latest in men's accessories. Think it'll catch on?"

Quinn squinted at his lapel. "I can hardly see it."

Tim glanced down. The tiny black hockey puck was almost lost in the herringbone pattern.

"Oh, well. Another of my fashion milestones down the drain."

Tim followed her out the door.

About time, Verran thought as he watched Brown and Cleary leave and head for the caf. I was beginning to think they'd never leave.

He waited in the bushes until they disappeared into the caf, then he slipped into the dorm and hurried up to Broads' Country.

No one about. Quickly he unlocked 252 and closed the door behind him. He turned on the metal detector and went immediately to the space between the window and the second bed, where he'd hit the floor when Cleary had surprised him last night. Slowly, carefully, he waved the business end of the detector over the thick carpet, keeping a close eye on the needle in the illuminated gauge in the handle.

It didn't budge.

He ran his fingers through the deep pile. This was the most obvious area. It had to be here.

When his fingers found nothing, he turned and crept across the room, carefully sweeping the detector over the carpet all the way to the door.

The only flickers from the needle turned out to be a penny and a dime.

Great. Just great. The detector was working fine, but no bug. Where the hell was it, then?

NOVEMBER

Claropril (ACE-1) the new ultra-potent ACE-inhibitor from Kleederman Pharmaceuticals, has captured a 20% share of the antihypertensive market a mere six months after approval.

Modern Medicine

The World's Longest Continuous Floating
Medical Bull Session
(II)

Tonight the session had wound up in, of all places, Harrison's room.

"He's not as bad as we all thought," Tim said as he led Quinn down the hall of the north wing's first floor. His sharp blue eyes were bright. He wasn't wearing his dark glasses as much as he used to. She preferred him this way. "Of course, he's hardly Mr. Warmth, either. Far from it, in fact. But at least he's articulate."

Quinn glanced at her watch. She was behind on her histology notes and had been in the middle of bringing them up-to-date when Tim had popped in and dragged her away to the bull session.

"Come on, Quinn," he'd said. "You need a break. Take five and add your two cents to the session. It could use some new blood."

"But my notes—"

"You want to crack like that guy Prosser who disappeared without a trace a couple of years ago? There's more to medicine than histology, you know."

"But if I don't pass, the rest won't matter."

"You'll pass."

She'd come along because she realized Tim was right. She would pass. Just passing had never been good enough for her and still wasn't, but she did need a break. Between classes, labs, studying, and working with Dr. Emerson, she was beginning to feel a bit frazzled. She'd thought about quitting the lab job, but the work was getting more interesting now, and she found the extra money came in handy for the sundries The Ingraham didn't provide.

Eight people were in Harrison's room. Quinn and Tim made it ten. They greeted Quinn with hellos but they had a cheer for Tim when he came through the door. He clearly had become a mainstay of these sessions. She marveled at his ability to make friends with almost anybody. And envied it.

"Tim, you're just in time." It was Judy Trachtenberg. Didn't she ever study? "Harrison here is going radical on us. He thinks chiropractors ought to be included in the tiering of care."

"Tiering?" Quinn said.

They quieted and looked at her.

"Tiers of eligibility," Tim told her. "You know. Alston mentions it every so often."

"Oh, right," Quinn said. Somewhere along the line Dr. Alston had turned "tier" into a verb: to tier. Last week he'd asked the class to assume a limited amount of medical resources, then directed them to create two sets of tiers: the first set listing levels of care in descending order of sophistication, the second set dividing the population into groups in descending order of their value to society. Quinn had found it a chilling exercise, but she'd considered it no more than that: an exercise in ethics. The bull session seemed to be taking it seriously.

"What do you think?" Harrison said. Quinn wondered if anybody knew his first name. "Yes or no on the back crackers?"

"Definitely yes," Tim said. "Acupuncturists too. We've got to find a tier for every therapy if this is going to work."

Quinn waited for the zinger, the gag line that would turn around what he'd just said. But it never came.

"All right," Judy said. "Where do we lump them?"

"With the physical therapists," Tim said. "Take away all their mumbo jumbo and look at what they do: physical therapy."

Quinn watched and listened in shock. "I thought you were against any kind of rationing," she said.

"I was," Tim said.

"Well, what happened?" Quinn realized that although she and Tim did a lot of talking, the future structure of health-care delivery was not a topic of conversation. She had no idea he'd come around 180 degrees.

"That was before I realized the full scope of the problem. The day is coming when there won't be enough care to go around. And that means some people are going to have to make do with lower levels of care. Tiering is the only way to decide who gets what, Quinn. The *only* way."

She heard murmurs of agreement and saw heads nodding in agreement all around the room.

"What are you saying? Someone gets past a certain age and we throw them to the wolves?"

"Nothing so blunt as that," Harrison said. "Age should not be the sole criterion. Overall value to society should be considered. Of course, the older you are, the fewer years you have left—*ipso facto*, your chances of contributing much are reduced. Plenty of people of all ages contribute nothing. The homeless, the drunks, the addicts, are the most obvious, but there are others, less obvious. People we never see, shut-ins who sit at home and do nothing. Should some couch potato on welfare get a coronary bypass while a hardworking mechanic who's the father of three has to go on working with chest pain? I don't think so."

"I don't think so either. But who's going to decide who gets stuck in which tier? Who's going to arbitrate human value?"

"You can bet we'll have something to say in it," Tim said. "Especially those of us who go into primary care. We'll be deciding who gets referred and who doesn't."

"But this tiering idea, this dividing people up and stacking them in order of how useful they are is so . . . cold." She turned to Tim. "What about compassion? Remember how we talked about finding a CPT code number for compassion?"

"Yeah," Tim said softly, his eyes suddenly distraught. "I remember. Trouble is, I don't know how I forgot."

Quinn didn't know what it was, but something in Tim's eyes unsettled her.

CHAPTER · 13

Quinn had a few moments, so she wandered across the lab to where Dr. Emerson was reading a journal article. He looked up at her approach and smiled.

"Taking a break?" he said.

Quinn nodded. "My computer's tied up with some number crunching on that reuptake program. It'll be another ten minutes or so till it's done."

"Very good." He nodded and returned to his article.

"Uh, Dr. Emerson," Quinn said, not sure of how to broach this. She'd rehearsed her opening all last night and most of today, but still she felt awkward. "Can I ask you a strange question?"

"Sure," he said, still reading. "Go ahead. I've always liked strange questions."

"What's going on here?"

He looked up at her over the tops of his reading glasses.

"I'd think you'd know the answer to that by now. We're putting 9574 through—"

"No. Not here in your lab. I mean in the school. In The Ingraham. What's going on here?"

Dr. Emerson put the journal down and removed his reading glasses. He stared at her.

"I'm not quite sure I'm following you, Quinn."

She dropped into the seat opposite him. "I'm not sure I'm following me either. It's all so vague." She groped for the right words, the appropriate analogy, but came up empty. "It's just that everybody here at The Ingraham seems to think alike, seems to have the same point of view."

"That's not so unusual, really," Dr. Emerson said. "It happens at many academic institutions. Certain points of view gain favor with an influential segment of a department, take root, bloom, and draw other like-minded individuals. As this group gains influence and tenure, those who strongly disagree with its positions tend to drift away, while those who agree or are indifferent stay on. Look how the deconstructionists came to rule the English department at Yale. Or—"

"But I'm not talking about a department. I'm talking about a whole institution—students and faculty alike."

"The Ingraham? Maybe you'd better explain."

Quinn took a deep breath. How was she going to explain this in a sane and coherent manner when it all sounded pretty crazy to her?

"Everyone's starting to sound like Dr. Alston."

Dr. Emerson burst out laughing. "Oh, I hope not! I truly hope not!"

"It's true. They're all starting to sound like his lectures. Why, just last night—"

Dr. Emerson put one hand on her arm and raised the other to wave someone in from the hall.

"Arthur! Come in, Arthur. I want you to hear this."

Quinn turned and started at the sight of Dr. Alston strolling through the door and approaching them. What was Dr. Emerson doing? Was he trying to get her in more trouble with Dr. Alston?

"You remember Miss Cleary, don't you?"

"Ah, yes," Dr. Alston said, nodding to her. "The object of my wrath a few weeks ago. I do believe I overreacted. My apologies, Miss Cleary."

"I'm glad you apologized, Arthur," Dr. Emerson said. "Because Quinn here just paid you a compliment."

Dr. Alston smiled thinly as he looked down at her. "Did she now? And what did she say?"

Quinn fought the urge to tell him not to refer to her in the third person. She was here in the same room and quite able to answer for herself.

"She thinks you're a very persuasive lecturer."

The thin smile broadened. "Is that so?"

"Yes. She says the whole student body is beginning to sound like you."

Dr. Alston's gaze became penetrating. "May I infer from your perspective that you have somehow managed to remain immune to the sway of my rhetoric?"

Quinn swallowed. This wasn't going well at all.

"I think you argue your points very well, but I find it difficult to accept the concept of rationing medical care on the basis of social and economic worth."

"Given the inevitability of such rationing," he said, his manner cooling quickly, "what criteria do you propose?"

"I don't think I'm qualified to make decisions of that magnitude," Quinn said. "I don't know if anybody is. But I've read where it used to be widely held that global communism was inevitable, how it was only a matter of time before Marxism took over the world. And now the USSR is gone. I'm sure there are plenty of other 'inevitabilities' that have never become reality."

"I'm sure there are too, Miss Quinn," Dr. Alston said, nodding slowly as he stared at her. His gaze made her uncomfortable. "I'm glad we had this little talk. You've given me something to ponder."

He nodded good-bye to her and Dr. Emerson, then left.

Quinn shook off a chill and turned back to Dr. Emerson.

"Am I such a Pollyanna?" she said. "I mean, why do I seem to be the only one in The Ingraham who isn't falling into line behind Dr. Alston's bleak outlook?"

"Knowing Arthur," Dr. Emerson said, "I'm sure he's wondering the very same thing."

As Louis Verran approached Alston's office in the faculty building, he wondered what Dr. Tightass wanted. Whatever it was, he knew it couldn't be good. Not from the tone of voice he'd heard on the phone a few minutes ago.

Please come to my office immediately, Louis. I have made a fascinating discovery that I wish to share with you.

Right. Verran had little doubt that the fascinating discovery meant Alston had tripped over a glitch in security and was going to rub his nose in it. He just hoped he hadn't somehow heard about the lost bug.

Dammit! Where the hell was it? They'd swept the halls on both levels of the dorm but still hadn't found it.

Verran knew he wouldn't have a decent night's sleep until he'd found the damn thing.

He knocked on Alston's door.

"Come," came the reply from the other side.

Come? Gimme a fuckin' break!

He stepped into the office—dark, oak-paneled, the largest in the building, befitting Alston's status as DME—and saw him be-

hind his desk, leaning back in his chair, his fingers steepled before
his mouth, looking like the proverbial cat with a bad case of canary
breath.

Verran took one of the chairs without asking. He noted with
satisfaction how Alston stiffened when he put his feet up on the
desk.

"What's up, Doc?"

"One of the dorm SLI units is malfunctioning—and please take
your shoes off my desk."

Verran dropped his feet to the floor to cover his relief. Alston
hadn't heard about or found the bug.

"Yeah? Which room?"

"I don't know the number, but I know the student's name.
You're capable of following up from there. But I didn't call you
here merely for informational purposes. A simple phone call
would have sufficed for that. The truth is, I'm more than a little
disturbed by the fact that if I hadn't learned of this by sheer hap-
penstance, she might have gone all semester without hearing the
night music."

Verran had to admit this was no petty matter. A malfunctioning
SLI undercut The Ingraham's very purpose. But Alston's notion
didn't necessarily equate with an established fact.

"What makes you think it's not working? I doubt the student
came up and told you."

Alston smiled. "In a way, she did. She told me she saw all her
fellow students swinging their points of view toward mine on certain matters, and she couldn't understand why." He leaned forward. "Obviously her viewpoints are *not* changing. Ergo, she's not
hearing the music. Conclusion: Her SLI is malfunctioning. Can you
dispute that?"

Vaguely uncomfortable now, Verran scratched his jaw. "No. It's
logical."

"My question, Louis," Alston continued, "is why didn't *you*
know about the malfunctioning unit?"

Verran shrugged. "All our SLI indicators are green. No signs
of trouble anywhere. Every unit got its usual overhaul this summer. Everything checks out fine every night."

Alston furrowed his brow. "But something is obviously awry.
I want you to check into it immediately."

Verran gritted his teeth. He didn't need Dr. Tightass to tell him
that.

"Right. Who's the kid?"

"First year. You're supposed to be watching her closely already. Quinn Cleary."

"Oh, shit!" Verran said. "Not two-five-two again."

Alston straightened. "Again? You've had trouble with Cleary before?"

Verran had to be careful here. He couldn't slip up and spill about almost getting caught—or about the missing bug.

"No, no. Not with her personally. Just her room. Her audio pickup went on the fritz last month and I had to replace it."

"Did you now?" He paused and leaned back. "Strange, isn't it?"

"What?"

"That two electronic devices should malfunction in the same room within a matter of weeks—in a room with only a single occupant." His tones became pensive, almost distant. "And that occupant . . . a young woman that I was against admitting in the first place. Very strange. I wonder . . . is something going on here?"

"She doesn't have any jamming equipment, if that's what you're thinking." He grinned at Alston. "You're not going paranoid on me, are you, Doc?"

"Not at all, Louis. I realize that coincidences occur, but I'm always suspicious when they do. It's the scientist in me, I suppose."

"Well, the first thing we should do, Dr. Scientist," Verran said, rising, "is make sure you've got your facts straight. So far as I know, room two-five-two's SLI is working perfectly."

"It had better *not* be, Louis," Alston said. "Or otherwise we've got ourselves a big problem. I do not want another problem, Louis. I had enough problems two years ago to last me a lifetime."

Verran nodded. This was one point on which he and Dr. Tight-ass were in complete agreement. That had been a nightmare.

"Amen, Doc." He turned toward the door. "I'll let you know as soon as I check it out."

"How are you going to work this?"

"I'll use the old exterminator ploy."

Alston nodded absently. "Odd, but lately it seems that every time there's trouble, this Cleary girl is involved. Why is that?"

"Beats me," Verran said as he stepped out into the hall.

"Am I going to regret letting her in?"

Verran closed the door and hoped Alston wouldn't regret it. Because if Alston regretted letting Cleary in, then inevitably Verran would come to regret it.

Of course, the one who'd wind up regretting it most would be the Cleary girl.

CHAPTER 14

"Don't lock your door, Quinn," Tim said as he heard the clink of her key chain.

"Why not?"

"They're spraying today."

"Oh, that's right."

Tim watched her tuck the keys back in her pocket. She looked great in her slacks and sweater, except that the sweater was too long—it covered too much of her. He sighed as he watched her. Today was going to be an especially long day, for tonight was the night they were taking off for A.C. A lot of quality time with Quinn—*overnight* time with her in his free room. He'd been indulging himself these past few weeks in some wild sexual fantasies—visions of those long, slim, dynamite legs wrapped tight around him—none of which, he knew, had the slightest chance of becoming reality, but still they managed to fuel his anticipation. He'd even picked up a pack of condoms, which he supposed was like buying a Pick-6 Lotto ticket—the chances of winning were six million to one, but that didn't stop you from thinking about what it would be like to be a multimillionaire.

He smiled. And as the lotto folks liked to say: You can't win it unless you're in it.

He stepped across the hall and took another look at the sign pinned to the bulletin board.

NOTICE

The exterminators will be performing their periodic spraying of the dorm. The second floor is scheduled first on Friday morning, November 18. All rooms must be vacated between 8 A.M. and noon. Please leave your room unlocked and remove all articles from your floors before leaving for morning classes that day.

Louis Verran
Chief of Campus Security

Something about the notice bothered Tim, but for the life of him he couldn't nail down just what it was.

"Seen any bugs around your room, Quinn?" he said.

"Not a one," she said as she left her door and came over to him. "And I don't want to."

"How about the other girls? Any of them mention being bothered by bugs?"

"Not that I recall. Why?"

"I don't know. Seems strange to start spraying on the second floor. I'd think if there was going to be an insect problem in the dorm it would start at ground level and work its way up."

"You're an expert on bugs now?"

"No. But if nobody's seen any—"

"Sounds like preventive medicine to me," Quinn said. "If you spray on a regular basis, you won't develop a problem. Not a bad idea, really. Besides, the stuff they're using is supposed to be colorless and odorless and nontoxic to humans once it dries." She tugged on his sleeve. "Come on. We'll be late for path."

Tim took one last look at the notice. Maybe it was Louis Verran's name on the bottom that bothered him. He hadn't told Quinn about his little run-in with Verran in her room that night. She'd already been upset about her confrontation with Alston and he hadn't seen any purpose in bringing it up.

But something about Verran's demeanor that night had lingered with him like a bad aftertaste. Tim had had a vague impression then that the man was hiding something. He'd looked guilty. Over the following weeks Tim had written it off as a misread, but then this notice: The second floor was going to be empty, all the doors unlocked, with Louis Verran in charge.

Was something going on?

Nah.

He followed Quinn toward the stairs.

Louis Verran stood at the door to room 252 and glanced at his watch: 9:16. Plenty of time left. He stepped back into the suite and watched Elliot checking the SLI units in the headboards. All the works were exposed and he was running his check, his long fingers pulling, poking, and probing the tangled wires and circuit boards.

"How's it look?" Verran said.

"Perfect so far, chief. I'm about halfway through and haven't found a thing. I got a feeling I'm not going to."

"Never mind your feelings," Verran said. "Just don't miss anything."

There *had* to be something wrong with the unit, something mechanical, something electronic, something that could be fixed. But if the problem wasn't with the unit, if the SLI wasn't on the fritz, then it had to be Cleary. A malfunctioning unit was one thing, but a malfunctioning student . . . ?

They'd had one of those two years ago. Please, God, never again.

He looked at his watch again.

"Don't rush, Elliot. Just do it right. Still plenty of time."

Tim sensed rather than saw Quinn lean over his shoulder.

"I've got to get back to the dorm," she whispered.

"Now?"

The clock on the auditorium wall said nine-thirty. Still ten minutes to go in Dr. Hager's pathology lecture on inflammation.

"I forgot my histo notes. I want to have them for the review."

Staying low, she edged out of the row of seats and started up the steps to the exit. Tim hesitated a moment, then got up and trailed after her.

"Wait up," he said in the hallway.

She turned, surprise in her eyes. "Tim? Where are you going?"

"With you."

"You forget something too?"

"No. I just . . . " How did he say this? He didn't want to tell her of his misgivings about Louis Verran. He was sure they'd sound pretty lame if he said them out loud. But he did not like the idea of her entering the empty dorm alone, even if it was a bright fall morning. "I don't think you should go alone."

She stopped and stared at him. "*What?* You've got to be kidding."

"No, I'm not kidding. They've got a bunch of outsiders wandering the halls."

"Campus security is there."

Tim was tempted to say that might be the problem, but resisted. "Yeah, but even The Ingraham's crack SWAT team can't be everywhere. One of the bug men could be a nut case. All the rooms are unlocked. He could catch you when you step into yours and . . . well, who knows?"

"My hero," she said. Then she touched his arm. "Thanks for the thought, but I—"

"No arguments," he said. "I'm going with you and we haven't got much time. Besides, I'm not letting some creep who's been sniffing too much bug spray ruin *my* weekend in A.C."

"Some hero!" she said, and laughed.

Tim loved the sound.

It took them less than five minutes to make it back to Women's Country. As Quinn pushed through the stairwell door ahead of him, she stopped and pointed down the hall.

"See? Nothing to worry about. You could have saved yourself the trip. There's the chief of security himself standing in my doorway."

I knew it!

Tim squeezed past her into the hall. He saw Verran, but the security man was no longer in the doorway to Quinn's room. He had just pulled it closed and was bustling toward them, his jowls jiggling, an anxious look straining his features.

"What are you two doing here?" he said. "You're supposed to be in class now."

"We're going right back," Quinn said.

"Didn't you read the notice? Rooms are to be vacated between eight and twelve."

"I'll only be a second," Quinn said, starting toward her room. "I just have to pick up some—"

Verran stepped in front of her, blocking her way.

"You can't go in there right now. He's right in the middle of spraying."

"Bullshit," Tim said.

He stepped around Verran and headed for Quinn's door. He'd had enough. Too many screwy coincidences here: Fifty-two rooms on the floor and they just happen to be spraying 252 when he and Quinn arrive unannounced, Verran obviously upset at their surprise return, and the unsettling fact that Verran didn't have to ask Quinn who she was and which room was hers.

Something was going on.

"Hey! Come back here!"

Tim heard Verran hurrying after him but didn't slow. He had a good lead. He'd be in Quinn's room well ahead of him. But as he was reaching for the knob, the door opened.

A tall, dark-haired man in his early thirties stood there. He wore gray coveralls with an oval patch on the left breast that said A-JACKS EXTERMINATING. He carried a toolbox in one hand and a two-gallon spray canister in the other.

He smiled easily at Tim. "Hey. How's it going?" then looked past him. "All set in here, Mr. Verran. Where to next?"

Verran hauled up next to Tim, puffing. "What? Oh, yeah. Good. We'll go to two-fifty-one next." He glared at Tim. "What's the idea of taking off like that? You got a problem or something?"

Tim saw Quinn come up behind Verran. She was giving him a funny look. What could he say? Something wasn't right but he hadn't the vaguest idea what.

He turned back to the exterminator and saw that he too was staring at him. Not at him, exactly—at his lapel.

"That's a neat-looking pin you got there," the bug man said. "Where'd you get it?"

"Found it," Tim said.

Tim wasn't in the mood for small talk, but the bug man seemed completely taken by the pin.

"Take a look at this, Mr. Verran," he said, pointing to Tim's lapel. "You ever seen anything like that?"

Verran came around and looked. Tim thought he saw him stiffen but couldn't be sure. What was so fascinating about a little black hockey puck?

"No," Verran said slowly. "Never." His voice sounded strained. "You want to sell that?"

"No."

Tim was irritated with the attention. He didn't want to buy or sell anything. He just wanted Quinn to get her notes and get out of here.

"You sure?" Verran said.

"Very sure. Is it okay if she gets her notes now?"

The bug man seemed surprised by the question. "Hmmm? Oh, uh, yeah. Sure."

Tim waved Quinn into the room, followed her in, then closed the door behind them.

"How's the room look?" he said.

Quinn glanced around. "Fine."

"Just as you left it?"

"I think so. The bedspread looks a little wrinkled, but otherwise—"

"Nothing missing?"

"Not that I can see." She looked at him closely. "Tim, are you all right?"

"I'm fine. Why?"

"Because you're acting—"

"Weird? Yeah, I know." He searched for a plausible explanation. "Maybe I've been cooped up on this campus too long. Maybe I'm getting Ingraham fever. I need a break, need to get away for a while."

"Well, you're getting away tonight, aren't you? We both are."

"Right. To A.C. And not a moment too soon."

"Okay. So hang on."

He gave her a smile. "I will." Then he sniffed the air. "You smell anything?"

"No. Should I?"

"They just sprayed in here, didn't they? Shouldn't we be smelling something?"

"The stuff they're using is supposed to be colorless and odorless."

So's water, Tim thought.

"Can I use your phone a sec?"

"Sure."

As Quinn dug her notes out of a drawer, Tim dialed 411. He turned his back to her and he asked in a low voice for the number of A-Jacks Exterminating. He didn't know whether to be relieved or disappointed when the operator came up with a number. When he hung up, Quinn was ready to go.

"All set?" she said.

"Yeah. Let's get out of here."

Before he closed the door behind them, he took one last look. Something had been done to this room, something more than bug spraying. But damned if he could figure what.

MONITORING

Kurt was laughing.

"What's so goddamn funny?" Verran said.

"This whole thing! Here we spend weeks combing the whole fucking campus for this bug you lost, and all the time this jerk's been wearing it like a stickpin on his coat!"

"At least it explains why we could never track it down," Verran said.

"Oh, God, I wish I'd a-been there . . . just to see the look on your face when you saw . . . " Kurt dissolved into helpless laughter again.

Even Elliot was grinning like an idiot.

Verran ground his teeth. Nothing funny about this, dammit. That Brown kid had been wearing the bug around campus for all to see. What if somebody had recognized it for what it was? Christ, what if Alston had spotted it?

Verran didn't want to think about it.

"Better get a grip on yourself," he told Kurt, "because it's going to be your job to get it back."

Kurt stopped laughing. "Why me? I didn't—"

"Tonight."

"Brown's taking off for Atlantic City tonight, chief," Elliot said.

"How do you know that?"

"Heard him talking with the Cleary girl about it. They're going together."

"Awright!" Kurt said. "Boffing the blonde! Wouldn't mind a piece of that action myself."

Verran motioned him to shut up. "Maybe our luck is starting to change. We can grab the bug back while he's out of town."

"What if he's got it with him when he leaves?" Elliot said.

Kurt snorted. "The way our luck's been running, that's the way it'll go down."

Verran couldn't argue with that. But maybe that could be worked to their advantage. What was the old saying? When somebody hands you a lemon . . .

"Here's what we'll do," he said. "We'll watch him leave. If he's wearing the same jacket as he had on this morning, we'll assume he's got the bug on him. You two will tail him to Atlantic City—"

"And whack him!"

Verran glared at Kurt for the interruption and started when he saw the .38 in his hand.

"Put that away!"

Kurt grinned. "Just kidding, Lou."

He watched Kurt replace the pistol in the bottom drawer of the center console, then continued. "As I was saying, tail him to A.C. and look for a chance to rough him up a little. Make it look like a mugging."

Elliot frowned "What if we see a chance to get it without any rough stuff?"

"Do it anyway."

Kurt ground a fist into his palm. "Awright!"

"I don't know about this, chief," Elliot said. "We could get pinched."

"Not if we do it right," Kurt said.

"I don't know," Elliot muttered. "I don't know."

Verran knew how twitchy Elliot got at the thought of winding up in a jail cell again.

"It'll be all right, Elliot," Verran said, clapping him on the shoulder. "I promise you."

Kurt grinned. "Don't worry, little buddy. I'll take care of you."

Verran swung on Kurt. This was almost like being a goddamn football coach—push one, restrain the other. "No permanent damage, Kurt. Just enough to get the cops involved. And make sure they get involved—even if you have to call them yourselves."

Elliot's expression was baffled. "How come?"

"I've got my reasons."

"I hope I'm not making a mistake," Quinn said as she dropped her overnight bag into Griffin's trunk.

She watched as Tim settled her bag next to his own, then slammed the trunk top.

"What do you mean?" he said.

"I mean that we're traveling as friends and there isn't going to be any hanky-panky."

He laughed. "'Hanky-panky'?"

She felt her cheeks reddening. "One of my mother's expressions. But you know what I mean. I just don't want any . . . misunderstandings. Understand?"

He hung his head. "You mean we're not going to have the night of wild, Dionysian sexual abandon that will finally give meaning to my miserable life?" He sniffed.

"Open the trunk," she said. "I'm out of here."

He grinned. "Only kidding!"

"You'd better be—otherwise you're going to be one very disappointed medical student."

"Let's go."

As Quinn moved toward the passenger door, she heard a car behind her. A black Celica GT-S pulled into the neighboring spot on her side. With all the empty slots around, she wondered idly why it had to park so close to them. A big blond fellow got out and gave them a friendly nod. He looked vaguely familiar, then Quinn recognized him as someone she'd seen around the security desk in the science center. Why was he parking in the student lot? She noticed him looking past her, directly at Tim, almost staring. Then he slammed his door and strode up the incline toward the administration building.

I wonder if he knows we're going away overnight? she thought.

Probably. Everyone else seemed to. You couldn't keep too many secrets at a place as small as The Ingraham.

And everybody seemed to think they were indeed going to A.C. for the wild night Tim had kidded about before. Judy Trachtenberg had caught her in the hall just a few moments ago, winking and nudging, speaking in a very bad cockney accent: "Gettin' away for a bit o' the ol' in an' out, are we?"

Quinn supposed it was a natural assumption. She and Tim were seen together a lot, and now here they were going off with overnight bags.

She settled into the front seat, belted herself in, and looked at Tim as he started the engine. She liked Tim, liked him a *lot*. She had a sense that his occasional sexist remarks and bluff attitude were a male thing, a front to hide the sensitivity perking below the surface. She was sure it was there; he'd let the facade slip a couple of times and she'd caught glimpses of it. Why did he feel he had to hide it?

Romance with Tim, a little sexual cuddling, or even sex . . . would that be so bad? There was an empty spot in her life, a void that she'd never managed to fill, a subtle, aching loneliness that she kept submerged in the torrent of activity that consumed her daily life. But in quiet moments, sometimes in those early morning hours when she'd awaken before her alarm clock, she'd feel the pang of that hollow spot.

She wasn't a virgin. That had ended in high school with Bobby Roca. She'd been sure he was the love of her life. They'd made lifelong promises to each other, and had wound up in his bedroom one Saturday night when his parents were away for the weekend. Her next period had been late and she'd been scared to death. She'd seen her whole future in medicine swirling down into a black hole and she was desperate for some support, some comfort, someone to lean on, just a little. Bobby had offered all the warmth and comfort of a snake. Worse, he actually blamed her. When her period finally arrived, a week late, she'd told Bobby to take a hike.

There'd been nobody since . . . nobody important, anyway. Not that there hadn't been opportunities, but she'd never let a relationship get off the ground. She wasn't sure why. Why did she take sex so seriously? So many of the girls at UConn had been so casual about it. They went out once or twice and sex just became part of the relationship. Male and female—what could be more natural? She knew it wasn't always so great for them, but neither was it the hardest thing in the world. Why wasn't it easy for her? Why did she attach so much importance to it?

Hadn't most of them been raised the way she'd been—the right man, the right time and place and circumstances?

Tim might be the right man, but this wasn't the right time in her life, and a freebie hotel room in Atlantic City after a night of watching Tim gamble would not be the right place and circumstances.

And overriding all of it was the weight of her concern for her career. She couldn't afford any sort of distraction now. This was not the right time in her life for a serious relationship—the only kind of relationship she knew how to have. Later. There would be plenty of time later. For now she had to remember to keep pulling back from Tim and keep her eyes—and the rest of her—focused on the future.

No foreign entanglements.

But snuggling close to him tonight, his arms around her . . . a nice thought, a warm thought. But it would remain just that: a thought.

"You're sure you saw it?" Verran said.

He was standing with Elliot and Kurt on the rise overlooking the student parking lot.

Kurt nodded. "It was there, right where Elliot said it was— same coat, same place. I could've reached out and grabbed it."

"That you'll do later on. In A.C. Follow them there. Watch them. Stay out of sight. Be patient. Wait for your chance and make it a good one. You got what you need?"

Kurt nodded. "Reversible jackets, gloves, ski masks, the works."

"Isn't there another way we can do this?" Elliot said.

He'd been quiet and edgy all day. Verran knew Elliot was picturing himself in a jail cell, but he didn't want to pussy out, so he was hanging in there with Kurt.

"This is no big deal, Elliot. And it's perfect if it happens up in Jersey. That way The Ingraham isn't involved in any way. And should there be any question, you were both here with me all night. Now get going. You don't want to lose them."

Verran watched them get into their separate cars and roar off. By tomorrow morning he'd have the missing bug back and he could rest easy again.

* * *

"Mmmmmm," Tim said as they came off the Delaware Memorial Bridge and turned onto New Jersey Route 40. "The road to Atlantic City. I can smell the money already."

Quinn looked around at the surrounding darkness as the four-lane blacktop quickly narrowed to two.

"Pretty desolate."

"This is mostly farmland. If you think it's dark here, my dear, wait till we get into the Jersey Pine Barrens. A million acres of nothing. *Then* you'll see dark. A.C. is still almost sixty miles off, so now's as good a time as any to plan our strategy."

"Strategy?"

"Sure. We're both going to play."

"Oh, no. I don't know the first thing about gambling. And I can't afford—"

"You'll be playing with my money. Here's how it works. In the casinos, blackjack is dealt—"

"Blackjack? I've never played blackjack."

"Sure you have. It's twenty-one. The guy who gets closest to a twenty-one value in the cards he's dealt, without going over, wins. Number cards are face value, picture cards are worth ten, and the ace can be worth one or eleven—your choice. You get dealt an ace and a picture card—say, a queen—that's twenty-one. That's black-jack, and you win automatically."

"Win what?"

"Money. If you just plain beat the dealer, you double your money. So if you bet ten bucks, you get your ten back, plus another ten. A blackjack pays even more."

"Who pays you?"

"The house."

"Whose house?"

"The casino! Quinn, where've you been for the past twenty-two years?"

"I've been lots of places." Why was Tim getting so worked up? "I just haven't been in casinos."

"That's obvious. And that's probably a good thing. But . . . " He wrinkled his nose as a pungent odor seeped into the car. "Whew! What's that?"

Quinn recognized it immediately. "Cows," she said. "Some-body's got a herd along here. You don't grow up on a farm without knowing that smell."

"Yeah? Well, they do call this the Garden State. But let me lay the situation out for you. We're going to be customers of the casino, and since the casino's business is gambling, we're going to be called gamblers."

"I'd rather be a customer."

"Bear with me, Quinn. We're going to go into the casino and sit at the table with other gamblers. But we're not going to play each other. We're going to play the casino—the house. The house will be represented by the dealer. The dealer is nothing more than a guy—or lots of times a woman—who is paid to be a machine."

"I don't get it."

"Dealers have no decision-making powers. If the cards they've dealt themselves total sixteen or less, they deal themselves another card. When the cards total more than sixteen, they take no more. The casinos have calculated that this strategy gives them the best odds of staying ahead of their customers. And they're right."

The whole concept baffled Quinn. "Well, if you know the casino—excuse me, the house—is going to win, why bother gambling at all?"

"An excellent question, Quinn. A question many gamblers have asked themselves countless times."

"It sounds to me like you should simply walk into the casino, hand your money to the dealer, and walk out again. You'd save yourself all the sweat and apprehension, and maybe you could do something useful with the extra time you had."

Tim stared at her, awe in his voice and a look of utter amazement on his face.

"You're not kidding, are you? You're really for real, aren't you?"

"The road, Tim," Quinn said, pointing through the windshield. "Please watch the road."

He faced front again. "How about excitement, Quinn?"

"What's exciting about losing money?"

"But that's just it. You don't *always* lose. Sometimes you win. And it's not so much the winning or losing but the process itself that matters. It's a chance to beat the system—or at least *a* system. And everybody likes to beat the system. Especially me."

"I think we've had this conversation before."

"Right. While we were waiting to hear if The Ingraham was going to accept you. That was when I told you that I can beat the casinos' system."

"Isn't it an old joke that if someone comes up with what he knows is a surefire, foolproof, can't-lose gambling system, the casinos will have a car waiting for him at the airport to take him directly to their tables?"

"Right. Because the casinos have got their own system: The structure of the payouts, the ceilings on the bets, the simple mathematics of the law of averages—everything is geared toward guaranteeing them the lion's share of the action that crosses their tables. But no casino's system is set up to handle a wild card like me."

Dustin Hoffman's face suddenly flashed before Quinn's eyes and she laughed. "You think you're Rain Man, don't you."

"I beg your pardon, Miss Cleary. I may be an idiot, but I am not an idiot savant. Rain Man and I work differently. His brain was number-oriented, mine is picture-oriented. But the end result is the same: After a few decks have been played, we both have a pretty good idea what's left in the shoe."

"Now I'm completely lost."

Tim sighed patiently. "Okay. Casinos don't deal blackjack from a single deck anymore since a bunch of people worked out a counting system that gave them a decent edge over the house."

"But?"

He held up a hand. "Let me finish. So the casinos started shuffling up to eight decks at a time and loading them all into this hopper called a shoe and dealing from that. Most folks can learn to keep track of a fifty- or hundred-card deck, but not *four* hundred cards. But I can."

"Your photographic memory," Quinn said.

"Yep. I remember every card that's been played."

"But what good is that?"

"Not much until you get down to the end of the shoe. But when we do get down to the last hundred cards or so, I usually know exactly what's left in the shoe."

"But if you don't know the order they're in, what good is it?"

"I don't need to know the order. All I need to know is if there's a predominance of high cards or low cards. If those last hundred or so cards are tilted heavily in either direction, that's when I make my move. *That's* when I make my killing and beat their system. And you're going to help."

"What do you mean?"

"Know what this is?" He held up his right hand; his thumb and pinkie finger were extended, the three middle fingers folded down. He wiggled it back and forth. "It's the Hawaiian hang-loose sign." He wiggled his hand again. "*In hoc signo vinces.*"

She knew the translation, but . . . "I still don't get it."

Tim reached over and patted her knee. "You will, Quinn. By the time we get to A.C., all will be clear. And then we'll both beat the system."

Atlantic City wasn't at all as Quinn had pictured it. The postcards and photos she'd seen over the years had shown sunny beaches, tall, new, clean buildings, and a wide boardwalk filled with smiling, happy people. The city she saw as they came in from the marshy salt flats was old, worn, battered, and beaten, with vacant storefronts, peeling paint, rotting shingles, and broken windows. Equally dilapidated people—most of them black—shuffled or slunk along the narrow, crumbling, littered sidewalks in the halogen glow of the streetlights.

"This looks like Beirut," Quinn said.

"Yeah, but it's a Beirut laid out by the Parker Brothers."

Despite the desolation, Quinn had to smile as they passed the avenues: Atlantic, Illinois, New York, Pennsylvania . . .

"Right. Monopoly. I've bought these streets plenty of times. But I'd be taking a lot better care of them if they were still mine."

"Consider this your reality check before stepping into the land of make-believe."

They turned onto Virginia, and moments later they were entering an Arabian Nights Neverland. Smooth, well-lit pavement lined with stone elephants led down a long, walled entry to a maharajah's palace—or rather a Hollywoodized vision of a maharajah's palace, with candy-colored cupolas and faux-Arabic script spelling out "Donald J. Trump presents the TAJ MAHAL." Tim pulled to a stop under the canopy, where turbaned attendants unloaded their baggage and whisked the car away to the hotel garage.

"Sort of like stepping out of Kansas into Oz, isn't it," Tim said as they followed their bags toward the registration desk.

Quinn thought of the desolation outside and the costumed attendants swirling around her now in the opulent lobby.

"More like entering the Masque of the Red Death."

Tim gave her a sidelong glance. "Nothing like an upbeat literary analogy to set the tone for the evening."

As the porter led them to the registration area, Quinn noted that the faux-Arabic script was everywhere—over the rest rooms and over the VIP check-in desk where they stopped.

"Can we have two beds?" Quinn said to the woman as Tim handed his comp invitation across the counter.

"I'll see what I can do, ma'am." She checked her computer screen. "Yes. That will be no problem."

"No problem for you, maybe," Tim muttered.

Quinn laughed.

As soon as the bellman was gone, Quinn tossed her bag onto the king-size bed near the window.

"I've got this one!"

Tim dropped his on the other. "Then I guess this one is mine."

Compared to the rest of the hotel, Quinn thought the room was rather ordinary. Almost a relief not to see minarets on the bed-posts.

"We can unpack later," she said. "Let's go downstairs. I'm not underdressed, am I?"

He laughed. "No way. There's not much in the way of a dress code on the gaming floor."

"Good. Are we ready, then?"

She was getting into the mood, giving in to a growing excitement. She couldn't help it. She wanted to see the casino and try out Tim's plan.

"Fine with me," Tim said. "But how about a quickie before we hit the tables?"

She could tell he was kidding—well, half-kidding. And she was almost tempted . . .

. . . *No foreign entanglements* . . .

She played indignant and pointed to the door. "Out."

"For good luck?"

"You told me you didn't believe in luck."

He hesitated. "I did, didn't I. Why do I say things like that?" Then he brightened. "But I'd sure as hell consider myself lucky if—"

She pointed to the door again. "Out!"

Quinn was taken aback by the casino's gaming floor. She'd expected the flashing lights and the noise, the bells, the clatter of the slots, the chatter of the voices, but she wasn't prepared for the crowd, for the ceaseless swirl of people, and the layer of smoke that undulated over the tables like a muslin canopy.

She paused at the top of the two steps that led down to the gaming floor, hesitant about mingling with the flowing crowd. Everyone down there seemed to know what they were doing, where they were going. Suddenly she felt a little lost. She grabbed Tim's arm.

"Don't lose me."

He patted her hand where it gripped his bicep. "Not a chance." He led her gently into the maelstrom.

"First we'll take a walk, get you oriented, then we'll find us a table and relieve Mr. Trump of some of his money."

Quinn couldn't say exactly what she had expected to see in a casino, but this was not it. Not by a long shot.

But it was absolutely fascinating.

She had always been a people watcher, and this was a people-watcher's paradise.

First they had to wade through the phalanxes of slot machines with their dead-eyed players, most of whom seemed old and not too well-dressed. Each stood—except for the ones in wheelchairs—with a cup of coins in the left hand and a cigarette dangling from the lips, as they plunked in coins and pulled the lever with the right hand. The machines dutifully spun their dials, and then the procedure was repeated. Endlessly. Robots playing robots. Even when the machines clanked coins into the trays, the players showed no emotion.

Quinn had a sense of *déjà vu*, and then she remembered an old silent film, Fritz Lang's *Metropolis*, in which laborers in the city of the future were shown working the machines of the future, pulling levers with soulless ennui.

But this was no dank subterranean factory. Dozens of huge, magnificent chandeliers were suspended in recesses in the mirrored ceiling. Lights flashed everywhere.

She heard excited shouting from a group of men crowded around a table.

"What's that?"

"Craps. I've tried to learn that game for years, but I still don't understand it."

"They sound like they're having fun."

"That's because they're winning. But you can lose your shirt before you know it in that game."

She followed him to the blackjack section, aisles of curved tables, some full, some empty.

"Can we get a nonsmoking table?"

"That's not one of my criteria," Tim said, "but I'll try."

"There's nobody at that one," she said, pointing to a table where a female dealer stood with her hands behind her back, staring blindly ahead over an empty expanse of green the color of sunlit Astroturf. She wore a purple vest festooned with gold brocade over a white shirt fastened at the throat with a gold brooch. All the dealers, male and female, were dressed identically. "We could have it all to ourselves."

"We don't want it all to ourselves," he said. "It'd take forever to work through the shoe."

"But she looks lonely."

"Quinn . . . "

"Sorry."

They wandered up and down the blackjack aisles. Quinn watched Tim's eyes flickering from table to table, searching.

"What are we waiting for?"

"I'm looking for the right table," Tim said. "It's got to be nearly full, and the dealer is just starting a new shoe." He stopped, staring. "And I think I just found it."

He led her to the right.

"But it's only got one seat."

"That's for you."

"What are you going to do?"

"I'll be standing right behind you, teaching you the game, waiting for another seat to open up."

Quinn saw cigarettes in the hands of two of the four players already at the table.

"About that nonsmoking table?"

"Quinn . . . "

"Sorry."

As Tim pulled out the end seat on the dealer's right and held it for Quinn, he scanned the cards on the table. This was the first hand. He'd seen one of the players placing the yellow cut card and had moved quickly, despite the table limits: minimum $10/maximum $500. He would have preferred something higher. Once the cards already played were photographed and filed in his memory, he squared Quinn at the table and dropped twenty $100 bills on the table.

"Hundreds," he said, and waited for Quinn's reaction.

As the dealer called out, "Two thousand in hundreds," she didn't disappoint him: She nearly gave herself a whiplash as she snapped her head around to look at him. Tim winked, pushed the black-and-green chips in front of her, then moved behind her where he had a good view of the table.

The other players were three deadpan middle-aged men with drinks in front of them—scotch or vodka on the rocks, Tim guessed—and an elderly, chain-smoking woman with orange hair.

"What do I do now?" she said.

"Bet a hundred. Put out one chip."

"That's a hundred dollars!"

"Please do it, Quinn." He winked at the dealer, a pretty blonde wearing a ton of eye shadow. "She's a beginner." The dealer favored him with a tolerant smile.

Quinn slid the chip forward and was dealt an eight and a ten. The dealer had a king showing.

"What do I do now?"

"Stick."

The dealer turned over a nine and raked in Quinn's chip.

"What happened?"

"We lost."

"We lost a hundred dollars? Just like that?"

Down the table, one of the other players groaned softly.

"Put out another chip."

"How about half a one?"

"Quinn . . . "

"Sorry."

She placed the chip and got a four and a five in return. The dealer had a seven showing.

"What do I do now?"

"Take a look: The very best she can do is eighteen. Since that's over sixteen, she has to stick. You're a sure loser with what you've got, so take another card when she comes around to you."

The dealer looked at Quinn, her eyebrows raised questioningly.

"I'll take another card, please."

Tim said, "Real gamblers say, 'Hit me,' or just tap their cards."

Quinn tapped her cards. "Hit me. Please."

Tim scanned the cards showing and noticed an indulgent smile on two of the other players.

A ten of clubs landed in front of Quinn. The dealer turned over a queen. She placed another green-and-black chip next to Quinn's.

"I won?" she said.

"You won."

"That means we're even. Maybe we should quit now."

"Quinn . . ."

"Sorry." She reached for one of the two chips in front of her.

"Let them ride," Tim said.

"Two hundred dollars all at once? I hope you know what you're doing."

The pit boss, dressed in a gray suit, stepped up to Tim's side and spoke in a low voice. "Is there anything the casino can do for you, sir?"

Tim had been expecting him. Two thousand tossed on the table tended to attract the right kind of attention. That was why he'd bought all his chips at once.

Tim shrugged. "Our room's already comped."

The pit boss nodded sagely. "In that case may we offer you dinner, perhaps? And the show? Julio Iglesias is here tonight."

"Dinner will be fine," Tim said.

The pit boss bowed and walked off.

Meanwhile, Quinn had been dealt a jack of clubs. Then came an ace of diamonds.

"Blackjack!" Tim said, and Quinn screeched excitedly as the dealer pushed three more chips in front of her.

"I *like* this game!" she said.

The others were smiling openly now, nudging each other. They loved her.

Of course they did. Tim put his hands on her shoulders and gently kneaded the tight muscles under the fabric of her blouse. How could they help but love her?

Quinn was feeling a little more comfortable with the game now. She'd caught the rhythm of the table, of the play, but she was behind in the winning category. Her pile of hundred-dollar chips had shrunk.

She didn't like this gambling thing. She didn't like any of it— the casino with its noise and congestion, the city around it, the people within it with their dead eyes and their cigarettes, their endless, air-fouling, breath-clogging, eye-stinging cigarettes.

And she would have been completely loaded by now if she'd taken advantage of the complimentary cocktails. Every few minutes a long-legged waitress in a short skirt and a feathered fez—it had taken a while for Quinn to get used to that fez—would be at her side, asking her if she wanted a drink. Quinn ordered her usual diet Pepsi.

She had a moment of uncertainty when the orange-haired lady quit her seat and Tim strutted to the far end of the table to claim it, taking half of her remaining chips with him.

"I guess it's time for me to show Mr. Trump how to play this game for keeps," he said in exaggerated basso voice, a perfect parody of macho overconfidence.

He gave her a reassuring wave from the other end, and she realized why he hadn't hesitated to move: The curve of the table gave her a clear view of him to her right. She missed the reassuring pressure of his hands resting on her shoulders but realized it was probably better if there was a little distance between them. It would make it easier to see the series of hand signals Tim had set up between them.

He'd said they'd be a very unpopular couple if the casino tumbled to what they were up to. That was probably the reason she had this prickling at the back of her neck, this feeling she was being watched. She'd glanced around a few times when the feeling had been exceptionally strong but had found no one staring at her.

Probably just a minor case of Timothy Brown–induced paranoia.

Quinn held her own through the next few hands without his direct guidance, then she glanced his way and noticed his left hand was splayed in the Hawaiian hang-loose configuration he'd shown her.

That was the signal to push her bets to the limit. A pulse of adrenaline shot through her. That meant the shoe was running out and Tim had calculated the remaining cards were heavily weighted one way or the other, predominantly high or predominantly low. She wondered which. Not that it mattered.

Whichever way it was, Tim had decided the time was right to make their move.

She watched him carefully now, her eyes darting repeatedly to his left hand, allowing him to direct her play.

She glanced at the plastic sign before her on the table.

MINIMUM BET: $10
TABLE LIMIT: $500

With an extreme effort she ignored the sick feeling that roiled through her stomach at the very thought of risking so much money on the turn of a card and pushed five $100 chips into the play area.

A queen and a two landed in front of her. What did Tim want her to do with that? Especially since the dealer had a five showing.

She glanced right and repressed a gasp as she saw that Tim had bet five hundred dollars too. Then she saw his left hand balled into a fist. She looked again to make sure, then took a deep breath. She hoped he knew what he was doing.

Her palms were slick with perspiration by the time the dealer came back to her. Quinn waved her off.

"I'll stick," she said, and her voice sounded hoarse. She knew it wasn't just from the smoke.

Right. First I'll stick, then I'll get sick.

The dealer flipped her down card—a jack. That gave her fifteen. She had to draw. *Like a robot*, Tim had said. Quinn held her breath . . . and watched her pull a king.

Busted!

The dealer placed a stack of five $100 chips next to Tim's bet, and another next to Quinn's.

Quinn felt too weak to cheer. She looked down at her watch. How long had that taken? Thirty seconds? She'd just made five hundred dollars in thirty seconds. How many summer weeks had she waitressed backbreaking double shifts and not made that much?

But then, as a waitress she'd never run the risk of *losing* money.

"You're beyond the table limit, miss."

Quinn looked up, startled. "What?"

"Five-hundred-dollar limit," the dealer said.

"Oh, sure. Sorry." Quinn picked up the winnings and left the original stack out in the bet area.

Then she stopped and turned around. That feeling of being watched was stronger than ever. But once again, no one but the dealer seemed to be paying any overt attention to her.

She shrugged off the feeling and braced herself for another nerve-racking hand.

They won three of the next four hands, then a yellow card popped out of the shoe and the play paused. Tim stood up and stretched.

"Maybe we should have had dinner, hon," he said. "I'm starved. Want to get something to eat?"

Hon? Quinn couldn't figure out what he was up to; then she glanced at the dealer and saw her shuffling a stack of cards.

"Uh, sure, *hon.* I know I could sure go for a big, fat, juicy steak right now myself, *hon.*"

Tim laughed out loud and began gathering up his chips. Quinn began stacking hers. She thought the pit boss was watching them a little too closely. Did he suspect?

"For a beginner you're one lucky little lady," said the old fellow next to her.

Quinn nodded toward Tim. "I have a great teacher."

Her pile was about the same size as when she'd sat down, but Tim had accumulated a pile of his own. Her hands shook as she stuffed them into her pockets.

She saw Tim take a chip and give it to the dealer. Quinn wondered why. The dealer hadn't been particularly friendly or helpful. She shrugged. Probably a custom. Like tipping a waitress.

She pushed one of her own chips across the table.

Tim pocketed his chips and guided Quinn away from the table. He wanted to throw his arms around her and kiss her, but he settled for putting his arm across her shoulders. He felt a fine tremor running through her. He squeezed her upper arm.

"Quinn," he whispered, "you were *great.*"

"I think I need a shower," she said.

"Not bad for less than an hour's work," he said.

"How much *did* we make?"

"I figure we're almost two thousand ahead. And that's just the start."

Quinn sagged against him. "I don't know how much of this I can take."

"Hang in there, kid. That's about what I do alone. For the two of us it's just a start."

"You mean to tell me you clear two thousand every time you come here?"

"Not every time, but most times. Sometimes it takes longer than others. Sometimes you'll nurse a shoe all the way along, and it stays even straight through, never swinging too far high or low. That's wasted time."

"But . . ." Quinn seemed to be having some trouble grasping the numbers. "If you take home two thousand dollars every time, and if you came here just once a week, you could . . ."

"Pull down six figures a year?" He shrugged. "Maybe. Don't think it hasn't occurred to me. Work one day, have the other six to spend the hundred thou you're taking home. Sounds great, doesn't it."

They wandered from the casino to the hotel section and strolled past the windows of the shops.

"I don't know," she said. "Does it?"

He noticed her watching him closely. He got the feeling the answer was important to her. But he didn't have to ponder a reply. Over the past few years he'd given the matter a lot of thought.

Still, he hesitated. He wasn't used to talking about himself—his real self. He'd spent his teen years cultivating an exterior that hid the sap inside. But this was Quinn and those big blue eyes were so close. Maybe he could risk it. Just a little.

"On the surface, yeah. It sounds ideal. But what have you got by the time you're old enough for Medicare?"

"I don't know," she said. "A pile of money?"

"Yeah. If that. Certainly not much else. There's got to be more to life than that, don't you think? Just making money isn't . . . *doing* anything. You haven't enriched anything but your bank account with your work. Like being a currency speculator or a gossip columnist, or something equally empty."

"So you chose medicine—so you could do something with your life?"

This was getting a bit too sticky and Tim felt himself instinctively pulling back.

"Well, I figure medicine's a good thing to have to fall back on. And at least I'll have something noble-sounding to tell the kids—*our* kids—"

"Bite your tongue!"

"—when they ask me what I've been doing with my life."

"Can't you be serious for two consecutive minutes?"

"It's not entirely beyond the realm of possibility, Miss Cleary, but let's not fit me for a halo yet. As I've told you, mostly I'm at The Ingraham because it's free and it's a way to stave off adulthood a little longer."

"Uh-huh." He sensed that she didn't buy that, especially since she was nodding slowly and smiling at him. A very big, very warm smile.

"Let's go outside," Quinn said. "I could use some fresh air."

Tim sighed. He'd been hoping she'd want to go up to the room. "Sure. This way."

"Aaaahhh!"

Quinn breathed deeply as she ran up to the railing on the leading edge of the Boardwalk and threw her arms wide to catch the cool onshore breeze from the Atlantic. She reveled in the clean, briny smell.

"Why can't they pump some of this into the casino?" she said.

Tim leaned on the rail beside her. "Because half the folks in there would probably keel over from an overdose of oxygen. Some of them haven't had a whiff of fresh air in twenty years."

She turned and looked at all the blinking lights, all the garish metallic colors on the cupolas of the Taj Mahal.

"Sort of adds new dimensions to the concept of gaudy, doesn't it," she said.

Tim laughed. "It could give garish a bad name."

They leaned and listened to the ocean rumbling beyond the darkened beach, watched the light from the gibbous moon fleck the water and glitter off the foamy waves. Quinn felt the tension of the blackjack table vent out through her pores. She noticed a stairway to their left.

"Let's go down on the beach, just for a minute." She kicked off her shoes. "I want to get some sand between my toes."

Tim followed her, grumbling. "I hate getting sand in my shoes."

At the bottom of the steps Quinn worked her feet into the cold, dry granules and again felt that prickle at the back of her neck, that feeling of being watched. She turned and saw two dark figures moving along the Boardwalk above them, hugging the rail, watching them. Something furtive about them . . .

She tapped Tim on the shoulder. "Maybe we should go back up."

"We just got here."

As Tim bent to empty the sand from his shoes, Quinn glanced up again. The two figures were at the top of the steps now, staring down at them, both definitely male, wearing knit watch caps. The lights were behind them so their faces were shadowed. They could have been sailors, but as she watched, they pulled their caps down over their heads—ski masks!—and began sprinting down the steps.

"Tim!" she cried.

She saw him turn at the sound of their pounding feet but he had no time to react before they were upon him. They knocked him onto his back in the sand, punched his face, then began tearing at his coat pockets, ripping them open. For a few heartbeats Quinn stood paralyzed with shock and terror—she'd never witnessed anything like this, had always thought it happened to other people—before she began screaming for help and beating on the backs of the assailants. One of them turned and shoved her back. The blow was almost casual, but it overbalanced her and her feet slipped in the sand and she went down. In the cold moonlight she saw chips falling and scattering on the sand next to Tim as she continued to cry for help. The smaller of the attackers began to scoop up the chips, while the bigger one kept battering Tim and tearing at his coat. Finally, after rocking Tim's head with a particularly vicious blow, the bigger one got to his feet at about the same time Quinn regained hers. He lunged toward her, but she leapt for the stairs, shouting nonstop for help, praying someone would hear, or maybe see, her. She was halfway up when he caught her, grabbing the waistband of her slacks and trying to pull them off her. With his other hand he began pawing between her legs. She jabbed back at him with her elbow but it glanced off his shoulder. She was losing her balance.

Suddenly Tim loomed up beside them, bloody nose, bloody mouth, and he was yanking the big one around and slamming his fist into the bump of the nose behind the mask. Quinn heard a crunch, heard a cry of pain, and then the smaller one was there, pulling his partner away, pointing toward the underside of the Boardwalk.

Quinn kept up her shouting. She craned her neck above the level of the boards and saw security guards rushing toward them from the casino entrance. When she turned back, the two muggers were already disappearing into the darkness under the Boardwalk. Then she saw Tim slump against the handrail, gasping, retching. Quinn darted to his side and hung there, not knowing what to do, where to touch him, where not to touch him, but knowing too well that her control was tearing loose and that all she wanted to do was throw her arms around him and cry.

So that was what she did.

MONITORING

Louis Verran snatched up the phone on the first ring.

"Yeah?"

"Chief—it's Elliot."

Tell me something good, Elliot!

"We got it."

Verran let out a long, slow sigh. At last. All this grief over a lousy bug.

"Where are you now? You made it out of town okay?"

"No problem." He sounded pumped, half-delirious with relief that he'd come through without getting pinched. "We're at a rest stop on the Delaware pike. We took him outside on the beach. It was too perfect to pass up. He put up a fight but we nailed him good. Then we ducked under the Boardwalk, ditched the ski masks, and reversed the jackets. Kurt ran north to his car and I went south to mine, just like we planned. Nobody gave us a bit of trouble. Very smooth, chief. Very smooth."

Of course it was smooth, Verran thought. You plan out all your moves ahead of time, it always goes smooth. Even if the A.C. cops could have got out an APB in time, they'd have been looking for two guys of unknown race wearing black or dark blue windbreakers. A lone white male driving out of town in a red jacket wouldn't get a second look.

"And the cops? You give them a call?"

"Didn't have to. The hotel fuzz was coming to the rescue just as we were leaving."

Perfect.

"Where's Kurt now?"

"He's in his car not ten feet from me, waiting to get home."

"Good. Both of you come straight here. I'm proud of you guys."

And besides, Verran wanted to see and feel that rotten lousy defective bug in his very own hand. Tonight.

CHAPTER · 16

"At least I didn't lose any teeth."

Tim sat on the bed with an ice pack against his right cheek. Quinn knelt beside him, her hands clasped between her thighs, still shaking inside. The room was warm but her hands felt cold; she felt cold all over.

"You could have lost your *life*."

They'd been to the hotel infirmary once, in and out of the hotel Security Office twice—she had to say the Taj Mahal had been genuinely solicitous, even though the mugging had occurred off its premises—and to the Atlantic City Police Department and back. They had filled out forms, given descriptions, and recounted the events leading up to and during the attack until they were both sick of talking about it.

The consensus was that it had been a random mugging, but Quinn remembered that feeling of being watched. She hadn't said anything to the police about it though. But she suspected the two attackers had watched them win heavily, seen them go outside to the deserted Boardwalk, and made their move.

Tim fingered the tears in his sport coat with his free hand.

"Look at this. Torn to shreds." He looked at her, reached out, and rubbed her arm. His warm touch felt good. "You okay?"

She nodded. "I only got shoved around a little. But I feel completely worn out." She felt as if she'd been inflated to twice her size and then had her plug pulled. A dull, throbbing headache topped it off.

"I know what you mean. But you got more than just shoved around. That goddamn creep!"

She didn't want to talk about it, even think about it. She put her hand over his. "You were very brave."

He snorted. *"Brave?* They had me down on my back and were punching my lights out."

"No. I mean after, when the big guy was attacking me. I know they hurt you, but still you got up and . . . came to help."

"I couldn't very well lie there and let him maul you, could I?"

"But you were hurt."

"Yeah, but I've seen all those John Wayne and Clint Eastwood movies. They sort of make you feel there are things you should do even though you know you're going to get hurt."

Quinn slid closer and leaned against him, resting her head on his shoulder.

"Does this hurt?"

"I'd say that's just what the doctor ordered."

Quinn felt oddly warm, with rushes of heat coursing through her. Short of breath too. All the good feelings she had for Tim crowded close around her, pressing her to him, and all the doubts and reservations she'd had, all the irritations he caused, were gone, blown away. They didn't matter any longer. Tonight they'd walked together through a fire. She felt *joined* to this man.

She lifted her head and kissed him on the lips, gently.

"Sorry," she said. "I don't know why I did that." And that was true. She hadn't planned it, or even thought about it. She'd just . . . done it.

"Do it again," he said softly. "But easy on the lower lip. It's killing me."

And what followed came very naturally, very slowly, with their clothes being shed bit by bit, like old skin, and the heat building incrementally but irresistibly till it pulsed and throbbed with an incendiary life of its own as they joined like longtime lovers who'd known each other forever.

Quinn lay facedown on the sheets and shivered in the dark as Tim's fingers traveled lightly up and down her spine. On one trip they continued farther down and he ran his hands gently over her rear.

"I always knew you had a—"

"Don't say it."

"—nice butt."

"You said it."

"It's true."

"I have a caboose butt on an Olive Oyl body."

"No, you've got a Bluto brain. You need therapy for your distorted body image."

She lay quiet, her thoughts in turmoil, as he continued his feather-light caresses.

"What have we done, Tim?" she said finally.

"What comes naturally."

"I'm serious."

"You mean, have we ruined a beautiful friendship?"

"Exactly."

He moved closer, sliding against her right side, crossing his knee over the backs of her thighs. His lips brushed her ear.

"I hope not. I desperately hope not. But we can't pretend this didn't happen."

"I know."

"Do you want to stop and never do this again?"

"No. God no. But every time you stop by the room, are you going to want to be like this? Am I? I didn't want to be involved, Tim. I really didn't."

"Are you involved?"

Quinn turned toward him and felt his chest hair brush her nipples as their legs entwined. She couldn't remember feeling this way about anyone else. Ever. This had to be love.

"Yes. Yes, yes, yes. Are you?"

"Have been since I first saw you at orientation last December. From that moment I knew it was going to be you and me. I didn't know how long it would take or how many different roads we would travel, but some part of me seemed to sense that we'd wind up together. You must have sensed something like that too."

Quinn laughed and hugged him closer—but gently. "No way! I thought you were an obnoxious brat, one of the last people on earth I wanted to have anything to do with. Just slightly ahead of Saddam Hussein."

"Thanks a lot." He nuzzled her throat. "But I have an idea. A compromise. We'll make it a rule between us that we don't make love on campus. When we can, we'll sneak away to the No-Tell Motel or something and go nuts, but at The Ingraham we stay strictly platonic."

Quinn tried to see his face in the dark. Was this one of his put-ons? She wished she knew because it sounded perfect to her.

"Where'd you come up with that?"

"Oh, I don't know. I just put myself inside a very practical, borderline-nerdy mind and tried to imagine what that mind could come up with.''

She punched him lightly on the shoulder and he winced.

''Ouch!''

''Sorry. But is that what you think of me?''

''Isn't that what you'd have come up with?''

Reluctantly, she had to agree.

He said, ''But there's got to be an angle we can work with this. Maybe we can apply to Dr. Alston for extra credit when we make our little off-campus trips.''

''Extra credit?''

''Sure. Extracurricular studies in anatomy. Or how about human sexuality lab? Gotta be worth something. In fact, I think I'm ready to earn a few extra credits right now.''

Quinn slid her hand down his abdomen. ''Yes, you are. Yes, you are indeed.''

MONITORING

"What the hell happened to you?"

Verran was staring at Kurt's swollen, purpling nose as he and Elliot arrived in the control room.

"The kid got in a lucky one when I wasn't looking." He sounded like he had a bad cold.

"Great. Just great. That means you're going to have to stay out of sight until that thing heals."

"What the hell for?"

"Because Brown saw you in the student lot before he left and your nose was fine then. If he knows he clocked one of the guys who attacked him on the nose, and then he sees you with a freshly busted beak—"

"Aw, he'd never put the two together."

"Maybe not. But these kids ain't here because they're dummies. Just to be sure, I'm keeping you on the graveyard shift till that heals up."

"Aw, Lou."

Verran held out his hand. "Where's the bug?"

Elliot leaned forward and dropped it into Verran's palm.

"Safe and sound, chief."

Verran stared at it. Such a tiny thing to cause so goddamn much trouble.

"Want me to see if I can fix it?" Elliot said.

"Are you kidding?"

Verran bent and placed the errant bug on the concrete floor, straightened, then ground it flat under his heel.

"That's the last time that little son of a bitch will give us any grief."

Elliot grinned and headed for his console, while Kurt went to find some ice for his nose. Verran surveyed the varicolored meters, terminals, and LEDs of his little domain with quiet satisfaction. Only one problem remained to mar his serenity: the Cleary broad.

Elliot had run an exhaustive, comprehensive check on her SLI unit yesterday and had found everything in perfect working order, but tightass Alston was still insisting that there had to be something wrong with it. Verran knew there wasn't. As far as he was concerned, the problem wasn't with the unit, it was with the girl.

And since it was Alston's responsibility to screen the students, that put the ball in his court.

Which was a big relief to Verran. He'd solved his own missing-bug problem; let Dr. Tightass figure out the Cleary problem.

As far as Louis Verran was concerned, it was back to business as usual in the control room.

DECEMBER

Most-active issues—
After a year of unprecedented growth, during which the company introduced three new successful products, Kleederman Pharmaceuticals stock hit 150 at the opening bell today and split three for one. It then surged another three points per share, closing the day at 53-1/8.

The Wall Street Journal

The World's Longest Continuous Floating
Medical Bull Session
(III)

Tim had dragged Quinn to another session tonight in Harrison's room. He told her the usual: She was working too hard lately and needed a break. But that wasn't the main reason. He simply needed to be with her a little more.

During the weeks since Atlantic City, despite the awful time he'd had keeping his hands off her, Tim had stayed true to his word and abided by their agreement: no sex on campus. But whenever he'd suggested some HSR lab—HSR being their code for human sexual response—Quinn never turned him down. She'd even suggested it a couple of times herself. After Thanksgiving break she'd told him she'd started on the pill, but still she insisted he wear a condom. One very careful lady.

They didn't get to the Quality Inn that often, but when they did she left Tim wrecked for days.

Those nights were like his wildest dreams come true. For all the no-nonsense prudishness Quinn projected when she was fully dressed, between the sheets she was a different species. Her inhibitions seemed to slough off with her clothes. She approached sex the way she approached everything else—seriously, practically, with boundless enthusiasm. She attacked it, she *studied* it—that was hardly a surprise—and wanted to try everything. Very little was taboo. She even rented triple-X videos for instruction, and she and Tim had spent exhausting nights mimicking the couples on the screen.

But for Tim the sex was the icing on the cake. It cemented the substance of their relationship, which for him was simply being with her, sharing her presence. He never seemed to get enough of her. Between the hours they were required to spend in class and in the various labs, plus Quinn's job as Dr. Emerson's research assistant, and the wasted hours grudgingly surrendered to sleep, there wasn't any time for them simply to be together. Sometimes they'd study together, holding hands when they weren't scribbling notes or turning pages, but her presence was too distracting for Tim to get much done.

He *hungered* for her presence. And that baffled him. He'd always been so self-sufficient. Now, when Quinn wasn't around, he felt incomplete. Tim wasn't sure he liked that.

But looking at her face now, at the disturbed and troubled expressions playing across it, he wondered if he'd been wise to include her in the bull session tonight. Her expression drifted toward horrified as Harrison elaborated on his ideas on the formation of a central government authority to oversee the equitable redistribution of all medical resources. Tim couldn't understand her reaction. Harrison's plan made perfect sense to him.

"I don't believe you people," Quinn said when Harrison took a breath. "You're all talking about 'redistributing' medical care like you're discussing natural resources."

"A country's medical care is a natural resource," Judy Trachtenberg said. "One of its most valuable resources."

"But it's *not* a natural resource," Quinn said. "It wasn't sitting underground waiting to be dug up. It's human-made. You're not talking about moving lumps of coal or steel around, you're talking about people—doctors, nurses, technicians. I don't know about you folks, but I don't become a national resource just because I've earned a medical degree. I'm not something to be shipped around at the whim of some appointee in Washington. I don't remember signing off my human rights when I became a student at The Ingraham."

The room was silent. The eight other occupants sipped Pepsi or munched pretzels as they stared at her.

"Easy, Quinn," Tim said.

"No. I won't take it easy." She was getting hot now. He could see the color rising in her cheeks.

She said, "Since when are all of you in favor of bureaucrats telling you who you can treat? What are we going to medical school for? To become glorified technicians? To spend our professional lives taking orders from a bunch of political appointees? 'Here, Brown. Fix this one here, but forget that one over there.' They'll shunt you here and shift you there and call you a 'provider' and a 'resource,' but what about the patients?"

The room was utterly silent. Tim saw eight uncomprehending faces staring at Quinn as if she were speaking a foreign language.

"Well," Harrison said slowly, "it's *because* of the patients—*for* the patients—that tiering is necessary. They can't all receive top-level care, so some will have to be satisfied with second-level care, and some with third-level care. And someone has to decide who deserves what level of care. No one's happy with that, but it's a reality that has to be faced. Hiding your head in the sand won't make it go away."

The crack annoyed Tim but Quinn simply laughed it off.

"Who's got his head in the sand? You're talking about social engineering. What next? Eugenics? Or maybe a new master race?"

Judy groaned. "We're not Nazis."

"Really? I wish you'd all wake up and smell the coffee. I mean, don't you think there'll be a temptation for some of us to 'tier' patients according to political, religious, and racial prejudices?"

Harrison cleared his throat. "I can't see that being a problem for an ethical physician."

"I agree," Quinn said. "But we're not all ethical—we're human. And we should be treating illness wherever we find it, not just in a select population. That's a God game I don't want to play."

"But it's going to be the only game in town," Harrison said. "That's why it's so important that graduates of The Ingraham go into primary care. That's where the front lines are. That's where we'll be exposed to both the useful and the useless members of society. That's where we can make a difference. And maybe we can even work it so that some of those useless folks *can* contribute to society." He turned to Tim. "You've been unusually quiet tonight, Brown. Any comments?"

Tim shook his head. "No, uh . . . just listening."

Tim avoided Quinn's eyes but knew she was giving him a strange look.

He deserved it. He *felt* strange. He'd had the oddest feeling while sitting here listening to the conversation. Schizoid. Dissociated. A deep part of him completely agreeing with Quinn and yet another part tugging him the other way. The only times he noticed this dichotomy in his attitudes was on those rare occasions when he discussed medical politics with Quinn, or when she stopped by the bull session. He'd attributed his attitude shift to the fact that he was now more conversant with the issues associated with the coming health-care crisis than he had been in September. None of the bull-session regulars seemed to differ much on the issue of tiering health-care delivery, simply on the mechanics of how to implement it. Quinn was becoming the gadfly, the devil's advocate they maybe needed to goad them into examining their premises.

Except no one was examining premises. Tim seemed to be the only one of the group even remotely receptive to Quinn.

But what had rocked Tim back on his heels was Harrison's last statement.

That's why it's so important that graduates of The Ingraham go into primary care. That's where the front lines are. That's where we'll be exposed to both the useful and the useless members of society. That's where we can make a difference. And maybe we can even work it so that some of those useless folks can *contribute to society.*

It had been a typical Harrison statement. That wasn't the problem. The problem was in Tim's head: The same statement—not the same sentiment, *the same statement*, word for word—had gone through Tim's mind in response to Quinn's question.

Almost as if he'd been coached.

Suddenly he wanted out of the session.

Not to walk out. To run.

MONITORING

"Guess who's on his way down?" Elliot said.

Louis Verran looked up from the daily status printout and groaned. "Don't tell me...."

"Yep."

"Shit," Verran said. He wasn't in the mood for Alston tonight. But then, when was he *ever* in the mood for Doc Tightass? "All right, pull that last bull-session tape. Maybe it'll get him off our backs."

Alston had developed this thing for the Cleary girl. He'd been on her case and had been dropping by the control room regularly since Thanksgiving, looking for anything and everything Verran could get on her.

"Good evening, gentlemen," he said, breezing through the door like he owned the place. "Any new elucidating snippets of tape for me, Louis?"

"As a matter of fact, yes," Verran said. "We found some good stuff for you this time." He turned to Elliot. "Got that tape cued up there? Let her roll."

Alston took a seat and cocked his ear toward the speaker, listening intently. Verran listened too, not so much to the words—he'd already heard them—as to the quality of the recording. Not bad. Pretty damn good, in fact. The kids must have been circled around the mike. Let Alston try griping this time about not being able to understand what they were saying.

Verran didn't record everything. Couldn't, and wouldn't want to if he could. Most of what went on in the dorm was studying and sleeping, the sound of pages turning followed by deep, rhythmic breathing. And when the kids were talking, it was usually about the most trivial, boring junk imaginable. So he sampled here and there. He'd rotate from pickup to pickup, eavesdropping from within the rooms or along the telephone lines, listening for anyone who might be talking about The Ingraham, or about any particular staff or faculty member. Happy talk was bypassed for the most part, but gripe sessions were always recorded. And any talk of a potentially compromising nature—sexual encounters, schemes to cheat on tests—was recorded and cataloged and filed away in Louis Verran's personal J. Edgar Hoover file . . . just in case.

The roving bull session tended to be as boring as all the other talk, except when a couple of them disagreed and got real pissed, but that only happened among newcomers early in their first year. After they'd all been here awhile, not only did the disagreements rarely get vehement, they rarely happened.

But when Verran had picked up the Cleary girl's voice in last night's bull session, he'd stopped his wandering ways and settled down to record the whole thing. Alston had said he was looking for any tidbits that would give him another look into Cleary's views on the future of medicine. Verran had recognized one of her rare participations in the bull session as a golden opportunity. Originally he had planned to tease Alston along with it, dangle the recording before him like a carrot before a mule. But when he'd heard Cleary sounding off like she did, he knew he couldn't wait. He had to dump the whole thing on Alston in one shot . . . and watch him squirm.

Verran tracked the growing concern on Alston's face as he listened. He barely moved. He was still sitting there listening even after Cleary had quit the session. He knew exactly what Dr. Tight-ass was thinking: *Who can I blame this on?*

But Louis was ready for him when Alston finally swiveled in his chair and faced him.

"What do I have to do, Louis, to induce you to repair that young woman's defective SLI unit?"

"There's nothing to repair."

"It's quite obvious to me, and I am sure it will be equally obvious to our overseers from the foundation, that you are not getting the job done."

Verran had suddenly had enough. He wanted to grab this twit and shake him until his brain rattled inside his skull. Instead, he squeezed the armrests of his chair.

"I'm not in the mood for games, Doc, so here's the story: Her unit checks out. Elliot and I went back to her room again last weekend while Cleary and her boyfriend were off campus boffing each other. It checks out. You hear that, Doc: Her SLI is in A-one shape. *Perfectamento.* So stop blowing smoke and tell me what you're going to do about it."

Alston was silent for a moment. His voice sounded tired when he finally spoke.

"What else can I do? She'll have to flunk out."

C H A P T E R · 17

T im was feeling restless, edgy. He couldn't handle studying tonight. He wanted to be with Quinn but she was
booking it for the anatomy practical tomorrow. So he
wandered.

He wound up in the north wing's first-floor lounge—soft,
shapeless leather couches, a dropped ceiling for acoustical effect,
snack and soft-drink machines lined up against the rear wall. Joe
Nappo was stretched out in front of the big rear-projection screen
watching some cop movie. Tim dropped into one of the rear seats.
He didn't recognize the movie but he did recognize Peter Weller's
face from the *Robocop* flicks. On the screen Weller was tearing his
apartment apart, looking for something. Tim didn't know what the
film was about and didn't care. He stared at the screen without
really following the action. He had other things on his mind.

Like his own mind, for instance.

His last bull session—the one Quinn had sat in on—still bothered him. It baffled him how he could *believe* one way and *think*
another. The shrinks had a term for it: cognitive dissociation. Two
conflicting points of view existing within the same person.

. . . On the screen Peter Weller pulled his telephones apart,
then began unscrewing the plates over the electrical outlets in his
walls. . . .

Tim realized he had two intellectual positions, one very much
like Quinn's, the other identical to Harrison's, warring within him.
The first seemed to spring from his gut, seemed to *belong* to him,
but it had been battered into the mud by the second position. He
might have forgotten it had ever existed had not Quinn's arguments caused it to stir. And that stirring had pointed up the vague
strangeness of Harrison's position. What was it doing in his head?

It sounded like an echo of everybody else who spoke up at the bull sessions.

Everybody else.

Tim had always prided himself on not thinking like everybody else. Yet he could sense himself becoming an intellectual clone of Dr. Alston. The guy was a charming and disarming lecturer, true, but he wasn't *that* good.

. . . On the screen Peter Weller was holding up something he had found. A small dark object. He was examining it, turning it between his fingers. The camera moved in for a close-up. . . .

Tim bolted upright in his chair.

"What the hell?"

The object in Peter Weller's hand looked startlingly familiar, like a tiny hockey puck on a pin.

"Hey, Joe," he said. "What is this?"

Nappo spoke without turning around. "Called *Rainbow Drive* or something like that."

"What's going on?"

"His partner got killed in the opening scenes and—"

"No. I mean now. What's he up to?"

"He just found out his apartment's bugged."

Tim stared at the screen in cold shock, then got up and hurried for the door. His thoughts swirled in a chaotic jumble as he trotted down the hall and burst into the chill December night outside. The sky was a clear bubble and the stars seemed to spin as he walked aimlessly along the paths between the buildings that made up The Ingraham. He jammed his hands into his pockets against the late fall chill.

A bug. His mind shied away from accepting the fact that his little stickpin had been an electronic pickup. He'd heard of them, but he'd never expected to see one in real life. Not at The Ingraham. Certainly not in Quinn's room. The possibility had never even occurred to him.

Was The Ingraham bugged? Or more specifically, was the dorm bugged? The very idea seemed ludicrous. A paranoid delusion of the first order. Because why in the name of sanity would anyone want to monitor the blatherings of a bunch of medical students? The idea zoomed past the ludicrous to the laughable.

And yet . . . *How come I'm not laughing?*

Because in some way he couldn't fathom, it seemed to dovetail with whatever it was that was making him so edgy lately.

Okay, he told himself. Let's run this through and follow the likely scenarios to wherever they lead. Let's assume the dorm is bugged. Or more specifically, since I found the bug in Quinn's room, that Quinn's room is bugged.

Why?

Who knows? We'll leave why for later. For now let's just get logical.

Premise: Room 252 is under electronic surveillance.

If we accept that premise, who would be in charge of that surveillance?

Obviously, Campus Security.

Who's in charge of Campus Security?

Mr. Louis Verran.

Who has been caught twice in Quinn's room when she was scheduled to be out?

Mr. Louis Verran.

Tim shook his head as the pace of his walking slowed of its own accord. This was getting scary. Syllogistic logic had its flaws, but this little syllogism hit too close to recent events: If room 252 is bugged, and if Campus Security is in charge of the bugging, and if Louis Verran is in charge of Campus Security, then one would expect Louis Verran to display an inordinate level of interest in room 252. Which he had.

Tim stopped short and watched his breath fume in the cold air as his thoughts raced through his mental pantries, grabbing incidents and observations from the shelves and tossing them helterskelter into the stew. He didn't like the aroma that was beginning to rise from the pot.

Fact: Louis Verran saw the bug in my lapel last month—that so-called exterminator with him had pointed it out. And twelve hours later I get rolled in A.C., supposedly for my winnings. But maybe those guys were after a different sort of chip. They put a lot of effort into ripping up my coat, and afterward, my little stickpin just happens to be missing along with my chips.

He swung around and headed back toward the dorm. Normally, the glow of the lights in the rooms would have seemed warm beacons beckoning him in from the cold. Tonight they looked like a multifaceted cluster of eyes, watching him.

Because if one room was bugged, why not more? Why not all the rooms?

He pushed through the entrance to the south wing and turned

toward the stairs to the second floor, heading for Women's Country. He had to tell Quinn. She had to know.

Then he stopped, unsure. Was that fair? Between classes, labs, and tests, plus her research job, she had enough on her mind. This would make her as crazy as it was making him. And maybe all for nothing. He could be wrong. Why dump any of this on her until he was sure?

But how could he be sure, unless . . . ?

If Quinn's room was bugged, there was a good chance his was too. Tim could think of only one way to find out: Tear it apart.

He headed for his room.

"I really appreciate this, Kevin."

It had taken a fair bit of doing, but Tim had convinced his roommate to bunk in with Scotty Moore for the night. Moore's roomie, Bill Black, had gone home for a long weekend due to a death in the family. Kevin, a good guy but a congenital straight-shooter, wasn't crazy about the idea. He was afraid it was against the rules, but he hadn't been able to find a rule against it. So he'd agreed, reluctantly.

"Yeah, well, it's okay this time, but don't make a habit of it."

"This is the only time I'll ask this of you, Kev," Tim said. "I swear."

He'd told Kevin that he and Quinn needed "some time alone together," and that the inhabitants of Women's Country were too damn nosy to allow them any "real privacy." Pretty thin, but it was the best Tim could come up with on short notice. He didn't feel he could wait until Kevin went home for a weekend; he wanted to search the room *now*. It worked, mainly because everyone knew that Quinn and Tim had a thing going on. Kevin read between the lines what Tim had written there for him and finally agreed.

"And you'll stick to *your* bed, right?" Kevin said.

"*Stick*? What on earth—"

Kevin's dark features darkened further. "I mean, you'll just use your own bed, right? You won't . . . do anything in mine?"

Tim held up three fingers. "Scout's honor."

"All right. But I've got to get back in here first thing in the morning."

"Have no fear, buddy. Everything will be exactly as you left it."

As soon as Kevin was gone, Tim ducked out and ran down to

the parking lot. He took the tool kit from his car trunk and lugged it up to the dorm. Back in the room, he locked the door and stood there, looking around.

Where to begin?

He decided to try the bedroom first. After all, wasn't it in Quinn's bedroom that he'd stepped on the bug he mistook for a stickpin?

He started with the furniture. Flashlight in hand, Tim crawled around the room, peering into every nook, cranny, corner, and crevice. He crawled under his bed and Kevin's, and when he found nothing on the underside of the frame, he pulled off the mattress and box spring and inspected the frame from above. He couldn't move the bed around because it was bolted to the headboard unit which was fixed to the wall, so he unbolted the bed frame from the headboard and gave it a thorough going-over. He emptied the closets, pulled out the nightstand drawers, cleaned out the book-shelves built into the headboard unit, took down the curtains, and dismantled the curtain rods.

Nothing.

Then he remembered what he'd seen in the movie. He attacked the telephone, dismantling both the base and the handset. Then he removed the wall plates from all the electrical sockets and light switches. He dissected the desk lamp and the gooseneck tensor lamp atop the headboard unit.

Nothing.

Hours after starting, Tim stopped and surveyed the carnage around him. It looked like Nirvana had shot a video here. He'd torn the place apart. All for what? He was tired—probably one of the last people awake in the dorm—and he was angry. There was something here. There had to be. Too many coincidences lately to be ignored. And he wasn't crazy.

He flopped back onto the mattress and box spring where they lay on the floor. He put his hands behind the back of his head and lay there staring at the ceiling, thinking: Where is the best spot to place a microphone if you want to pick up every sound in the room? Someplace centrally located with no possibility of being covered and muffled . . .

Tim's gaze drifted past the light fixture in the ceiling, then darted back to it.

Of course!

He jumped to his feet and stood on his mattress, but it was too much of a stretch to reach the fixture. He pulled a desk chair over, and he was there. As he loosened the central screw on the frosted-glass diffuser, he wondered if it was just coincidence that the glass on these fixtures hung an inch below the ceiling. A sensitive bug positioned up here would pick up every word said in the room.

When the glass came free, Tim set it on the bed, then squinted at the two 60-watt standard bulbs. He couldn't see much in the glare, plus they'd been on for hours and were hot. He craned his neck, this way and that, trying to check it from all sides, but saw nothing.

Damn, he thought. Not only was it the perfect place, but it was the last place. He gave up and was fitting the diffuser back on its spindle when he spotted something in the tangle of wires behind the bulbs. A tiny thing—black like the one he'd found in Quinn's room, only this one's face was more beveled—with its pin inserted into the insulated coat of a wire above the bulb sockets. Completely unnoticeable, even to someone changing a bulb.

"Jesus."

Tim could barely hear his own voice.

An uneasy chill rippled through his gut as he stared at the bug. He realized then that deep within he hadn't expected to find any-thing. He'd been suspicious, there were unanswered questions, but this whole exercise had been something of a game. His hunt was not supposed to yield a real bug. Nestled in the unspoken rules had been the assumption that he would do a thorough search and find nothing, and then the game would end, leaving him frustrated at having no hard evidence to back up his suspicions.

But the game was no longer a game. Hard evidence was half a dozen inches from his nose. He stared at it a moment longer, then stepped down to the floor and sat on the corner of the bed.

Now what?

Report it? To whom? Certainly not Louis Verran. And what did one bug prove? No, the best way was to spread the word, have everybody check out their ceiling fixtures, and then present all the bugs en masse to the administration, even though they were prob-ably involved as well. But even if they weren't, what could they do? What could they say? He could imagine what they'd say:

Yes, you have indeed found electronic eavesdropping devices in the rooms, but that doesn't prove anyone is actually listening. It's got to be some sort of elaborate practical joke. Because in the final analysis, why on earth would anyone want to listen to the incidental conversations of a group of medical students? *We* certainly don't. We can't imagine anything more boring.

Neither could Tim.

But that opened the door to another question: If the administration had nothing to do with the bugging and didn't care what was being said in the dorms, why did it insist that all Ingraham students live here for their entire four years as medical students?

It didn't make sense.

Unless there was something else going on.

He'd been puzzled by the seemingly alien thoughts taking hold in his mind. What if they'd been planted there?

Tim shook his head. This was getting wilder and wilder. The bug was one thing, but . . .

. . . but what if the people behind the bugging were interested in hearing what was coming *out* of the students as a way of monitoring what they were putting *in*?

Nah. The whole idea was too farfetched. Besides, how could they possibly put ideas into your head? Where could they hide the equipment?

His gaze drifted to the only piece of furniture in the room he hadn't disassembled.

The headboard unit.

Before attacking that, he replaced the glass diffuser on the ceiling fixture without touching the bug—better not to tip off the listeners that they'd been found out. Then, screwdriver in hand, he approached the headboard.

MONITORING

"Yo, chief."

Louis Verran looked up from his copy of *Shotgun News* and saw Elliot motioning him to his console. He rose, dropped the magazine on his seat, and waddled over.

It had been a very routine night so far. *Less* than a routine night. Nothing much of interest going on in the dorm, what with all the first- and second-year kids studying for their first-semester finals. Even the bull session was in a lull.

Dull. Just the way Verran liked it.

"What's up?" he said, leaning over Elliot's chair and scanning his readouts.

"Something's going on in room one-two-five."

"Yeah? Let's listen."

"No. No chatter, chief. But I've been picking up strange noises all night long."

"Yeah? Like what?"

"Like all sorts of scrapes, squeaks, scratches, and sounds like furniture being moved."

"Somebody's redecorating?"

"I don't think so. Especially since I'm almost sure he was fooling with the ceiling fixture."

Great, Verran thought. Just what we need.

"The pickup still working?"

"Yeah. Perfectly."

"All right." Verran let out a deep breath he hadn't realized he'd been holding. "So even if he was fooling around with the light fixture for whatever reason, he didn't find nothing."

"I can't say that for sure," Elliot said. "All I can say is he didn't *touch* the pickup. But I wish I could say the same for his SLI."

Verran felt a sheen of cold sweat break out between his shoulder blades and spread across his back.

"Stop beating around the fucking bush, Elliot. What's wrong?"

"It went dead about five minutes ago. I'm not getting any feedback from it at all."

"You run the troubleshooting program?"

"Sure. First thing. But you can't do a software troubleshoot on a dead unit."

"Shit!" Verran said. Was this how the year was going to go? First Alston bitches about Cleary's unit when nothing was wrong, and now they had a unit that was genuinely on the fritz. "What do you think's wrong with it?"

Elliot gave him a sidelong glance. "You really want to know?"

"Of course I want to know!"

"I think it's being tampered with."

Verran reached for a chair and gently lowered himself into it. He hadn't wanted to know that.

"You mean he's into the headboard?"

Elliot nodded. "Not only into it, I think he unplugged the unit."

"Who?" Verran said. "Who the fuck is it?"

"Brown."

Brown. Verran rubbed a trembling hand over his eyes. It was happening again. Just like two years ago.

"I should've known. Where's Kurt?"

Elliot glanced at his watch. "Not due in for another hour yet."

"Call him. Get him down here right away. Tell him we need him pronto."

"Take it easy, chief. This could all be a false alarm."

"False alarm, my ass! That Brown kid has been trouble since the day he stepped onto this campus. We've got to do something about him."

Brown has a roommate, he thought. Is he in on this too? Christ, two of them at once. What was he going to do?

As Elliot made the call, Verran pressed a hand against the right side of his abdomen, trying to ease the growing pain there. His ulcer was kicking up again. It had started two years ago, now it was back full force, mostly because of the Brown kid and his girlfriend, Cleary.

Trouble. Nothing but trouble.

And if Elliot was right about Brown opening up the back of his headboard, the shit was really going to hit the fan.

All right, Tim thought as he stared at the maze of wires running throughout the rear section of his headboard, I've found it. But *what* have I found?

It hadn't been easy getting into the base of the headboard. Steel bolts with recesses in their heads had been used instead of conventional slotted or Phillips-head wood screws; they'd been wound tightly into steel bushings. Apparently these headboards had been custom-made to take a *lot* of punishment. But Tim had found an Allen wrench in his toolbox that did the trick—not with ease, but after an hour of cursing and earning a few fresh blisters, he'd managed to loosen the panel and expose the innards.

He knew something about electronics—he'd poked through his share of PCs, stereos, and VCRs—but he'd never seen anything like what lay behind the panel. Wires and circuit boards, okay, but what was that big black shiny disk facing the bed? It reminded him of a giant subwoofer.

Whatever it was, he knew he was out of his depth. Something big was going down here. He was too beat to open up Kevin's headboard, and besides, he was sure he'd find the same thing. The same damn science-fiction rig was probably inside every damn headboard in the whole damn dorm.

Something clinked against the window then, and Tim jumped. He stared at the drawn curtains. Was someone on the other side? His was a first-floor room. The windowsill was chin level to a man of average height. If someone wanted to check out what he was up to in here, the first thing to do would be to try to look in the window.

Steeling himself, Tim stepped to the curtain and pulled it aside. Cold air trapped between the glass and the curtain swirled around him, raising gooseflesh on his arms, but thankfully there were no faces peering through the panes. Nothing but darkness out there.

I'm getting jumpy.

He closed the drapes and turned back to the exposed workings within the headboard. Maybe he had good reason to be jumpy. What if there was a trip switch of some sort within that mess of wire in there that set off an alarm somewhere when the headboard was tampered with?

Maybe he should get out of here.

Tim was scared now. He felt himself shivering and his hands shook as he pulled on a sweater. He wished he'd never begun this search, wished he'd left well enough alone.

But dammit, things hadn't been well at all. Somebody had been tampering with his mind, skewing his values. How could he have let that go on?

But now he had to tell Quinn. She had to know what was going on, what they were doing to people's heads here.

Funny thing about that, though . . . Quinn seemed unaffected. She'd stayed the course . . .

. . . which might explain why Verran kept returning to her room. Maybe the thing in her headboard wasn't working.

He had to tell her. He glanced at his watch. Late, but this couldn't wait. He snatched Quinn's room key off his dresser and shoved it into his pocket. They'd traded keys a while back—he'd given her a set to his car and she'd given him one to her room so he could use it anytime he wanted to be alone when she was out.

But he couldn't talk to her there, or anywhere else in the dorm. Where? He grabbed a scratch pad and a pen as he left. He hoped he could figure out a safe place to talk by the time he reached the second floor.

"Wha—?"

Abruptly, Quinn was awake and she didn't know why. She lifted her head and looked around the darkened room, listening. She felt extremely vulnerable in the dark, especially since she was wearing only an oversized T-shirt and a pair of panties. But nothing was moving, nothing—

She heard the hall door click closed.

Someone's here!

She reached for the phone beside her.

"Who's there? Tim, is that you?"

The light went on in the front room and Tim's voice drifted through the open door.

"Just me, Quinn." His voice sounded strange . . . strained.

She glanced at the radio alarm. The red LED display read 2:34.

"Do you know what time it is?"

He stepped through the door and flicked on the light.

"I'm sorry it's so late, but I couldn't sleep."

Quinn squinted in the sudden glare. "Must you?"

"Yeah. I want to look at you."

When her eyes adjusted, she stared at him and gasped. He looked ghastly—pale, haggard, and . . . frightened.

"Tim, what's wrong?"

"Nothing. I just had to see you."

As he finished speaking he held his index finger to his lips and thrust a notepad toward her.

"What . . . ?"

He tapped the finger against his lips insistently and pointed to the pad. Quinn stared at the block printing.

THE ROOM IS BUGGED!!!!

"*What?* You've got to be—"

He was frantically jamming his finger against his lips now. She looked at him and shrugged, completely bewildered. Was this one of his gags or had he gone off the deep end completely?

He took the pad and scribbled lengthwise on the next sheet.

MAKE SMALL TALK!

Quinn gaped at him. He appeared to be in genuine distress. She fumbled for something to say.

"Uh . . . you ready for the anatomy practical?"

He gave her the okay sign and began writing on a third sheet as he spoke.

"Sure. You know me. I'm a quick study. Nothing to those practicals."

He held up the new note.

MEET ME IN THE ~~ANATOMY LAB~~ MY CAR AND I'LL EXPLAIN EVERYTHING

"Yeah. I wish I had a memory like yours," Quinn said as she grabbed the pen and pad from him and jotted her own note.

ARE YOU FOR REAL??

His slow, grim nod gave her a chill.

He yawned loudly as he retrieved the pad, scribbling as he spoke.

"Well, I've bothered you long enough. I'll leave you alone and see if I can get some sleep."

He handed the pad back to her.

I'LL WARM UP THE CAR

She nodded. "Good idea. See you soon."

Tim flashed her another okay sign, waved, and left her there in her bed, wondering what on earth had come over him. She sat for a moment or two, staring at the pad he'd left with her, flipping through the bizarre series of notes. She decided the only way to find out what was going on was to meet him in his car.

She jumped out of bed and began to get dressed.

"Can you hear me, chief?"

It was Elliot's voice, transmitting via the pickup in room 125.

Louis Verran stood in the control room with his face all but pressed against the fabric of the speaker.

"You know damn well I'm listening," he said irritably, though he knew just as damn well that Elliot couldn't hear the reply.

"Listen, we're in the bedroom of one-two-five. We couldn't see anything through the window—he almost caught us doing the Peeping Tom thing—so we came inside when he left. I was right, chief. He's got the whole place torn apart, including the headboard."

"Shit!" Verran said. "Shit, shit, SHIT!"

"We don't know where he is now, but we can guess. We're going to go looking for him. Out."

"Yeah," Verran muttered. "Out."

This was bad. Very bad. Kurt and Elliot would have to find Brown and bring him in before he talked to anyone.

And Louis Verran would have to pick up the phone and call Dr. Arthur Tightass Alston and tell him that the nightmare scenario from two years ago was starting a rerun.

His intestines coiled into a Gordian knot as he reached for the receiver.

Tim checked his pockets as he galloped down the stairs and realized he didn't have his car keys. He'd have to stop off at his room.

When he opened his door, the room was dark. Had he turned the lights out? He didn't remember. As he reached for the switch someone grabbed his arm and yanked him inside. The shock and sudden terror of it stole his voice. He heard the door slam behind him, and now he was in complete darkness. He started to yell but someone rammed a fist into one of his kidneys and all that escaped him was an agonized groan. As the pain drove him to his knees, gasping, retching, his arms were pinned behind his back.

Here it comes, he thought. A bullet through the brain.

But then something—a rag of some sort—was forced into his mouth. He heard the *scritch* of tape being pulled from a roll, and then a piece was pressed over his mouth. He had to breathe through his nose. Air whistled in and out of his nostrils. He fought panic as he listened to another piece of tape being torn from the roll. If they covered his nose he'd suffocate. But this piece went across his eyes. And then he felt metal bands tighten around his wrists.

Handcuffs. His panic ebbed toward mere terror. They weren't going to kill him.

At least not yet.

Quinn knew something was wrong before she reached the parking lot. As she hurried down the slope, she spotted Tim's car in its usual spot, but the motor wasn't running. She approached Griffin cautiously and peered within.

Empty.

She touched the hood and found it cold.

What's going on, Tim? What are you up to?

She shivered in the chill breeze. She'd thrown on a sweatsuit and a jacket but still she was cold. She'd just got out of a warm bed from a dead sleep and her body wasn't ready to handle this drop in temperature.

She heard a creak as one of the dorm's outer doors opened and closed.

Finally!

She looked toward the darkened dorm, expecting Tim to appear on the slope, heading her way. She heard the squeak of wheels, like someone rolling a wagon along the walk up there, thought she saw a shadow or two move across the space between the dorm and the caf, but it was gone before she could focus. She waited, but still no Tim.

Who else would be wandering around the campus at this hour?

Meet me in the car. That was what the note had said. Tim had said he was going to warm it up.

That gave Quinn an idea. She pulled out her key ring and picked out Tim's car keys. She opened the door and got inside. The cold of the vinyl raced through the fabric of her sweats, chilling her rear and the backs of her thighs. She started the car and pushed the thermostat up to the maximum.

If Tim wasn't going to heat up the car for her, she'd heat it up for him. But she wished he'd hurry. It was creepy out here.

She pushed down the door lock and rubbed her hands together, waiting for the heat.

Come on, Tim. Come out, come out, wherever you are.

Tim tried to keep the encroaching panic at bay by cataloging what he knew.

First off, he was still alive. That was a good start.

Second, he was unharmed—relatively. His left flank still ached and throbbed from that one nasty kidney punch—which he now assumed had been dealt to shut him up—but after that he'd been handled roughly but without any evidence of malice. His abductors didn't seem to have anything personal against him. It was all pretty businesslike. Tim wasn't sure whether or not he should take heart from that.

Third, he was still on campus—where, he wasn't sure. After binding and gagging him, they'd dumped him into one of the laundry hampers the maids used for dirty linen and wheeled him out of the dorm—just the way convicts used to break out of prison in the old B movies. He'd bumped and rattled along a series of fairly level concrete walks, so he'd assumed he was traveling among the buildings of the campus. Then he'd been pushed uphill a short distance, into a building, into an elevator for a short trip down, along a hallway, and into this room, where he'd been strapped into a padded armchair that creaked like wood when he shifted his weight.

His best guess: He was in the basement of the science center.

Suddenly the tape was ripped away from his mouth. Tim spit out the gag and gulped air. He waited for the blindfold tape to be removed but it remained untouched.

"Who are you?" he heard someone ask him.

The tantalizingly familiar voice startled him with its matter-of-fact tone.

"What?" Tim's tongue was dry from the cloth gag, and he sounded like a frog who'd been singing all night. He worked up some saliva to moisten it.

The question came again. "Who are you?"

Now he pegged the voice: Louis Verran's. He found a certain grim satisfaction—if no comfort—in realizing that his suspicions were now proved correct.

"You know damn well who I am—" He almost added Verran's name but caught himself. Maybe the blindfold had been left on for a reason. Maybe he'd be endangering himself by revealing that he recognized his interrogator.

"I want you to say it. Say your name."

Okay. He'd cooperate. No harm in that.

"Timothy Brown."

"From what college did you graduate, Mr. Brown?"

"Dartmouth."

"And which is your room here on campus?"

"Room one-twenty-five."

"All right," Verran's voice said, moving closer. "He's all yours."

Tim grimaced with pain as the tape was ripped from across his eyes, taking some of his eyebrows with it. He squinted in the unaccustomed glare, but gradually the light and shadows began to take form.

"Mr. Brown, Mr. Brown, Mr. Brown," said a tired voice he recognized instantly. "Whatever are we going to do with you, Mr. Brown?"

Tim blinked to bring the figure standing before him into focus.

"Dr. Alston!"

"Yes, Mr. Brown."

"You're in on this?"

Dr. Alston pulled up a chair and seated himself facing Tim. He looked utterly relaxed, completely in control.

"In on what, Mr. Brown? Just what is it you think is going on here?"

Tim glanced around. He could have been in an electronics hobbyist's heaven—or hell. Monitors, speakers, computers, equalizers, oscilloscopes, white, red, and green blinking lights, wires, cables, and an array of other equipment he couldn't identify. Louis Verran was off to the right, watching a monitor. Tim tried to pull his arms free, but they were securely bound—wrists, forearms, and biceps—to the armchair. He noticed wires connected by clamps to his fingertips. Were they going to shock him? He wiggled his fingers, trying to shake off the clamps, but they held firm.

He looked at Alston, who smiled.

"No, Mr. Brown. We have no intention of torturing you. But we do want to make sure you stay put until we are through with you."

No question about staying put. He was trapped. Caged like a lab animal. The realization was a sick, sinking sensation in his chest. But at least Dr. Alston was a safe, sane, respected physician, researcher, and academician.

Wasn't he?

Alston said, "Again: What do you think is going on?"

"I don't know," Tim said. "But I do know you've got The Ingraham bugged six ways from Sunday."

Dr. Alston smiled that thin, cold smile of his as he lounged in his chair. " 'Six ways from Sunday.' How quaint. I assure you, we do not have The Ingraham bugged."

"The dorm, then."

"The dorm, yes. And you've discovered that, haven't you? What else have you discovered, Mr. Brown?"

Tim saw no use in lying about dismantling the headboard. The two goons who'd mugged him must have seen it.

"Something in the headboard."

"*What* in the headboard?"

"I don't know."

"You're the brainy medical student, Mr. Brown. What do you think?"

Might as well let it all hang out, Tim thought.

"I think you're brainwashing us."

Tim saw Dr. Alston stiffen and straighten in his chair. He was no longer lounging.

Bingo.

"What on earth could lead you to such a farfetched conclusion?"

"You really want to know, or are we just killing time?"

"I quite sincerely want to know, Mr. Brown. It's important to me."

Tim believed him. Briefly he ran down the suspicions he'd developed about the stickpin/bug, the change he'd perceived in his own attitudes, his search of his room, and what he'd discovered.

Dr. Alston listened with visibly growing agitation, glancing frequently at Verran, who was partially insulated in the earphones of his headset and seemed absorbed in his readouts.

"So am I to understand it that if you hadn't stepped on that misplaced bug, you would still be a model student here at The Ingraham?"

"Not quite," he said. "One of the other students at the bull sessions hasn't shown any change in attitudes." Tim didn't want to bring Quinn into this, so he changed her sex. "His unchanged opinions made me aware of the change in mine."

"He's not talking about a 'he,' " Verran said in a low voice. "He means Cleary, the girl in two-five-two."

"Ah, the redoubtable Miss Quinn Cleary. Her name keeps popping up. By the way, why isn't she here?"

For the first time since the tape had been pulled from Tim's eyes, he saw Louis Verran look up from his readouts.

"She's not supposed to be here."

"I wanted her brought here," Dr. Alston said.

"Kurt and Elliot are too busy with damage control right now to play footsie with her."

"I specifically told Kurt I wanted her brought in."

Verran swiveled in his chair and stared at Dr. Alston.

"Kurt? You told *Kurt* to bring her in? He's a fucking animal!"

Tim clenched his fists as a ball of lead dropped into his stomach. Kurt? Who was Kurt?

Dr. Alston sniffed. "He won't do anything rash when he's operating on my direct orders."

"Don't be too fucking sure of that."

Dr. Alston waved Verran off. "Never mind."

Tim said, "If anything happens to her—"

"What?" Dr. Alston said, turning to him. "You'll do what? I'll tell you what you'll do, young man. You'll do nothing but sit here and listen as I explain to you what's really happening here at The Ingraham. And once you've heard the whole story, I'm sure you'll feel quite differently about it."

But Tim couldn't listen. All he could think about was Quinn and what this Kurt animal might do to her.

Quinn flicked on the courtesy lights and checked the dashboard clock: 3:02 A.M. The car heater was going, she was warm, but still no Tim.

Her concern was mounting with every passing minute, like a knot, tightening in her chest. Tim . . . he'd looked so strange, so frightened. And those notes about the room being bugged. Was he having some sort of breakdown?

And where *was* he? He'd said to meet him here. She'd read the note correctly, hadn't she? She wished she'd brought those notes with her, but she'd left them on her bed.

She thought back, trying to picture the note about meeting him in the car. He'd had something else written first and then crossed out. The anatomy lab. That was it. He'd wanted to meet her in the anatomy lab first but had changed his mind.

Maybe he'd changed it back. Quinn saw no use in sitting in Griffin any longer. She turned off the engine, stepped out into the cold air, and trotted up the slope to the center of the campus. She passed through the darker shadows between the caf and the administration building, skirted the pond with its newly formed skin of ice, and made a beeline for the lighted doors of the class building. They were unlocked, as usual. She hurried down the lighted hall.

She found one of the double doors to the an lab open when she got there. Her spirits lifted. They normally were kept closed. That could only mean Tim was already here.

But the lights were out.

"Tim? Tim, are you in here?"

Silence replied. She flipped on the lights.

"Tim?"

The an lab was empty except for the rows of sheet-covered cadavers on their tables.

Quinn moved forward, hesitantly. She'd grown accustomed to the place during the day, but at this time of night—morning, rather—it was creepy.

"Tim?"

The lab was empty, no question about it. She made her way toward their table in the far corner of the room. Someone had been here and left the door open. Maybe it was Tim. Maybe he'd left her a message at their table.

But no, Dorothy lay just as they'd left her. No note pinned to her sheet.

Tired, baffled, worried, Quinn sighed and leaned against the table. Where could . . . ?

The lights went out.

Quinn spun in the sudden darkness and saw the entry doors swinging closed. A human-shaped shadow flitted across the rapidly narrowing wedge of light flowing between them from the hall.

It wasn't Tim. Tim liked jokes but he wasn't cruel. This was *not* Tim.

She wanted to scream but suppressed it. What good would screaming do? There was no help within earshot, and it would only give away her position.

With her heart punching against the base of her throat, she ducked and fumbled her shoes off. The concrete floor was cold through the socks on her gliding feet as she moved to her left, away from Dorothy, using the rear wall of the lab as her guide.

Whoever was in here with her hadn't removed his shoes. She could hear him scuffing along the floor, moving at a diagonal from her, heading directly for Dorothy.

She thought, Oh, God, Dorothy, I wish you were alive. I wish you could sit up and take a poke at this creep, whoever he is.

As the scraping steps continued to move away from the entry doors, Quinn edged back and around, gradually circling closer to the front of the lab, using the sliver of light leaking between the doors as a beacon to guide her. A few more minutes and she'd be able to make a break for those doors.

The lab went silent. The whispered scraping from the intruder's shoes died and Quinn froze, hovering in the darkness, afraid to move, afraid even to breathe for fear of giving herself away.

Shoes in hand, she dropped into a crouch, listening.

Where was he? Why had he stopped? Had he found the area around Dorothy deserted and was he deciding which way to go next? Or had he taken off his own shoes and was he at this instant slipping toward her?

Suddenly a flashlight beam lanced through the darkness, ranging back and forth above the tables, coming her way, moving closer. It was gliding down the aisle on the far side of the table she was crouched behind, approaching, coming even, then passing by. Quinn was about to exhale with relief when the intruder suddenly roared in triumph and swung the light around, shining it directly in her face.

There was no holding back this time. Quinn cried out in terror as she recoiled from the glare and instinctively batted at the light. Her shoes were still in her hand and they connected, sending the flashlight flying. It landed with a crash and a tinkle of broken glass, and abruptly the an lab was dark again. As she rose, a clutching hand brushed her arm; she yanked the sheet off the nearest corpse, tossing it at the intruder, tangling him in it. He stumbled and went to his knees. She slid the half-dissected corpse off its table and pulled it on top of him.

As he cried out in shock and loathing, Quinn turned and ran for the doors, her socks slipping on the floor. She heard scrabbling footsteps behind her and lunged for the light sliver, felt her palms slam against the doors, sending them swinging open into the light, but she wasn't home free, she knew. The building was empty and she was as vulnerable as ever, so she kept running, careening around the corner—

—and colliding into someone, someone male and heavy, someone with two strong hands that gripped her shoulders and pulled her upright, someone with white hair and round, rimless glasses—

"Dr. Emerson!"

"Quinn!" he said. "What on earth . . . ?"

She was so relieved she wanted to cry. She clung to him.

"In the anatomy lab!" she said, gasping for air. "Someone in there! After me! Had a light!"

He disengaged her arms. "After you? Are you sure?"

"Yes!"

"Here? On campus? This is intolerable!"

He started down the hall, toward the lab, but Quinn pulled him back. She was afraid for him.

"No, don't. He might still be there. Let's get out of here."

"Very well," he said. "You come to my office. We'll call Campus Security from there and have them check it out." He took her arm and led her toward the front doors. "By the way, what on earth are you doing here at this hour?"

"I was supposed to meet Tim—"

"Oh, yes. Mr. Brown. Your cadaver mate. A little last-minute cramming before the practical?"

Quinn didn't know how much to tell Dr. Emerson. She didn't want him thinking Tim had gone crazy. As they stepped out into the chill air, she slipped back into her shoes and ducked his question by asking one of her own.

"I know why I'm here at this hour," she said. "But why are you? You don't have a practical tomorrow."

"I don't sleep well. Haven't since my wife died. Maybe I don't need as much sleep as I used to."

Quinn had heard he was a widower, but this was the first time he'd mentioned it.

He tapped the frayed notebook protruding from the side pocket of his coat. "I came to retrieve this from Lecture B. Then I was going over to Science for a while."

"More work on 9574?" Quinn said.

He nodded. "I suppose. But I'll gladly postpone that." He pointed toward the administration building across the pond. "We'll stop in my office, we'll call Security, I'll make us some tea, and you'll tell me exactly what happened tonight."

Quinn nodded in the darkness. She'd like that. She felt safe with Dr. Emerson.

But where was Tim?

Tim watched Dr. Alston pace back and forth before him.

"You've heard my lectures, Mr. Brown," he said. "You're a bright young man. I trust I don't have to go into too much detail about the grim future of medical care and the delivery of medical services during the span of your productive years."

"I don't care about any of that," Tim said. "I want to know about Quinn."

"Forget her for now. You must listen to me and—"

Tim glared up at him. "How can I listen to you when she might be in trouble? Get real, Alston."

"Oh?" he said with arched eyebrows. "It's 'Alston' now, is it?" He turned to Verran and sighed. "Louis, see if you can learn the status of the Cleary girl."

Verran said, "I'll signal Kurt to call in."

He went to another console and tapped in a code, then they all waited in silence, a sweaty, anxious silence for Tim—until a bell rang. Verran flipped a switch and muttered into the mike on his headset. Then he turned to Dr. Alston.

Tim's heart leaped at his first words.

"She got away," he said. "Kurt almost had her but your buddy Dr. Emerson happened by at the wrong moment, and so Kurt had to let her go."

"Walter?" Alston said. "He has a talent for saying and doing the wrong thing at the wrong time. What's he doing here at this hour?"

"I dunno," Verran said with a shrug. "Maybe—"

The phone by his elbow jangled. He picked up on the second ring.

"Campus Security . . . Yes, sir. In the anatomy lab, you say? . . . Yes, sir. We'll get right on it."

He grinned at Alston. "Speak of the devil. That was your friend Emerson on the phone, telling me that a 'Miss Cleary' reported being chased through the anatomy lab by an unknown intruder. He says the girl is staying with him—drinking tea, he said—until we've checked the matter out."

"At least we know where she is." He turned to Tim. "Satisfied?"

"How do I know any of it's true?"

Alston smirked. "Look at where you are, and look at where I am. I don't have to lie to you, Mr. Brown."

"Okay, okay," Tim said. Quinn trusted Dr. Emerson. If he was looking after her, she was probably all right. "What do you want from me?"

"Your attention. Listen to me with an open mind and then we'll see what you think when I'm finished."

"I already know what I think."

"But you're intelligent enough to be influenced by logic, and logic is what I'm going to give you."

"How about unstrapping me from this chair?"

"All in good time. First, you listen." He began to pace again. "I'm going to tell you everything. But in order for you to fully grasp the import of what I have to say, you'll have to have some background."

"That's usually helpful."

"When Mr. Kleederman set up his foundation—years before you were conceived, Mr. Brown—he peopled its board not only with a former senator, but with an international array of high government officials and other influential men in industry and labor who shared his cause, his vision. Kleederman Pharmaceuticals was already well established in the U.S. by that time, but even then he saw the writing on the wall: The new drug-approval process was going to thicken into a stagnant quagmire unless intelligent changes were made. But he knew those changes would never be made, so he embarked upon a course to find a better way to bring new pharmaceuticals to the sick of the world despite the interference of their own governments."

"And perhaps in the process," Tim said, "move Johann Kleederman from the ranks of mere multimillionaire to multi*billion*aire?"

"I don't believe he is driven by money. I doubt that he and all his heirs can spend even the *interest* on his fortune. No, he truly has a vision. Disease is a scourge upon mankind. The tools to defeat it merely wait to be discovered. Yet petty bureaucrats entangle new compounds in endless miles of red tape, delaying their use for years. Mr. Kleederman finds that unconscionable, and so do I."

"Everybody seems to have a bitch about the FDA, but what's that got to—"

"The bedrock of the Kleederman vision is Kleederman Pharmaceuticals. From there he branched out into medical care, building nursing homes, buying up failing hospitals within easy reach of major cities and converting them to medical centers that have become paradigms of compassionate, top-quality care. Those medical centers have always operated under the rule of providing that top-quality care to everyone, regardless of ability to pay. That's why they're always located near urban centers—to allow access to the neediest cases from the inner cities. Mr. Kleederman gathered the medical centers, the nursing homes, and the pharmaceutical company under the conglomerate umbrella of Kleederman Medical Industries. KMI funds the Kleederman Foundation, which in turn funds the Ingraham College of Medicine."

"Fine," Tim said. Alston hadn't told him a damn thing he didn't already know. "But none of that explains the bugs, or the contraptions in our headboards."

"Tell me, Mr. Brown: Do you have any idea what it currently costs to bring a new drug to market in the United States?"

"That doesn't answer my question."

"Do you know?"

Tim didn't, so he picked a number out of the air. "Fifty million."

"Oh, if only that were so!" Alston said, laughing. "Actually, the figure is closer to a quarter of a billion—two hundred thirty-one million dollars, to be exact."

Tim blinked at the staggering figure. "Okay, I'm impressed, but you've got seventeen years under patent to get your money back."

"Not true. We have nowhere near seventeen years. It takes twelve years, from synthesis to FDA approval, to bring a new drug to market . . . twelve years before you can recoup dollar one on a new drug. But the patent clock begins running as soon as the compound is registered, so you try to hold off registering a compound as long as you can. But still it frequently takes a full seven years from registration to final approval. That leaves you only ten years with exclusive rights to sell a product you developed from scratch."

"I haven't seen the pharmaceutical companies standing in line to file for bankruptcy."

"With the price regulation President Clinton's talking about, you may. But profits aren't the point. At least not the whole point. I'm speaking of an enormous waste of resources. And a tremendous human cost as beneficial drugs sit unrecognized while their useless brothers go through exhaustive animal trials only to be discarded because they are ineffective in humans; and even when the useful compounds are identified, they sit on the shelf, beyond the reach of the people they could help, while their paperwork drags through the quagmire of the approval process. For every ten thousand investigational compounds, only ten—*ten!*—make it past rodent and primate studies. That's an enormous loss in and of itself. But then consider that of the ten surviving compounds, only one makes it through human studies and gets to market. A one-in-ten-thousand success rate, Mr. Brown. A ninety-nine-point-ninety-nine percent failure rate. What's your gambler's opinion of those odds, Mr. Brown?"

"Sort of like dropping a marble off the edge of the Grand Canyon and trying to hit a particular ant on the bottom."

"Precisely. And people wonder why new drugs cost so much. That lone surviving compound has only ten years to make up all the negative costs of the nine thousand nine hundred ninety-nine compounds that didn't make it, plus show enough profit to convince the stockholders that this research-and-development merry-go-round is worthwhile. But without R and D, there'd be no new drugs at all."

"Isn't the answer obvious?" Tim said. "Lengthen the patent life for new drugs."

Alston's smile was sour. "A few lucky compounds do get an

extension, but it's a form of noblesse oblige rather than a legal right. The pharmaceutical companies have spent decades lobbying for more time . . . to no avail."

"Then get the FDA to speed the approval process."

"We're already paying for extra staff at the FDA—to keep the line moving, as it were. Any further suggestions?"

Tim thought a moment, bringing his economics courses into play. "Only one other way I can see: Narrow the field."

"Meaning?"

"Find a way of weeding out the useless compounds earlier in the process. That will cut your front-end expenses."

Alston grinned and clapped his hands. "Mr. Kleederman would be proud of you! Exactly his solution! Running an investigational compound through the endless mandatory animal studies only to learn later that it's completely worthless in humans is a sinful waste of time and money."

"So what are you talking about? Trying it on humans first?" He was afraid of the answer.

"Of course not."

"Good. For a moment there—"

"We run it through some rodents and primates to make sure it's not toxic, *then* we try it on humans."

Tim stared at him, not wanting to believe this.

"The problem, of course," Alston went on, "is the supply of human subjects—*sick* human subjects. Obviously we can't evaluate a drug's efficacy against disease by giving it to healthy people. That's where The Ingraham's graduates come in."

Tim saw a mental image of the "Where Are They Now" board, and the pieces began to fall into place.

"All those inner-city clinics, the nursing homes . . . "

"Precisely. The inner cities especially are loaded with disconnected people of no social significance who do not care for their health and are consequently rife with diseases—some of them might be described as ambulatory pathology textbooks. We needed a way to funnel those patients to the Kleederman medical centers where investigational compounds from Kleederman Pharmaceuticals could be tested on their many and various conditions. Since we could not count on enough run-of-the-mill physicians to come through for us, no matter how much of a bounty we offered them, the foundation decided to produce a custom-designed model of physician to serve its needs. And the only way they could see to do that was start their own medical school. They bought Laurel Hills Hospital, turned it into a top medical center, built a medical school adjacent, and *voilà*, The Ingraham."

"So you admit it, then!" Christ, it was true. No reason for Alston to make this up. "You *have* been brainwashing us!"

" 'Brainwashing' is such a loaded term, Mr. Brown. 'Attitude adjustment' is much more palatable. You see, with its well-connected board, the foundation had access to all sorts of government agencies. The Vietnam War was going full swing then, and one such agency developed something called a subliminal learning and indoctrination unit for use on U.S. troops before they went overseas—to give them the proper attitude toward the war effort and their Viet Cong enemies. But the SLI proved impractical for that use. It worked, but it took years to achieve its maximum effect, so the project was defunded. The foundation saw a use for the SLI units and intercepted them on their way to the scrap heap. They hired the original designers and technicians to perfect them and retool them to the foundation's needs, and the units have been in use at The Ingraham with great success for almost two decades now."

"That's brainwashing," Tim said. "Pure and simple."

"No. Attitude adjustment. We don't wash your brain, we don't change who you are, we simply mold your attitudes concerning the appropriateness of certain sickly individuals reimbursing society for all the benefits they have reaped but never contributed to; or of allowing other individuals with but a few useless years left to help make this world a better place as they take leave of it. We also incite in you a desire to practice where you are most likely to run across such patients. And when you do find a disconnected individual suffering from one of the more common ailments that afflict mankind, you feel a compulsion to refer that individual to the nearest KMI medical center."

Tim thought of Dorothy, the cadaver he shared with Quinn. Her doctor had been an Ingraham graduate who referred her to the medical center next door. She didn't leave it alive. Had she been a human guinea pig? And he thought again of all those Ingraham graduates working the inner-city clinics across the country, all connected to KMI medical centers. This was *big*.

He swallowed his loathing.

"So all this talk about rationed medical care has been a smoke screen."

"Not completely. Rationed care is on the way, I guarantee it. But that was merely a vehicle to introduce the concept of social tiering to your conscious minds while the SLI units were whispering it to your unconscious."

"How? I've never heard of a subliminal method that's a hundred percent effective."

"None is. But the Ingraham system *works*—not by chance, but by careful selection of its students."

Dr. Alston pulled a chair closer and sat a few feet before Tim, leaning forward, his face and hands more animated than Tim had ever seen them. An air of suppressed excitement crackled around him. He was really into his story now.

"The special entrance exam is the key. Because The Ingraham is the so-called 'twenty-four-karat medical school,' all the best pre-med students in the country apply here. From those applications we choose the brightest and most outgoing, and we invite them here to spend the day and night before the entrance exam—actually, we insist on it, but we're euphemistic about it. While they're asleep in the dorm the night before the exam, we introduce them to the SLI unit by implanting information in their unconscious minds about a nonexistent formula called the Kleederman Equation. In the exam the following day we ask them three questions about the Kleederman Equation. Those who answer them correctly reveal themselves as being susceptible to the SLI's influence. In one fell swoop we've identified the susceptible subgroup out of our applicant population. We choose our students exclusively from that." He barked a laugh. "Isn't it brilliant?"

You son of a bitch, Tim thought. You son of a *bitch*!

"Not so brilliant," Verran said. "What about Cleary?"

Tim stiffened at the mention of Quinn's name. "What about her?"

"We've had some trouble with the SLI unit in your girlfriend's room," Alston said.

"The unit's working fine," Verran said. "The kid's not responding."

Alston seemed uncomfortable. "At this time I am unable to explain Miss Cleary's apparent imperviousness to the influence of the SLI. She answered two of the three Kleederman Equation questions on her test and got them both right. She couldn't have done that unless she was susceptible to the SLI. There's a variable here that I haven't been able to identify. But I will. I assure you, I will."

Tim repressed a smile as he realized *he* was the variable. He'd marked the correct answers on Quinn's sheet as he'd passed on his way to hand in his test. Quinn hadn't had the faintest idea what the Kleederman Equation was.

But the inner smile died in the heat of Tim's mounting anger as it dawned on him how he'd been duped and manipulated—how they'd *all* been duped and manipulated by the Kleederman Foundation, by The Ingraham's administration.

But how far did this conspiracy go? How deep did it reach? It was big, no doubt about it. Johann Kleederman controlled a multinational empire, and apparently people like former senator Whitney jumped when he spoke. So it went high, but how far down The Ingraham's academic tree did it reach? The Ingraham wasn't a complete front. There was a real medical center attached, and genuinely important research like Dr. Emerson's was going on here.

"Is *everybody* on staff part of this?"

"Heavens, no. The fewer people aware, the less likelihood of a leak. Only key personnel in Administration, the admissions committee, and part of the clinical staff answer to the foundation. The rest have no idea."

Who was friend, who was foe? Tim wondered. And how could you tell?

Alston was still crowing. "But occasional glitches aside, we've been extraordinarily successful here at The Ingraham. As a result, every city of any consequence has Ingraham graduates delivering health care to its neediest citizens."

"How do you people do that to us and live with yourselves?"

"Quid pro quo, Mr. Brown. You get the world's finest education at no cost, and—"

"No *cost*? What about our souls?"

"Please don't be so dramatic. Your soul, should such a thing exist, remains quite intact. All we get in return are a few referrals."

"Right. Referrals to an early grave."

"Come, come. You make the medical centers sound like death camps. They are *anything* but. These are sick people being referred to us. And we treat their illnesses."

"With experimental drugs!"

"That very often work. We cure people every day."

"And the ones you don't?"

"Then we try another."

"How many deaths on your hands, Alston?"

He shook his head with annoyance. "Look, Brown, I'm not some megalomaniacal comic-book villain. This plan was already in development when I came to The Ingraham. The foundation's board, composed of some of the keenest minds in industry, labor, and government, arrived at this policy after months and years of debate. There's nothing haphazard or whimsical here. It's all been carefully thought out."

"How'd they get you?"

"They recruited me. They'd heard me speak, read some of my articles critical of FDA policies and protocols; they scouted me, hired me, watched me very closely, and eventually let me in on their grand plan. I joined them—enthusiastically. I believe in what we're doing here. We're bringing amazing new therapies to medicine, to the world. This is the most important thing I will ever do with my life. And I'm proud to do my part."

Am *I* being recruited? Tim wondered. He decided that it might be in his best interests—and Quinn's as well—to bite back any critical remarks and feign a growing sympathy with Alston's point of view.

"But I don't see how this can work."

Alston smiled. "Oh, it's *already* working, Mr. Brown. Kleederman's ability to bring a whole array of new products to market has made it the top pharmaceutical company in the world. Consider all the benefits being reaped by patients on adriazepam and fenostatin and carbenamycin—compounds that would still be lost in the investigational jungle if not for our program. Lives have been saved by those drugs. And thousands upon thousands of people are living better lives because of them."

"I never looked at it that way," Tim said, nodding slowly, thoughtfully, hoping he looked and sounded convincing. "Maybe you're not as crazy as you sound."

"Crazy?" Alston frowned. "I see nothing crazy about trying to remain on the leading edge of technology and therapeutics. Do you want to practice with second-rate tools, Mr. Brown?"

"No. Absolutely not." No lie there.

"Then we must be willing to take risks."

Risks, Tim thought. Right. But with whose lives?

"It's a glorious challenge. Enormously exciting. But if you're not with us, you're against us. So what do you say, Mr. Brown? Do you want to be part of this? Do you want to join Mr. Kleederman in advancing the frontiers of therapeutics and leading medicine into the twenty-first century?"

What will happen to me if I say no? Tim wondered.

He had relaxed while listening to Dr. Alston's spiel, but suddenly he was afraid. He knew too much. If he went to the papers, the FBI, or even the AMA, he could blow the lid off The Ingraham and, at the very least, undo the decades of effort and millions of dollars Kleederman had invested in this intricate, monstrous conspiracy. The scandal could conceivably topple KMI itself.

They had to get rid of him . . . unless Tim convinced Alston that he'd play along. And now he realized why Alston had taken all this time to explain everything to him—he didn't want to have to get rid of Tim. It was easier, much less complicated to simply enlist him. And Alston's monstrous ego had absolute faith in his ability to make Tim see the light. He was offering Tim a chance. Tim saw no choice but to take it.

And he *would* play along. He'd be a model Ingraham student until he saw an opening, then he'd get the hell out of here and blow the whistle loud and clear.

"Count me in," Tim said.

Alston was watching him closely. "Why should I believe you?"

Tim met his gaze. "As you said, why should I want to practice with second-rate tools?"

"Don't answer my question with another question. Convince me, Mr. Brown."

"You're the one who's convincing, Dr. Alston. You've made a powerful case. And by the way, can we possibly arrange some KMI stock options for me?"

"Can I take that to mean that you will continue your studies here as if nothing has happened, that you will never reveal what you know about The Ingraham?"

"You can."

Alston stepped over to where Verran was concentrating on his console.

"Well, Louis. What do you say? Can we take Mr. Brown at his word?"

Verran shook his head. "He's lying."

Tim's stomach plummeted at the words. They were spoken not as opinion but as fact.

"I'm not!" Tim said. "How can you say that?"

"The chair's a lie detector, kid," Verran said. "And it says you're lying through your teeth." He pressed a button and spoke into a microphone. "All right, guys. Time to move him."

His gut squirming now, Tim began struggling in the chair, writhing, straining at the straps around his arms, but they wouldn't budge.

"Damn you!" Alston said. His face was contorted with genuine anger as he leaned close to Tim. "Why couldn't you have gone along? Your shortsightedness forces us into an untenable position. We must now take extreme measures to protect ourselves."

"L-like what?" Tim had never stuttered in his life, but he was starting now.

"You'll see."

Alston pulled a syringe and a small vial of clear fluid from his pocket.

Panic became a rapier-taloned claw, raking at the lining of Tim's gut.

"What's that? What're you going to do?"

Alston said nothing as he filled the syringe and approached him. Tim made a desperate, futile attempt to squirm away from the needle as Alston plunged it into his deltoid without bothering to roll up the overlying shirtsleeve. Tim flinched at the sting of the point, the burn of the fluid emptying into his muscle from the syringe.

Part of his brain was screaming that he was going to die, going to die, going to die, while another part refused to believe it. Then the door opened and two men came in. Tim recognized both. One was the blond security guard he and Quinn had seen in the parking lot before going to Atlantic City, and the other had been the phony exterminator in Quinn's room.

The big blond guy stalked forward and stopped in front of Tim.

"His number's up?" he said to Verran.

Verran nodded. He didn't look too happy. "Yeah, Kurt. His number's up and gone."

"Good," Kurt said. "That means no more Mr. Nice Guy."

He cocked his right arm and punched Tim in the face.

Amid the sudden blaze of pain, Tim heard Alston say, "Stop that immediately! What's gotten into you?"

"This is the son of a bitch who broke my nose."

"That's no excuse to mistreat him, especially considering what's about to happen to him."

Perhaps it was the injection, perhaps the punch, perhaps Alston's remark, or perhaps it was a combination of all three. Tim passed out.

Quinn watched anxiously as Dr. Emerson spoke into his phone. She noticed that his tweed jacket was worn at the elbows, his corduroys were rumpled, and he needed a shave. He looked tired.

"Very good. I'll tell her. No, that won't be necessary. Thank you." He hung up and turned to her. "That was Security. They've combed the anatomy lab and the entire class building without finding anyone. Whoever it was must have been scared off."

The news brought Quinn no sense of relief.

"I'd rather they'd caught him," she said. "Now they probably think I'm some sort of hysterical female."

"I'm sure that isn't so. They say they think it was a thief, sneaking through the building, looking to steal whatever wasn't nailed down. You just got in his way, that's all. Security even offered to send over someone to escort you back to the dorm. I told them not to bother." He began to push himself up from his chair. "Come. I'll walk you back myself."

"No, please," Quinn said. "I'll be all right." She glanced out the window at the approaching dawn. "The sun's almost up. I'll be fine."

"Are you quite sure? It's really no trouble—"

"You've done enough already," she said. She drained her teacup as she rose. "Thanks for your help."

"It was nothing, child. Absolutely nothing. Any time you need my help, you just call."

Funny thing about Dr. Emerson calling her "child." She didn't mind.

"I hope that won't be necessary."

"By the way," he said as she reached for the doorknob, "Security wants you to stop by as soon as you can and give them a description of your assailant."

"I don't know what I can tell them. All I saw was a shadow and a flashlight."

"They need to make a report to the local authorities, so tell them what you can. You never know what tiny snippets will lead to an identification."

"Will do."

Quinn waved, stepped out into the hall, and hurried toward the exit.

The pre-dawn air was cold and clear and a rime of frost had crystallized on the grass. Quinn broke into a jog toward the dorm, her breath steaming and streaming around her. She couldn't help anxious glances left and right at the shadows tucked behind the shrubs and foundation plantings. Security had said the intruder was gone, but Security was supposed to keep intruders from getting on campus in the first place.

Despite her lingering anxiety, it felt good to move, to run, to inhale cold air and feel it swirl through her bronchial tree, clearing her lungs and her brain. Last night's fright seemed remote, almost as if it had happened months ago, to someone else. All of the night's strange events had taken on an air of vague unreality.

But what about Tim? What had he been thinking last night? Such erratic behavior—it gave her the willies, especially in someone she'd come to care for so much. And where had he been all this time? Probably back in his bed sound asleep. She smiled. She'd kill him.

She trotted directly to his room and raised her fist to pound on the door, but stopped herself when she realized she'd probably wake Kevin and most of the residents on this end of the floor. She could wait.

Quinn trotted up the stairs to her own room. It would be nice to grab a few winks to make up for some of her lost sleep, but she knew the caffeine in Dr. Emerson's tea wouldn't let her do that. Maybe she could bone up a little more for the anatomy practical. But first . . .

She searched through her rumpled sheets and blankets for the notes Tim had written her when he'd popped in last night. She wasn't going to let him forget how crazy he'd acted. She'd hold on to them and perform dramatic readings whenever the situation warranted.

But where were they? She was sure she'd left them right here by the pillow. She tore the bed apart. She looked under the bed. She checked all her pockets.

Gone.

She sat on the edge of the bed, dumbfounded. Where on earth . . . ?

Unless Tim had come back and taken them.

She slapped her thighs. That did it. She reached for the phone. Sorry, Kevin, but you're about to get a wake-up call. Blame it on your crazy roommate.

Ten rings. No answer.

Uneasy now, Quinn ran back downstairs and began knocking on Tim's door, calling his name. She wished now she'd accepted one of his room keys when he'd offered it, but she hadn't felt right taking it when he had a roommate, even someone as easygoing as Kevin.

"Hey, Quinn. What's up?"

She turned and gasped. "Kevin!"

He was coming down the hall dressed in a T-shirt and boxer shorts, his pillow slung over his shoulder.

"You two have a fight?"

"Where's Tim?"

He grinned. "Hey, you spent the night with him, not me."

"What are you talking about? I just got here. I called a minute ago and there's no answer."

His grin vanished. "You kidding?"

"No. Open up, will you? He was acting awfully strange last night."

Kevin already had his key in hand. He unlocked the door, and Quinn pushed ahead of him, rushing through the front room to the bedroom.

"Oh, God."

Neither bed had been slept in. The room looked just like all the bedrooms looked after the maids were finished. She ran to the closet and slid the door aside. It wasn't empty, but there were a lot of unused hangers on the rod.

"Where is he, Kevin? What did he say to you last night?"

Kevin told her about Tim asking him to bunk down the hall so the two of them could have some time alone together.

With her terrified heart pounding against the wall of her chest, Quinn pushed past Kevin and ran full tilt for the parking lot. She slid to a halt on the frosty grass at the top of the rise. Even from up here, even in the skim-milk light of pre-dawn, she could see that Griffin was gone. She searched the rest of the lot for it, but no gray Olds Cierra anywhere. Tim's invisible car was nowhere to be seen.

"Tim!" she called to the dawn, knowing there would be no reply but compelled to cry out for an answer.

Where are you? What's wrong with you? What have you done?

Her voice rose to a scream that echoed down the hill.

"*Tim!*"

"I warned you there'd be only trouble if you went to that school. You remember that, don't you?"

Quinn groaned within. She'd told herself she'd regret it if she called her mother, but after the way the day had gone, she needed to talk to someone. She felt as if she were losing her mind.

She'd stumbled through the day in a daze, unable to concentrate on her classes. Her mind was on Tim and where he could be, and how he was, and why he hadn't made any of his classes and missed the practical. Between every class, when she wasn't calling Tim's room, praying he'd pick up the phone, she was out on the slope overlooking the student parking lot, searching for a glimpse of Griffin.

The thought of eating repelled her, so she'd used her lunch hour to stop by the Security Office, ostensibly to make her report on the incident in the anatomy lab, but mainly to see if they had any idea of where Tim might be.

Mr. Verran looked exhausted, more hangdog than ever. He didn't seem the least bit concerned by Tim's disappearance.

His attitude was: "So? He's skipped a few classes and took off on a long weekend. He ain't the first student to do it, and he won't be the last, I promise you."

Quinn knew he was wrong. Tim might have a cavalier attitude about studying, but he didn't miss tests.

Mr. Verran wouldn't hear of reporting Tim as a missing person. There was a twenty-four-hour minimum before anyone would start looking for him. Quinn left the Security Office angry and frustrated at her inability to convey to anyone the fearful urgency exploding inside her.

After staggering through the anatomy practical and realizing she'd barely passed, she'd called Dr. Emerson and asked to be excused from her research duties for the afternoon. He told her, by all means stay out—after last night's ordeal, he wouldn't dream of asking her to come in. He thought she was still strung-out from the incident in the lab. She didn't tell him about Tim.

After a halfhearted attempt at dinner, she scanned the parking lot once more, then returned to her room and called Matt at Yale, praying he'd heard from Tim—or better yet, that Tim was right there, lounging by the TV, drinking a beer.

But Matt hadn't heard a word from his old roommate and was dumbfounded. She made him promise to call her the minute he heard anything. *Anything.*

The next call had been the toughest: Tim's folks. Mrs. Brown answered and quickly passed it to her husband. Mr. Brown was hostile at first, and why not? He'd never met Quinn and didn't want to hear what she was telling him. But something in her voice must have carried her feelings along the wire—her fear for Tim and genuine bafflement as to his whereabouts—for he began to soften, to really listen and ask questions. By the end of the call he was somber and subdued. He took Quinn's number and said he would call her if he heard from his son.

After that she'd sat on her bed in her darkening room. Despite the voices drifting in from the hall—someone laughing, someone shouting—the dorm seemed empty. She felt alone in the universe. She'd had a sudden, irrepressible urge to call her parents, to make sure they were okay, to reassure herself they still existed, and to affirm that she herself was real.

"Yes, Mom," she said. "I know you warned me. But you said something would happen to *me.* This is a friend of mine."

Her mother's voice softened. "I've gathered from how you've spoken of him that Tim is more than just a friend."

"Well, yes."

"Do you love him?"

"I . . . I think so." Quinn knew so but couldn't go into that now with her mother. She missed Tim desperately, and if she began talking about her feelings for him, she'd break down completely. "He's very special."

Her mother's voice suddenly turned plaintive. "Come home, Quinn. Come home now before the same thing happens to you."

The change in tone startled her as much as the words.

"Mom, what are you talking about?"

"Something terrible's happened to your friend, Quinn. Can't you feel it?"

"Don't say that, Mom. You can't know that. You're scaring me."

But what was truly frightening was that Quinn *did* feel it, a deep, slow, leaden certainty in the base of her neck that something unimaginable had befallen Tim. She couldn't tell her mother that, couldn't let her think that she too might be experiencing "the Sheedy thing." Not after disparaging it for so long.

"I'm already scared, Quinn. I've been living in constant fear since you left for that awful place."

It was almost as if her mother knew about the incident in the an lab last night. But how could she? Quinn hadn't mentioned it. And this was why.

"But it's *not* an awful place, Mom. It's one of the most highly respected medical schools in the world. How can you say that?"

"It's just a feeling I have."

"I've got to go, Mom. I didn't get much sleep last night. I'll call you if Tim shows up."

"Call me anyway, Quinn. Call me every day. Please."

"Mom—"

"*Please?*"

The naked anxiety warbling her mother's words forced Quinn to relent. "Sure, Mom. Every day. I'll do my best."

She hung up feeling more worried and fearful than before. She checked to see if her door was locked, then she angled the back of a chair under the knob. Without undressing, she crawled into bed and pulled the covers over her head. She cried for a while. Eventually, she slept.

An insistent pounding on her door yanked Quinn from her sleep. The room was bright. She glanced at her clock: after nine. She'd slept almost twelve hours. Rubbing and slapping her face to rouse herself, she stumbled to the door, moved the chair away, and pulled it open.

She almost screamed, she almost fainted, she almost threw herself into his arms, but then she realized it wasn't really Tim, so she leaned her trembling body against the doorjamb and gaped at him.

"Quinn Cleary?"

She recognized the voice through the pounding in her ears.

"You must be Mr. Brown."

Tim's father was young, or at least young-looking. He had Tim's lean body and dark brown hair and eyes. On a good day he might have passed for Tim's older brother. But this obviously was not a good day. He looked haggard and worn, as though he'd been driving all night. And he looked wound too tight, as if he were barely holding himself in check, barely restraining himself from exploding and flying off in all directions. Mr. Verran stood behind him in the hall like a watchful mastiff.

"Yes," Mr. Brown said, extending his hand. "Have you heard anything from . . . ?"

"No. Nothing." His palm was moist against hers as she shook his hand. "I keep hoping the phone will ring, but . . . "

"I know." He released her. "Mr. Verran has graciously agreed to drive me to the Sheriff's Office to make out a missing-person's report on Tim. Since you were the last one to see him, I was hoping—"

"Of course." She knew she should wash up, change the wrinkled clothes she'd slept in, but that would mean more time before people began looking for Tim, and too much time had been wasted already. "Just let me grab my purse."

Quinn sat with her cold hands clamped between her thighs, watching and listening and thinking this couldn't be really happening as Deputy Southworth of the Frederick County Sheriff's Department sat before them filling out forms. The three of them clustered around his desk, one of four in a large open area. Quinn yearned for an enclosure. This was private. This was about Tim. But the deputy was cool, professional, and appropriately sympathetic as he quizzed Mr. Brown on what his department considered useful and relevant about Tim: vital statistics; physical characteristics; scars; medical history; Social Security, driver's license, and credit-card numbers; hobbies, vices, a list of close friends, and on and on. Quinn noticed that Mr. Brown did not mention gambling. Perhaps he didn't know.

Most of all, the deputy needed pictures. Mr. Brown had come prepared with an envelope full of wallet-size graduation photos.

Next the deputy asked Mr. Verran if he could add anything.

Quinn sensed a strained atmosphere between the two. The Ingraham security chief shrugged.

"Not much. I checked his record before coming down. He gets good grades and seems to be well liked by everyone who knows him. He does stay out all night rather frequently though. More than any other student in The Ingraham."

Quinn felt the flush creep into her face and hoped nobody noticed. She knew exactly where Tim went on those overnights, what he did, and with whom. She hoped no one else knew. And she wondered how Mr. Verran managed to keep such close tabs on Tim's comings and goings.

His father apparently wondered the same thing.

"Really?" Mr. Brown seemed genuinely surprised. "That's news to me. How do you know?"

"The gate in and out of the student parking lot. Every kid with a car gets a card to work it. The card is coded with his name. The gate records the date and time and card owner every time it opens."

"Do you know if he goes alone or with somebody?"

"The gate doesn't tell us that."

Which isn't an answer, Quinn thought. She had a feeling Mr. Verran knew she'd been in the car with him most of those times— at least the times since Atlantic City—but was glad he hadn't mentioned it.

Wanting to swing the talk away from overnight jaunts, Quinn said, "Do you think Tim's disappearance could have anything to do with the break-in at the anatomy lab last night?"

"A break-in?" Deputy Southworth said, looking sharply at Mr. Verran. "I hadn't heard about that."

"Nothing was really broken into," Mr. Verran said quickly. "Nothing stolen. More of a trespasser than anything else. I filed the incident report with the sheriff's secretary yesterday. It would have been completely minor except that Miss Cleary wandered into the building when he was there, and he frightened her." His voice lowered to a growl. "I don't take kindly to trespassers frightening students at The Ingraham. He'd better pray I don't catch him on the campus."

The deputy turned to her. "Well, we haven't heard from you yet, Miss Cleary. What were you doing out at that hour?"

"I was looking for Tim."

Suddenly she was the center of attention.

Quinn had been dreading this moment since Mr. Brown had asked her to accompany him here. How much should she tell them? Certainly not about their relationship, their intimacy. That was none of their business, had nothing to do with Tim's disappearance. At least, God, she hoped it didn't. She didn't know if she could be sure of anything anymore.

But what about the last time she'd seen Tim, that bizarre scene in the wee hours of yesterday morning when they'd sat there saying one thing while writing other things on the notepad passing back and forth between them because Tim thought the room was bugged? She didn't want to repeat it, any of it. It made him sound deranged. And he wasn't.

But Tim certainly hadn't been himself that night. Had he broken with reality? Was he crouched in the dark somewhere, cold and hungry, hiding from some army of imagined enemies?

The thought of it brought her to the verge of tears.

She had to tell them. It might offer some clue into Tim's state of mind at the time, and that might lead them to where he'd gone.

Deputy Southworth said, "When was the last time you saw your friend Timothy Brown, Miss Cleary?"

Quinn told them all about it—the scribbled notes, waiting in the car, going to the anatomy lab, the intruder, Dr. Emerson. Everything.

The office was tomb-silent when she finished.

"Bugged?" Mr. Brown said finally. "He told you he thought the room was *bugged*?"

"He wrote it," she said, her mouth dry from telling her story. "On the notepad."

"Do you still have those notes?" the deputy asked.

She shook her head. "That's the weird thing. I went back to my room to look for them but couldn't find them. I was sure I'd left them on my bed."

"*Bugged?*" Mr. Brown said again. He turned to Mr. Verran. "Where on earth would he get an idea like that?"

The security chief shrugged. "I couldn't tell you."

The deputy said, "Did your son have any history of mental illness, Mr. Brown? Has he ever been under a psychiatrist's care?"

"No, never." He seemed offended.

"They're under a lot of pressure at The Ingraham," Mr. Verran said. "Every once in a while one of the kids cracks."

"This isn't the first time this has happened," the deputy said.

"It isn't?" Mr. Brown straightened in his chair. He turned to the security chief. "You mean *other* students have disappeared without a trace?"

Mr. Verran looked acutely uncomfortable. "Two years ago we had a second-year student run off before finals."

"Proctor, wasn't it?" Deputy Southworth said.

"Prosser." Mr. Verran pressed his hand against his lips and stifled a belch. "Anthony Prosser."

"Did he ever turn up?"

"I'd heard that he did," Mr. Verran said. His eyes were watching the scuffed tile floor and Quinn wondered what was so interesting there. "The family doesn't keep in touch with me, so I couldn't swear to it, but I believe I'd heard something to the effect that he'd returned home." He cleared his throat. "So you see—"

"Listen to me, both of you," Mr. Brown said. Quinn saw angry fire flashing in his eyes. "We just had Tim home a few weeks ago at Thanksgiving. He was as sane and relaxed as could be, and happier and more content than I've ever seen him. My wife and I both noticed it and even mentioned it to each other. And one thing that young man has never felt is academic pressure. He's always been able to stand toe-to-toe with any course and take whatever it could dish out. Nothing like that was going to send him wandering off in some sort of fugue state. If he said a room was bugged, you can bet he had damn good reason to think so."

"I'm sure you're right," Deputy Southworth said. He rose and extended his hand across the desk. "Mr. Brown, I'm going to get this missing-person report out immediately. We'll put out an APB on his car and run a check on his credit card. I'll file it with the feds because in a state this size it's a good bet he's already crossed the state line. I have the number of your hotel and I'll be in touch as soon as I hear anything."

"Come on." Mr. Verran rose from his own chair, speaking sorrowfully. "We've done what we can here. I'll drive you both back."

Mr. Brown didn't move. He stood by the desk like a statue. Quinn saw his throat working, his eyes blinking back tears. She fought the urge to throw her arms around him and tell him he had the greatest son in the world and not to worry because everything would be okay, that nothing bad could happen to Tim because she wouldn't let it.

But she allowed herself to touch only his elbow, and to say,

"Let's go, Mr. Brown. You never know. Maybe Tim's waiting for us back at the dorm."

He gave her a weak, grateful smile. "Yeah. Maybe he is."

Neither of them believed it.

Quinn was sitting, staring out the window at the afternoon sky but seeing nothing, when someone knocked on her door. It was Mr. Brown. With him were Mr. Verran and another man she'd never seen before.

"Quinn?" Mr. Brown said. "Could I trouble you to let this man"—he nodded toward the stranger—"check your room for bugs?"

He said it with the same tone one of the supers might have mentioned checking her bathtub for leaks.

She stifled a gasp. A queasy sensation settled in her stomach. Tim had said something about the room being bugged, and now here was his father, actually looking to prove it. She gave Mr. Brown a closer look. His face seemed to have turned to slate. In the hall behind him stood Mr. Verran, and he did not look too happy.

"Sure," she said. "I guess so."

"All right, Don," he said to the stranger. "Do it."

The man stepped past Quinn and produced a wand of some sort. It was black and had a loop at the end, reminding her of the electric contraption her father used to start the briquettes in their charcoal grill. He began waving it about the room, along the walls, all around the fixtures. There was something ritualistic, almost shamanistic about the procedure.

"What's he doing?"

"Sweeping the room, looking for electronic pulsations, microwave transmissions."

The feeling of unreality swept over Quinn again as she watched. Almost in a trance, she followed him into the bedroom and watched as he scanned every object in the room. She wished she'd thought to pick up the place. But you so quickly get used to a maid, and the maids had the weekends off.

Don did a visual search, and even disassembled the telephone.

When he was finished he nodded pleasantly to her and returned to the front room, where Tim's father waited. Mr. Verran was still outside the door in the hall, hovering, watching.

"Not a blip," the man called Don said. "The place is clean, just like your son's."

Mr. Brown nodded. He seemed neither pleased nor displeased. He turned to Mr. Verran.

"I had to know. You understand that, don't you? I had to know for sure."

"Of course I understand," Mr. Verran said. "A hundred percent. I'd've done the same thing myself."

As Don slipped past him into the hall, Mr. Brown turned back to Quinn. "Thank you, Quinn."

"Has there been any word? Any word at all?" She felt foolish asking—they'd only completed the report a few hours ago—but it was a compulsion she could not deny.

"No." His eyes were bleak, his mouth a thin, grim line. "Not a word."

"Will you . . . ?"

"I'll let you know if I hear anything." He touched her arm and managed a smile that was heartbreakingly close to Tim's. "Thanks for caring."

As soon as the door closed behind him, she broke down and cried.

Quinn had dozed only sporadically through the night, so she was already up and showered when someone knocked on her door Sunday morning. She ran to it, hoping, praying. . . .

It was Mr. Brown. He wasn't smiling, but he didn't look quite so grim.

"I think we've found him," he said.

Quinn's knees were suddenly weak. Her heart began pounding in her ears. As the room threatened to tilt, she reached behind her, found a chair, and sat down.

"He's . . . he's all right?"

"We don't know. They found his car at the airport south of Baltimore."

"BWI."

"Right. It's in the long-term lot. They checked with the airlines and learned that he purchased a one-way ticket to Las Vegas Friday morning."

Visions scuttled across Quinn's brain: Tim in his dark glasses, sitting at a blackjack table, drink in hand, lights strobing all around him as he grinned and flashed her his Hawaiian hang-loose signal.

"And a further check of his credit card shows he arrived and rented a car from Avis. Signed for a week's rental."

"Vegas," Quinn said softly, still trying to comprehend.

"Yes. I don't understand any of it, but I'm so relieved to know he's alive. For days now I've had these visions of Tim lying in a ditch somewhere."

Quinn said nothing. She was too numb with relief to speak.

"We learned something else," Mr. Brown said with a sidelong glance in her direction. "A report from the Atlantic City Police Department."

Quinn closed her eyes. Her name was on that report as well. She supposed she should have known that would come to light eventually.

"Maybe I should have said something before," she said. "But I didn't see that it had anything to do with—"

"Does Tim have a gambling problem?"

She looked at Tim's father and found his eyes intent upon her. The answer was important to him.

"I don't know if I'm fit to judge that, but—"

"Was he getting in with the wrong kind of people?"

"No. Why do you say that?"

"Well, he's been staying out all night a lot, and he got beat up outside a casino."

"We were mugged. If I hadn't wanted to go down on the sand, it never would have happened. And truthfully, Mr. Brown, Tim isn't really interested in gambling. He's never once mentioned going back since then. He's more interested in beating the system with his memory than in gambling itself."

Mr. Brown smiled for the first time. "That memory of his. He was always playing games, doing tricks with it." He extended his hand. "I'm glad I stopped by, Quinn. Even though there's still a lot of questions left to be answered, you've eased my mind some."

"Where are you going?"

"To Las Vegas. I can't sit back and wait. I've got to go looking for him."

Take me with you! Quinn wanted to say. She'd go herself if she had the money.

"You'll call me as soon as you find him?"

He nodded. "Better yet, I'll have him call you himself." He waved and let himself out.

Quinn remained in the chair, staring at her trembling hands. Las Vegas . . . what on earth . . . ?

At least she knew he was still alive.

Why didn't she feel better?

She sat there for she didn't know how long, her mind almost blank. Finally she stood and shook off the torpor. She couldn't give in to this. She had to keep moving.

A walk. That was what she needed. Fresh air to clear her head and help her think straight. As soon as she stepped outside, she headed for the student lot. It had become a habit now, a compulsion: Whenever you're outside, check the lot. Maybe you'll see Griffin easing through the gate.

She checked. No Cierra.

Quinn followed the walk around the pond and found herself nearing the science center. She checked the pocket of her coat for her wallet. Her security card was in it. She thought, Why not? She needed a distraction, something to do with her mind besides worry about Tim. Sorting, filing, setting up the data on 9574 for analysis might distract her, make the time go faster. Trying to study now would be nothing but wasted effort.

And maybe Dr. Emerson would be there. It was a good possibility—9574 had become his life. You never knew when you'd find him in the lab. She hoped he'd come in today. His presence alone had a soothing effect on her. He was a deep-set rock to cling to in all this chaos.

Up on the fifth floor she passed Ward C with her usual quick glance through the window to make sure all was well within, then continued down the hall.

She stopped. Something had changed in Ward C. She couldn't say what, but there was something. . . .

She walked back and looked again. Immediately she knew what was different. There were eight patients in Ward C today. A new burn victim had arrived since she'd last been up here.

Quinn continued down the hall toward the lab, wondering what catastrophe had befallen that poor soul.

MONITORING

"I wish the hell I knew what they talked about in there," Louis Verran said as he watched Timothy Brown's father leave the dorm on the video monitor.

"Well," Kurt said, stretching languidly after his flight back from Vegas, "you're the one who wanted the bugs pulled from those two rooms."

"And a damn good thing I did too! You two guys have any idea how I felt when Brown's old man showed up with that industrial-espionage consultant? I damn near blew lunch."

"Why? The rooms were clean. Nothing to worry about."

"Oh, really? You two guys haven't exactly been models of efficiency lately. You had to put Brown's SLI back together and replace the headboard, cut the power to his roommate's SLI, clean out all our bugs, and make like maids and neaten everything up. That's a lot of stuff. You could've missed something."

"But we didn't. And don't forget whose idea it was to check out the girl's room."

"Okay, okay. I admit it. That was a good thought."

A *damn* good thought. Verran rubbed a hand across his queasy stomach. If Elliot hadn't checked Cleary's room, they wouldn't have found the notes. And then when Brown's father had shown up with that sweeper, Verran had quickly ordered the power cut to *all* the SLI units in the building.

Not that the sweep would have picked up the bugs anyway. The electrets were nonradiating. Plus, the dorm phone taps were all off premises.

Altogether a bad weekend though, spent worrying all night about who else the Brown kid might have told. But nobody new had made any noise about it yet, so it was pretty safe to assume that they'd managed to keep the lid on everything.

The only ongoing risk would be Deputy Ted Southworth. Verran knew The Ingraham's security measures rubbed the Sheriff's Department the wrong way—they saw Verran's crew as some sort of vigilante force—but Southworth had had a special hard-on for The Ingraham since the Prosser thing two years ago. He'd asked an awful lot of pointed questions when Prosser had disappeared, and he'd made it clear he wasn't satisfied with the answers.

He turned to Kurt. "You ditch the rental good in Vegas?"

"Just like you said: Wiped clean as a whistle and sitting smack-dab in the middle of the MGM Grand parking lot."

Verran nodded. Hide in plain sight. That was the best way. The Vegas hotel lots were always loaded with rented cars. It would be a long time before that one was picked up. And when it was, no one would suspect a damn thing.

"All right, then," he said, leaning back. "I think we've got everything under control again. They all think the kid has a gambling problem and is still alive and making the scene in Vegas. The father's off our backs, looking for him out in Nevada."

Kurt yawned and said, "All we've got left to worry about is the girl. What do we do about her?"

"We don't chase her around the anatomy lab again," Verran said sharply. "That's for sure."

"Hey, Alston wanted me to bring her in."

"Yeah, well, it's just as well you flubbed it."

"I'd've had her if Emerson hadn't wandered by."

The door to the control center opened then, and Doc Alston walked in. He looked pale as he dropped heavily into his usual seat.

"I've just been on the phone with Senator Whitney and two of the board members."

"All at once?"

"A conference call." His hand shook as he rubbed his high forehead. "And they are *not* happy—with either of us. Not happy at all."

Verran felt his heart begin to hammer. Two board members and the senator on the phone at once. Someone was majorly pissed. And that someone could only be Johann Kleederman himself.

As much as he disliked Alston, Verran could not help feeling a twinge of sympathy for him.

"Did you explain?"

Alston nodded. "I explained my heart out. Believe me, it's not easy explaining away two near disasters in two years."

"Will they be . . . calling me next?" His mouth went dry at the thought.

"I don't think so. I think I settled everything."

If that was true, he *owed* Alston. But . . .

"They always want to blame someone," Verran said, watching Alston closely. "Who's getting the blame?"

"I managed to spread it around. I told them this has to be expected. If they want only the cream of the intellectual crop, it's inevitable that every so often one member of that crop is going to spot an inconsistency and follow it up."

"And they bought it?"

"Of course. It's true, and the logic is inescapable. They were somewhat mollified when I told them that we intercepted Brown before he told his girlfriend much of anything. I hope that is still true, Louis."

"Yeah. Truth is, I don't think we ever had a real worry there. Turns out Cleary doesn't know squat. And it also turns out a good thing Brown's father brought in his electronics man yesterday. Cleary stood right there in that room and heard him say there were no bugs. So even she's convinced her boyfriend's cuckoo."

"Do we replace the bugs?" Elliot said.

"Not yet. She's alone in the room, so she doesn't do any talking anyway. And we've got the off-premises tap on her phone. So I say we leave things as they are for the moment." He looked at Alston. "You agree?"

Alston nodded. "She wasn't responding to the SLI anyway. Might as well leave her room entirely cold until I can think of a way to get her out."

"You got it," Verran said.

"But I want her phone monitored twenty-four hours a day."

"No problem. I'll have Elliot hook up a voice-activated recorder to her line and we'll check it all the time."

"That will do, I suppose. But I want someone to know where she is every minute of the day," Alston said. "Got that?" He fixed Kurt and Elliot each with a hard stare, then looked at Verran. "Every minute."

"You're the boss," Verran said.

F loating. In darkness. Falling through a limitless black void with no sense of movement or direction, without so much as the sensation of air passing over his skin.

I'm alive.

Tim didn't know the hour, the day, or even the month, where he was or how he got there, but he knew he was alive.

Or was he? In this formless darkness in which he could feel nothing, hear nothing, could he call this being alive?

Cogito, ergo sum.

Okay. According to Descartes, he was alive. But was he awake or dreaming?

He seemed to be awake. He was becoming aware of faint noises around him, of movement, of an antiseptic odor. He tried to open his eyes but they wouldn't budge. And then he realized that he didn't know if he was lying on his back or his belly. He couldn't feel *anything*.

Where the hell was he?

And then he remembered . . . he had passed out after being punched in the face in the early hours of Friday morning. Suddenly he wanted to shout out his rage, his anger. But how could he? He couldn't even open his mouth.

Wait. That must have been a dream. Had to be—the bug in the fixture, the weird device in the headboard, the grilling by Dr. Alston, the man's elaborate Kleederman conspiracy. All a nightmare.

Get these eyes open and the whole thing would be over. He'd see that ugly fixture in the ceiling of the bedroom, the one in his dream he'd thought was bugged. And then he could roll over and see his roomie conked out in the other bed. Good old Kevin.

The eyes. He concentrated on the lids, forcing them to move. Light began to filter through. He kept at it, and the light brightened

slowly, like the morning sun burning through fog. But this wasn't
sunlight. This was paler. Artificial light. Fluorescent.

Shapes took form. White shapes.

And then he saw himself, or at least his torso, lying in bed on
his right side, under a sheet.

That's more like it.

He tried to roll over, but his body wouldn't respond. Why not?
If he could just—

Wait. His left arm, lying along his left flank, draped over his
hip—it was wrapped in white. Some sort of cloth. Gauze. And his
right arm too, lying supine upon the mattress, was wrapped in
gauze to the fingernails. Why?

Maybe he was still dreaming. That had to be it. Because although he could see his gauze-wrapped arms, he couldn't *feel*
them—couldn't feel the gauze, couldn't feel the pressure of their
weight on his hip or the mattress, couldn't feel *anything*. Almost
like having no body at all.

Then he saw the transparent tube running into the gauze from
an IVAC 560 on a pole beside the bed. An IV.

He was on IVs! That meant he was in a hospital. Jesus, what
had happened to him? Had he had an accident?

He spotted another tube, also clear but larger gauge. This one
coiled out from under the sheet and ran down over the edge of
the bed. The yellow fluid within it flowed downward, out of him
and over the edge.

A catheter. He'd been catheterized. He'd seen those rubber
tubes with the inflatable balloon at the tip. His insides squirmed
at the thought of one of those things being snaked up his penis
and into his bladder. Apparently it had already been done. Why
couldn't he feel it sitting in there?

Tim dragged his gaze away from himself and forced his eyelids
open another millimeter to take in his surroundings.

He wasn't alone. There was another bed next to him, half a
dozen feet away. And a white-swathed body under the sheet. And
beyond that, another. And another. All mummy-wrapped, with
tubes running in and out of them. And beyond them all, a picture
window, looking out into a hallway.

Tim realized he'd seen this place before. But he'd seen it from
another perspective, from the hallway on the far side of that
window.

I'm in Ward C!

He wanted to scream but his larynx was as dead as the rest of him.

Tim battled the panic, bludgeoned it down. Panic wouldn't help here. He tried to think. He *had* to think.

The dream, the nightmare of being bound and gagged, and then listening to Dr. Alston while strapped into that chair in the basement of the science center, that all had happened. And now he was a prisoner in Alston's private preserve.

At least they hadn't killed him.

But maybe this was worse.

Tim shifted his eyes down to his body. He saw white gauzy fabric all around the periphery of his vision—his head was wrapped like the rest of his body. Another faceless Ward C patient. And something else: snaking up past his right eye . . . a white tube. It seemed to go into his nose. A feeding tube, snaking through a nostril, down the back of his throat, and into his stomach.

Farther down his body he saw the gentle tidal rise and fall of his chest. Quinn had told him the properties of the anesthetic Dr. Emerson was developing, and how it was being used on the patients in Ward C. Obviously he'd been dosed with it as well.

What had she said? She'd called it 9574 and it supposedly paralyzed all the voluntary muscles while it let the diaphragm go on moving—like in sleep. But it didn't have complete control of him. He'd managed to open his eyes, hadn't he? He could move his eyeballs, couldn't he?

He drew his gaze away from the ward about him and looked at himself again.

He had to get control of his body. He could move his eyeballs and eyelids. But he needed his hands. He searched out his right hand where it lay flopped out before him on the mattress, palm up. If he could move it . . .

Maybe start small. Just a finger. One lousy finger. He picked his little finger, the pinkie. He imagined himself inside it, crawling through the tissues, wrapping himself around the flexor digiti minimi tendon and pulling . . . pulling for all he was worth. . . .

And then it moved. It *moved!*

He tried it again. Yes, the tip was in motion, flexing and extending, back and forth. The arc was no more than maybe a centimeter, but he could move it, dammit, he could *move* it. And he could actually feel something down there. A faint tingle. He was regaining control. He was going to get out of here. And then he was going to bring the walls down.

"Good morning, Number Eight. About time you woke up."

A nurse, dark skin, brown eyes, her nose and face behind a surgical mask, her hair tucked into a surgical cap, was looking down at him. Tim's eyes fixed on her blue eye shadow, so glossy, almost luminous. The eyes smiled down at him.

"Time to turn you, Number Eight. But first—" She held up a syringe filled with clear fluid. "Time for your two o'clock dose."

She poked the needle into the rubber tip of the Y-adapter on the intravenous line and emptied the syringe into the flow.

She patted his shoulder—he felt nothing. "I'll be back in a sec to turn you."

Tim watched her go, then returned his attention to his tingling fingers. He watched his pinkie finger move again, but this time the arc seemed smaller. He had to keep working at it. He tried again, struggling, pushing harder, but this time it wouldn't budge. And the tingling, the parasthetic, pins-and-needles sensation in his hand had faded.

. . . *Time for your two o'clock dose* . . .

The nurse's syringe. It had been loaded with 9574. The fresh dose had turned him into dead meat again. They had him on a round-the-clock schedule.

Movement . . . at the window into the hall. Someone standing there, looking in. His eyes focused so slowly.

Quinn! Jesus, it was Quinn, looking right at him. Didn't she recognize him? But no, how could she? He was swathed head to toe in gauze. He tried to shout, begged his hands to move, but his voice remained silent, his limbs remained inert.

Fear, frustration, terror, and rage swam around him. Helpless . . . he was utterly helpless.

And then Quinn turned and walked on.

Tim's vision blurred. He knew a tear was running down his cheek, but he couldn't feel it.

Matt Crawford turned from the floor-to-ceiling view of the harbor and crossed his living room. He'd been putting it off all day. By nine o'clock he could hold out no longer. He picked up the phone and called Quinn.

What a nightmare wild man Brown had started by running off to Las Vegas. Both his parents were ready for rubber rooms. Matt had spoken to Tim's mother just yesterday and all she'd done was cry; she'd heard from Tim's father in Vegas but his search for Tim was getting nowhere. Apparently Tim hadn't used his credit card again after renting the car at the airport.

And Quinn . . . Quinn had sounded like someone on a ledge. When she'd called him last Friday, there'd been something in her voice when she spoke Tim's name, something that said she was worrying about someone who was a lot more than just a friend.

No question about it, Quinn had been *hurting*. And that could only mean . . .

Quinn and Tim . . . he hadn't let it sink in at the time, but maybe it *was* possible. She did sound brokenhearted that he'd left . . . left *her*.

And Tim. What the hell was he thinking about with this Las Vegas stunt? Matt knew the guy, knew how he liked to keep you off balance, be unpredictable, but this went way beyond anything he'd done since Matt had known him.

And that was what had been bothering Matt since Friday. This wasn't like Tim. This was something else. This smelled bad.

Matt listened to the phone ringing. Quinn picked up on the third ring. When he said hello, she all but jumped through the phone, the words frantically spilling out.

"Matt! Is it about Tim? Have you heard from him? Did they find him?"

He'd intended to ask her point-blank if she and Tim had something going on. Now he didn't have to. He wasn't sure how he felt about this. Quinn had never been his, so why did he feel as if something special had been stolen away from right under his nose?

"No, Quinn. Nothing yet. I just called to talk to you and see how you're doing."

"I'm okay."

"Are you?"

She didn't answer, at least not with words. Matt heard soft sobbing on the other end.

"You miss him that much." It wasn't a question.

Her voice was a gasp. "Yes."

"He'll be back soon."

"I'm afraid, Matt." She was getting her voice back now. "I've got this horrible feeling I'm never going to see him again."

She sounded so lost. This wasn't like the Quinn he knew. Was this what love did to you?

"You'll see him. He's got to come back soon."

"You really think so?" She sounded like a shipwrecked sailor groping for a piece of floating debris.

"I guarantee it. When are you getting in Friday?"

Christmas break was a few days away. Maybe he'd drive out to Windham County and try to cheer her up.

"For Christmas? I won't be leaving until next Friday."

"The twenty-third? Our break starts the sixteenth. Why so late?"

"Well, I'm working on this project. I can get overtime if I stay, and I thought if Tim comes back, I ought to be here."

Matt resisted the impulse to say that's crazy, that if Tim's old man finds him in Vegas, he'll bring him straight back to New Hampshire.

"You're going to hang around an empty campus?" He hated the thought of her being alone in a deserted dorm. "You think that's a good idea?"

"It's not empty, and you sound like my mother."

"Sometimes mothers make a lot of sense."

"I just got off the phone with her. She's got one of her 'feelings' and wants me to come right home."

"Is that so bad?"

"Do you have any idea how quiet a farm gets in the winter?"

"How about I come visit you down there?" he found himself asking without thinking.

"No, Matt. You've got better—"

"What's better than visiting an old friend who sounds like she needs a friend?"

"That's nice of you, Matt, but really, I'll be busy in the lab and there's not much to do around this part of Maryland if you aren't working. I appreciate it, and I'll be fine. And I promise to call you as soon as I get back home. Then the three of us can go out together and catch up."

"The three of us?"

"Sure. Tim will be back by then. He's got to be. He wouldn't stay away through Christmas."

"Right," Matt said slowly. "Sure. The three of us. That'll be great."

I hope you're right, Quinn, he thought as he hung up a few minutes later.

The phone rang almost immediately. Matt didn't recognize the voice at first.

"Matthew? This is Lydia Cleary. Quinn's mother."

Why on earth was she calling? She sounded upset.

"Hi, Mrs. Cleary. I was just talking to Quinn."

"Oh. That's why your line was busy. I was speaking to her earlier and she says she's going to stay down there next week."

"She told me."

"Matthew, you've got to get her home. Something terrible is going to happen to her if she stays there. Just like it happened to that friend of hers."

Cold fingers did a walk along Matt's spine.

"What do you mean, 'happened' to Tim? Tim took off for Las Vegas."

"I don't know about any of that. I just know something bad's happened to him, and the same will happen to Quinn if she stays down there. You know how stubborn she is. She won't listen to me."

"She won't listen to me either."

"Maybe if you go down there, Matthew. Maybe she'll listen to you then, and you can bring her back. I know it's a lot to ask . . ."

"It's not a lot," he said, trying to soothe the growing agitation in her voice. "Not a lot at all. I'll leave as soon as they cut me loose on Friday."

"Oh, thank you, Matthew." She sounded ready to cry. "I'll be eternally grateful for this."

He eased himself off the phone, then sat there, wondering, feeling uneasy. Her sense that something had 'happened' to Tim rattled Matt. And she was so convinced the same was going to happen to Quinn. Superstition, of course, but still . . .

Matt decided then to leave for Maryland Friday afternoon without telling Quinn. He'd catch her by surprise and work on her all weekend. By Sunday he'd have her packed up and ready to go.

In a few days he'd have Quinn home safe and sound. But what about Tim? He wished he could do the same for Tim.

Tim, old buddy, where the hell are you?

Tim existed in a timeless space of boredom, rage, and terror. Sometimes he slept, and dwelt in a nightmare in which he had no body.

Sometimes he was awake, and dwelt in a nightmare in which he could not feel his body.

The staff took good care of that body. Three times a day, every shift, his limbs were put through their ranges of motion to keep the joints limber and prevent contractures. He was turned back and forth, his position changed every few hours to prevent pressure ulcers in his skin. And whenever they were in the ward, all the nurses spoke to him constantly, like girls talking to their dolls.

And that was what Tim began to feel like. He couldn't feel, couldn't reply, couldn't move on his own. He was a giant Ken doll.

Despite all the care, he was afraid for his body. What had they done to it? Had they scorched his skin? Was he now a burn victim like the others? He felt nothing. If only he could feel *something*— even pain would be welcome—he might know.

And Tim had begun to fear for his mind. Imprisonment in an inert, mute body was affecting it. Every so often he would feel his mental gears slip a few cogs, would catch his thoughts veering off and have to reel them in from wild, surreal tangents filled with giant floating syringes and stumbling, mummified shapes. He knew one day—one day too soon—those thoughts could slip their bonds and never come back.

Focus. That was the only thing that kept his mind in line. Focusing on movement, on brief, tiny increments of victory over the drug that crippled his nervous system.

He'd learned to recognize the signs that his previous dose of 9574 was wearing off. Mostly it was a tingling, beginning in his fingertips and toes and spreading across his palms and soles. When the sensation came, he focused all his will on his fingers. Sometimes he was positioned so he could see them, but many times he wasn't. He didn't let that stop him. For most of the day his hands didn't exist. But when the tingling came, it told him where they were, and then he could locate them, focus on them, make them the center of his world, and demand that they obey him.

Tim couldn't be sure, but it seemed to him that the episodes of tingling were lasting longer, starting a little sooner before each new injection. What did that mean? Was he building up a tolerance to the drug? Was his liver learning to break it down faster? He'd read that the liver could "learn." When a new substance was introduced into the bloodstream, the liver's job was to break it down and dispose of it. At first it would metabolize the substance slowly. But as the substance made more passes through the liver, the enzymes within the hepatic cells adjusted and became increasingly efficient. That was why a teetotaler could get tipsy on a single glass of wine while a drinker might down half a bottle with little or no effect: The teetotaler's liver has no experience breaking down ethanol, but it's routine for the drinker's.

Tim knew he had a good tolerance for alcohol—always had. Maybe that indicated an especially efficient liver. Maybe his liver was learning new ways to clear the 9574 from his blood, and getting a little better at it every day.

He clung to that thought. It wasn't much of a hope, but at least it was hope. And he needed all the hope he could muster. His hands were tingling now. He was lying on his back, staring at the ceiling, so he couldn't see them. But he knew where they were now. There was another sensation today. A dull pain on the outer aspect of his left thigh. He ignored that. It was his hands that concerned him. He focused on them, concentrating his will. . . .

"Is Number Eight awake?"

That voice. He knew that voice!

"Yes, Doctor."

Alston. Dr. Arthur Alston. Tim wanted to roar the name, wanted to spring up and hurl himself at his throat, but all he could do was lie here and feel the growing tingle in his hands.

"When's he due for his next dose?" Alston's voice said.

"Not for another twenty minutes."

"Give it to him now. I've got a little debriding to do here, and I don't want him twitching."

Suddenly Dr. Alston's face loomed over him. He was wearing a surgical mask and cap.

"Hello, Brown. I'm terribly sorry it had to come to this, but you gave me no choice. This, by the way, is the last time you'll be referred to by your name. From now on, you're the John Doe in bed eight. Don't look for rescue from the Ward C staff. These nurses have been handpicked by the foundation. They don't know your real name, but they do know you're not one of our usual burn victims, and they know you're here because you're a threat to the foundation."

Tim would have groaned if he could. The nurses too?

"Is that surprise I see in your eyes, Brown? A male-chauvinist reaction? Do you see some reason why professional women such as these nurses can't share the goals pursued by the foundation?

We all have many common goals here in Ward C. Perfecting the semisynthetic burn grafts is just one. We are all committed individuals, and we all work toward those goals in our own way. But it's a group effort."

Alston sounded so sane, so rational. Tim would have much preferred a mad-doctor persona. It would have been easier to take. This was so damn unsettling. It almost made Tim feel like the deviate. Almost.

Dr. Alston's face was replaced by the mocha-skinned nurse's. Her eyes crinkled warmly as she smiled behind her mask. She did something out of Tim's sight. He guessed it was another dose of 9574. When the tingling in his fingers and toes faded, he knew he was right.

"All right, Marguerite," Alston said. "He should be ready now. Turn him on his side and we'll get to work."

Tim's stomach gave a little heave, and the room did a quick spin as hands he could not feel rolled him off his back and onto his right side. The picture window into the hall swam into view, but the curtains were drawn.

"Watch out for the N-G tube," Alston said. "Good. Don't worry, Number Eight. That feeding tube is only temporary. We'll put in a deep line for TPN soon. That's total parenteral nutrition—something you would have learned about in your clinical training over the next few years."

Clinical training . . .

Tim realized he'd never see his clinical training.

"Right there," Alston said to Marguerite. "Perfect. And now the tray, please."

Tim's mind screamed out to know what Alston was doing. He must have sensed Tim's thoughts. He spoke from somewhere behind him.

"Just because you've been reduced to a vegetative state doesn't mean your days of usefulness as a productive human being are through. Quite the contrary. You're earning your keep, Number Eight. And you're making a significant contribution to the well-being of your fellow man."

Tim sensed movement behind him, heard a rustle, the soft clank of a metal tray.

"You see, one of the ongoing problems we've had with fully researching the new grafts has been our inability to test them on fresh burns. Since the grafts must be grown from cultures of the victim's own skin cells, they are, *ipso facto*, unavailable for treatment of a fresh burn. We could keep a bank of grafts for people at high risks for burns—fire fighters, for instance—for immediate use should a burn occur, and I'm sure that such a program will come into being eventually, but at this early stage it's not feasible. So what we've needed for a while is another test subject whose skin grafts can be cultured in advance and then tested on fresh burns of varying severity and surface area."

Another test subject? Tim thought.

"You do realize, don't you, that you're not the first student to learn too much. We've had a few unfortunate incidents in the past when the subliminal intrusion of the SLI unit has triggered unsuspected psychosis in a student, but until now only one other student has learned as much as you. That was Anthony Prosser, two years ago."

Tim remembered the phrase he'd heard a few second-year students use: to pull a Prosser. It meant to go over the wall and never be heard from again.

Everybody probably thinks I've pulled a Prosser.

"Anthony has been known as Number Five for two years now."

Two years!

"During that period he has made an enormous contribution to our graft research. But now . . . " Tim heard Alston sigh. "Now he's given all he has to give. Now he just lies there, completely mad. But we're not abandoning him. We'll take care of him as long as he lives."

Give? What did Prosser give?

"So, as unfortunate as it was that you had to stumble on our little secrets here at The Ingraham, in a way it proves rather timely. We were just beginning to perfect our acute-stage grafting techniques when Number Five ran out of undamaged skin. You can take over where he left off."

Tim's brain was screaming. *They're going to burn me!*

"We've been culturing your skin cells since you arrived. Yesterday we added a sedative to your afternoon dose of 9574. While you were unconscious, I inflicted a thirty-six-square-inch third-degree burn on the lateral aspect of your left thigh."

Ward C—what Tim could see of it—blurred and swam before his eyes. They'd *already* burned him!

"I felt it was kinder to put you out during the procedure. Even though you'd feel nothing, you'd still smell it. The odor of burning human flesh is rather unpleasant, especially unpleasant when it is your own. I spared you that. We're not cruel here, Number Eight. We bear you no ill will, no malice. In fact, we feel sorry for you. You are the victim of a particularly vicious and ironic Catch-22: The very attributes of intellectual curiosity and sharply honed analytical brilliance that once made you an asset to The Ingraham have now caused you to become a liability. We couldn't let you go, and we couldn't kill you—despite what you must think of us, we're not murderers, Number Eight. So we chose this method of neutralizing your threat to the foundation and The Ingraham. You still have your life, and in a very important way, you're still contributing to the medical well-being of your fellow man. Which was one of the reasons you came to The Ingraham in the first place, isn't it, Number Eight?"

But you did kill me, Tim thought. You must have. Because this is worse than death. This is hell.

MONITORING

Louis Verran noticed the red light blinking on the recorder. He nudged Elliot.

"How long's that been lit?"

Elliot glanced up at it and shrugged. "Beats me."

"When was the last time you checked it?"

"This morning when I came in. Wasn't blinking then."

With an effort Verran kept his voice low and even.

"Well, it's blinking now. And when it's blinking, it means the recorder's been activated. And when the recorder's been activated it means Cleary's been on the phone. And in case you forgot, we're monitoring all her phone calls. So do you think you could spare some time from your busy schedule to listen to it?"

"Sure, chief."

Verran shook his head. The best goddamn high-tech voice-activated recorder wasn't worth shit if nobody listened to it.

He watched Elliot slip on the headphones and replay the conversation. He looked bored. Finally he pulled them off.

"Same old crap, chief. Her mother wants her to come home Friday. Her old boyfriend wants her to come home too, even offered to come down and get her, but she blew him off. She's staying."

"She should go. She's bad news, that kid."

"She thinks Brown's coming back and she wants to be here." Elliot grinned. "She's got a looooooong wait, huh?"

"Yeah," Verran said. "But as long as she's waiting, you keep an eye on that recorder. Anytime you see that light blinking, you listen right away. Not later. *Right away.*"

Verran almost felt sorry for Cleary. Her boyfriend was never coming back. There was no way out of the place Alston had put him.

im watched the day-shift nurses—the dark-skinned one called Marguerite and another whose name he hadn't caught yet—string garland and holly around the window on the hallway. They worked on the far side of the window; apparently Christmas decorations weren't allowed in the antiseptic confines of Ward C. They were laughing, smiling, presenting a Norman Rockwellesque portrait of holiday cheer.

Who on earth would believe what they were involved in on this side of the window?

And what would a Rockwell portrait of my right thigh look like? Tim wondered.

All the shifts told him how well the graft was taking, as if he cared. How long since Alston had burned him? How long since he'd placed the graft? If only there was a clock here. Or a calendar. Tim's only measure of time was his injections. He knew today was Friday—he'd heard Marguerite say "TGIF" this morning—but *which* Friday? Was it one Friday before Christmas, or two?

He was betting on two. That made today the sixteenth of December. Maybe.

He hadn't been placed on his left side since the graft. He'd been on his right side, faced toward the hall window for the past few hours. Never since his arrival had he been rotated to the spot directly in front of it. Each of the other seven patients on Ward C got a regular turn there, but Tim was always kept near the back. Why?

Because of Quinn, he guessed. Even mummy-wrapped as he was, there was still a chance she might recognize him if she got within a couple of feet.

The thought of her was a deep ache in his chest. He liked being positioned so he could see some activity—anything but hours of staring at the ceiling—but he hoped Quinn wouldn't pass by. He longed for the sight of her, but each time she walked on after pausing at the window, a part of him died.

He preferred watching Marguerite and the other nurse decorating the window.

Go on, ladies. Do a good job. Take your time. Take all the time you want.

Because the longer they stayed out there, the longer it would be before his next dose of 9574.

Already his hands were tingling to the wrists. He'd begun concentrating on his left fingers the instant the tingling began. He knew they lay on his left hip. He wished he could see them, to measure his progress.

And he *was* making progress—no question about that. He could feel his fingers moving, feel the pinkie flex, then straighten . . . flex, then straighten. He just wished he knew how much movement he'd gained. He didn't know how far he could trust his proprioception—he needed to *see* those fingers move to believe it.

Tim noticed one of the nurses—Marguerite—looking in his direction. He froze his hand in position. Had she seen the movement? He prayed not. If they saw the 9574 wearing off, they'd give him another shot of it. They might even start keeping a special eye out for movement. And if they saw too much, they might up his dose.

Tim was sure that would push him over the edge into madness. All that kept him sane were these moments when he could feel something, *do* something. He spent his day waiting for these moments. He lived for them. If they were taken away . . .

Marguerite turned and said something to the other nurse and they both laughed. They went on decorating the window. Good. She hadn't seen him. He could go on moving his fingers.

He switched his concentration to his left thumb.

. . . flex . . .

. . . extend . . .

. . . flex . . .

. . . extend . . .

Snow.

As she hurried toward Science, Quinn brushed at a flake that had caught in her eyelashes. The Baltimore radio stations were all talking about the big snowstorm charging in from the Midwest.

Pennsylvania and New Jersey were slated to take the brunt if the storm stayed on its present course, with Maryland collecting a few inches from the periphery.

Normally, she'd be excited. Quinn loved snow, loved to ski. During college, whenever a snow hit New England, she and a couple of friends would hop in a car and head for Great Barrington, where her roommate's family had a ski condo.

But she felt no interest, let alone excitement, in the coming storm. It didn't matter. Not much seemed to matter anymore.

One thing the threatened snowfall did accomplish was the cancellation of the Friday afternoon labs. Since this was the last day before Christmas break, the administration had decided to let the students get a head start on the storm.

Everyone who was going home, that is. For Quinn it meant an early start in Dr. Emerson's lab. She'd had lunch, helped a couple of friends load up their cars, and waved them off to their Merry Christmases.

Merry Christmas.

Not bloody likely.

Another reason for not going home until the last minute: Quinn wasn't feeling very Christmasy—anything *but* Christmasy. And Mom always did Christmas up big, decorating the first floor as though she were entering it in a contest. Everything would be so cheery and warm and happy, and Quinn knew she'd be a horrible wet blanket. If she was going to mope, better to do it in private.

She shook herself. This had to stop. Everything was going to be fine, everything was going to be all—

Why did you leave me, Tim? Why did you make me care about you and then run off like that? Why?

She bit back a sob.

"I'm okay," she said softly. "Really. I'm okay."

She groaned as she entered Science. The entry vestibule and the lobby were festooned with Christmas ornaments. There wasn't going to be any getting away from the Season to Be Jolly.

Nobody was at the security desk. One of the male guards was holding a ladder while Charlene stood on the top step and taped a strand of golden garland to the wall. They recognized Quinn and waved her through.

Fifth was no better. Santa faces, Merry Christmas greetings, plastic mistletoe, fake holly, and tinsel garland hung all over the place.

Quinn kept her eyes straight ahead, glancing left only briefly when she passed the newly decorated Ward C window, trimmed with tiny Christmas bulbs, blinking chaotically.

She stopped as a thought struck her: Here I am in the dumps about my Christmas . . . what about *theirs*? Her gaze roamed the ward, coming to rest on the patient against the far wall. He appeared male, and his body was long and slim.

Like Tim's, Quinn thought with a pang.

He was lying on his right side, facing her. She couldn't make out his eyes between the folds of gauze wrapped around his head, but he seemed to be looking at her.

Quinn!

Jesus, it was Quinn. And she was staring directly at him. If only he could reach up and yank the gauze off his face, or screech her name, or just wave and attract her attention. Anything but lie here like a goddamn asparagus and watch her walk away again.

His hand . . . his left hand . . . if he could get it to move now . . . *now*, when he needed it . . . to signal her . . . something definitive . . . something that wouldn't look like some sort of random muscle twitch . . . if only he knew sign language. . . .

And then Tim realized that he did know a sign language of sorts.

Quinn stared at the bandage-covered face, trying to read something there. She had a feeling he was staring back at her, trying to tell her something. His body looked slack, utterly relaxed, yet she sensed a bridled intensity about him.

Movement caught her eye. His left hand was twitching where it lay on his left hip. The fingers were curling into a fist. No, not all of them. Just the middle three. The thumb and pinkie finger remained extended.

And then, ever so slightly, the hand wagged back and forth.

Quinn felt a smile begin to pull on her lips. Why, it almost looked like—

As she cried out, her knees buckled, and she fell against the window with a dull *thunk* that echoed down the hall.

Tim's Hawaiian hang-loose sign . . . the patient on the far side of Ward C was looking her way and doing a crude version of the shake-a-shake-a signal Tim had used in the casino.

Suddenly hands were gripping her upper arm, supporting her.

"Are you all right?"

Quinn looked up and saw a nurse holding her arm, steadying her as Quinn straightened and leaned against the window frame.

"I . . . " Her throat locked, refusing to let another syllable pass.

"You look terrible," the nurse said. "You're white as a ghost."

I've just *seen* a ghost, she thought.

She was shaking, dripping with perspiration. Bile surged against the back of her throat but she forced it back down.

"What's wrong?" the nurse was saying, looking at her closely. "Are you a diabetic or hypoglycemic?"

I probably look like I'm having an insulin reaction, Quinn thought. I almost wish I were.

She shook her head and started to say something, to ask about that patient at the far end of Ward C, then bit back the words.

It couldn't be Tim. Not in Ward C with the burn patients. Anywhere but Ward C.

If she said anything about it, they'd think she was losing it. Hallucinating. Breaking with reality. Word had already spread around The Ingraham about Tim having a breakdown and running off—pulling a Prosser. The administration would think she was cracking too. They'd send her home. Maybe for good. One breakdown per class was more than they wanted to deal with.

"My period," she said, improvising. "I always get bad cramps the first day."

The nurse's face relaxed. "I get some whoppers myself. Come on over here. I'll give you a couple of Anaprox."

Keeping one hand on the wall to steady herself, Quinn followed her to the nursing station, where she sat, blotted the beaded perspiration from her face with a paper towel, and choked down the two blue tablets.

After a few minutes she felt strong enough to move on. She thanked the nurse and made it down the hall to Dr. Emerson's lab, where she told Alice that she didn't feel well enough to work today.

Alice took one look at her and bounded out of her seat.

"I should say you don't! You look awful! You might have the flu. Dr. Emerson won't be in until tonight, so you get right out of here and over to the infirmary right this minute. As a matter of fact, I'll take you there myself."

"That's all right. I'll be okay. Just tell Dr. Emerson I'll be in tomorrow."

Alice shooed her out and Quinn stood outside the lab, looking down the hallway. The elevators were on the far side of Ward C. She was going to have to pass the window to get to them.

She wasn't sure she could handle that.

But she didn't feel strong enough for the stairs right now, so what choice did she have?

None.

Taking a deep, tremulous breath, Quinn straightened her spine and marched back down the hall. The nurses' station was empty as she passed it, and she intended to keep walking past Ward C, but when she reached the window she had to stop. No way she could breeze by without one more look.

Both nurses were in there now, standing around the patient who'd signaled her. Marguerite was just removing a syringe from his IV line. Was something wrong?

Quinn pressed closer to the glass. The blinking lights bordering the window made it difficult to see, but she still could make out the patient's left hand, the one that had been stretched into the hang-loose sign—it now hung limp and lifeless. As she watched, the nurses gently rolled him to his left and repositioned him on his back. Everything so normal. Just another day of routine patient care on Ward C.

The nurse who had helped Quinn a few moments ago looked up and smiled at her. Quinn gave her a friendly wave, then forced herself to walk on.

Half-dazed, still weak and shaky, feeling as if she were in a dream, Quinn found the elevator-control slot and slipped her card into it.

What had just happened here? What was real? What was not? The questions whirled about her in a maelstrom of confusion. Nausea rippled through her stomach and inched up toward her throat. She feared she might get sick right here in the hall.

She had to get out of here, back to the dorm. Back to her room, where she could lock the door, crawl into bed, pull the covers over her head, and think.

Maybe Mom and Matt had been right. Maybe it wasn't such a good idea to stay down here the extra week.

When she got outside, the snow was falling heavily. Everything was covered with a thin coat of white. At any other time she might have stopped to appreciate the silent beauty of the scene. But now she broke into a careful run for the dorm.

* * *

Tim stared at the ceiling.

What was wrong with Quinn? She'd been looking right at him as he'd given her the hang-loose signal. She'd even reacted as if she'd seen it, looked as if she'd been about to faint, but she'd done nothing.

Nothing!

Maybe she hadn't really seen it, or maybe she didn't *believe* she'd seen it. It didn't matter which. He'd never get a chance like that again. It was over. Might as well pack in the hope and forget about ever getting out of here.

Still staring helplessly at the ceiling's mottled whiteness, Tim felt himself tumbling into a black hole of despair.

This isn't a highway, Matt thought. This is a parking lot.

The New Jersey Turnpike wasn't exactly stopped dead, but for an hour now it had been moving too slowly for the speedometer to register. As far ahead as he could see, the three southbound lanes were a stagnant river of glowing brake lights fading into the falling snow.

Not falling, exactly. Racing horizontally was more like it. And lots of it. The windows on the passenger side of Matt's Cherokee were caked with an inch or better of white. It was piling up on the road and the shoulders.

Matt banged impatiently on the steering wheel and glanced at the dashboard clock. Nine o'clock. He should have been there by now. Instead he was just south of Exit 7A, only halfway through Jersey. And the longer he stayed here, the worse it was going to get. He'd played all his CDs twice, and the radio had nothing but traffic reports about the snarl-ups all over the East Coast and weather reports about how much worse it was going to get during the next few hours.

This little jaunt was turning into an ordeal.

A sign on the right with logos for Roy Rogers, Big Boy's, and Sunoco told him that the "Richard Stockton Service Area" was two miles ahead. Matt glanced at his gas gauge and saw it edging onto E. At his present pace those two miles could take an hour, maybe more. Running out of fuel now would be the icing on the cake.

He edged the Cherokee to the right and began riding along the shoulder at around twenty miles per hour. It wasn't legal, but at least he was moving. He just had to hope he didn't run into a cop. A ticket would be the candle on the icing on the cake.

He slammed on his brakes and skidded to a halt as a beat-up, twenty-year-old Cadillac DeVille with New York plates pulled out in front of him and stopped. Matt flashed his high beams and honked, but the Caddy didn't budge. He had two choices: Sit here behind the guy, or try to slip past him on the right, but that meant risking the snowy slope that dropped away from the shoulder at a good forty-five-degree angle.

He got out and walked up to the Caddy. The driver window rolled down as he approached and a bearded face glared at him.

"Don't fuck with me, man."

"How about letting me by," Matt said. "I'm trying to get to the service area."

"You wait like the rest of us."

"I'm going to run out of gas."

"Tough shit."

Matt stared at him a moment. Everyone was fed up, but this guy was looking for a fight. Matt was tempted to help him find it, but for all he knew, there could be three others like him in that car. He looked at the big, heavy Caddy, at the snowy slope beyond it, and had a better idea.

Without a word he returned to the Cherokee. He put her in four-wheel drive and slowly eased to the right. The Cadillac responded, moving right to block him. Matt edged farther onto the slope, and the Cadillac mimicked him, matching Matt's every rightward move.

When he was sure all four of the Caddy's tires were on the slope, Matt pulled sharply to his left, darting back uphill. The heavier car tried to respond but its rear wheels spun uselessly on the snow. It began to fishtail as it slipped farther down the slope, swerving ninety degrees until it was sliding back-end first, its rear wheels spinning madly. It stopped with a jolt in the gully at the bottom, its headlights pointing skyward.

Back on the shoulder again, Matt gave two quick toots on his horn and drove away.

"All I wanted to do was get by," Matt said softly.

No one bothered him the rest of the way to the service area.

"What's the problem up ahead?" he asked as the attendant filled the Cherokee's tank. He had stringy blond hair and was maybe nineteen. "It can't be just snow."

"It ain't. Scanner says a tractor trailer jackknifed coming down the Exit Six on-ramp."

"Six? That's where I get off. Damn, I'll be here forever."

"Maybe longer. We heard that four cars piled into the truck.

There was a fire and everything. A real mess. If I was you, I'd find a parking spot, get a comfortable seat in Roy's or Big Boy's, and figure on spending the rest of the night there."

Uh-uh, Matt thought. He saw a set of headlights glide across the overpass just south of the service area.

"Will that road take me to the Pennsylvania Turnpike?"

The attendant followed Matt's pointing arm and nodded.

"Yeah. Eventually. If you could get on it. But there's no off-ramp to that road. Like the man says: You can't get there from here."

"Suppose I make my own ramp?"

The attendant looked at the Cherokee, then back at Matt.

"There's a cornfield back of the service area here. With four-wheel drive you just might be home free."

"I'm not heading home, but at least I'll be free of the turnpike."

"Hope it's real important to get where you're goin'. You bust an axle or blow a tire out in that field, you'll have a lotta explaining to do in the morning."

"I've got a friend in need," Matt said.

The attendant grinned. "And you're the friend indeed, right?"

"You might say that."

"I got my break in a couple of minutes. I'll show you a way out the back."

Matt shoved a twenty into his hand.

"Show me now."

Quinn sat cross-legged on the bed in her darkened room and watched the snowflakes tumble through the bright cones from the dorm's exterior floodlights. She wished she could glide out the window like one of the kids in *Peter Pan* and get lost in the storm.

Then she wouldn't have to think about that patient in Ward C, and the hand signal he'd made for her.

It was Tim.

As crazy as it sounded, it had to be Tim. The more she thought about it, the more convinced she became.

He was Tim's height, had Tim's build, and he'd given her the signal, the Hawaiian hang-loose that only Tim would have known to give.

Quinn's first impulse had been to run to the police, to call Deputy Southworth and demand that he charge into Ward C and save Tim from whoever had imprisoned him there for whatever reason.

She'd made it as far as her door before having second thoughts. And third thoughts.

She imagined the conversation with the Sheriff's Department:

"Who do you think kidnapped your boyfriend and imprisoned him in the burn ward, Miss Cleary?"

"Dr. Alston, I guess. He's in charge of Ward C."

"Why would The Ingraham's dean of medical education want to do something like that?"

"I don't know. Maybe because Tim discovered the place was bugged."

"But his own father brought in an expert who couldn't find a shred of evidence of electronic surveillance."

"He's there in Ward C. I know he's there."

"How do you know that, Miss Cleary?"

"I was watching one of the Ward C patients when he gave me a secret hand signal Tim and I used in Atlantic City."

"A secret hand signal. I see. Did you get close to him? Did you see his face?"

"No, but—"

"Why were you watching this particular patient?"

"He's built like Tim. He reminded me of Tim."

"You really miss your boyfriend, don't you. You really wish he was back."

"Yes, but—"

"We understand, Miss Cleary. We'll be sure to look into this matter very soon. But don't call us. We'll call you when we find something. Good night."

So now Quinn was back on her bed, staring into the swirling wilderness and racking her brain for a way to convince the police that Tim was in Ward C.

If indeed he was in Ward C.

Sometimes you see what you want to see.

What if she did manage to convince Deputy Southworth to barge into the science center and they found out the new Ward C patient was a farm boy from West Virginia who'd been riding a tractor when the fuel tank exploded under him? What would happen then?

The Ingraham would probably kick her out.

And then where would she be? She'd still be without Tim, but she'd be without a medical education as well.

Quinn could come up with only one solution: She had to be

able to go to the Sheriff's Office and say she had looked into the patient's face and it was Timothy Brown.

And that was just what she was going to do. Tonight. After the change of shift.

It was the only way.

She shivered. It wasn't cold in the room. She was terrified.

Matt rubbed his burning eyes. His arms were leaden, his fingers cramped from gripping the steering wheel, and his right leg throbbed from incessant switching between the gas and brake pedals. He glanced at the dashboard clock.

I don't believe this, he thought. After midnight and I haven't hit Gettysburg yet. And it's *still* snowing like crazy.

After getting lost twice in the rural backroads of western New Jersey, he'd finally made it to the Pennsylvania Turnpike. That too had been slow going, with accidents eastbound and westbound, but at least it had been moving—a big improvement over the Jersey Pike.

But he'd made his big mistake around Harrisburg when he got off the Pennsy Pike and headed south toward Maryland. He'd had three choices: Route 83, Route 81, or Route 15. The first two were major roads, but 83 would swing him too far back east, and 81 would take him too far west; Route 15 ran right between the other two and offered to bring him closest to The Ingraham in the fewest miles.

But Route 15 was only two lanes, lined with dark sleeping houses and snow-coated trees bending their laden branches low over the road. Matt had been crawling for miles, with hours more to go, most likely.

This is crazy, he thought.

The best thing to do would be find a motel and spend the night. Forget about The Ingraham for tonight and get some sleep. The roads would be clearer in the morning.

He pulled onto the shoulder and yanked the cellular phone from its cradle between the bucket seats. He fished out a slip of paper with Quinn's number and punched it in.

If he wasn't getting there till tomorrow, he wanted to make sure she didn't zip off to Baltimore or the like for the day.

The signal was shaky but he recognized her hello.

"Hey, Quinn, it's Matt."

"Oh, Matt. Thank God you called. It's Tim! I think he's here!"

"What? He came back?"

Matt was stunned. But beneath the shock was a strange mix of emotions, an uneasy balance between relief that Tim was back and anger at him for running off in the first place.

"No. I don . . . ink he ever went away. . . . "

The signal was breaking up. Through the static Matt thought he'd heard her say something about Tim not going away.

"Come again, Quinn? I didn't catch that."

"I th . . . s here, at . . . ngraham . . . ink they're hiding him."

"Quinn—"

" . . . m going . . . ind out . . . sure . . . night . . . Sheriff's . . . Southworth . . . "

And then he lost the signal completely. He tried the redial button a couple of times but couldn't make a connection. Either he was on the fringe of the local cellular transmitter zone, or the storm was doing it. Whatever, he'd lost the connection.

But even through the static Quinn had sounded strange. Frightened. Almost deranged.

Something about somebody hiding Tim at The Ingraham? What was happening to her?

To hell with knocking off, he thought as he put the Cherokee back in gear. He'd push through to The Ingraham tonight. A glance at the dashboard clock, and he corrected himself: This morning. It was almost 1:00 A.M.

Quinn waited for Matt to call back. She'd barely been able to understand him. He'd sounded as if he'd been calling from a car phone. But why would he do that from Connecticut?

She waited awhile, and when he didn't call again, she decided it was time. Enough waiting. Time to *do*. She had everything ready, lined up on the bed: her sneakers, her security pass card, and her penlight. All she had to do was put on her coat and slip into her boots.

Her hands shook as she slid the leather boot tops over her calves. One part of her mind was scolding her for even thinking of engaging in such a foolish, no-win stunt—if she didn't find Tim but was caught by Security, she'd be in deep trouble with Dr. Alston and maybe even Dr. Emerson; if she did find Tim and got caught, she'd be in even deeper trouble, because she'd know something she shouldn't, and the people who had shanghaied Tim would have to do the same to her.

But she *wasn't* going to get caught. She could do this. She *had* to do this.

Because another part of her was prodding her on, telling her she couldn't last another night wondering if that had been Tim in Ward C, couldn't go on with another day of her life until she knew the truth.

But what did she want the truth to be? Did she truly want to find Tim tonight? If that was Tim in Ward C, at least she'd know he was alive and know where he was. But she didn't want to find him *there*. Because that would mean there was something hideous about The Ingraham. Knowing that would put her in jeopardy and Tim in greater peril than he was already.

I have to know, she thought as she slipped into her coat. I won't have a moment's peace until I *know*.

With her sneakers jammed into the pockets of her overcoat, Quinn exited the dorm at a dead run, ducking past the camera in the lighted doorway and dashing outside to where the powdery snow was gusting through the frigid air. The flakes seemed smaller now, and there were fewer of them falling, but the wind was re-arranging them, building dunes around the shrubs and between the buildings, and scraping the open areas clean.

She had decided against the direct route to Science along the walks around the pond on the central campus. That would mean running the gauntlet of security cameras on all the flanking build-ings. She opted instead for the rougher, woodsier route behind the class building to approach Science from the rear. She was a little concerned about her footprints at first, but when she turned to see how much of a trail she was leaving, she saw the wind busily filling it in almost as soon as she completed a step.

When she reached Science, Quinn paused in the darkness out-side the cone of light in front of the emergency exit door on the west side and looked around. No one about, nothing moving ex-cept the flakes. Still, she felt as if she were being watched. She knew there was a camera over the door, but were there others about? She wished she'd bothered to take note of their positions during the months she'd been here, but who'd have thought it would ever matter?

She pulled her security card from her jeans and took a deep

breath, then she marched up to the door, slipped her card into the slot, and entered. She eased the door shut behind her but kept her snowy boots as close to the threshold as possible. Quickly she pulled her sneakers from her coat pocket and laid them on the floor. Then with repeated, nervous glances down the hall, she began pulling off her boots. She hated standing here in the fully lighted, deserted corridor, sure to be spotted by anyone who walked into the rear end of the building's lobby, but she didn't dare leave a trail of wet footprints in the hall.

She also figured this gave her an excuse in case anyone in Security had been monitoring the camera on the west side of Science during the two seconds she'd been on-screen. If someone came to check, instead of a skulking interloper they'd find a student standing in plain view, changing her shoes. Quinn even had a story ready: She couldn't sleep so she'd come over to see if Dr. Emerson was around and if she could put her insomnia to good use.

But no one had come to investigate the door by the time she got into her sneakers, so she carried her boots over to the stairwell door, unlocked it with her card, and ducked inside. She left the boots in a corner and started up the steps, pulling off her coat as she climbed.

On Fifth Quinn carded herself out of the stairwell, blocked the door open with her coat, then crouched in the corner and checked the hall. Most of the overheads were out; only those by the nurses' station were on. Softly glowing night-lights were spaced low on the walls along the hallway. A Neil Diamond song was playing softly on the radio at the nurses' station.

Quinn crept down the hall. So far she hadn't broken any rules. If they caught her now, her insomnia story would still hold up. She glanced into Ward C as she passed the window, but it was dark in there. The only illumination came from the vital-signs indicators, IVAC infusion pumps, and cardiac monitors over the beds. She tried to identify the patient she suspected was Tim, but in this light they were all indistinguishable.

She stayed close to the wall as she edged toward the nurses' station. Neil Diamond's baritone had segued into Michael Bolton's caterwaul on the radio—apparently one of those easy-listening stations. She knew there were two nurses on the late shift; she heard the muffled sound of their voices behind the music. They didn't sound as if they were at the desk, so she chanced a peek around the corner at the station.

Empty.

The music and the voices were coming from the little lounge room behind the med cabinet. That was where the nursing staff gave report, relaxed, and listened to the control board for alarms from the monitors in the ward.

This was her chance. She had to act now, before they came out onto the floor again. As the two nurses broke into soft laughter, Quinn moved. Without giving herself time to change her mind or lose her nerve, she dropped into a crouch, scurried around the corner, and ducked through the door into Ward C.

Now you're over the line, she thought as she eased the door closed and felt her terrified heart beating a mad tattoo against the inner wall of her chest. Now you've got *big* trouble if you're caught.

For a few seconds Louis Verran didn't know where he was. He jerked forward in his chair and looked around. He was in Monitoring.

Christ! He'd dozed off.

He rubbed his eyes. Good thing he was alone. If Kurt or Elliot had caught him, they'd have given him a helluva razzing. But Elliot was in Baltimore on some R&R and Kurt was sacked out next door in the on-call room.

Goddamn Quinn Cleary.

They all should have been getting some R&R. Christmas break wasn't a break for Security, as a rule, not with all those applicants rolling through here next week. Christ, it seemed like a treadmill at times. But at least they used to get off the first weekend of Christmas break. Not this year. Because Cleary was staying, and because Alston wanted close tabs on her, only one of them was off tonight. Elliot had drawn the high card.

Verran got up and stretched. His gut burned. He needed a break. He *craved* a break. He was still feeling the stress of last week—hauling in the Brown kid, putting him in storage: None of it was his cup of tea. He hadn't figured on any rough stuff when he took this job—who'd have thought? It was rare, but the potential was always there, and it never failed to set his stomach acid production a few notches higher.

He grabbed for his bottle of Mylanta and unscrewed the cap. As he tilted back his head to chug a couple of ounces, he saw the red light blinking on the recorder.

Shit! She'd been on the phone. When the hell had that happened?

He hit the Rewind button, put on his headphones, and listened.

An incoming call from her friend Matt. Lots of static. Those two had already talked earlier in the day. Verran relaxed and smiled. Maybe old Matt was trying to move in on the absent Tim. But the smile vanished when he heard Cleary mention Tim.

"It's Tim! I think he's here!"

Acid surged anew into Verran's stomach.

"I don't think he ever went away." . . . *"I think he's here, at The Ingraham. I think they're hiding him."* . . . *"I'm going to find out for sure tonight. If something happens to me, call the County Sheriff's Office. Ask for Deputy Southworth."*

Verran tore off the headphones. Where had she got those ideas? And when had her friend called her? There was no timer on the recorder.

. . . *I'm going to find out for sure tonight* . . .

Christ! She could be upstairs in Ward C right now.

He grabbed the phone and dialed her dorm room. If she picked up, okay—he could sit down and carefully consider his next move. If not . . .

Half a dozen rings and no answer. He began to sweat. Four more and he slammed down the receiver. If she wasn't already here, she was on her way.

He dialed the Ward C nurses' station. Doris answered.

"This is Verran. Anybody strange wandering around up there?"

"Strange?" Doris laughed. "There's *nobody* wandering around up here but us chickens."

"Check Ward C anyway."

"Mr. Verran, there's no way—"

"Check it *now*, goddammit!" he said through his teeth. "We may have a trespasser."

He could hear her swallow. "Yessir."

He hung up and began shouting for Kurt.

Got to make this fast.

The penlight trembled in Quinn's hand, its narrow beam wobbling ahead of her as she moved among the Ward C occupants, weaving her way toward the rear of the room to where she'd seen the patient who'd signaled her.

As she approached the bed, she heard a phone begin to ring out at the nurses' station. She flashed the light on the patient's bandaged face. Only the eyes were visible; they were closed in sleep, and the lids did not open in response to the light. Holding her breath, Quinn hooked a finger under the facial bandages and pulled down.

The nose came free. It wasn't Tim's.

She pulled farther down, exposing a pale, shiny area of scar tissue. She jerked her hand away. Not Tim.

She stood there in the dimness, confused and uncertain: *crushed* because it wasn't Tim, which meant he was still among the missing; *elated* because it wasn't Tim, which meant he wasn't the victim of some grisly plot.

She rearranged the bandages into their original position. How could she have been so terribly wrong? She'd been so *sure*.

She stepped back from the patient to make sure she was in the right spot. Yes. This was it. This was where she'd seen—

Wait. She flashed her light along his body. This patient was short and heavy. The one who'd signaled her had been long and lean.

Like Tim.

As she turned to survey the darkened ward, she saw a shadow appear at the window in the door. Quinn dropped to the floor. A heartbeat later the door swung open and the overhead lights went on.

Kurt stood blinking in the glare of the lights.

"Jesus, Lou. I was sound asleep."

Verran envied him. He could have used a few solid hours of sleep himself.

"Enjoy the memory. That's the last you're going to have for a while. Our friend Cleary's on the loose."

"What's that supposed to mean?"

"Don't ask me how, but she suspects we've got Brown. I heard her on the phone. She's on her way here—may be here already."

"Fuck damn!" Kurt said. "I knew we should've taken her out with the Brown kid."

"That's not our decision. Besides, the situation is still salvageable. From what I gathered, she doesn't *know* Brown's here. If we intercept her, send her back to the dorm, then move Brown out, we can make her look like a nut case and kick her ass back to Connecticut."

"Why go to all the trouble?" Kurt said. "Let me handle it. I'll see to it she's found in the woods fifty miles from here—a rape-murder victim. Our worries'll be over."

Verran stared at the big blond man. Sometimes Kurt really frightened him.

"Just do as you're told. She's not in her room. I called Fifth and they're checking Ward C. She didn't get by the security desk in the lobby, so she's probably on her way."

"What about the side door?" Kurt said, turning to his console. "The bitch pulled a fast one like that on me once before." He tapped away at his keyboard, then pointed to the screen. "There she is: the west door, ten minutes ago."

Christ, no!

"Get upstairs! Stop her! If she gets into the ward and finds him, our asses will be in a sling!"

Tim watched the whole sequence of events and could do nothing. Real life was reduced to television, and he was a passive, helpless viewer. Couldn't even change the damn channel.

His tingling hands had awakened him but he'd wished they hadn't. He'd been too depressed over the day's events—*non*-events, rather—to work his fingers in much more than a desultory fashion. No hope, no future—what difference did it make how well he could move his fingers? Even when the tingling reached his elbows, the highest yet, so what?

So he lay there in the darkness, staring at the blinking lights around the hall window, but from a different angle this time. They'd moved his bed at the end of the day shift, rotating him to the side of the room farthest from the door. The current shift had propped him up on his right side again.

When he saw a familiar blond head bob past the hall window, he thought he'd fallen back to sleep and was dreaming. But when he saw her slip through the door and begin flashing a penlight, he prayed it was real. It *had* to be real.

He wanted to laugh, he wanted to cry, he wanted to shout with booming joy. There was a God, there was a Santa Claus. Quinn was here! She'd seen! She believed!

Then he wanted to scream at her when she approached the wrong bed.

Over here! Over here! They moved me over here!

He watched her flash her light in the other patient's face, saw her flinch back when she realized it wasn't him. Silently he begged her not to think she'd been seeing things this afternoon and give up. When she started looking around again, he knew there was still hope, but he was bewildered when she suddenly dropped into a crouch.

Then the lights came on and he understood.

Squinting, Tim watched the nurse called Doris step inside the door. She appeared wary as she stood with her hands on her hips, surveying the ward. Tim couldn't remember a night when the overheads had been turned on like this. Had she heard something? Was she looking for Quinn?

Maybe it was his own cardiac monitor that had brought her in. His heart was tripping along at a breakneck pace.

He could see Quinn crouched beside Number Four's bed, statue-still, barely breathing.

Jesus, she had guts. How many women—how many *men*— would brave this place at night to search for him?

Apparently satisfied, Doris turned off the lights and closed the door behind her.

Quinn's shadow popped up almost immediately and she began to flash her penlight at the patients around her.

Over here, dammit!

Maybe she caught the thought. Or maybe she spotted the madly flashing rate light on his cardiac monitor. Whatever the reason, she came directly toward him and shone the light in his face.

She didn't have to pull at his bandages. She seemed to know as soon as she saw his eyes.

"Oh, Tim!" It was a whisper encased in a moan.

She bent and clutched his shoulders and buried her face against his neck, sobbing.

"Oh, Tim, it's you, it's you, I knew you'd never leave me like that."

He felt his own sobs welling up in his chest with nowhere to go, searching for a voice, an exit. His vision blurred and he was startled to feel the wetness of tears on his cheeks. Sensation was returning to his face.

If only he could speak. Because as wonderful as this was, she had to go now.

Okay. You've found me. Now get out of here, get somewhere safe and call the cops, the FBI, the CIA, the Pentagon, just make sure you're safe first!

And then over Quinn's shoulder, through the blur of tears, he saw the other nurse, the one called Ellie, walking past the window in the hallway. She stopped abruptly and stared into the ward. She leaned closer to the window and cupped her hands around her eyes for a second or two, then she jerked away from the window and darted back the way she had come.

But Quinn hadn't seen a thing.

She had to get out of here, had to run! He had to let her know! Tim tried his voice again, knowing he couldn't make a sound, yet he had to try.

"Go."

The word shocked him. His voice sounded like a tree limb scraping against a stucco wall, but it *was* his voice.

Quinn straightened and stared at him. "Tim! Can you speak?"

He tried to tell her that a nurse had seen her but his lips and tongue wouldn't cooperate. He had to keep it simple.

"Go!"

"Not without you. I'm never—"

Then the overheads came on.

Quinn whirled in the sudden burst of light and saw two nurses—one heavy and blond, the other thin and brunette—standing inside the door, gaping at her.

"*Now* do you believe me?" the thin one said.

"Who are you?" said the heavy one. "And what are you doing here? Do you realize how you're endangering these patients?"

Quinn was tongue-tied for an instant. She'd had a story set to use had she been intercepted before she reached Ward C, but nothing for why she was actually in the ward. She realized that they didn't know who she was. Why should they? The only times she'd ever been on Five Science were in the afternoon. She could be anybody. So she blurted the first thing that came to mind.

"I thought they might be lonely," she said as lamely as she could. She tried to look dazed, out of it as she shuffled toward the nurses . . . toward the door. "But no one will talk to me."

The nurses glanced at each other, then the heavy one spoke again. She seemed to be the head nurse for the two-woman shift.

"You could have brought an infection in here."

"Oh, no," Quinn said with intense sincerity as she continued her approach. "I wash my hands every day. But they still wouldn't talk to me. Will you talk to me?"

Another glance flashed between the nurses, then the thin one spoke.

"Of course we'll talk to you." She pulled open the door to the nursing station. "Come on out here. We've got coffee and doughnuts and we'll talk as long as you like."

Quinn gave a sleepy smile as she walked between them and out the door . . . and kept walking. She turned to her right toward the hallway.

Someone grabbed her shoulder. "Not that way." It was the heavy nurse. "The lounge is over here."

"That's okay," Quinn said, shrugging off the hand. "I don't feel like talking anymore."

"Wait!"

Quinn pulled away and began running down the hall, ignoring the shouts behind her as she headed for the exit stairs. She could see the door was still propped open by her coat, and she complimented herself on her foresight. She was scared, but her adrenaline was flowing now and she knew she could outdistance either of the nurses here in the hall. Before they could phone the lobby and get Security moving, she ought to be down the stairs, out into the snow, and pelting across campus toward the dorm. Once back in her room, she'd barricade the door and call the Sheriff's Office. She'd blow the lid off Ward C and expose everybody involved in this horror and then Tim would be free and they'd be together once more and she wouldn't care if she never saw The Ingraham again.

She was halfway there when the door opened the rest of the way and a blond man stepped over her coat and into the hall. Quinn recognized him immediately as someone from Campus Security—the one she and Tim had seen in the parking lot before leaving for Atlantic City last month.

His sudden grin had a nasty twist to it. "Well, well, well. I've been looking for you, sweetheart."

Quinn's sneakers squeaked as she skidded into a turn and ran the other way. The heavyset nurse had been close behind her, but Quinn's sudden change in direction took her by surprise, and she slipped and fell. Quinn dodged around her and headed back the way she had come.

Panic was beginning to crowd her now, nipping at her heels.

She wouldn't make it into the stairwell at the other end of the hall. She'd have to use her card to unlock it, and the blond guy would be all over her while she was trying to get it into the slot. Maybe the lab—

As she passed Ward C again, she spotted the little lounge behind the nurses' station. Maybe she could lock herself in there, and if they had a phone . . .

But the thin, dark-haired nurse was at the station, on the phone, undoubtedly to Security. When she saw Quinn coming, she dropped the receiver and moved to intercept her. Quinn didn't think she could duck around the nurse so she barreled right into her, sending her flying backward into the meds cart, knocking it over. She had a brief glimpse of the bottles and syringes flying off the top, smashing on the floor, the drawers below falling open, spilling their contents, adding more liquid and broken glass to the mess, then she ducked into the lounge, slammed the door behind her, and locked it.

She whirled, found the phone, lifted the receiver, hit 9, then dialed 4–1–1. If only she'd thought to memorize the number of the Sheriff's Office.

She got a busy signal. How could Information be busy at this hour?

As fists began pounding on the door, she hung up and tried again, only this time she listened after she hit the 9 for an outside line: busy signal. Someone in Security had blocked phone access to the outside.

A heavy weight slammed against the door. The molding by the doorknob cracked.

Quinn began to shake. Her stomach hurt. She was trapped. And she was going to end up like Tim, she knew it.

Another slam against the door, a bigger crack in the molding. Desperate now, ready to try anything, she jumped up, twisted the lock switch in the doorknob to the Off position, turned the knob ever so slightly to free the latch, then stepped aside, flattening herself against the wall just to the right of the knob.

The door slammed open with a violence that almost ripped it off its hinges as the blond man hurtled into the room, out of control, stumbling wildly.

Quinn was on her way out the door immediately. She didn't see him land but heard the crash of tumbling furniture, then groans and angry curses behind her as she dashed once more into the hall. The two nurses were there, blocking her way, their eyes wide with surprise at the sight of her. They clutched at her arms but she shook them off and darted behind the station counter, taking the longer, flanking route to the hall. She would have made it too, if her sneaker hadn't slipped on the wet floor. She prevented a fall by grabbing the counter, but the delay gave the heavy nurse a chance to reach the other end of the station and cut her off.

As Quinn straightened she noticed three fist-sized multidose bottles of a clear liquid near her right hand. She grabbed one and flung it at the big nurse. It struck her in the shoulder, bounced off, and smashed. Quinn grabbed another, spun, and winged it at the thin nurse, who deflected it with her hands. That too smashed. Quinn turned again and threw the last at the heavy nurse, who ducked. It sailed over her head and shattered against the far wall. Before the nurse could straighten, Quinn was past her and again sprinting down the hall.

This time she made it to the stairwell. She grabbed her coat as she passed, pulled it on, and fumbled her pass card from the pocket as she bounded down the steps. She ignored her drying boots as she burst from the stairwell onto the first floor. She jammed the card into the emergency-door slot and ran out into the icy air.

At first she ran through the snow without a destination—down the hill toward the campus buildings, anywhere as long as she was putting distance between herself and Science. Then she heard the exit alarm sound from the science building—someone had come through without using a card. She turned and saw the long trail she'd left in the snow and the big blond guy from Security running down the hill, following it. She might be able to outrun him, but she'd never lose him, not in this snow.

She heard a whimper of fear and realized it had come from her.

Ahead lay the faculty office building. One of the windows was lighted. Dr. Emerson's?

"Oh, God, please, God!" she said softly, pushing her speed to the red line.

She skidded into the entry door, yanked on the handle—it opened. She ran inside, locked it behind her, then kicked off her sneakers. Wet footprints were as easy to follow as a trail in the snow. She padded down the hall in her socks toward Dr. Emerson's door. She burst into his office without knocking and slammed the door behind her.

Dr. Emerson jumped in his seat and looked up at her.

"Oh, Dr. Emerson, thank God you're here!"

"Quinn!" he said, pulling off his glasses. "What on earth's wrong?"

"You've got to hide me! Security's after me! You've got to call the Sheriff's Department!"

"What are you talking about?"

"Tim Brown! He didn't run off to Vegas. He's still here, in Ward C!"

"Preposterous! Who told you such a thing?"

"I *saw* him, Dr. Emerson. I just came from Ward C, and Tim Brown is *there*!"

Shock and confusion warred across Dr. Emerson's features.

"But why . . . ?"

"I don't understand why. None of this makes any sense. I just know he's there and Dr. Alston's using your compound to keep him there and we've got to get him out." She was starting to cry. She didn't want to, but she was so afraid, and the sobs seemed to have a will of their own. "So please, *please*, call the sheriff!"

Dr. Emerson closed his eyes and shook his head, as if trying to shut out something he didn't want to hear.

"This is terrible," he muttered. "This is awful." He looked heartbroken.

"What's wrong?"

"Nothing. This just confirms my worst fears." He rubbed a hand over his eyes, then straightened in his chair. "Very well. Hide in that closet over there if you wish. I still can't believe this, but I'll make the call. But I won't tell the authorities a thing. I'll try to get someone from the Sheriff's Office here, and you can tell him yourself. Is that fair enough?"

"Yes! Oh, yes! Thank you!"

Quinn hurried over to the closet, stepped inside, and closed the door behind her. On the far side of the door she heard Dr. Emerson pick up the phone and dial. She listened as he spoke.

"Sheriff's Office? Yes, this is Dr. Emerson at The Ingraham. I have a very frightened young woman in my office who feels she is in some danger. Could you send a car over immediately? Yes, I'm in room one-oh-seven in the faculty building. Thank you." He hung up and said, "They'll be here shortly."

Quinn breathed a deep sigh of relief and slid to a sitting position on the floor of the closet. She hadn't been sure she could trust anyone connected with The Ingraham, including Dr. Emerson. Now she chided herself for doubting him, even for an instant.

It's almost over.

All she had to do now was sit tight here until the sheriff or a deputy came, then lead them up to Ward C and show them the missing Timothy Brown. And then heads would roll.

Maybe she'd learn what this nightmare was all about. Because that was exactly what this was like—bizarre, scary as hell, surreal, and it made no sense at all.

Outside in the office, a door opened.

"Where is she?" a voice said.

Dr. Emerson, sounding very old and very tired, replied, "In the closet."

Quinn was rising to a standing position when the closet door was flung open. She screamed when she saw the blond security guard standing there, smiling at her.

No! It can't be! Can't BE!

She tried to dart past him, but he grabbed her arm and squeezed her biceps. Quinn winced with the pain.

"Don't hurt her," Dr. Emerson said.

"Are you kidding?" the guard said. "After all the shit she's put me through tonight? Thought I busted my arm up there on Five Science. All because of her."

As she was dragged past his desk toward the hall, Quinn stared at Dr. Emerson in shock and disbelief.

"You? You too?"

He wouldn't meet her gaze. He stared instead at his desktop. His betrayal was a knife through her heart. Her terror receded and the hurt poured out of her.

"How could you? I thought you were a decent man, a *great* man! I thought you were my *friend!*"

Finally he looked up at her. His face was stricken, filled with grief. There were tears in his eyes.

"So did I. But there are some processes that cannot be stopped once they are set in motion."

Quinn's hurt suddenly turned to fury. It flared up, fueled by the growing fear for her life, and suddenly she was shoving the security man, wrenching her arm from his grasp with a sudden burst of strength that took her as much by surprise as it did him.

She was free, and she was running again, but with nowhere to go.

Quinn glanced over her shoulder and saw the guard racing after her, arms and legs pumping, teeth bared, face a mask of rage. She screamed and stretched her legs to their limit, but her socks gave her little traction on the polished floor. He gained quickly this time and tackled her just as she was banking into a turn in the hall.

His weight slammed her to the floor, knocking the air out of her as they slid into a wall. He lurched to his knees and hovered over her, panting, murder ablaze in his eyes as she struggled to breathe.

He grabbed the front of her hair. "I've had enough shit from you for one night!" he said.

Quinn felt her scalp burn as he yanked her head up. Before she could reach up to grab his arms, he slammed her head down against the floor. Jagged bolts of white light arced from the back of her skull along both sides of her brain and met in the space behind her eyes, then plunged into darkness, dragging Quinn with them.

inally!
Matt felt the crushing fatigue begin to lift as he turned off the road and up the drive toward The Ingraham's gates. It had stopped snowing, and there were only six inches or so on the ground here. The going became much faster and easier once he'd crossed into Maryland and pushed south of Emmitsburg. The roads from there on had been plowed sporadically, but at least none of them was blocked by four-foot drifts like a few up in Pennsylvania.

The guard in the gatehouse looked at him suspiciously as he pulled up to the brightly lighted entrance. He seemed reluctant to open the window to his heated cocoon.

"Help you?"

"Yeah. I'm here to visit a first-year student named Cleary."

"They've all gone home for Christmas break."

"She's still here. She's expecting me."

"I wouldn't know about that. I'm afraid I can't let you on campus at this hour."

"I've come all the way from Connecticut. I would've been here hours ago if I hadn't got stuck in the storm. Please give her room a call. Two-fifty-two."

The guard shrugged, slid his window closed, and dialed his phone. And waited. And waited. Finally he shook his head and hung up. He opened the window again.

"No answer. Like I told you: They've all gone home for the break. Won't be back till after the first of the year."

An uneasy feeling began to worm through Matt. Even through the static Quinn had sounded frightened. And why not? The things she'd been saying . . .

Matt had spent the hours since their abortive phone call trying to piece together the fragments he'd heard. The more he'd thought about them, the more unsettling they became.

It's Tim! I think he's here! . . . I don't think he ever went away. . . . I think they're hiding him here. . . .

They were enough to shake up anybody.

"I know she's here. I spoke to her a couple of hours ago. Call her again."

He shook his head. "I already let it ring a dozen times. If she was in that room, she would've picked up."

"Then maybe something's happened to her. Maybe—"

"The only thing that's happened to her is she's gone home for a couple of weeks."

"But she could be hurt. Let me go up and check on her."

The guard shook his head with deliberate slowness. "Nobody goes wandering around this campus without an escort, and there's nobody to spare for an escort at this hour. You come back after eight when the day shift's on and they can help you out. Right now, I suggest you turn around and take the road two miles farther west to the Quality Inn and spend what's left of the night there."

"But—"

The guard shut his window.

Matt stared at him, then glanced at the red-and-white-striped gate a few feet ahead. He was tempted to slam the Cherokee into gear and drive right through that slim, brittle-looking two-by-four. But what would that do? He'd get kicked off the campus before he learned anything, and probably be banned from ever entering again. He did not need that.

Maybe the Quality Inn was a good idea. But before he headed down the road again, there was one more thing he had to do.

Hoping the local cellular transmitter was working, he picked up the car phone and dialed Quinn's number. He counted a dozen rings, then let it go on ringing after that. Finally, when he couldn't stand the sound any longer, he hung up. But her words from hours ago echoed and reechoed through the canyons of his brain.

It's Tim! I think he's here! . . . I don't think he ever went away. . . . I think they're hiding him here. . . .

Either Quinn had gone paranoid, and that seemed unlikely—about as unlikely as Tim dropping out and flying to Las Vegas—or there was something nasty going on at The Ingraham.

Matt rubbed his eyes.

God, I'm tired.

He was too exhausted to think straight right now. Maybe it would all make sense in the morning. It sure as hell didn't now. But he'd be back at eight on the dot to find Quinn and straighten out this whole mess.

He was shifting into reverse when he heard the vibrato *thrum* of a helicopter. He looked up and saw the lights descending toward the helipad behind the medical center. When he'd been here last year he'd seen ex-senator Whitney land in one. Matt doubted he'd be coming to The Ingraham at this hour. Probably a medevac shipping in an emergency case.

Great things, helicopters. Snow-choked roads didn't slow them down a bit.

Matt turned the Cherokee around and went in search of the Quality Inn.

Tim lay on his right side in an agony of suspense. He'd seen Quinn leave the ward flanked by the two nurses, flash past the hall window with a nurse in pursuit, run back the other way chased by the blond bastard who'd punched him in the face that night ages ago when he was strapped in the chair talking to Dr. Alston.

Nothing had happened for a few minutes. He'd heard heavy banging vibrating through the walls, then the faint sound of glass breaking, then he'd seen Quinn run by the window again. Soon after, but not too close behind, the blond security goon had followed.

That was the last he'd seen of Quinn.

She got away.

Tim had been repeating that over and over, making a litany of it. She had to have got away. She couldn't have expended all that courage, braved all those risks, just to be caught and dragged downstairs to face Alston in Verran's little hidey-hole. That would be too cruel, too unfair.

No, she got away, and the cops would be here soon.

But just in case Quinn had been caught, Tim was doing his damnedest to get his arms and legs working. His 2:00 A.M. dose of 9574 was late. Had to be. How else to explain the gnawing pain in his left thigh where Alston had burned and grafted him? *Pain.* When had Tim last experienced an iota of physical discomfort? And how else to explain this sudden ability to flex his elbows,

shrug his shoulders, bend his knees? The joints were stiff and painful, but they did move. The daily physical therapy had kept them
limber.

The important thing was, he could *move* them. On his own. And
he kept moving every joint he could, repeatedly flexing and extending, back and forth. But he had to be careful. They'd left the
lights on, so any movement could be seen. He saw some of the
other patients moving, twitching, jerking, like B-movie mummies
in the earliest stages of reanimation. But none seemed to have anywhere near his degree of mobility. So as he worked his limbs Tim
kept his eyes trained on the window and the door. He couldn't let
the nurses catch him moving. They'd dose him right back into
flaccidity.

Quinn's escape must have upset the dosage schedule—must
have upset a *lot* of things out there. She'd probably thrown their
whole routine into chaos.

What a gal. Tim grinned—yes, grinned. He could feel his facial
muscles move, feel his cheeks crease with the smile. *Can I pick 'em,
or what?*

He wiped the grin and froze his limbs as he saw a head appear
in the door window. The door opened and Doris, the shift's head
nurse, walked in. She strode directly to Tim's bed. She frowned as
she looked down at him.

"Do you have any idea how much trouble your girlfriend
caused up here tonight?"

Not entirely, but I hope it's a lot. He felt the muscles in his hands
begin to fasciculate. He was glad they were hidden under the
sheet.

"Is that graft on your leg hurting you? Feel it? It's only a fraction of what your fellow patients are going to be feeling soon. And
it's all your girlfriend's fault."

What was she talking about?

"She went crazy out there. Broke near every vial of injectable
we have. *Threw* them at us."

Good for her.

"So as a result, we have none of the special neuromuscular
agent we've been using left on the floor."

No 9574! Tim restrained himself from pumping a defiant fist in
her face. *Yes!*

"But not to worry. There'll be more along as soon as Dr. Alston
opens up the third floor for us. And then you'll get your dose,

Number Eight. A little late, but better late than never, ay?" She smiled sourly. "And who knows? Maybe your girlfriend will be up here by then, and she'll be getting her own dose of it."

Tim squeezed his eyes shut and fought his hands from creeping up and covering his ears.

Oh, no. Not Quinn. Not here.

"Well, you didn't really think she got away, did you? Not a chance. Kurt caught up to her, but I doubt that's the last we've seen of her." She sighed. "Why couldn't the two of you have just let things be? Why'd you have to go snooping about? It puts us all in a terrible position. Believe me, nobody's happy with this situation. This is not what we're about."

She turned and walked among the other patients, reassuring them, checking their IVs and their dressings. Suddenly the room began to vibrate. It took Tim a moment to recognize the sound: a helicopter. Who'd be coming in by helicopter at this hour—whatever it was? Doris must have wondered too. She bustled out to the nurses' station, turning off the lights as she closed the door behind her, leaving the patients of Ward C in the dark.

Tim lay still for a few moments, dazed and sickened by the news that Quinn was a prisoner; then he burst into furious activity, moving his limbs, rubbing his hands together, massaging his muscles. He'd lain here like a lump long enough. He had to do something, had to think of something he *could* do despite his weakened state. How long did he have before Doris returned with a fresh supply of 9574? An hour? A few minutes?

Whatever the answer, he had to be ready for her.

"Do I have to tell you how upset Mr. Kleederman is, Arthur?"

Quinn heard the distantly familiar voice through the thick, sick, unrelenting pain that hammered against the inner wall of her skull. She was on her back; the feel of the cushions against her shoulders and buttocks was very much like a couch, but she had no idea where that couch was.

Wherever the couch was, the air smelled stale, like old cigar smoke.

"No. Not at all. Your very presence here at this hour is testimony to that."

A new voice. Quinn knew that one: Dr. Alston. No surprise there. She'd guessed he was in on this. But Dr. Emerson . . .

She fought a sob and forced her eyes to open a slit. She saw

Dr. Alston half turned away from her. The man he was speaking to was tall, sleek, well-dressed, with not a single one of his salt-and-pepper hairs out of place. Even through the web of her eyelashes, Quinn recognized him immediately: former senator Whitney.

"We need a major overhaul of the screening process, Arthur."

"The screening process works extremely well," Dr. Alston said. "But it's not perfect. No system dealing with human variables can be perfect."

Through her lid slits Quinn saw the senator point her way without looking at her.

"This will be the third student to disappear in two years, Arthur. Three in two years. Sooner or later, and I fear it will be sooner, someone is going to become suspicious and begin asking questions. Someone is going to demand an investigation. With my connections and the combined influence of our board, we can bury a certain amount of that sort of thing. But one suspicious parent coupled with one loudmouthed reporter, and we could have the makings of a disaster for the foundation. Tell me, Arthur: How do we explain two students disappearing this year?"

"I . . ." Dr. Alston didn't seem to have an answer.

"And she does have to disappear, Arthur. She doesn't know The Ingraham's mission and methods, but she can bring charges of kidnapping, unlawful imprisonment, battery, and who knows what else against us. If you can think of another way out of this, I'll gladly present it to the board. I don't like this, any of it, but you and I know how the board decides on these matters: She's got to go."

Quinn knew she had to be hallucinating. A former U.S. senator and a respected professor at one of the world's premier medical schools were discussing the necessity of making her "disappear." This couldn't be true.

Then came a third voice, also familiar: "I think I've got the answer."

Security Chief Verran was speaking from somewhere to her right.

"Well, don't keep us in suspense, Lou," Whitney said. "How do we settle this?"

"We put the two disappearances together. Link them. Make them *one* disappearance."

Dr. Alston had turned to face Verran, who Quinn still couldn't see.

"We're listening," Whitney said.

"I've already set it in motion. I got hold of Elliot in Baltimore. He says there wasn't much snow down there and the airport never shut down. So I sent him out to BWI to get the Brown kid's car out of the long-term lot and drive it back here."

"What?" Dr. Alston said. "Are you insane? That will only serve to point the finger directly at us!"

"Let him finish, Arthur," Whitney said.

"Thank you, Senator. My plan is to say the Brown kid came back, picked up his girlfriend Cleary, and the two of them drove off together. We haven't seen them since."

"I see," Whitney said. "So even though we've got two missing students, it's really only one incident. I like it. Excellent thinking, Louis."

"But we've still got a car to get rid of," Dr. Alston said.

"I'm sure we can hide it for a while until things cool down, then find a way to destroy it," Whitney said.

"Destroy it tonight."

A new speaker, a fourth voice.

Verran's voice said, "What do you mean, Kurt?"

The blond man who had chased her and knocked her out stepped into Quinn's field of vision.

"Crash and burn. It's the perfect night for it. We inject a little booze into the guy's bloodstream, pour a little down his throat. The two lovebirds go racing down the icy road, skid into a tree, the gas tank explodes, *boom*, they have to be identified by their dental records. No disappearances. No questions. A tragic case of drunk driving. Case closed."

Quinn watched Dr. Alston and the former senator look at each other, saw their gazes meet, then break away. Her heart began to pound.

Why aren't they saying anything? The man's talking about a double murder. Why isn't anybody telling him to shut up?

Whitney broke the silence. "No. That's out of the question."

Thank you, God! A voice of sanity!

The man called Kurt shrugged. "Just a thought."

Silence. Complete except for the low electrical hum of the equipment that filled the room.

Suddenly Whitney said, "You could ... handle this?" He kept

his eyes down, not looking at Dr. Alston, not looking at Kurt, look-ing at no one.

"Sure," Kurt said. "No problem." His tone was apropos to someone discussing who was going to make a run to the nearby Pizza Hut.

Another silence, chilled and calculating this time, was shattered by the ringing of the phone. Quinn jumped and hoped nobody noticed.

From her right Verran spoke monosyllables into the receiver, then hung up.

"It's Doris up on Fifth, Doc," Verran said. "She's howling for that fresh supply of juice you promised her."

"She'll have to be patient," Dr. Alston said.

"She says the natives are getting restless."

"Oh, very well," Dr. Alston said peevishly. "Call her and tell her to meet me on Three. I'll be right back."

"First we settle this," Whitney said. "I think the car crash sounds like the answer."

"Now wait a minute," Dr. Alston said. "Do you realize what you're saying?"

Whitney spun on him. "Of *course* I do, Arthur! And I don't like it any more than you! I *loathe* it! But extreme problems sometimes call for extreme solutions."

"But we're talking murder here."

"Really. And I suppose you'd prefer that we transfer this latest transgressor to your private abattoir, where you can slice and dice her to your heart's content in the name of science."

Dr. Alston's head rocked back as if he'd been slapped in the face. "I resent that! My research will save burn victims, improve the quality of countless lives. This . . . this car ride will accomplish nothing!"

"It may well save The Ingraham," Whitney shot back. "It will certainly protect the foundation. Isn't that enough? *More* than enough?"

Dr. Alston said, "I know the foundation is quite willing to take extreme measures to protect itself, but—"

Whitney leaned into his face. "Or shall I set up a meeting be-tween you and Mr. Kleederman and the board of directors so you can discuss your reservations with them face-to-face?"

Dr. Alston shook his head glumly, shrugged, and turned away, moving toward the door.

Spicules of ice crystallized in Quinn's veins as former senator Jefferson Whitney pronounced sentence.

"All right, then. We'll wait for the car to arrive. Then we'll leave the matter in Kurt's hands."

Tim retched.

As his reflexes began to return, the nasogastric feeding tube snaking through his nose, down the back of his throat, and into his stomach had begun to trigger his gag reflex. The retching was becoming intolerable. He had to get it out.

He reached his right hand up, wrapped his fingers around the glossy plastic tubing, and began pulling. The sensation was indescribably nauseating, like extricating a thick white tapeworm from your gut via your nose. Tim's stomach heaved, his esophagus spasmed, his throat tried to close around it, but still he pulled, relentlessly dragging on the tube until he felt its soft, blunt end scrape against the back of his throat. Then, accompanied by a final retch, it slithered through his right nostril and dropped free onto the mattress, trailing a thick glob of mucus.

Tim grimaced as he watched it slink over the side rail and fall to the floor.

Now the IV.

His fingers pushed aside the overlying gauze on his forearm and fumbled with the tape over the IV site. His gross motor control was returning, but his nervous system didn't seem ready for fine manipulation yet. No matter. He'd simply have to bull through this. One way or another, that IV was coming out.

He wriggled his index finger under the tape and ripped it up, exposing the hub of the IV needle and more tape. He guided his twitching fingers around the tape and hub, grasping them as one, then he yanked back. The needle pulled free painlessly, dribbling clear fluid across the sheet while a droplet of blood welled in the puncture site.

Tim jabbed the IV needle into his mattress, then dammed the blood flow with his thumb. He didn't want any telltale red splotches on his arm. He maintained the pressure for what he guessed was a minute, then checked the site: no more bleeding. He sucked the blood off his thumb, then pushed the tape and gauze back into place.

Okay, he was ready. But first he decided to try something radical: He pushed himself up on both elbows, grabbed the side rails, then pulled himself to a sitting position.

The room pinwheeled clockwise while the bed did its own tilt-a-whirl in the opposite direction. He felt seasick and ridesick; he closed his eyes but the feeling of spinning into the void pursued him. He'd figured his inner ear would pull this sort of stunt on him after his being flat for so long, but he hadn't imagined it would be this bad. He clenched his teeth against his rising gorge and held on for the duration of the hell ride. He wasn't going to let go.

Finally the vortical movement slowed. When it stopped, Tim dared to open his eyes. The room was steady. He dropped back onto the mattress, gasping, sweating. He'd done it. In a couple of minutes he'd try it again. In the meantime he'd keep working his limbs, keep stretching and contracting those muscles. And all the while he'd be waiting.

Tim was surprised at how good he'd become at waiting.

As tired as Matt was—exhausted was more like it—sleep would not come.

He lay among the mute shadows of the motel room and listened to a snowplow scrape by on the road outside. He knew why he couldn't sleep—because he *shouldn't* sleep. He should be up and out and doing something.

Because the more he lay here and thought about it, the surer he was that Quinn was in trouble. Big trouble. She'd sounded so frightened on the phone, and now it looked as if she'd disappeared.

He'd replayed their fragmented cellular-phone conversation countless times in his mind, looking for an answer, and with each run-through it sounded progressively more disjointed and bizarre. But the last two words he'd heard kept nudging him.

. . . *Sheriff . . . Southworth . . .*

Matt threw off the covers and sat on the edge of the bed. It was obvious he wasn't going to get any sleep, so he might as well get up and do something. Get into motion. Even if he wasn't accomplishing anything, at least he'd feel better about himself. He pulled out the slim Frederick County phone book, looked up the number of the Sheriff's Office, and dialed. A man who announced himself as Deputy Harris answered, and Matt asked for Sheriff Southworth.

Harris laughed. "The sheriff's name is Clarkson. But there's a *Deputy* Southworth."

"Is he around?"

"Won't be in till eight."

"Could you call him at home?"

"I don't think he'd appreciate a call at this hour. Can I help you?"

Matt hesitated, then figured, What the hell. He told Deputy Harris about Tim's disappearance—Harris was familiar with that—and about his phone call to Quinn.

"And now Quinn's gone too," Matt said.

"We don't know that yet," Harris said.

"But she did mention the name Southworth. Couldn't you give him a call? Maybe Quinn told him something."

"I guess I could give Ted a buzz," Harris said slowly. "He's been following the Brown case...."

"Please do."

Matt gave Harris his room number at the motel should he or Southworth want to get back to him, then hung up and waited.

Not a long wait. The phone rang three minutes later.

"You the one who just called the Sheriff's Office?" said a deep voice.

"Yes. Deputy Southworth?"

"That's me. Start talking."

Tim froze as the door opened and the lights came on. Ellie, the skinny nurse, entered, pushing a wheeled tray ahead of her. Tim watched the door swing shut behind her. She was alone. He was relieved to see her instead of Doris. He didn't know if his plan would work on the bigger woman.

As she headed in the direction of Number One, she glanced Tim's way and stared. Tim kept his face slack and expressionless.

"Well, look at you, Number Eight. Looks like you've been busy while I'm out."

She turned and wheeled the tray toward Tim. He noticed a row of filled and tagged syringes lined up on the tray—eight of them. She stopped the tray beside the bed and gazed down at the feeding tube on the floor.

"Now how did you manage that?"

Tim's right arm and the IV line were under the sheet. His left arm lay on top. He moved his left index finger back and forth.

"Oh, I see. Getting a teeny bit of movement back, are we? So are the others. Well, we'll fix that. Looks like the new supply arrived just in time."

Tim watched her check the IVAC flow rate, then shut it off and swab the rubber injection port on the Y-adapter with alcohol. She then selected a syringe from the tray, pulled off the needle protector, jabbed the point into the port, and pushed the plunger home, emptying the barrel's contents into the line.

As she restarted the flow, Tim pulled the IV needle out of the mattress with his right hand. Then he reached up with his left hand, grabbed a fistful of the starched white uniform over Ellie's breastbone, and yanked her toward him. Her eyes widened with shock that changed to pain and fear when Tim rammed the IV needle through her uniform and into her abdomen.

She started shouting, struggling, but Tim pulled her farther over the bed rail, levering her kicking feet off the floor and pressing her face against his chest, muffling her cries in the gauze that swathed him. He watched the IV continue dripping, hoping the 9574 was flowing into her abdominal cavity, hoping it was being absorbed into the bloodstream via the peritoneal lining, praying it would work soon because he didn't know how long his weakened muscles could keep this up.

Suddenly, as if someone had pulled her plug, Ellie went limp. Tim loosened his grip, saw her eyes looking out at him from a slack face, and knew the 9574 had gone to work. Ellie would not be a problem for the next six hours.

He released the nurse and let her slip to the floor like a stuffed toy. He propped himself up on an elbow and grabbed one of the syringes from Ellie's tray.

Then Tim lay back and began waiting again. He hoped it didn't take Doris too long to come looking for her co-worker.

"Elliot!" Verran said to the slim, dark man who had just arrived. "What took you so long?"

Still feigning unconsciousness and watching through her barely parted lids, Quinn immediately recognized the newcomer as the exterminator who had been in her room with Verran.

"In case you forgot, chief," Elliot said, "there's been some snow."

"Never mind that," Whitney said. "Did you bring the car?"

"Left it in one of the public lots by the hospital."

"Very good." Whitney turned and looked at the others. "You all know what to do. I'll return to Washington now. I'll be expecting a call imminently, informing me that this matter has been satisfactorily disposed of. I will pass the news on from there."

Then he brushed past Kurt and Dr. Alston and strode through the door.

"There's a guy in a big hurry," Elliot said.

Verran nodded. "Yeah. A rat deserting the ship. He wants to be out of state when it goes down."

"When what goes down?" Elliot said.

Verran jerked his thumb at Quinn. "Her and the Brown kid. They're going to have an accident in that car you just brought in."

"Shit," Elliot said. His gaze darted nervously about the room. He was visibly upset. "I didn't sign on for anything like this."

"None of us did," Verran said. He rubbed his upper abdomen, as if in pain.

"We've no other choice," Dr. Alston said. "We've been given instructions and I'm afraid we're stuck with them."

"Right," Kurt said. "So let's stop standing around like a bunch of biddies, and let's figure out how, when, and where we're gonna do this. We haven't got much darkness left."

Quinn listened in horror as they discussed the mechanics of situating the two of them in the front seat of Griffin, running it off the road into a tree, and making sure the gas tank blew up. She looked for a way out, but there were four men between her and the exit. No way she could get past them. But a chance might present itself later if they thought she was still out cold. Maybe she could get free and get to a phone, or find somebody who could get a message to the Sheriff's Office. . . .

A lump formed in her throat as she remembered Dr. Emerson, and how she'd thought he'd called the sheriff for her. . . .

"All right," Verran said. He sounded tired and unhappy. "We can't put this off any longer. Let's get it over with. Elliot, get up to Five and wheel Brown down here. I'll call up and have Doris transfer him to a gurney for you."

With Elliot gone, there were only three men left in the room. Come on, Quinn thought, mentally urging the rest of them to leave. Don't any of you have someplace to go?

But Verran and Dr. Alston sat in glum silence while Kurt whistled, clipping his fingernails.

* * *

"Ellie?"

Tim closed his eyes as he saw Doris stick her blond head through the door and scan the ward. He heard her step inside and walk over to the prep room.

"Ellie, where are you?"

He heard Doris's footsteps turn in his direction, stop abruptly, then—

"Oh, my God! Ellie! Ellie, what's wrong?"

He opened his eyes then and saw Doris beside the bed, bending over the unconscious nurse. The white fabric of her uniform was stretched across the expanse of her back. The strap of her bra was a whiter band across her ribs. Holding the syringe like a dagger, Tim snaked his arm through the bars of his bed's safety rail and poised the needle over Doris's back. He hesitated. This was a gamble. He didn't know if the 9574 would be absorbed from the pleural cavity. But that wouldn't matter if he hit a rib and bent the needle.

He clenched his teeth and remembered Doris's words to him earlier. *And who knows? Maybe your girlfriend will be up here by then, and she'll be getting her own dose of it.*

Here's *your* own personal dose, bitch, he thought, and plunged the needle into the right side of her back, just above the bra strap. He felt the point graze a rib, then pop through into the lung cavity. Immediately he rammed the plunger home.

Doris jerked and reared up, clutching at her back, reaching around her side and over her shoulder, trying frantically to get to whatever was causing the sudden stabbing pain. When she turned and saw Tim up on his elbow, looking at her, Doris's eyes bulged.

"You!"

She began to gasp for air. And then she saw the tray of syringes next to the bed. She coughed.

"Oh, no! Oh, NO!"

Tim grabbed for her as she lurched away from the bed, but his fingers only managed to brush her sleeve, then she was tottering out of reach toward the door, wheezing loudly, her hands still clawing at her back, trying to reach the syringe that was still buried to the hub between her ribs. She staggered against the door and almost fell but leaned on the frame and pulled it open. She squeezed through the narrow opening and stumbled out to the nurses' station.

"Damn!" Tim croaked as she disappeared from view. If she got to a phone . . .

He fumbled at his side rail, found the release, and lowered the rail. Slowly he pushed himself up to a sitting position. Everything remained stable—the practice runs had helped. He let his legs drop over the side of the bed. The room spun for half a minute and he grabbed fistfuls of sheet to keep from falling off. When his equilibrium returned, he slowly slid his legs down to the floor. His knees wobbled but held as they accepted the unaccustomed burden of his weight. The tile floor was cold but Tim wouldn't have cared if it had been ice—it felt wonderful to be on his feet again. All around him, his fellow Ward C residents were moving under their sheets.

Still holding on to the bed for support, he took a tentative step toward the door. He wished his legs were shorter, stumpier, so they'd hold him better, but his present models were doing the job. He took a second step—

—and searing agony shot through his penis and pelvis.

Grunting with the pain, Tim doubled over and would have fallen if the bed hadn't been there to lean on. Gasping, bleary-eyed, his breath hissing between his clenched teeth, he looked down to see what—

The catheter. He'd forgotten the urinary catheter.

He groaned and backed up one, two shaky steps. He didn't have time for this. Doris could be out there right now calling the security goon squad. But he wouldn't get far dragging his urine-collection bag along like a purse. He had to disconnect it.

As he turned, searching for the bag, he spotted Ellie's bandage scissors protruding from the side pocket of her uniform. He stretched over and fumbled in the pocket. He came out with the scissors and a credit card. No, not a credit card, a security passkey, just like Quinn's. That might come in handy.

But now the scissors. Slowly, carefully, he got the handles situated in his fumbling fingers and managed to cut through the brick-colored tube protruding from the tip of his penis.

A tiny stream of clear water shot from the severed end. Tim knew these catheters were multibored. A thin tube ran within the wall of the larger tube, ending in a small sack at the bladder end. After the catheter was inserted into the bladder, water was injected along the tube, inflating the balloon and locking the catheter in the bladder. By cutting the catheter, Tim had deflated the balloon. But did he have the courage to remove it?

He had no choice. Gritting his teeth, he grabbed the distal end and pulled.

It wasn't quite like dragging barbed wire through his urethra, but it came close. He shuddered twice as he was forced onto his tiptoes, and then it was out. He tossed it aside without looking at it, then sagged against the bed, but only long enough for a few ragged gasps. Then he straightened his knees and grabbed the remaining syringes from Ellie's tray; with those in one hand and the security key in the other, he wove his way across the ward like a drunk on Rollerblades.

Tim pushed on the door and found Doris on the floor behind the nurses' station counter, the syringe still protruding from her back, the phone still on its cradle.

Had the 9574 hit her nervous system before she'd had a chance to call? Tim hoped so.

From outside in the night he heard the *thrum* of a helicopter again, this time rising and fading. Whoever had flown in before was flying out again.

No time to lose. He shuffled to the elevator and shoved Ellie's card into the slot. When the car arrived, he stepped in, inserted the card into the interior slot, and pressed the basement button. If they were holding Quinn in the science center, she'd be in the basement.

As the doors closed, Tim thought he heard the hum of the cables in the neighboring shaft. He wondered who else was riding the elevators at this hour.

As his car started down, Tim leaned against the rear wall, bracing his elbows on the handrail. He was startled by his reflection in the metallic doors. Even taking into account the distortion of the uneven surface, he was one hell of a sight. He looked like Kharis the mummy after a run-in with a mob of angry villagers. The gauze wrappings over his left thigh were soaked with blood; apparently the graft was bleeding. There was even a splotch of blood over his genitals, probably oozing from his penis after his none-too-gentle removal of that catheter. He had no desire to examine either area closely.

He pawed the gauze from his face but left the rest in place. It was the only clothing he had.

He suddenly realized he might need a weapon of some sort

beyond a loaded syringe. Something heavy. He hit the 3 button just in time, and the car stopped. He stuck his card back in the slot and pressed the Off button. The lights went out and the car went dead. He stepped into a dim hallway, lighted only by widely spaced night-lights along the floor. He shuffled up and down, trying doors. He wasted five precious minutes or more looking for something, anything he might use as a club. He would have been grateful even for a broom handle. But everything was locked.

He returned to the elevator, flipped on the power, and continued down. He'd have to rely on his syringes of 9574. Trouble was, they took so damn long to take effect.

As the car slowed to a halt, Tim glanced up at the floor indicator. *L* was lit.

"Oh, no!" he cried softly, jamming his palm against the basement button. "No!"

When the doors opened on the lobby, he'd be in plain view of the security desk.

Louis Verran's stomach rumbled and shot him another stab of pain—just in case he'd momentarily forgotten about his ulcer. He reached for his Mylanta. The soft blue bottle felt light. He shook it. Empty. He tossed it in the trash and rubbed his ample, aching gut. Christ, he had more acid bubbling inside than a Delco warehouse. He reached for a cigar, then changed his mind; that would only aggravate his stomach.

He'd left the CIA to get away from stress situations, from pressure, from dirty jobs. The Ingraham was supposed to be like semi-retirement, but it was beginning to make the Company look like play school.

He glanced over at the girl, Cleary. He had a feeling she was coming to, but she hadn't stirred. Kurt must have clocked her good. When he'd carried her in, limp as a dishrag, blood smeared over the back of her head, Verran had thought she was already dead and had nearly panicked trying to figure out what to do with the body.

Wasted worry, it turned out. But now, thanks to Kurt and the senator, she was going to be truly dead, and soon.

More pain as another surge of acid found a tender spot in his stomach lining and torched it.

He used to think of himself as one of the good guys. Now . . .

He looked across the room at Kurt scraping away at his cuticles and Alston flipping through one of Kurt's skin mags. He certainly hadn't been hanging out with the good guys.

But Christ, there was no other way to silence the girl so soon after her boyfriend's disappearance. And Cleary had to be silenced. She could put all their heads in a noose.

Verran sighed and burped. You do what you have to do, and then you try to forget about it and hope you never have to do it again.

The phone rang. It was Elliot.

"We got trouble, chief."

"Aw, no," Verran groaned. "What now?"

Across the room Kurt stopped fooling with his nails, and Alston rested his magazine in his lap. Both stared Verran's way.

"I'm on Five and we've got two doped-out nurses on the floor and Ward C is shy one patient—Brown."

"Oh, Christ. Where is he?"

"I've checked this floor from one end to the other, and he's not on Five, I can tell you that."

"But he couldn't get off. It's a secure floor."

Kurt put his nail clipper away; Alston dropped the magazine and rose to his feet.

"What is it, Louis? What's happened?"

Verran concentrated on the phone and waved at Alston to shut up.

Elliot said. "He's off, chief. Trust me on this."

"Then find him, dammit!" Verran said. "Go down to Four and start looking. We'll start on One and work our way up. Get moving!"

As he hung up, Verran decided to go on the offense. He pointed to Alston.

"You fucked up again, Doc. Brown is on the loose."

"That's impossible! He was dosed with . . ." Alston's voice trailed off.

"Right. But they ran out of the stuff, didn't they."

"Good Lord!"

"It's okay," Verran said. "We'll seal the building until we find him. But it's a damn good thing the senator left when he did."

Alston nodded mutely.

Verran had an awful feeling, wondering what else possibly could go wrong, when the phone rang again.

"I'll bet that's Elliot," he said. "Probably found Brown in the bathroom or something."

It wasn't Elliot. It was Bernie from the lobby security desk. Since Bernie wasn't part of the big picture at The Ingraham, Verran immediately began inventing explanations in case he'd found Brown wandering around. But that wasn't the problem.

"Mr. Verran, there's a couple of men here to see you."

At this hour? Verran's mouth went dry.

"Who?"

"I only got the name of one. He says he's Deputy Southworth from the Frederick County Sheriff's Office, and he wants to talk to you."

"Tell him . . ." Verran wanted Bernie to tell Southworth to get lost, or come back later, but knew that wouldn't work. Southworth hadn't come here in the wee hours of the morning to chitchat. "Did he say what he wants?"

"Yeah. He wants to talk to you about the disappearance of one of the students."

"At this hour? He wants to talk about Timothy Brown at *this* hour?"

"No, sir. He says he wants to ask you about someone named Quinn Cleary."

Verran almost dropped the phone. For a few heartbeats his voice failed him as acid bubbled up and seared the back of his throat.

"Tell him I'll be right up."

Verran hung up and turned to the others. Suddenly he was exhausted. When was this going to end?

"A couple of guys from the Sheriff's Department are upstairs asking about a missing student named Cleary."

"Cleary?" Alston said. "How on earth does anyone know she's gone?"

"We are about to find out. Kurt, you stay here and keep an eye on her. The doc and I will go up and see what this is all about."

"You let me do the talking," Alston said as they hurried toward the stairs to the lobby. "I'll handle this yokel."

"You do that, Doc," Verran told him. " 'Cause I don't feel much like talking."

As they stepped out of the stairwell and into the lobby, Verran spotted Southworth immediately, but the guy with him wasn't another deputy. He could have been one of the Ingraham students, but Verran didn't recognize him.

And then he got a sudden, awful feeling that this was the guy Cleary had been talking to a few hours ago. But that couldn't be. He'd been calling from Connecticut. Hadn't he?

Verran told Bernie to take a break. As Bernie headed for the security lounge on Second, Verran introduced Alston to Southworth, who in turn introduced the kid as Matt Crawford, an old friend of Quinn Cleary's.

Yeah, that was the one. But how the hell had he got here so fast—and in the snow, no less?

As they were all shaking hands, Verran heard the elevator bell sound behind him. His stomach acid began another dance as everyone turned to look. All he needed now to cap off the night would be Timothy fucking Brown standing there in the elevator, staring out at them. He forced himself to steal a glance over his shoulder, and sighed quietly when he saw the empty car.

As the doors slid closed again, he turned back to Southworth to see what he knew. He desperately wanted something for his stomach. He was ready to trade his left hand for a roll of Tums.

As the elevator doors closed and he was once again safely sealed in the car, Tim released the breath he'd been holding. Just before the doors had opened on the lobby, he'd flattened himself against the side wall by the control panel. He hadn't been able to see the security desk, and the security desk hadn't been able to see him. But he'd heard voices out there and knew he'd acted not a second too soon.

Tim maintained his position by the control panel as the elevator continued its descent to the basement. When it stopped, he flattened himself against the wall again, planning to check out the immediate area before leaving the car.

As the doors opened, he heard a muffled shout of pain. It came from behind one of the doors down the hall on the left.

But it wasn't Quinn's voice. It was a man's.

Quinn's hopes had risen when she'd heard that Tim had escaped; they'd leapt higher when Verran said there were a couple of deputy sheriffs up in the lobby. Now they soared as Verran and Alston walked out.

That left only one man to get past. But big blond Kurt was the most formidable.

She spied on him through her lashes: For a moment he stood at the door to the hall, watching Alston and Verran head for the first floor, then he closed it and approached her. Quinn closed her eyes.

"C'mon, baby," he said, his voice close as he shook her shoulder. "Wake up and play. Ol' Kurt's got something for you. Something you're gonna love."

Quinn repressed a shudder and willed her body to remain limp as his fingers moved to her throat and began unbuttoning her blouse.

"You're too fine to waste without a little taste. Ol' Kurt's gonna get some of you before you become a french fry."

He opened her blouse and pushed up her bra. Quinn locked a scream in her throat as his rough palm cupped over her left breast and squeezed.

"Mmmm, they ain't big, but any more than a handful's wasted, right? C'mon, honey. Wake up. Ol' Kurt wants you to know what's happening. He ain't into humping corpses."

He leaned over her and began nuzzling her neck as he unbuckled the belt on her slacks.

"Wish the hell you were wearing a dress," he mumbled against the flesh of her throat.

Quinn couldn't take any more. She came unglued. She opened her eyes and saw his ear an inch away from her lips.

In a panic, she bit it.

She more than bit it. She locked her teeth onto the earlobe and ground down with every ounce of strength in her jaws. She grabbed two fistfuls of his shirt and held on, rising off the couch with him as he reared up, howling in pain, trying to beat her off. Despite the pounding impacts of the blows, Quinn held on. Her rage and terror were in control now and refused to allow her to let go. Finally, with a violent shove, he broke her grasp and sent her sprawling against the console.

He leaned against the wall, groaning in pain, blood running down his cheek and neck from under the hand he had clasped over the side of his head.

"My ear! You bitch! You bit my fucking ear!"

Quinn felt something soft in her mouth. She spit, and gagged when she saw a bloody earlobe splat on the counter. Thoughts of AIDS skittered fearfully across the surface of her mind but vanished in the urgent need to get out of this place and away from this beast.

Quinn tried to dart past Kurt but she wasn't quick enough. His hand caught her arm and he whipped her around, sending her sprawling back onto the couch. He came toward her with his right fist balled, his arm cocked, and murder in his eyes.

"You just made the biggest fucking mistake of your goddamn life!"

Quinn screamed and raised her arms to protect herself, then gasped in shock as a familiar face appeared over Kurt's shoulder.

Tim was pushing his legs as fast as he thought they'd safely carry him—he couldn't afford to fall now—but when he heard a faint, high-pitched scream that sounded like Quinn's voice, he ditched all caution and broke into a tottering jog.

He reached a door marked ELECTRONICS, threw it open, and saw Kurt, the big blond son of a bitch who'd punched him in the nose. His back was to Tim, but there was no mistaking him. He was leaning over a woman on the couch. Her blouse was pulled open, one breast was exposed, her mouth was all bloody, and she was screaming.

Quinn!

Tim almost lost it then. Any other time he would have leapt on Kurt's back and begun flailing away at him, but he knew he hadn't the strength to do much more than annoy him. Restraining himself, he uncapped one of the syringes in his hands and slipped up behind Kurt. As he raised it over the exposed back, he prayed this dose worked a little faster than the one he'd emptied into Doris's pleural cavity. With a grunt of effort he drove it into Kurt's chest and pressed the plunger almost immediately.

But the needle struck a rib and bent, jamming the plunger. Kurt let out a howl and straightened up. He whipped his right arm around as he turned, leading with his elbow. Tim tried to duck but his reflexes weren't up to it yet. The flying elbow caught him on the side of the head, sending him sprawling against one of the consoles. The remaining syringes slipped from his grasp as the room dimmed and wobbled.

"Well, I'll be damned!" Kurt said. "Look who it is: the asshole from Ward C."

With the whiteness of his rage-contorted face accentuated by the glistening crimson smear painting his left ear and side of his neck, Kurt was a fearsome sight as he closed in on Tim.

"You've got no idea how much I'm going to love kicking your troublemaking ass!"

Tim looked around for the syringes and spotted them on the floor by his feet. If he could get to one, maybe he could inject Kurt in the belly. But as he reached down, Kurt's right fist caught him with a solid uppercut to the face that knocked him to the floor. His vision swam and he lost sight of the syringes, of Quinn, of everything but the berserk monster looming over him.

For a few heartbeats Quinn couldn't move. One moment she'd been cowering on the couch, waiting to be bludgeoned by Kurt's fists, the next Kurt was turning away from her and battering Tim.

Tim! He was down now, huddled against the wall, virtually defenseless as Kurt began kicking him. She had to do something.

As she rose from the couch, she automatically tugged her bra down over her breasts, but she left her blouse unbuttoned. She needed a weapon, something she could use as a club—or a knife. She noticed a syringe dangling from the back of Kurt's shirt. As she watched, it slipped from the fabric and fell to the floor.

Quinn spotted a number of other syringes scattered on the floor and her mind began to race. Obviously Tim had brought them. He'd tried to inject Kurt with one. What was in them? A sedative? A poison? Or . . .

. . . 9574?

Of course!

She snatched a pair off the floor, uncapped both, dropped into a crouch, and crept up behind Kurt where he was viciously driving those big boots into Tim's slumped, defenseless body.

"Stop it!" she screamed as she plunged one of the needles to the hub into the back of his thigh and emptied it.

It wasn't an intravenous injection, but if nothing else it would stop him from kicking Tim.

Kurt grunted and lurched around, clutching at the back of his thigh. Quinn tried to jab him with the other needle, but he took an off-balance swing at her and she had to duck away.

And then she saw that the door was wide open and the path to it was clear.

She ran.

"I'm going for help, Tim!" she shouted as she passed him.

Tim lay slumped on the floor, a still, bloodied form. She didn't know if he heard her or not, wasn't sure he was still conscious— or even alive. A sick, cold anger added its own power to the terror already fueling her feet. Kurt had hurt Tim. She'd get him for that.

Heavy, pounding footsteps behind her shattered her little fantasy and yanked her back into horrific reality. She had a good lead on Kurt but she didn't know where she was going. The elevator was out of the question.

The stairs! Where are the stairs?

She lost a few steps as she slowed, reading the signs on all the doors. And then she saw the Exit sign. She lost more ground pulling open the door, ground that Kurt did not lose because he caught the door before it closed—

—and he grabbed Quinn as she reached the first landing.

He snagged her ankle and wrenched it back and up, trying to topple her. Quinn clung to the railing with her free hand and twisted around to look down at him. With the blood oozing along the side of his neck and soaking into his collar, and with a grin as triumphant as it was ferocious, Kurt looked like an escaped lunatic. He had her now. He'd won. And there was no hint of mercy or compassion to be found in the glacial blue of his eyes. She was going to pay dearly for what she'd done to his ear.

"No!" Quinn shouted, and defended herself with the only weapon she had. She stabbed at him with the syringe, backhanded, blindly, squeezing the plunger as she struck. It sank deep into his right eye socket.

Two things happened immediately:

Quinn released the barrel and recoiled in horror at the sight of the syringe jutting from Kurt's stunned, horrified, agonized face.

Kurt released her ankle and his hands darted toward his face.

They never made it. Both hands stopped within inches of his face and remained there, fingers splayed, trembling. His expression was a mixture of shock and dismay. The tremor spread to the rest of his body as it shuddered and shook like a fish on a hook. And then his body stiffened. Slowly he teetered backward like a felled redwood and landed headfirst on the steps behind and below him. With a sickening snap his head bent on his shoulders to very nearly a right angle. His body shuddered once, then lay still.

Quinn stood trembling on the landing, unsure of which way to turn, torn between running back to see if Tim was all right and climbing the rest of the stairs to the lobby to find Deputy South-worth.

She chose the latter. The only way to save herself and Tim was to break through The Ingraham's iron shell of security and drag in the outside world.

She just hoped the deputy was still there.

Louis Verran was actually allowing himself to relax. The subdued lighting of the lobby—they cut half the switches after Science closed down for the day—lent it a quiet, peaceful atmosphere. Almost like church.

Cleary's friend, Crawford, didn't really know that much. He'd only heard snatches of Cleary's end of the conversation on his car phone. And Verran had to hand it to Doc Alston—he handled Southworth beautifully.

A bad moment came when Dr. Emerson walked through the front doors. He looked dazed, like a guy in shock. Almost looked as if he'd been crying.

"Walter," Alston said. "What on earth are you doing here at this hour?"

But Emerson said nothing. He walked past like a zombie, eyes straight ahead, on a beeline for the elevators. Verran held his breath. Emerson was one of the faculty members who knew the score at The Ingraham, but he was a bit too unpredictable for Verran's liking.

But Emerson kept his mouth shut. He stepped into the elevator and went up to Fifth.

And Verran vented another sigh of relief.

"You see?" Alston said to Southworth as the elevator doors closed behind Emerson. "I'm not the only faculty member here at this hour."

"Fine," Southworth said, "but let me get this straight: Mr. Verran called you in because Timothy Brown had reappeared?"

"Not quite," Alston said with exaggerated patience. "Louis does not 'call me in,' as it were. He called to *inform* me that Mr. Brown had returned. I *decided* to come in to see Mr. Brown for myself. As director of medical education, I thought it my duty to question him about his missed tests and classes and to warn him of his imminent risk of failure. He wanted to hear none of it. All he wanted was to collect Ms. Cleary and take her skiing."

"I don't believe any of this," Crawford said.

Alston shrugged dramatically. "I don't know what else I can tell you, young man. Mr. Brown returned, picked up Ms. Cleary, and the two of them drove off together. I certainly disapproved, but I had no power to stop them."

"Just when did Brown show up?" Southworth asked.

"Just before midnight, Ted," Verran said, jumping in. "I called Dr. Alston right away."

"And that would explain that fragment you heard from your friend," Alston told Crawford. "About Tim being here. That was what she meant. Your mutual friend had returned."

"No," Crawford said, shaking his head. "That doesn't hang together. Quinn said—"

Alston raised his hand. "None of us can be sure what Ms. Cleary said. *You* were tired; *she* was tired and overwhelmed by her friend's return. I suggest we all get a good night's sleep and discuss this further in the morning."

Southworth looked at Crawford. The deputy had been pretty quiet, soaking up everything in his usual low-key way. No telling for sure what Southworth was thinking. Ever.

He said, "I think Dr. Alston's got a point there. I'll put out a bulletin on Brown's car and we'll wait and see if they're picked up. Meanwhile, if you want to do anything, try hanging around the airport and see if they show up there."

Verran loved the idea, but Crawford didn't look too happy with it. Finally, he gave a reluctant shrug.

"All right. I'll try that. None of this makes any sense, but if they're not here, I guess they're not here."

Alston stepped forward and put a hand on Crawford's shoulder, guiding him toward the doors as he spoke.

"Don't you worry, young man. We'll find them. The Frederick County Sheriff's Department is second to none in its dedication and expertise. If your friends are still in Maryland, they'll locate them. And if they contact The Ingraham, I promise, you'll be the first to know."

That's it, Doc, Verran thought. Lay it on thick. Say whatever you have to say, just get them the hell out of here.

And then, behind him, through the door to the basement stairs, Louis Verran thought he heard a female voice shout *No!* But it was so faint he couldn't be sure he'd actually heard it.

No matter. Southworth and Crawford hadn't heard it. They were almost to the doors.

Keep going. Keep going.

A dozen or so feet and they'd be gone.

Half a dozen feet . . .

They were at the doors, passing through . . .

A sound behind him. A door opening. Verran turned and thought his heart was going to stop as his worst nightmare became real: the Cleary broad, her shirt flapping open, blood smeared around her mouth, bursting into the lobby. Verran made a grab for her, but he was far too slow. And he was too stunned by the sight of her. Had that jerk Kurt tried something on her? And if so, where the hell was he? What had happened downstairs?

Not that it mattered. The end of his cushy job at The Ingraham, and no doubt the end of his life as a free man, was sprinting across the floor toward Southworth and Crawford, screaming at the top of her lungs.

"Matt! Oh, God, Matt! Matt, Matt, *Maaaaaaatt!*"

She leapt into Crawford's arms, and they hugged like a long-lost sister and brother while she babbled a mile a minute.

Suddenly Southworth was no longer low-key. He grabbed Alston by the shoulder, turned him around, and shoved him back toward the security desk. Verran felt his stomach acid explode and wanted a place to hide.

"Seems we've got a little bit of a discrepancy here, Verran," Southworth said as he and the others reached the desk. He stood two feet back from the counter with his hand resting on the grip of his pistol—still in its holster, but the meaning of the gesture was not lost on Verran. "This young lady says she's Quinn Cleary— and Crawford here confirms that—and she says Tim Brown is being held downstairs as a prisoner. What the hell do *you* have to say about that?"

"Somebody call an ambulance," Cleary was saying as she buttoned the front of her shirt. "Tim's hurt. He needs help."

"Show me where," Crawford was saying. "Maybe we can—"

"Everybody stay put!" Southworth said. "I want some answers here."

The deputy was reaching for the radio remote on his left hip when Verran heard that sound again—the stairway door opening. Who was it going to be now? Brown himself? This was turning into a goddamn circus.

No. It was Elliot. And oh shit, he had a gun. He raised it in a professional two-handed grip and aimed it at the deputy. But Verran saw the way the barrel wavered and knew Elliot was on the edge of panic.

"Your gun, Southworth," Elliot said. "Take it out and put it on the counter."

Southworth remained cool, didn't move. "This isn't going to help," he said softly.

"Do it!" Elliot's voice cracked on the first word.

Southworth's face looked more annoyed than anything else as he removed his revolver from the holster and placed it on the counter.

"Take it, chief," Elliot said, then he glanced at Alston. "And now I want to know what's gone down here. When I went up to Fifth a little while ago, everything was under control. I come back down, and there's a dead guy in Monitoring"—Cleary moaned and began to cry on Crawford's shoulder—"and I find Kurt on the stairs with a chewed-up ear and a broken neck. What the fuck's happening?" He glanced back at Verran again, then at Southworth's .38, still on the counter. "Go ahead, chief. Take the gun."

"I don't want it." As Elliot stared at him wide-eyed, Verran said, "It's over, Elliot."

"No way!" he said, shaking his head violently. "I'm not going back inside! We can . . ."

And then he ran out of words as he finally realized what Verran had known the instant he'd seen Quinn Cleary dash into the lobby.

"No," Verran said softly. "We can't."

Alston was moving. He reached around Verran and picked up the .38 by the barrel.

"Louis is right, Elliot," Alston said. "The dominoes have begun to fall." He turned to Southworth and lifted the gun. "I'm going to borrow this, Deputy. You may have it back in a few minutes."

He strolled to the stairway door and made his exit.

Fright and confusion swirled across Elliot's face.

"What's he . . . ?"

Verran jumped as a single gunshot from the other side of the stairway door answered his question.

"Oh, shit!" Elliot said.

And then he was running for the front doors.

Before Elliot was through them, Southworth had his radio in hand and was calling for backup and emergency medical assistance, and putting out an APB on Elliot. As he returned the remote to his belt, he jabbed an index finger at Verran.

"Stay put."

Verran could only nod. His whole world was falling apart. He wished he had the guts to end it like Alston, but knew he'd never be able to pull that trigger.

Strangely enough, his stomach didn't feel so bad right now.

With Matt at her side, Quinn crowded close behind Deputy Southworth as he headed for the stairwell.

"We've got to get to Tim," she said.

He couldn't be dead. She didn't care what Elliot had said, Tim was alive. He was *alive.*

She kept repeating the phrase, hoping that would make it true.

The deputy opened the door, looked into the stairwell, then closed it again. His face was a shade paler as he turned to them.

"We'd better take the elevator."

Quinn clung to Matt as the deputy used her security card to take them down to the basement. A residue of the overwhelming joy she'd felt upon finding a familiar face in the science-center lobby still trickled through her anguish for Tim. She couldn't get over Matt's being here. How had he managed to come so quickly? Not important now. She'd find out later. Right now she had to get to Tim.

"How was he when you left him?" Matt said.

"He . . . he wasn't moving."

Deputy Southworth's expression was grim as the car stopped and the doors began to slide open.

"Maybe you'd better let me—"

Quinn slipped through the doors as soon as the opening was wide enough to let her pass. She wasn't waiting for anybody.

She ran to the room where she'd been a prisoner and skidded to a halt at the door. Tim lay huddled against the angle of the wall and the floor, his back to her, one arm splayed out at an unnatural angle. He was perfectly still. She couldn't see his chest move. There was blood . . .

She screamed. *"Tim!"*

The body jerked, the limp arm stiffened, the thumb and pinkie finger straightened, and waggled back and forth.

Quinn didn't know whether to laugh or to cry as she knelt beside him and slipped her arms around him.

"Oh, Tim."

"Just a couple more questions," Deputy Southworth said.

Quinn fidgeted in her seat behind the counter. The police had taken over the security desk as a command center.

"Okay, but just a couple."

She was anxious to get over to the hospital and see Tim. The EMTs had wheeled him out of the basement on a gurney. He'd looked awful. She wondered how his X rays had turned out.

Matt had gone along with Tim, and after they were on their way, the people from the morgue had removed the two bodies from the stairwell. The state police led Louis Verran away in handcuffs. New nurses were brought in to care for the patients in Ward C. Things were settling down. Quinn had wanted to go with Matt and Tim but the deputy needed a statement.

"Now . . . is there anyone else you can think of who might be directly involved in this?"

"Only one." Quinn's throat constricted at the thought of him. "Dr. Emerson. He's over in the faculty building. Or at least he was."

She told him what had happened in Emerson's office.

Deputy Southworth stopped writing.

"Dr. Emerson . . . first name Walter? Old guy?"

"That's him. Why?"

"He came through here shortly after we arrived. Took the elevator. Does he have an office upstairs?"

"A lab. On Fifth."

"I wonder why we haven't seen him. We've had people all over the fifth floor."

"He's probably locked in his lab." *With the other rats.* "But . . ." Quinn fished in a pocket for her key ring, then held it up. "I have the key."

She rose from her seat and started for the elevators.

"Wait a minute," Deputy Southworth said. "I'll take those."

Reluctantly, Quinn handed over the keys.

"All right," she said. "But I'm going with you. I want to be there when you arrest him."

Southworth smiled as they stepped into the elevator. "You've really got it in for him, don't you."

Quinn nodded grimly. She saw nothing amusing in his betrayal. She had put her life in Dr. Emerson's hands, and he'd handed her over to her executioners.

On Fifth she led the deputy down the hall to Dr. Emerson's lab. The Christmas decorations on the walls and doors seemed hollow now, devoid of any warmth or meaning, almost sacrilegious. She stood close by Southworth's shoulder as he unlocked the door and edged in behind him as he stepped through.

"There he is," she said as she saw the familiar figure sitting at one of the computer consoles. "That's him."

She slipped past Southworth and approached Dr. Emerson from the side. He didn't look up.

"It's all over, Dr. Emerson," she said, fighting the tears that sprang into her eyes, angry at her voice for teetering on the rim of a sob. She was supposed to be angry, vindictive. Why did she feel so sad? "It didn't work. I'm still around."

He didn't move, simply sat and stared at the screen.

Then Quinn noticed the chrome pole on the far side of him. And the bag of clear fluid suspended from it. And the clear plastic tubing running down into his arm.

She touched his shoulder, shook him gently. His body sagged and started to topple to the side.

"Holy—!" Southworth said. He lunged forward and caught Dr. Emerson's body before it fell.

Quinn stood frozen, staring at the computer screen and the words that had been entered there.

To Whom It May Concern: If my calculations prove correct, this should establish beyond a doubt that 9574 does indeed have an LD.

" 'LD'?" Southworth said after easing Dr. Emerson to the floor.

"Lethal dose."

Quinn's voice sounded as empty as she felt. All her emotions seemed burned out, used up. She felt like a hollow, desiccated husk.

"Can I go now?" she said.

She needed very badly to be with Tim.

EPILOGUE

"**A**ny news?" Quinn said as Matt stepped through the door to Tim's hospital room.

Late-morning sunlight glared off the white of the bedsheets and the polished floor. She sat on the edge of the bed, holding Tim's hand, not simply because she was so glad to have him back, but because it was one way of keeping him in bed.

Tim was a lousy patient. He had six broken ribs, a cerebral concussion, and a large third-degree burn on his left thigh, but he wanted out of the hospital. Now. Only Quinn's restraining presence and the weakness of his atrophied muscles kept him in place.

He'd spent much of the morning explaining to the state police and the FBI all he knew and what had happened to him. Quinn had been at his side, listening in awe to his incredible tale of mind control at The Ingraham and human experimentation on a national scale.

At first the various law-enforcement agents had seemed uniformly skeptical. But when they returned for follow-up questions after investigating Verran's control room and dismantling a few of the headboards in the dorm, they were obviously believers.

Matt waved a copy of the *Baltimore Sun* as he dropped into a chair. "KMI and the Kleederman Foundation are stonewalling. They say the charges are preposterous, and even if they should prove to be true, Kleederman and the directors know nothing."

Anger tightened in Quinn's chest.

"You mean he's going to get away with it?"

Matt shrugged. "I called my father and talked it over with him.

He says unless some pivotal conspirator spills his guts, it's going to be rough getting convictions on the higher-ups. After all, they're pretty well insulated and it's your word against a billionaire businessman with an international reputation, a former U.S. senator, and the other big shots on the board."

Tim said, "I don't see Verran as the type to make a deal, do you? They haven't caught that Elliot guy yet, and Alston and Emerson removed themselves. We don't know who else was in on it here and who wasn't. And without written records, where does that leave us?"

"Probably with a lot of lower-echelon indictments, according to my father," Matt said. "But once they start asking questions around the KMI medical centers, someone's bound to crack, and then the truth about the experimentation will come out and the whole network will collapse."

"And maybe the investigations will work their way back to Kleederman himself," Tim said, setting his jaw. "Criminal charges, civil suits, whatever they can do to hound that son of a bitch into the ground."

Quinn squeezed his hand. "Easy now." And then a thought struck her. "What about the graduates?"

"Right," Tim said softly. "What about them? All the 'Where Are They Now' docs. Those poor bastards."

"Why do you say that?" Quinn said.

"They're the real victims. None of it's their fault, but their reputations will be ruined or, at the very least, highly suspect."

"Don't count on it," Matt said. "They won't believe they've been brainwashed, and frankly, I doubt there's any way to *prove* that someone's been brainwashed. They'll say they were never affected by any silly science-fiction machine, or they'll say none of those contraptions were in *their* headboards when *they* were students at The Ingraham. And unless somebody turns up some written records, who's to say those SLI units or whatever they're called weren't installed last summer?"

"So they'll go on as they are?" Quinn said.

"They're still well-trained physicians. They'll go on giving the inner-city populations excellent medical care—even better care now that the patients they're subconsciously compelled to refer to the medical centers will no longer be pharmaceutical guinea pigs."

"So it's over?" Quinn said, finally letting the relief seep through her. "Really over?"

"For all intents and purposes, yes," Matt said. "You two pushed over the first domino. Just a matter of time now before they all go down. It's over."

NEW MEDICAL SCHOOL OPENS

(Budapest) A new international charitable organization, The Eastern Europe Medical Care Foundation, has announced the opening of a tuition-free medical school in Budapest and a string of medical centers located in Hungary, Romania, Czechoslovakia, and Poland to bring the benefits of modern medical care to the poor, the disadvantaged, and the disconnected of Eastern Europe.

The Frankfurt *Allgemeine Zeitung*